THE BEAUVOIR SERIES

"THE USELESS MOUTHS" AND OTHER LITERARY WRITINGS

THE BEAUVOIR SERIES

Coedited by Margaret A. Simons and
Sylvie Le Bon de Beauvoir

A list of books in the series appears at the end of this book.

Simone de Beauvoir

"THE USELESS MOUTHS" AND OTHER LITERARY WRITINGS

Edited by Margaret A. Simons
and Marybeth Timmermann

Foreword by Sylvie Le Bon de Beauvoir

UNIVERSITY OF ILLINOIS PRESS
Urbana, Chicago, and Springfield

First Illinois paperback, 2021

1 2 3 4 5 C 5 4 3 2 1
∞ This book is printed on acid-free paper.

The Library of Congress cataloged the cloth edition as follows:
Beauvoir, Simone de, 1908–1986.
[Bouches inutiles. English]
The useless mouths, and other literary writings / Simone de Beauvoir; edited by Margaret A. Simons and Marybeth Timmermann; foreword by Sylvie Le Bon de Beauvoir.
p. cm. — (The Beauvoir series)
Includes bibliographical references and index.
ISBN 978-0-252-03634-7 (cloth : acid-free paper)
I. Simons, Margaret A.
II. Timmermann, Marybeth.
III. Le Bon de Beauvoir, Sylvie.
IV. Title.
PQ2603.E362B613 2011
842'.914—dc22 2011012405

PAPERBACK ISBN 978-0-252-08595-6

The editors gratefully acknowledge the support of a grant from the National Endowment for the Humanities, an independent federal agency, and a Matching Funds grant from the Illinois Board of Higher Education. The volume also received a translation grant from the French Ministry of Culture.

IN MEMORY OF HAZEL BARNES,
ELIZABETH FALLAIZE,
AND ELEANORE HOLVECK

Contents

Foreword to the Beauvoir Series *ix*
Sylvie Le Bon de Beauvoir

Acknowledgments *xi*

Introduction *1*
Margaret A. Simons

1. The Useless Mouths (A Play) *9*
   Introduction by Liz Stanley and Catherine Naji
2. Short Articles on Literature *89*
   Introduction by Elizabeth Fallaize
3. Existentialist Theater *125*
   Introduction by Dennis A. Gilbert
4. A Story I Used to Tell Myself *151*
   Introduction by Ursula Tidd
5. Preface to *La Bâtarde* by Violette Leduc *165*
   Introduction by Alison S. Fell

6. What Can Literature Do? *189*
Introduction by Laura Hengehold

7. Misunderstanding in Moscow *211*
Introduction by Terry Keefe

8. My Experience as a Writer *275*
Introduction by Elizabeth Fallaize

9. Short Prefaces to Literary Works *303*
Introduction by Eleanore Holveck

10. Notes for a Novel *327*
Introduction by Meryl Altman

Contributors *379*

Index *385*

Foreword to the Beauvoir Series

Sylvie Le Bon de Beauvoir

TRANSLATED BY MARYBETH TIMMERMANN

It is my pleasure to take this opportunity to honor the monumental work of research and publication that the Beauvoir Series represents, which was undertaken and brought to fruition by Margaret A. Simons and the ensemble of her team. These volumes of Simone de Beauvoir's writings, concerning literature as well as philosophy and feminism, stretch from 1926 to 1979, that is to say throughout almost her entire life. Some of them have been published before, and are known, but remain dispersed throughout time and space, in diverse editions, diverse newspapers or reviews. Others were read during conferences or radio programs and then lost from view. Some had been left completely unpublished. What gives them force and meaning is precisely having them gathered together, closely, as a whole. Nothing of the sort has yet been realized, except, on a much smaller scale, *Les écrits de Simone de Beauvoir* (*The Writings of Simone de Beauvoir*), published in France in 1979. Here, the aim is an exhaustive corpus, as much as that is possible.

Because they cover more than 50 years, these volumes faithfully reflect the thoughts of their author, the early manifestation and permanence of certain of her preoccupations as a writer and philosopher, as a woman and feminist. What will be immediately striking, I think, is their extraordinary *coherence.* Obviously, from this point of view, *Les cahiers de jeunesse* (*The Student Diaries*), previously unpublished, constitute the star document. The very young 18-, 19-, 20-year-old Simone de Beauvoir who writes them is clearly already the future great Simone de Beauvoir, author of *L'invitée,* (*She Came to Stay*), *Pour une morale de l'ambiguïté* (*The Ethics of Ambiguity*), *Le deuxième sexe* (*The Second Sex*), *Les Mandarins* (*The Mandarins*), and *Mémoires* (*Memoirs*). Not only is her vocation as a writer energetically affirmed in these diaries, but one also discovers in them the roots of her later reflections. It is particularly touching to see the birth, often with hesitations, doubt, and anguish, of the fundamental choices of thought and existence that would have such an impact on so many future readers, women and men. Torments, doubt, and anguish are expressed, but also exultation and confidence in her strength and in the future—the foresight of certain passages is impressive. Take the one from June 25, 1929, for example: "Strange certitude that these riches will be welcomed, that some words will be said and heard, that this life will be a fountain-head from which many others will draw. Certitude of a vocation."

These precious *Cahiers* will cut short the unproductive and recurrent debate about the "influence" that Sartre supposedly had on Simone de Beauvoir, since they incontestably reveal to us Simone de Beauvoir *before* Sartre. Thus, their relationship will take on its true sense, and one will understand to what point Simone de Beauvoir was even more herself when she agreed with some of Sartre's themes, because all those lonely years of apprenticeship and training were leading her to a definite path and not just any path. Therefore, it is not a matter of influence, but an encounter in the strong sense of the term. They each *recognized themselves* in the other because each one already existed independently and intensely. One can all the better discern the originality of Simone de Beauvoir in her ethical preoccupations, her own conception of concrete freedom, and her dramatic consciousness of the essential role of the Other, for example, because they are prefigured in the feverish meditations, pen in hand, which occupied her youth. *Les cahiers* constitute a priceless testimony.

I will conclude by thanking Margaret A. Simons and her team again for their magnificent series, which will constitute an irreplaceable contribution to the study and the true understanding of the thoughts and works of Simone de Beauvoir.

Acknowledgments

Simone de Beauvoir's *"The Useless Mouths" and Other Literary Writings* is dedicated to the memory of Hazel Barnes, Elizabeth Fallaize, and Eleanore Holveck for their pioneering contributions to our understanding of Beauvoir's literary-philosophical work. This volume would not have been possible without the generous support of a Collaborative Research Grant from the National Endowment for the Humanities (NEH), an independent federal agency; a Matching Funds grant from the Illinois Board of Higher Education allocated by the Graduate School of Southern Illinois University Edwardsville (SIUE); and a translation grant from the French Ministry of Culture. We are very grateful to Michel Rybalka for directing us to Beauvoir's texts housed in the Margaret Clapp Library, Wellesley College, and the Department of Special Collections, Memorial Library, University of Wisconsin-Madison; and to Ezio Vailati for his assistance with the Leibniz quotes in "Notes for a Novel." We would like to thank the SIUE students from France who worked on the audio transcriptions, and Sarah Gendron for transcribing the fragmentary "Notes for a Novel." We would like to give special thanks to Sylvie Le Bon de Beauvoir, coeditor of the Beauvoir Series, for her laborious work on transcribing the Notes and continuing encouragement; and to Joan Catapano, our longtime editor, for her unwavering support of the Beauvoir Series.

"THE USELESS MOUTHS" AND OTHER LITERARY WRITINGS

INTRODUCTION

Margaret A. Simons

This volume of literary writings by Simone de Beauvoir (1908–86), the renowned French existentialist author of *The Second Sex*, opens with a drama. Beauvoir wrote her 1945 play, *The Useless Mouths*, during the final year of the Nazi Occupation of France when food shortages were acute. Her story of the anguish of choice for a besieged medieval town facing starvation is also a surprisingly feminist tale of courageous women who stare down death and inspire the male leaders of the town to do the same.

The play doesn't provide the only drama in the volume: there are lots of surprises including several texts discovered only after Beauvoir's death. Her short novel from 1965, "Misunderstanding in Moscow," not published in France until 1992, seems destined to become one of Beauvoir's most popular works of fiction. Set in Moscow during the era of détente, "Misunderstanding" is an unconventional love story of an elderly French couple as they confront their fears of aging and reaffirm their love.

The surprising discovery by the renowned Sartre scholar, Michel Rybalka, of two of Beauvoir's previously unknown texts housed in American university libraries is another source of drama. "Notes for a Novel," tentatively dated from 1928, was found in the University of Wisconsin at Madison library. Described by Meryl Altman as notes for a "heroine's text" and "a love story that is also a Bildungsroman or novel of development," this early fragmentary text shows Beauvoir working out her own ethics and epistemology focusing on what she will later call "the problem of the Other." The Wellesley College library was the site of another discovery: a set of 78 rpm records containing Beauvoir's 1947 lecture, *Existentialist Theater.* Accompanied by readings from plays by Sartre and Camus (not included here), Beauvoir's lecture invites comparisons with Sartre's discussion of *The Useless Mouths* in his 1946 New York lecture, "Forgers of Myths."[1] Another recording transcribed here for the first time is "A Story I Used to Tell Myself," a 1963 interview on Beauvoir's autobiography in which, as Ursula Tidd observes, Beauvoir writes herself into a tradition that was still "a predominantly male preserve." Together, the transcriptions of these recordings bring us, as Dennis Gilbert remarks, Beauvoir's "true, living voice."

Clues in Beauvoir's posthumously published *Lettres à Sartre* led to my discovery of another previously unknown text, "New Heroes for Old."[2] In this 1947 article on postwar French literature, originally published in English for American readers, Beauvoir describes how the various schools of French writing from the French revolution to World War II have been shaped by their times—an historical analysis reflective of the wartime transformation in Beauvoir's own philosophy.

Such insight into her own thought is often provided by Beauvoir's prefaces to works by other authors, several of which are included here. Beauvoir's 1964 "Preface" to *La Bâtarde*, for example—in which she reads Violette Leduc's autobiography as demonstrating "the reworking of one's destiny by one's freedom—" has been described as more reflective of Beauvoir's philosophy than of Leduc's life. This preface, which brought a wider audience to Leduc's work, also sheds light on Beauvoir's life and her relationships with women. As Alison S. Fell writes, the preface is "the culmination of a collaboration that had begun more than twenty years earlier," a period during which Beauvoir became Leduc's mentor and literary advisor in a nurturing relationship that deserves to be better known.

Beauvoir's confrontation with her critics is another source of drama in this volume. A criticism that spans the decades of these texts is the charge that the existential novel, with its focus on action and philosophical questions, forsakes the aesthetic function of literature. In her 1947 article, "American Renaissance in France," Beauvoir responds to critics "scandalized" by the popularity of American novels in France. She defends the admiration of postwar French writers for American novels that "express the truth of life in its crude materiality." In the traditional French novel, she explains, language had come "to be regarded as an end in itself" and "literature had become a purely abstract domain" reducing life to analytic or poetic concepts and leading to the "dead-ends" of "academicism and preciosity." For Beauvoir, "the true mission of the writer" is "to describe in dramatic form the relationship of the individual to the world in which he stakes his freedom."

Beauvoir responds to a similar attack almost twenty years later, in the eagerly awaited translation of Beauvoir's contribution to a 1965 debate on the topic, "What Can Literature Do?"[3] In this case her critics are proponents of the "new novel" who see literature as an end in itself, an exploration of language, and who attack the goal of communication in "engaged literature" as a merely instrumental use of language to convey information. Beauvoir emphasizes the value of communication in her response, arguing that literature is "the privileged place of intersubjectivity" and the only form of communication "capable of giving me the incommunicable"—"the taste of another's life." Beauvoir makes an analogous defense of autobiographical writings as a literary work and not simply a communication of facts, in her 1966 Japan lecture, "My Experience as a Writer." Here she argues, in part, that only the "literary quality" of an autobiography can overcome the problems of a chronological account, by capturing the interest of the reader who, alone, can realize a "living synthesis" of the discrete moments of the author's life.

One of the first criticisms leveled against Beauvoir's existential novels is that she used literature to merely illustrate a philosophical thesis. An October 1945 review article, for example, praised her 1943 metaphysical novel, *She Came to Stay*, for describing a discovery (of the existence of the Other), the meaning of which remains ambiguous at the novel's conclusion. But the review condemned her 1945 novel, *The Blood of Others* as a "thesis novel," in which we witness not the discovery of an ambiguous truth but a definitive moral "conversion" to political responsibility.[4] In a December 1945 interview Beauvoir was asked about the risk that characters in a philosophical novel would be reduced to "incarnated ideas," to which she replied: "I know well that this is the pitfall [*l'écueil*] of the metaphysical novel."[5]

Beauvoir addresses this criticism in *Existentialist Theater* (1947); she argues as she does in her 1946 article, "Literature and Metaphysics," that authentic philosophical literature, like a scientific experiment, does not illustrate a preexisting theory but leads to discoveries for the author as well as the reader.[6] "New Heroes for Old" (1947) also addresses the charge, denying that the philosophical novel is a "thesis novel." "To describe a novel as 'metaphysical' is not to define it as the pure exemplification of a theory; it is only to indicate that the author [. . .] gives his heroes a metaphysical dimension—defines them [. . .] primarily according to their attitude in the presence of the great realities: death, the existence of others, suffering, life."

In her 1966 Japan lecture, "My Experience as a Writer," Beauvoir implicitly challenges the traditional reading of *She Came to Stay* as merely an illustration of Sartre's philosophy, by recounting the novel's origination in her own "concrete psychological experience." When "a friend I was very fond of [. . .] was somewhat hostile to me. [. . .] I discovered something that everyone knows," she writes, "the other's consciousness exists; [. . .] in his world I am an object with which he can more or less do as he likes." Beauvoir's continuing work on the philosophical novel is evident in her 1966 lecture, "My Experience as a Writer," where she rejects the charge that her prize-winning 1954 novel, *The Mandarins*, is a thesis novel "which preaches a lesson." "I gave Henri the sense of an action to be done, the taste for life, the taste for engagement. [. . .] On the contrary, I gave Anne, the female protagonist, a sense of nothingness, death, the futility of all things. [. . .] In the end I do not prove either of them right. [. . .] [The novel] says nothing but rather shows a whole set of difficulties, ambiguities and contradictions which constitute the lived meaning of an existence."

The most intriguing drama in this volume may come not from Beauvoir's responses to critics but from the clues found here to a puzzle that has baffled scholars for decades: how to understand Beauvoir's denials that she was ever a philosopher or wrote philosophy, given that she earned a graduate degree in philosophy, taught philosophy for many years, and wrote existentialist novels and essays. Beauvoir's denials of her philosophical work apparently begin in 1958 with the first volume of her autobiography, *Memoirs of a Dutiful Daughter*, where Beauvoir states that she "preferred literature to philosophy" and would not have been pleased "if someone had prophesized that I would become a kind of female [Henri] Bergson; I didn't want to speak with that abstract voice which, whenever I heard it, failed to move me."[7] In the next volume of her autobiography, *The Prime of Life* (1960), she writes of her interests in 1935: "Why was I not tempted to try my hand at philosophy? [. . .] I did not consider myself a philosopher. [. . .] I wanted to communicate what was original in my experience. In order to succeed in that, I knew that I had to orient myself towards literature."[8] Beauvoir continued to deny her philosophical work, drawing a sharp line between literature and philosophy, and between her work and that of Sartre, throughout the remainder of her life, as in our 1979 interview: "Sartre was a philosopher, and me, I am not;

and I never really wanted to be a philosopher. [. . .] I have not constructed a philosophical work. I constructed a literary work. [. . .] On the philosophical plane, I was influenced by Sartre. Obviously I was not able to influence him, since I did not do philosophy. [. . .] When I wrote my novels, I was never influenced by Sartre, because it was my lived and felt experience that I rendered."[9]

But the texts in this volume, along with other recent posthumously published texts, show that Beauvoir's autobiographical writings and post-1955 interviews misrepresented her work in philosophy. An entry from Beauvoir's recently published 1926 diary, for example, reveals Beauvoir's admiration for Henri Bergson's philosophy. She describes his philosophy in his 1889 essay, *Time and Free Will: An Essay on the Immediate Data of Consciousness,* where he defines reality as a temporal becoming, as a "great intellectual rapture. Whereas in reading other philosophers I have the impression of witnessing more or less logical constructions, here finally it is palpable reality that I touch, and I find life anew."[10]

Several texts in this volume demonstrate Beauvoir's continuing work in philosophy and her enduring admiration for Bergson's philosophy. Beauvoir's "Notes for a Novel" (1928), draws deeply on Bergson's philosophy. As Meryl Altman observes: "questions about the stability of the self, the relation between the social self and the deep self, and the persistence and coherence of the self through time, are Henri Bergson's questions." Bergsonian themes run throughout Beauvoir's works from the 1960s as well, including "Misunderstanding in Moscow," with its descriptions of the ways in which one's experience of time changes with one's situation. Beauvoir's definition of the authentic function of literature as an activity "to disclose the world" to men, in the opening passage of "What Can Literature Do?" reflects Bergson's philosophy as well as Husserl's phenomenology, as does her claim that "Each of us grasps but a moment" of truth. In "What Can Literature Do?" Beauvoir's description of reality is profoundly Bergsonian: "reality is not a fixed being; it is a becoming. It is, I repeat, a swirling of singular experiences that envelop each other while remaining separate."

The texts in this volume show that Beauvoir continued to write philosophy and to present herself as a philosopher, despite the sexism that prevented public recognition of her original philosophical work in *She Came to Stay*. Beauvoir's decades-long response to the "thesis novel" criticism discussed above demonstrates that her efforts to resolve the problems of writing philosophy in a novel continued through 1954, while her work on the philosophical problem of communication evident in her writings from the 1960s can be traced back to the larger problem of the Other that she began working on in her 1926 student diary and her 1928 "Notes for a Novel."

In *She Came to Stay*, Beauvoir portrayed the collapse of metaphysical solipsism in the realization of the existence of other, separate consciousnesses. With that realization came a new problem of how to establish connection with the Other and overcome the threat of isolation—a problem that gained urgency for Beauvoir during the Occupation. In the texts in this volume ("New Heroes" is one example), Beauvoir often cites the existence of other consciousnesses, along with death, life, and suffering as examples of metaphysical realities, of universals in human existence. Communication emerges as an important theme in her postwar writings (*The Useless Mouths* is one example) as a means of overcoming isolation and establishing connection with others. In *Existentialist Theater*, Beauvoir could be describing her own wartime transformation in recounting Orestes' move away from a rootless, abstract freedom to a situated awareness of his social responsibility in Sartre's play, "The Flies."

Communication is an important theme of the texts from the 1960s as well, not only as the central problem of "Misunderstanding in Moscow," but also in Beauvoir's discussions of literature. In Beauvoir's preface to Leduc's autobiography, for example, she writes of Leduc's writing that "The failure to connect with others has resulted in that privileged form of communication—a work of art." In "What Can Literature Do?" Beauvoir writes that "If literature seeks to surpass separation at the point where it seems most unsurpassable, it must speak of anguish, solitude, and death, because those are precisely the situations that enclose us most radically in our singularity. We need to know and to feel that these experiences are also those of all other men. Language reintegrates us into the human community; a hardship that finds words to express itself is no longer a radical exclusion and becomes less intolerable."

If there is a lesson to be learned from the clues in this volume to Beauvoir's autobiographical misrepresentation of her work in philosophy, it might be, as Elizabeth Fallaize observes in her introduction to "My Experience as a Writer": "the writing of autobiography is indeed a construction rather than a recording of meaning." Ursula Tidd, in her introduction to "A Story I Used to Tell Myself," makes a similar point about Beauvoir's constructing herself in her memoirs. A fitting conclusion to these remarks may be drawn from Meryl Altman's observation about interpreting Beauvoir's fragmentary "Notes for a Novel": "To a large extent these are puzzle pieces which the reader's conjectures must reassemble: a good reminder perhaps of the extent to which despite her voluminous texts 'Beauvoir' remains a character we (readers and feminists) create, assembling dispersed fragments and collating versions in a process of interpretive collaboration that can never be completely finished."

NOTES

1. Jean-Paul Sartre, "Forgers of Myths," in *Sartre on Theater*, ed. Michel Contat and Michel Rybalka, trans. Frank Jellinek (New York: Pantheon-Random House, 1976), 33–43.

2. Simone de Beauvoir, *Lettres à Sartre*, ed. Sylvie Le Bon de Beauvoir, 2 Vols. (Paris: Gallimard, 1990), 2:344–46; for an English translation, see Quintin Hoare, *Letters to Sartre* (New York: Arcade Publishing, 1992).

3. See Toril Moi, "What Can Literature Do? Simone de Beauvoir as a Literary Theorist," *PMLA* 124:1, January 2009:189–98.

4. Maurice Blanchot, "Les romans de Sartre" ("Sartre's Novels"), *L'arche*, no. 10, October 1945, reprinted in *La part du feu* (The Work of Fire) (Paris: Gallimard, 1949), 200, 203–4.

5. Dominique Aury introduces Beauvoir as "écrivain et philosophe existentialiste" (existentialist writer and philosopher), in "Qu'est-ce que l'existentialisme? Escarmouches et patrouilles" ("What Is Existentialism? Skirmishes and Patrols"), *Les lettres françaises*, December 1, 1945:4.

6. See Simone de Beauvoir, "Literature and Metaphysics," in *Philosophical Writings*, ed. M. A. Simons, M. Timmermann, and M. B. Mader (Urbana: University of Illinois Press, 2004), 270–71.

7. Beauvoir, *Mémoires d'une jeune fille rangée*, Folio (Paris: Gallimard, 1958), 288; *Memoirs of a Dutiful Daughter*, trans. James Kirkup (New York: Harper and Row, 1959), 208.

8. Simone de Beauvoir, *La force de l'âge* (Paris: Galllimard, 1960), 253–55; translated by Peter Green as *The Prime of Life* (New York: Lancer, 1962), 265–66.

9. Margaret A. Simons, "Beauvoir Interview (1979)," in *Beauvoir and The Second Sex; Feminism, Race, and the Origins of Existentialism* (Lanham, Maryland: Rowman and Littlefield, 1999), 9–10.

10. Simone de Beauvoir, *Diary of a Philosophy Student: 1926–27*, trans. Barbara Klaw and ed. Barbara Klaw, Sylvie Le Bon de Beauvoir, and Margaret A. Simons (Urbana: University of Illinois, 2006), 66.

1

The Useless Mouths (A Play)

INTRODUCTION

by Liz Stanley and Catherine Naji

> *"I finished a play. It had been begun three months earlier, and the title I gave it was* Les bouches inutiles. *Ever since I had attended the rehearsals of* The Flies *I had been thinking of writing a play."*[1]

The Background

Les bouches inutiles (*The Useless Mouths*), Simone de Beauvoir's only play, opened with a benefit performance on October 29, 1944, at the Théâtre des Carrefours.[2] It has considerable importance for understanding Beauvoir's writing, the development of her philosophical ideas particularly. However, as Virginia Fichera has pointed out, "Although it is a major work exploring the relationship between sex and gender predating *The Second Sex* by about four years, unfortunately it has been neglected by critics and scholars of her work."[3] The play deals with the ethical consequences of treating some people as worthless and useless, something still of considerable social relevance, and it also reveals much about changes occurring in Beauvoir's philosophical thinking. Around the time it was written, her ideas shifted from a pre–World War II solipsism, toward a postwar moral and political engagement, something usually not seen as happening before publication of *The Second Sex*. However, in *The Useless Mouths* Beauvoir is thinking aloud about such matters, particularly concerning her developing ideas about self-and-other and a relational view of social relationships.

The plot of *The Useless Mouths* concerns the breakdown of social bonds in an *in extremis* situation and is set in medieval Flanders in the fictional city-state of Vaucelles, which had revolted against the rule of the Dukes of Burgundy. As it opens, there has been a long siege and the townspeople are facing starvation unless the King of France helps them. There are three leading Aldermen, Louis, Jacques, and François, who lead the town Council. Louis is married to Catherine, herself a significant figure in the revolt. They have two wards, Jean-Pierre and his sister Jeanne. Catherine wants Jeanne to marry Jacques, although Jeanne is unhappy about this. Their daughter Clarice is in love with Jean-Pierre, but rather childishly hides it; and although Jean-Pierre is in love with her, he cannot cope with emotional commitment. Their son Georges is a disaffected tough who wants power without responsibility, and he also has inappropriate feelings for Clarice. These characters represent different varieties of dictatorship and tyranny (Louis, and very differently François), of nihilism (Georges, and in another sense François), of solipsism (Jean-Pierre, and also Clarice), of bad faith (Jean-Pierre's sister Jeanne, but also Catherine and Clarice), and of inauthenticity (Jean-Pierre, also Catherine). The play's action is propelled by four events that occur in rapid succession: Jean-Pierre's return from secretly visiting the French court, the Council's decision to expel "the useless mouths" from Vaucelles, Georges forcing his attentions on Clarice and then killing Jeanne when she overhears this, and François attempting to usurp power and become dictator of Vaucelles. "The useless mouths" include all the women. The men defend their decision to expel them because the women's deaths will enable Vaucelles to live, while the terrible ironies involved are pointed up by the town's name: when this is said it is heard as "vaut-elle," which in a play on words implies the question "does she have worth?"

As with the work preceding it, *The Useless Mouths* evidences Beauvoir's interest in working in cross-genre forms so as to produce philosophy in ways additional to the conventional one.[4] So as well as discussing the play as a contribution to her philosophy, we also indicate its part in her developing thinking more generally. As a young woman, Beauvoir was interested in puppet theater, and the background to its writing was a series of radio dramas she researched and wrote in 1943, two of which were set in the Middle Ages.[5] However, the specific context was the German Occupation of France. When *The Useless Mouths* was performed in late 1944, the Occupation had just ended and a sea change in the military fortunes of the Allies versus the Nazis and their sympathizers was apparent. Alongside this, there was a sense of expectation among critics, readers, and audiences in Paris regarding the intellectual ideas named—and somewhat reluctantly adopted by Sartre and Beauvoir—as Existentialism. Beauvoir later commented that, "without having planned it, what we launched early that fall turned out to be an 'Existentialist offensive.' In the weeks following the publication of my novel, *The Age of Reason* and *The Reprieve* appeared, as well as the first numbers of *Les temps modernes*. Sartre gave a lecture—'Is Existentialism a Humanism?'—and I gave one at the Club Maintenant on the novel and metaphysics. *Les bouches inutiles* opened. We were astonished at the furor we caused . . ."[6]

Beauvoir enjoyed the theater and went to many productions, particularly those associated with the studio theater movement. In the late 1930s and the 1940s she moved in progressive theater circles, including her long-standing friendship with the actor-director Charles Dullin and his partner the actor-writer Simone Jollivet, and her close friendship with Olga Kosakievicz. Kosakievicz was training at the Atelier under Dullin; then, following her appearance in 1943 in Sartre's *The Flies* (*Les mouches*), she played the part of Clarice when *The Useless Mouths* was performed. During the Occupation, a number of studio theater plays, most importantly Anouilh's *Antigone*, had straddled the divide between entertainment and politics, writing and resistance, being and doing, and, like *The Flies*, had a palpable influence on audiences.

The Useless Mouths came near the end of a fertile period during which Beauvoir wrote a short story cycle (*When Things of the Spirit Came First*), two novels (*She Came to Stay* and *The Blood of Others*), an uncompleted play about a city, the longer philosophical essay *Pyrrhus and Cineas*, followed by *The Useless Mouths*, and the "Introduction to an Ethics of Ambiguity."[7] And although she later returned to these other kinds of writing, she never wrote another play. This was largely because of her hindsight feelings about her "moral period" and its didacticism, which she characterized as treating moral or philosophical ideas abstractly and removed from grounded situations. However, *The Useless Mouths* in fact deals with a very grounded situation, and given this, it is surprising that she did not return to playwriting as a means of exploring "the situation" and how it imposes itself.[8]

Philosophical Context and Ideas

Beauvoir and Sartre mutually influenced each other, regularly reading and discussing each other's work in draft. In the 1940s, there were some interesting differences between the approaches to "the problem of the other" and "freedom" that each was developing. Beauvoir's work leading up to *The Use-*

less Mouths shows her increasingly positioning the relationship between self and the other in a relational way, which we use the term "self-and-other" to characterize. In *Being and Nothingness*, Sartre explores how one's being-for-others appears through the experience of shame, which demonstrates the existence of the other.[9] In doing so, he sees freedom in terms of absolute freedom and then has to find ways around this to explain how in practice people do not perceive themselves "free" in this sense. Beauvoir takes a different tack by "socializing" freedom in three respects: by recognizing that some kinds or categories of people are systematically denied freedom in society; by insisting that the freedom of self is by definition interdependent with that of others; and as a consequence by developing what we think is usefully termed as an ontological ethics around what above we called "self-and-other."[10] These ideas are foregrounded in *The Useless Mouths*, which provides an exposition of Beauvoir's refreshingly direct way of getting to grips with apparently insoluble philosophical issues.

Beauvoir thought such matters important, writing *Pyrrhus and Cineas* to provide the basis for an existentialist ethics as she interpreted this. Looking closely at characters and events in *The Useless Mouths* shows that its central concern too is a strongly ethical one, concerning the people seen as "the useless mouths" and their place in a just society, which is what Vaucelles finally becomes. In the play, Beauvoir explores the meaning and consequences of divergent ethical and philosophical ideas. She does this in part through characters who embody philosophical positions, in larger part through exploring how these characters react to a situation in which a cataclysmic decision is made and its terrible consequences are about to be enacted: the useless mouths will be forcibly expelled from Vaucelles and left to die or be killed by the besiegers, so as to enable its "useful" citizens to survive. The positions adopted by its characters change because of this decision—as one event follows another, so what look like static viewpoints begin to shift. This is because this decision overturns everything people had previously assumed about social bonds: it demolishes their beliefs about the nature of the social contract and forces them to realize the ethical consequences that will follow the decision. As their knowledge and understanding change, their sense of self changes as well. The crucial concern here is who is seen as useful or useless to society, and who should be accorded worth. What the play's unfolding events make clear is that this evaluation is *not* about who should die, but instead that some categories of people are seen as fundamentally useful or useless, not because of what they do, but because of *who they are*.

In Vaucelles, usefulness is apparently defined in relation to work—but in practice only *some* activities performed by *specific* categories of people are seen as useless. And so, although it might appear that the useless mouths are defined as such in relation to seemingly objective measures, it becomes clear that this evaluation is actually the product of gender and power divisions and is ontologically founded. That is, all females are defined in an *a priori* way as useless by virtue of their sex category membership, while only some kinds of males are seen as useless (boys, old men, and the sick) because they cannot work. And what is defined as work is only the activities that healthy adult men engage in, activities that no women can do.

In *The Useless Mouths* and other writing leading up to *The Ethics of Ambiguity*, published in 1947 with its introduction appearing initially in 1946, Beauvoir developed an ontological ethics that centers on concrete situations and their contingencies and how people as individuals and as members of social groups can best act as moral or ethical agents. The play pivots on the presupposition that self is actually self-and-other, and explores what happens in a particular situational reality when self is treated in an individualist and solipsist way. This is spelled out in the tableaux vivants—formal and stylized scenes that show characterization, meaning or an event in a condensed and usually rather static way—that structure it. Beauvoir's uses and reversals of didacticism and use of other writing genres to express her philosophical arguments suggest the influence of Kierkegaard at this time. In December 1940 and January 1941, Beauvoir's letters to Sartre indicate that she was closely reading Kierkegaard's work alongside Kant's, following her equally detailed reading of Hegel's work starting around July 1940.[11]

Kierkegaard proposes that ethics has to recognize the situational nature of social life because the ethical subject requires a framework of social practices and institutions; and that while the universal does not lie outside the individual in an external absolute, it cannot be collapsed into solipsist moral intentions either.[12] Consequently Kierkegaard sees a Hegelian sinking of self into the spirit or *Geist* of an age as evading recognizing people's moral responsibilities. Kierkegaard proposes instead that people are self-determining participants in the existential process, and his ethics foregrounds a resolute engagement in this process, recognizing both social forces and contingencies and the importance of individual moral responsibilities and taking a stand in extreme situations. The Kierkegaardian influence on *Pyrrhus and Cineas* is unmistakable. Beauvoir wrote this dialogue to indicate two opposing but plausible viewpoints. This is strikingly similar to the epistolary dialogue in Kierkegaard's *Either/Or* between A, the representative of a philosophical position on aesthetics, and B, an older person who reads and comments on A's work.[13] The message of *Pyrrhus and Cineas* is more individualist concerning human action, subjectivity, and freedom than that of *The Useless Mouths* although completed only a short time earlier, suggesting the latter was something of a watershed.

The philosophical ideas in *The Useless Mouths* follow Kierkegaard in positing a self-directing individual capable of exercising free will and intentionality. They are also influenced by Hegel's concern that ethics should be rooted in civic life, in reciprocal social relations, thereby reconciling the claims of individual conscience with those inherent in a socially based conception of moral life. There is, however, a lonely and responsible "I" at the center of Kierkegaardian thinking, which positions self as a relation to its own self and an inner anxiety, with this influencing Heidegger and through him Sartre. But Beauvoir in *The Useless Mouths* departs from the Kierkegaardian notion of self, because solipsist boundaries between self-and-other are dissolved when the necessity of common humanity is finally realized by the men of Vaucelles. This is most tellingly played out in the changing relationship between Jean-Pierre and Clarice once the decision to expel the useless mouths becomes known. At this point they both reject their earlier, although rather different, solipsist positions and Jean-Pierre makes a key statement concerning the self-and-other relationship: rather than solipsism characterizing the human condition, there is an indissoluble interconnection.

Beauvoir's thinking about self-and-other and an ontological ethics changed rapidly at this time not least because of the particular concrete situation she was living in, Paris during the Nazi Occupation. *The Useless Mouths* deals with an *in extremis* situation that paralleled the terrifyingly real *in extremis* situation of regulation, deportations, and executions in occupied France. The play consequently focuses on something of direct practical and ethical significance for its author and her audiences: how to respond to a tyrannous regime, which accorded little value to people conceived as "other" and which engaged in brutal genocidal acts against the many categories of people seen as useless and worthless. Beauvoir's ontological ethics are developed around the circumstances of extremity in Vaucelles and whether it is possible to entirely avoid complicity with a tyrannous regime. The fundamental ambiguity and contingency of social life is central to the play because people's behaviors and intentions often have unclear or uncertain meaning, and the consequences of resistance can be lethal for third parties. Here Beauvoir addresses the crucial matter of what commitment actually entails, when the results may mean life and death, not only for the person who acts but other people too.

The Prime of Life charts Beauvoir's move away from solipsism and her growing awareness of the importance of ambiguity and contingency in human affairs and the significance of situation. On this, she commented that, "I objected when people talked to me about Frenchmen, Germans, or Jews: for me there were only individuals. I was right to reject essentialism. . . . But the universalist notions to which I turned bore me equally far from reality. What I lacked was the idea of 'situation,' which alone allows one to make some concrete definition of human groups without enslaving them to a timeless and deterministic pattern."[14] She had in fact arrived at the concept of situation some time before writing *The Useless Mouths*, but the impact of the Occupation underpinned the very concrete exploration of situation that occurs in it.

The German Occupation, Collaboration, and *The Useless Mouths*

> *"For most, food was* the *primary concern in France throughout the occupation. One can appreciate the impact of major food shortages in a country where meals are the focus of daily life . . . Allocations—determined by age and activity—diminished during the occupation years. Simone de Beauvoir was among the many women for whom concerns about finding food became a major obsession . . ."*[15]

The Nazi Occupation began in June 1940 when German forces entered Paris and ended in August 1944. The terms of the Armistice amounted to a German political diktat: although there was nominally a French Government, it carried out German commands, with the total costs of the Occupation borne by the French economy.[16] Between 1938 and 1942, milk consumption halved, bread prices almost doubled, the purchasing power of the franc nearly halved, the cost of living increased by some 166 percent, and the incidence of tuberculosis and other diseases of poverty increased dramatically. Food was scarce and expensive, rations were differentially allocated by age and economic activity, and a huge black market came into existence. A *service du travail obligatoire* (Compulsory Work Service or STO) was introduced, compelling France to send many of its nationals to work in Germany, initially involving 250,000 people and around a million by 1944. An apparatus of discrimination against Jews was instituted and affected all formal encounters between the occupied population and their German rulers. Strict curfews were introduced and an *Ausweis* or internal passport was required for even limited journeys in the occupied zone, as well as between it and Vichy France. By early 1942, Jews were obliged to wear a yellow star and the first mass roundups and deportations started. Alongside this, the Gestapo operated a draconian system of policing backed by hostage-taking, torture, and the rubber-stamping of summary execution for even mundane anti-German acts.

The Occupation impacted on communications at all levels, including the censoring of newspapers and other media. The highly centralized relationship between Paris and the rest of France aided this; the national media was quickly controlled and thereafter communicated a mixture of ordinary material and pro-Nazi propaganda. Cinemas, for instance, showed a mixture of French films and German news propaganda, and radio stations broadcasted a similar cocktail, accustoming people to the ordinariness and apparently factual nature of propaganda news content. Many artists and intellectuals were seduced into turning a blind eye, in accepting money and work contracts. While censorship was tightly controlled, at the same time the propaganda involved was often in packaging and presentation rather than specifying content, making it all the harder for people to draw a line between what was collaboration and what was not.

The Occupation affected all aspects of life, from the most draconian of military and policing encounters to the everyday essentials of shopping and eating. Women were particularly affected, because conventional divisions of labor assigned them responsibility for domestic matters, and because they provided much of the labor force working in the bureaucracies, shops and markets, restaurants, and so on, where French people and the German occupiers interacted. The nature of the Occupation also meant that, to some degree, in some part of people's lives, complicity was almost impossible to avoid: German soldiers and administrators worked, shopped, ate, visited tourist attractions, and went to the theater and cinema, and many Parisians found themselves getting along with or even liking some of them. The moral issues involved were complex, particularly in a situation in which even mild resistance could unleash reprisals on third parties. Two aspects of this bearing on *The Useless Mouths* are Sartre's initial incomprehension of the ethical ambiguities involved and Beauvoir's job writing radio programs for a national radio station.

Beauvoir commented that, when Sartre returned to Paris in March 1941 from being a prisoner of war, he was "armed with principles" and unable to comprehend that "just to be alive implied some sort of compromise," particularly in relation to food and other necessities.[17] For most people, including Beauvoir, food became *the* primary concern. At the start of the Occupation, she had been angry with her father for taking no responsibility for domestic matters and consequently avoiding knowledge of what the German measures actually entailed at a day-to-day level. She also commented about rescuing bad but still edible food Sartre threw away and in effect provisioned him without him really realizing what this took. At least in part, the centrality of food and its scarcity in *The Useless Mouths* was a riposte to the men who abrogated responsibility to women, and certainly it was no accident she dedicated it to her mother, writing to her that, "I am writing a play which is almost finished . . . The subject is . . . a little town in Flanders that is being besieged and where everybody is dying of starvation. They decide to get rid of the children, the women and the old people . . . And then they realize they can't sacrifice half the population that way . . . When it appears in the fall, I will dedicate it to you."[18]

In mid-1943 Beauvoir was forced to leave her teaching post.[19] She later wrote that she was unable to remember how she obtained a job in August or September 1943 writing for Radiodiffusion Nationale, known as Radio-Vichy. There were actually two national radio stations, Radio-Vichy and Radio-Paris. The latter shared the Nazi ideology. However, Beauvoir correctly commented that the unwritten rules meant that people could work for Radio-Vichy without being seen as collaborators depending on what they actually did for it, and that she was involved only with a neutral program concerned with music and song in the Middle Ages. It has been suggested that Beauvoir tried to ensure the transcripts of the broadcasts would not be found. However, Ingrid Galster has traced these transcripts and demonstrated that Beauvoir was entirely accurate about their content.[20]

Not surprisingly, there was considerable discussion about the difficult line between small complicities and actual collaboration. In the context of ensuring economic and physical survival, ethical sensibilities could become flattened. The temptation to use available opportunities to earn money, get food, and get by in reasonably good health was considerable; silence about the "vanishings" of Jews and perceived resistors involved a stronger level of acceptance or turning a blind eye; and not protesting at public acts of brutality and violence a stronger level still. Collaboration, then, encompassed a wide range of kinds and degrees of complicity and it was possible to slide from one to another almost imperceptibly. *The Useless Mouths* deals with many of these themes, locating them in a setting apparently far removed from the Occupation but which permitted their ethical implications to become more visible.

The play has two levels of meaning, about the historical past and the political present, with the latter apparent only indirectly, to enable it to pass the German Censor (although in the event, the Occupation ended before this was necessary). Certainly its original audiences would have immediately grasped the strong "there and here" relationship between the tyranny in Vaucelles and that in Paris.[21] And while Beauvoir makes an ethical and political point in *The Useless Mouths* about the lack of value and humanity accorded to women, she also uses this analogously regarding the Nazi treatment of Jews. Indeed, she is making a wider point about domination more generally and its expression through positioning some categories of people—women, the old, the sick, the young—as by definition worthless. In *The Useless Mouths*, the intended expulsion of the women is a product of the power dynamics operating in Vaucelles around notions of usefulness and personhood, rather than implying there was a different basis for oppressive acts toward women.

It is not just decisions that bring about the genocide of whole groups that *The Useless Mouths* is concerned with, because the everyday low-key nature of much complicity with a ruling group is indicated around class and gender divisions. Thus Catherine and Clarice, wife and daughter, respectively, of Louis, one of Vaucelles' ruling Aldermen, had been unaware that a system of unjust governance existed because they had assumed they shared the same category membership with him. It is only when wider events make clear they are by definition (because women) among the useless mouths that they realize that injustice had existed all along, and they had supported it. Similarly, the fact that resistance could have unintended consequences for third parties is explored in relation to fundamental issues about the self, freedom, and commitment. Thus Jean-Pierre initially insists that intentional action has multiple consequences, much like a bomb that explodes and impacts well beyond its point of detonation. His stance is principled radical solipsism and he determinedly remains disengaged so his behavior does not negatively affect other people: he tries to have clean hands by avoiding close relationships and emotional commitment. But, as Catherine emphasizes, this results in his implicit acceptance of the immoral decision to expel the useless mouths: he either actively resists this, or tacitly he gives consent. In spite of the ambiguities and uncertainties, action has to be taken to resist the immorality of an unjust state if people are to avoid the collaborationist position of bad faith, the Hegelian idea of submitting one's will to a greater force.

The Studio Theater Movement and Its Influence

Developments in contemporary theater in France as well as politics and philosophy influenced Beauvoir in writing *The Useless Mouths* and impacted on its form and content.[22] Performance as a means of engaging with contemporary political events and appealing to a popular audience were very much part of the studio theater movement, with its "mythic theater" component being particularly important in this. The work of Jean Cocteau (whose *Les monstres sacrés* [The Sacred Monsters] was first performed February 1940), Jean Girandoux (whose *Electre* [*Electra*] was first performed May 1937 and *Ondine* May 1939), and especially Jean Anouilh (whose *Antigone* was first performed February 1944) were central here. Mythic theater explored the analogies between classical and contemporary issues, and its approach to *mise en scène* or direction enabled different levels of meaning to unfold through the developing (ethical, political) awareness of a play's characters. Sartre's *The Flies* was an influence on Beauvoir too. About watching Dullin rehearsing her friend Olga in one of its leading roles, she commented, "I knew the text almost by heart, and I found its gradual transformation into a living play immensely exciting: I was fired with the urge to write a play too."[23] She responded in particular to audience reactions to Sartre's *No Exit* (*Huis clos*), first performed in May 1944, stating, "I very much wanted to see *The Useless Mouths* put on. At the preview of *Huis clos* I had been stirred by the thunder of the applause; it was much more immediate, more intoxicating than the scattered echoes wakened by a book."[24]

French theater earlier had been dominated by realist boulevard productions, supported by powerful traditionalist reviewers who dominated public and press responses to theatrical productions and performances. However, in 1927 the *Cartel des quatres* was formed, involving the independent producers Georges Pitoëff, Charles Dullin, Gaston Baty, and Louis Jouvet. This Group of Four director-producers operated independently of the aesthetic stranglehold of traditional theater; their studio theaters pursued very different production values, supported by a smaller but loyal target audience who shared their political as well as aesthetic values. Studio theater involved a strong *mise en scène*, with the directors providing their interpretation of the text but in a way that stayed faithful to the writer's intentions. It also promoted a more naturalistic style of acting, encompassing pauses, silences, and other subtleties, to bring out the symbolic dimensions of an unfolding drama. Studio theater, then, demolished the realist/symbolic divide of earlier French theater and combined realistic sets and acting styles with antirealist plots and situations, and mythic theater revived classical dramas and staged new plays reworking classical themes and plots. With this as a background, Beauvoir became interested in how she might use a play to explore the philosophical aspects of an unfolding "situation" in the philosophical sense of the term.

Beauvoir's interests as a theater-goer, the relationship between the tableau vivant structure and the ideas contained in *The Useless Mouths*, the play's direction by Michel Vitold, and its cast members including actors Lucien Blondeau and Jacqueline Morane, all indicate that Beauvoir aligned herself with the studio theater movement at this time. Mythical theater had become an important part of the studio theater movement, with the "theater of resistance" of early 1940s Paris developing its ideas about a play having different levels of meaning—one articulated on the surface, the other beneath it which audiences could perceive analogically, for antifascist purposes. The key work here is Jean Anouilh's *Antigone*, first performed in February 1944, although other plays with double meanings preceded it, including Claude Vermorel's *Jeanne avec nous* (Joan of Arc with Us) (first performed January 1942) and Sartre's *The Flies* (May 1943). Given the enormous acclaim that Anouilh's work received, and that his *Becket* at the Vieux-Colombier was to have been succeeded by *The Useless Mouths*, Beauvoir and especially her director Michel Vitold would have been influenced by it.

The Useless Mouths was to have opened at the Vieux-Colombier under the management of Baty, but shifted to the Buffes du Nord. This theater was strongly associated with the socialist-influenced *théâtre populaire* or *théâtre d'action*, which announced to theater critics, reviewers and audiences alike that Beauvoir and her play were also part of a political commitment, with its politics very visible because the first night performance was given as a benefit for the orphaned children of people who had been deported to Germany.[25] *The Useless Mouths* moved to the Buffes du Nord principally because Vitold and Baty had a major falling out.[26] Anouilh's *Becket* overran at the Vieux-Colombier, thereby postponing the opening of Beauvoir's play. Alongside this, although Baty had earlier promoted studio theater values, by 1944 he was known for radically departing from the text of plays he produced, while Vitold held firmly to studio theater values.

When *The Useless Mouths* was in rehearsal, Vitold and Beauvoir became lovers and spent much time together, talking through how best dramatically to put across its ideas about contingency, situation, freedom, and ambiguity.[27] Earlier, in 1939 and on holiday with Sartre in Germany, Austria, and Alsace, Beauvoir had attended the Oberammergau passion plays. Although the passion plays ran for many hours each day, audience attention did not waver. From this developed her interest in the tableau vivant form as a means of putting her ideas across through focused emphasis, with this structural aspect of *The Useless Mouths* as well as its core ideas chiming with studio theater values. Beauvoir had been struck that although the plays encompassed vast crowd scenes, their tableaux vivants enabled this to be combined with intense focus on particular characters, in moments of concentration that she described as "dumb and motionless," but which were also located in a strong narrative flow of events that swept audiences along. And within this, contingency and situation were crucial because the (cosmic) context of the passion plays is that freedom is severely circumscribed by factors beyond individual choice or will. Beauvoir later commented that the overall effects "were achieved by a most remarkable blend of precision and 'distancing.'"[28]

The connections here with studio theater ideas about intensity of performance are strong, and Vitold's direction of *The Useless Mouths* pointed up these aspects. Vitold's particular style of directing was clearly important to Beauvoir and in a pre–first-night interview she commented, "What strikes one first of all when you see Vitold working is his extraordinary integrity, he never allows a light effect, a movement of the crowd, an attitude that is not in the text to be added: he works only from the text, he reveals hidden meanings . . . emphasizes the resonances . . . he obtains a type of aesthetic transposition which is neither stylization nor realism . . . it is only with a certain use of space and time—attitudes, movement, rhyme, silences—it is through atmosphere that certain sentiments, certain situations—limits can be created or made to exist."[29]

The Play's the Thing

The Useless Mouths has two acts and eight tableaux vivants. Act I is composed of three tableaux vivants and takes place on a single day. Act II commences the morning after, with its five tableaux continuing through the day and into the evening, the last taking place at two o'clock in the morning of the following day. It is a very "writerly" play. Its writerly aspects include its often elaborate and always significant uses of semicolons and colons, which are forms of punctuation that work solely in writing and not in speaking. They also include the ways that the complexly layered events and scenes in each tableau are related to the other tableaux and to the play as a whole. How the tableaux vivants are interconnected with those that precede and follow is indeed crucial to the way ideas are developed, including how issues about particular ways of being a self, and about particular moral positions, are pointed up within the flow of events and the characters' responses to these. This also helps convey Beauvoir's philosophical ideas beyond the specific situation they are presented through.

The structure of the play and its tableaux vivants is in fact well-suited to Beauvoir's writerly purposes in also putting across delineated philosophical positions. What some contemporary reviewers described as the play's stiltedness was actually her conscious use of formalism: the tableaux vivants are a formal and stylized way of focusing on particularities in a linked formation. Beauvoir uses this in two ways. Structurally, she does so by breaking up each act into a series of tableaux and signaling that each of these is "about" a particular emphasis or viewpoint in the narrative flow. And dramatically, she uses these moments of focus to signal transition points that propel the dramatic action forward. The result is that *The Useless Mouths* is both very realistic (it takes place in a real-world historical setting, its characters talk to each other rather than declaim to the audience, it contains speaking silences and meaningful pauses rather than being always filled by talk and action) and also highly symbolic (by using a distant time period to put across timeless ideas with then-contemporary relevance).

Beauvoir read widely on the Middle Ages for the radio programs mentioned earlier. Many of her ideas about Vaucelles are based on Ghent, the most powerful of the Flanders city-states, with the others being Bruges, Antwerp, Lille, and Oudenburg; and Beauvoir visited these places while on holiday with Sartre in 1943. Vaucelles, like the Flanders city-states, received its charter from its feudal lord, the Dukes of Burgundy. Like the Flanders city-states, Vaucelles has guilds of highly skilled craftsmen who operate monopolies, while its lower-level artisans are underprivileged and disaffected. Also Vaucelles, like the Flanders city-states, is ruled by a group of Aldermen led by its "Three Members," with these roles occupied by Louis, Jacques, and François in the play. In the Flanders city-states, their belfries had great symbolic power because they housed their archives and charters. In Vaucelles, building a belfry is the symbol of its independence, because it has revolted and overthrown Burgundian rule. Its belfry has a literal purpose in the play, because its bell will be rung when the siege is ended by the King of France and his troops, while its symbolic purpose is to represent what work is. Work is ensuring the building of the belfry, with this also providing the definition of usefulness and value in Vaucelles. This work is useful and valuable, and it is what men do. However, the consequence of seeing work in such terms is to position women as by definition not working, and therefore as useless and without value.

The Useless Mouths is historically well-grounded, with the fictional Vaucelles built up around a creative use of the historical facts. Its resoundingly ironic name, its symbolically important but actually totally useless belfry, its many small betrayals of human fellow-feeling, and its men's collaboration in the self-serving decision to expel the so-called useless mouths, add considerable verisimilitude to its portrayal. Also, watching and hearing what was unfolding on the stage, its analogy between a fictional city in a play and a real city under the Occupation must have been both striking and audacious. And while Beauvoir later represented the critical response as hostile,[30] many reviewers actually mixed positive comments about the play itself and its innovativeness with critical assessments of its production.[31] Ph.D.'s review in *L'ordre* (Order), for instance, commented, "The eccentricity of this theater, the uneven quality of its previous shows and the mediocrity of its present troupe diminishes the chance of success for *The Useless Mouths*. How come in all Paris there wasn't to be found at least ten directors fighting for this manuscript? If there is any justice, if the public . . . is still in a state to appreciate its worth, *The Useless Mouths* will triumph on the Boulevard de la Chapelle. If not, rest assured it will triumph abroad and will return to Paris on a major stage."[32]

The more critical comments were made about Vitold's direction and the inadequacies of the theater, although the studied nature of the tableaux vivants and their effects on characterization and performance were also mentioned. D's review in *Le théâtre*, for instance, commented that it is "[A] play about ideas, a very 'writerly' play and strongly thought out. Michel Vitold's direction alternates between being too solemn or too violent and struggles uncomfortably against the emptiness and the silence that arise between too many tableaux."[33] However, while Jean Walter's review in *Plaisir des hommes* recognized the play's strong structure of ideas, this is seen as negatively affecting characterization, suggesting that "it would have been better to develop the characters one by one than a text phrase by phrase," and also commenting that the theater's acoustics were terrible and the actors could not be heard.[34] While the more negative reviews might have stung, Beauvoir would certainly have been aware that they came mainly from traditionally minded critics of the kind that the *Cartel des quatres* had been formed to counter, and that they were judging *The Useless Mouths*, a studio theater production, against boulevard theater values. Indeed, what comes across now is that such critics did not understand what *The Useless Mouths* was about, treating it as a conventional but gloomy "show" rather than a philosophical play.

Looking beyond the immediate 1944 evaluations by theater critics and reading it in today's context, *The Useless Mouths* is engrossing, particularly when read aloud; its dramatic action is absorbing, and it "works" as a piece of writing. At the same time, this does not necessarily mean it will work as *a play*, a drama written for performance before an audience that will immediately respond positively or negatively to it. It is important to recognize here that present-day audiences respond to new productions of companion studio theater productions, such as *Antigone* or *No Exit*, much more positively than their 1940s counterparts; audience tastes have developed considerably and what was considered avant garde then has now become part of mainstream theater. However, the jury must necessarily remain out on whether *The Useless Mouths* is a good play or not until it is actually revived, in French or in English or both, and performed once again on stage. But considered as a contribution to Beauvoir's developing ideas, *The Useless Mouths* inhabits clearly pivotal space and marks what was with hindsight a transition point in her thinking. It has what became one of her hallmarks, as a mixed-genre piece of writing, in its case combining philosophy with the dramatic form; and importantly, it shows Beauvoir's move from the solipsism of earlier work, toward a concept of self-and-other and the ontological ethics of her later writing.

Increased attention to Beauvoir as a philosopher has not yet led to *The Useless Mouths* becoming a well-known part of her oeuvre. Beauvoir's comments about the play have played a part here, with her criticisms taken literally and her positive comments often disregarded. In the latter, she highlighted the attention given to the importance of "situation," the emphasis on freedom being neither an absolute nor a given, and the argument that ethics has to recognize the fundamental ambiguity of social life, all clearly resonant in her later work.[35] Her "condemnation," to use Beauvoir's own word, focused on its idealism and didacticism, which she thought had led to the same mistake in the play that she perceived in *The Blood of Others*, that her characters were just ethical viewpoints.[36] Kruks has suggested that the ethics Beauvoir developed in *Pyrrus and Cineas* was as "empty" as the Kantian ethics she was ranging herself against.[37] However, this really cannot be said of *The Useless Mouths*, written shortly after, for what emerges from the *in extremis* situation it represents is neither an extreme individualist existentialism nor an empty abstract Kantian approach but a grounded, collective and shared ethics. The problem the play turns on may not be resolvable and the people of Vaucelles may die; uncertainty remains. But, finally, they act together as a collective ethical unity.

On Translations

Beauvoir's letters to Nelson Algren show there had been an earlier English translation of *Les bouches inutiles* that was never published. On September 27, 1947, she wrote to him that, "I saw a young English man who has just translated my play *Useless Mouths* and would like to have it acted in England. I'll send you his translation;" on September 28, 1947, she added, "I'll send you tomorrow morning the translation of my play which was acted in winter 1945. . . . I know it has many faults but I should like you to read something from me;" and on October 14, 1947, she responded, presumably to some critical comments, that, "I understand very well what you say about the play. Even in French it is a little stiff. Some critics liked it very much and others disliked it as much, but nearly everyone agreed it was too stiff and didactic. I think you would find me better in the novels: I tried to put in them much more of myself. . . ."[38] There also seems to have been a German translation too, for on October 4, 1950 she wrote to Algren that, "I have *Blood of Others* given in Germany, in a long two hours radio-cast, worked about carefully last year by a nice woman . . . it could make it quite good. *Useless Mouths* is going to be given on the radio, too."[39]

This was followed by an English translation by Claude Francis and Fernande Gontier, published in 1983 as *Who Shall Die?* and now out of print and very difficult to obtain.[40] Their translation used the same French text as we did, the 1945 Gallimard first edition of *Les bouches inutiles*, and we read their version well after finishing our own translation because it took many months to obtain a copy of it. However, once we read it and compared it with our own work, we were struck by some significant differences. The most important is the very different way they and we interpret the philosophical crux of the play. Francis and Gontier's translation is called *Who Shall Die?*, although this has a very different meaning from Beauvoir's own title, *Les bouches inutiles, The Useless Mouths*. They see who dies as what the play is about, whereas for us—and we think for Beauvoir—this concerns who has worth in an ontological and ethical sense, who is deemed to have social value and thus to be a fully human subject or self.

Thinking in terms of "who shall die" we think fails to perceive the *categorical* nature of the decision to expel "the useless mouths" from Vaucelles, with this misperception then guiding other aspects of Francis and Gontier's translation. Their omission of the play's dedication is a case in point, for in dedicating it to her mother, one of the useless mouths on two counts (sex and age), Beauvoir was pointedly rejecting Nazi ideas about usefulness and value. Their omission of a short but resonant remark from one of Vaucelles' ruling Aldermen, François, is another, for his statement shows the sea change in his philosophical position: he now sees women as useless, having earlier evaluated the building of the belfry in these terms. The remark is omitted probably so this actor does not have to stay on stage for a lengthy period without speaking. But without it, François' behavior later in the play, when he becomes a would-be dictator seeking to overthrow the established order, makes little sense. Francis and Gontier's translation also masculinizes English renditions of the French, and by doing so ignores structural features of French as a language. In fact Beauvoir is extremely precise in her usage, and where she is defeated by the "maleness" of some words in French she leaves ample hints as to whether she intends a masculine form or not, whereas Francis and Gontier straightforwardly use male forms. Their approach was "of the time" and then-usual practice, although being challenged by the 1980s; however, our point is that such an approach runs against the grain of what Beauvoir wrote and the precision of her French.

Regarding our own translation practices, one of us (Naji) is a hybrid speaker of French and English (also Arabic), one of us (Stanley) is a native English speaker, and we have worked by "triple translating." This has involved translating the original text into English, and then translating the English back into French, the better to gauge its successes and limitations, and then repairing the latter in the translated version. Our translation practices have also involved translating orally. That is, we talked out every small detail of translation and constantly read aloud the results to each other. We always translated orally each sentence and then the whole of each speak-act by each character. In addition, we read aloud and revised particular sections within each tableau while the translation as a whole was in progress; then we read aloud and revised every tableau; then we did this for the entire play; and at every point in this process we compared and contrasted what we had done by returning to Beauvoir's original text. In addition, each of these stages of translation occurred on a number of occasions, as did returning to the original French and immersing ourselves in it.

In translating like this, we have balanced being true to Beauvoir's text with producing a translation that is believable to present-day readers and audiences. Walter Benjamin's comments are very much consonant with our own approach when he proposes that, "the language of a translation can—in fact, must—let itself go, so that it gives voice to the *intentio* of the original not as reproduction but as harmony. . . . A real translation is transparent; it does not cover the original, does not block its light, but allows the pure language, as though reinforced by its own medium, to shine upon the original all the more fully."[41] We too have striven for intention and harmony, rather than a strict reproduction kind of translation, which attempts what he calls "covering" the original and which produces a stiff and wooden result, "blocking the light." Moreover, being attentive to its own medium, as Benjamin puts it, has involved us in translation practices that not only focus on the details of the text but are also attentive to the historical, political, and cultural context in which the play was written and performed. Our intention has been to produce a translation that works at a number of levels: as a piece of writing; as a play, that is, as text for potential performance; and as a cross-genre form that combines a play with a philosophical message.

In working in this way, we were mindful of Beauvoir's comment in a newspaper interview published immediately before the first performances of *The Useless Mouths*, that everything about its writing was studied, deliberate, and intended.[42] Indeed, the more detailed our knowledge of the text has become, the more this comment seems exactly right: this was a text she crafted with great care, much deliberation, and considerable exactitude. Our translation practices have stayed close to Beauvoir's intentions and the intellectual and political project underpinning her writing of *The Useless Mouths*. This is to convey the consequences when a society perceives some people as by definition useless, without value, and therefore dispensable. The ethical import of *The Useless Mouths* is that no separation between ends and means is possible, let alone ethically desirable; and that a self is not divided into being-for-self and being-for-others, but instead involves self-and-other and an ontological ethics. These ideas are put across through successive events as responded to by the inhabitants of Vaucelles, and our translation carefully follows the thread of Beauvoir's thinking across the play's two acts and their tableaux vivants, teasing out in English the many allusions and nuances in the original text. Such things are easy to lose in translation, even easier to iron out if searching for a completely smooth translation, and we have endeavored to avoid this by staying close to Beauvoir's philosophical project. Our translation of the play's title is crucial in this.

The Useless Mouths depicts the moral order of Vaucelles as one where all females *by definition* have no use and so no value, but when males are seen as useless this is *not* because of their category membership as male, but due to subsidiary factors like youth and ill health. Accordingly, we have translated its title as "*the* useless mouths" because the unfolding drama of the play is constituted by the growing realization on the part of some characters that "useless" is not an evaluation that might be attached to any person, but instead signifies an entire category of people who are by definition, as this kind of person, morally valued as useless and worthless. In other words, we have followed the same logic as was used in translating Beauvoir's *Le deuxième sexe* as "The Second Sex" and not "Second Sex," which would have had a very different meaning and depart significantly from Beauvoir's analytical purposes. Our strategy throughout has been to "follow Beauvoir," and it is clear that in *The Useless Mouths* she was analyzing the situation of women in categorical terms well before she is usually seen to have done so.

In producing this new translation of *The Useless Mouths*, we have been encouraged and enabled by the excellent scholarship on Beauvoir's philosophy published over the last few decades. Howsoever *The Useless Mouths* is finally evaluated within the complete oeuvre of Beauvoir's writings, as the result of this new scholarly work English-speaking readers are now better equipped to appreciate her ideas in this play than ever before, and we are very proud to have played a small part in this.

NOTES

1. Simone de Beauvoir, *The Prime of Life*, trans. Peter Green (Harmondsworth: Penguin, 1965 [1960]), 587.

2. Simone de Beauvoir, *Les bouches inutiles: pièce en deux actes et huit tableaux* (Paris: Gallimard, 1945). Le Théâtre des Carrefours was originally named Les Buffes du Nord and later reverted to this name.

3. Virginia Fichera, "Simone de Beauvoir and 'The Woman Question': *Les bouches inutiles*," *Yale French Studies* 72 (1986): 52–54.

4. See the other contributions to this volume for confirmation.

5. One program, "A Fair in the Middle Ages," featured a brouhaha of voices, the shouts of merchants, and the cries of animals, over which well-known songs of the comic tradition in the Middle Ages were heard, with a bourgeois couple visiting a fair and talking to other people. The other was set in Paris at night and featured a penniless young prostitute who was befriended by a student and taken to eat and drink in a nearby tavern; again, music was used together with conversations between characters. For the radio programs, see Ingrid Galster, *Beauvoir dans tous ses états* (Beauvoir in All Her States) (Paris: Editions Tallantier, 2007), 111–34. For Beauvoir's reading on the Middle Ages, see Beauvoir, *The Prime of Life*, 540, 587–90; and Simone de Beauvoir, *Force of Circumstance*, trans. Richard Howard (Harmondsworth: Penguin, 1968 [1963]), 23–44, 56–60, 70–75.

6. Beauvoir, *Force of Circumstance*, 46.

7. For these essays in new translations, see the contributions to Simone de Beauvoir, *Philosophical Writings*, ed. Margaret A. Simons (Urbana: University of Illinois Press, 2004). For

these novels, see Simone de Beauvoir, *When Things of the Spirit Come First*, trans. Patrick O'Brian (New York: Pantheon, 1982 [1979]); Simone de Beauvoir, *She Came to Stay*, trans. Yvonne Moyse and Roger Senhouse (London: Flamingo/Harper Collins, 1984 [1943]); and Simone de Beauvoir, *The Blood of Others*, trans. Yvonne Moyse and Roger Senhouse (New York: Knopf, 1948 [1945]).

8. For an interesting discussion of Beauvoirian ethics in connection with *Pyrrhus and Cineas*, see Sonia Kruks, "Introduction to Moral Idealism and Political Realism" in Simone de Beauvoir, *Philosophical Writings*, ed. Margaret A. Simons (Urbana: University of Illinois Press, 2004), 167–73.

9. Jean-Paul Sartre, *Being and Nothingness*, trans. Hazel E. Barnes (New York: Gramercy, 1956 [1943]).

10. As proposed in Liz Stanley, "Rejecting the legend, re-reading Beauvoir, reworking existentialism: the case for ontological ethics," *European Journal of Women's Studies*, 3 (1996); and Liz Stanley, "A philosopher manqué? Simone de Beauvoir, moral value and 'The Useless Mouths'," *European Journal of Women's Studies*, 8 (2001).

11. Simone de Beauvoir, *Letters to Sartre*, ed. Sylvie Le Bon de Beauvoir, trans. Quentin Hoare (London: Vintage, 1991 [1990]).

12. For a useful introduction, see Patrick Gardiner, *Kierkegaard* (New York: Oxford University Press, 1988).

13. Søren Kierkegaard, *Either/Or*, trans. Robert L. Perkins (Macon, Ga: Mercer University Press, 1995 [1843]).

14. Beauvoir, *The Prime of Life*, 167.

15. M. Collins Weitz, *Sisters in the Resistance* (Toronto: Wiley, 1995), 39.

16. For helpful accounts of the German Occupation, see J. Adler, *The Jews of Paris and the Final Solution* (Oxford: Oxford University Press, 1989); A. Beltran, R. Frank, and H. Rousso, *La vie des enterprises sous l'occupation* (The Life of Businesses during the Occupation) (Paris: Belin, 1994); M. C. Weitz, *Sisters in the Resistance*; I. Ousby, *Occupation: The Ordeal of France 1940–1944* (London: John Murray, 1998); and also Jean-Paul Sartre's essay, "Paris sous l'occupation" ("Occupied Paris"), in *Situations III* (Paris: Gallimard, 1949).

17. Beauvoir, *The Prime of Life*, 479–80.

18. This is in a letter to her mother, dated just "Monday"; see Deirdre Bair, *Simone de Beauvoir: A Biography* (London: Vintage/Random House, 1991), 267.

19. This was primarily because of the revelation of a sexual relationship with a pupil, but also because the collaborationist regime in the Education Department saw her as additionally morally subversive in assigning Proust and Gide for her pupils to read. See Galster, *Beauvoir dans tous ses états*, 97–111.

20. They were found in the Bibliothèque Nationale, Département des Arts du Spectacle; for details, see Galster, *Beauvoir dans tous ses états*, 113.

21. Divisions in the Flanders city-states are usefully discussed in Peter Arnade, *Realms of Ritual: Burgundian Ceremony and Civic Life in Late Medieval Ghent* (Ithaca: Cornell University Press, 1996); Mary Ehler and Maryanne M. Kowaleski, *Women and Power in the Middle Ages* (Athens, Ga.: University of Georgia Press, 1988); and William TeBrake, *A Plague of Insurrection: Popular Politics and Peasant Revolt in Flanders, 1323–1328* (Philadelphia: University of Pennsylvania Press, 1993).

22. On issues and strategies in French theater of the time, see Jacques Guicharnoud, *Modern French Theater, from Giraudoux to Genet* (New Haven: Yale University Press, 1967),

Harold Hobson, *The French Theater of Today* (London: George Harrap, 1953); Harold Hobson, *French Theater Since 1830* (London: John Calder, 1978); Dorothy Knowles, *French Theater of the Inter-War Years* (London: George Harrap, 1967); and David Whitton, *Stage Directors in Modern France* (Manchester: Manchester University Press, 1987).

23. Beauvoir, *The Prime of Life*, 538.

24. Beauvoir, *Force of Circumstance*, 56.

25. See A. Collingnon, "Bouches inutiles aux Carrefours," *Opéra*, October 31, 1944. Manuscript no. R supp. 1717, scrapbook of press cuttings; Bibliothèque de L'Arsenal, Paris.

26. Discussed interestingly in Beauvoir, *Force of Circumstance*, 23–35.

27. This and other background to the play is discussed in Beauvoir, *Force of Circumstance*, 23–39.

28. Beauvoir, *The Prime of Life*, 196.

29. See the "Interview" with Beauvoir in *Le pays* (The Country), October 1, 1945; our translation. Manuscript no. R supp. 1717, scrapbook of press cuttings; Bibliothèque de L'Arsenal, Paris.

30. Beauvoir, *Force of Circumstance*, 59–60.

31. There were approximately forty reviews; these appeared in, among others, *Le soir* (The Evening), *Plaisir des hommes* (Men's Amusements), *Le monde* (The World), *Courrier de Paris* (The Paris Courier), *La dépêche de Paris* (The Paris Dispatch), *Le figaro* (Figaro), *Populaire-la scène* (The Populist—Stage Section), *L'écran* (The Screen), and *Le pays*. See Manuscript no. R supp. 1717, scrapbook of press cuttings; Bibliothèque de L'Arsenal, Paris.

32. See Ph.D., "Le théâtre" ("The Theater") *L'ordre*, November 8, 1945; our translation. Manuscript no. R supp. 1717, scrapbook of press cuttings; Bibliothèque de L'Arsenal, Paris.

33. "D" in "Points de vue" ("Points of View") *Le théâtre*, November 15, 1944; our translation. Manuscript no. R supp. 1717, scrapbook of press cuttings; Bibliothèque de L'Arsenal, Paris.

34. Jean Walter in *Plaisir des hommes*, November 7, 1944; our translation. Manuscript no. R supp. 1717, scrapbook of press cuttings; Bibliothèque de L'Arsenal, Paris.

35. See the discussion in Beauvoir, *The Prime of Life*, 547–50.

36. Beauvoir, *The Prime of Life*, 587–90.

37. Kruks, "Introduction to Moral Idealism and Political Realism," 167–73.

38. For these letters, see Simone de Beauvoir, *Beloved Chicago Man: Letters to Nelson Algren 1947–64*, ed. Sylvie Le Bon de Beauvoir (London: Victor Gollancz, 1998 [1997]), 68–70, 71–73, and 80–81, respectively.

39. Beauvoir, *Beloved Chicago Man*, 377–79.

40. See Simone de Beauvoir, *Who Shall Die?*, trans. Claude Francis and Fernande Gontier (Florissant, Missouri: River Press, 1983).

41. Walter Benjamin, "The Task of the Translator. An Introduction to the Translation of Baudelaire's Tableaux Parisiens," in (ed.) Hannah Arendt, *Illuminations*, trans. Harry Zorn (London: Pimlico, 1999 [1923]), 79.

42. Beauvoir states this in the "Interview" in *Le pays*, October 1, 1945. Manuscript no. R supp. 1717, scrapbook of press cuttings; Bibliothèque de L'Arsenal, Paris.

THE USELESS MOUTHS

by Simone de Beauvoir

TRANSLATION AND NOTES BY LIZ STANLEY AND CATHERINE NAJI

A play in two acts and eight tableaux

To my Mother

Characters

Character	Actor
Louis D'Avesnes	Lucien Blondeau[1]
Jacques Van Der Welde	Roger Bontemps
François Rosbourg	Georges Vitsoris
Jean-Pierre Gauthier	Jean Berger
Georges D'Avesnes, son of Louis	Jean-Roger Caussimon
The Captain	
The Site Foreman	
Soldiers, masons, drapers, deputies, ordinary people.	
Catherine, wife of Louis	Jacqueline Morane
Clarice, her daughter	Olga Dominique
Jeanne	Marise Manuel
Women of the people	

The events take place in the 14th century, in Vaucelles, a town in Flanders.

The play was performed for the first time in November 1945 under the directorship of MICHEL VITOLD, in the Théâtre des Carrefours.

FIRST ACT

First Tableau

A lookout post under the ramparts of Vaucelles,[2] *at the foot of a tower. Three soldiers around a fire. They are stamping their feet to keep warm.*[3]

FIRST SOLDIER:[4] It's freezing!

SECOND SOLDIER: I'm hungry. Isn't the angelus bell going to ring soon?

FIRST SOLDIER: Once we've eaten, it's even worse; we're just as hungry as ever and we've nothing left to look forward to.

SECOND SOLDIER: If something was happening, at least it would take our minds off it.

A woman accompanied by a child comes in and huddles up[5] *against the wall.*

THIRD SOLDIER: We're here, we don't move, the Burgundians don't move either. This siege has lasted for a year now! It will never end.

FIRST SOLDIER: It *will* end. We can't live for long on straw and husks.

A Sentry comes down the ramparts pushing Jean-Pierre Gauthier ahead of him.

THIRD SOLDIER: Where is the Captain? We've caught a Burgundian spy.

GAUTHIER: It's *me* who's the spy!

THIRD SOLDIER: Gauthier!

SECOND SOLDIER: It's Jean-Pierre Gauthier!

GAUTHIER: I'm really glad to see you! It was devilishly cold in that ditch. Quick, give me some good hot soup.

FIRST SOLDIER: Come and sit down next to the fire. You look frozen.

THE SENTRY: I want to hand this man over to the Captain.

FIRST SOLDIER: But I'm telling you, it's Gauthier.

THE SENTRY: Nobody has the right to breach the walls.

THIRD SOLDIER: Stubborn as a mule.

SECOND SOLDIER: All right; I'll go and fetch the Captain for him.

He goes into the tower. An old woman comes in and lines up next to the first woman.

FIRST SOLDIER: Have you seen the King of France?

SECOND SOLDIER: When will he come to defeat the Duke?

GAUTHIER: I'll tell that to Master D'Avesnes. Give me some soup.

FIRST SOLDIER: It's that . . . we don't have any soup.

GAUTHIER: Give me anything I can eat, with a good drink of wine.

The soldiers look at each other, embarrassed.

SECOND SOLDIER: We haven't got any wine.

THE SENTRY: But where has this fellow come from?

FIRST SOLDIER: We have to wait for the angelus bell.

GAUTHIER: What, there's nothing to eat here? Nothing to drink?

THE SENTRY: He understands nothing.

FIRST SOLDIER: Twice a day we're given a soup of boiled husks and some bread made from straw.

Two women pass them and join the others.

GAUTHIER: We have come to this?

SECOND SOLDIER: Yes, the King of France has to hurry himself.

GAUTHIER: What are these women doing?

SECOND SOLDIER: Every day they come to beg a little food. I don't like to see them!

He turns his back.

THE CAPTAIN: But yes, it's Gauthier. (*To the Sentry.*) Go and inform Master[6] D'Avesnes. (*The Sentry leaves.*) Did you get back without too much trouble?

JEAN-PIERRE: It wasn't difficult to get across the Burgundian camp. But our town is well guarded.

THE CAPTAIN: What's being said about us in Paris?

GAUTHIER: The bourgeoisie[7] admire us, but they wouldn't have the audacity to overthrow their King and govern themselves. They don't think enough and they are too prudent.

THE CAPTAIN: Not everybody is capable of what we've done here.

THIRD SOLDIER: For that, we had to be tough. If our plot *had* failed, we'd all have been hanged.

SECOND SOLDIER: But it's the Duke's Bailiff that was hanged! (*They laugh.*) Another great day!

GAUTHIER: We're going to have others just as great!

SECOND SOLDIER: You think so?

FIRST SOLDIER: Will we ever be at the end of our troubles?

GAUTHIER: Yes, that day will come. Soon we'll be happy and free men.[8] We will work for ourselves, we will live for ourselves.

THE CAPTAIN: All the other towns[9] will envy us; we will set a great example to the world. Keep your hopes up: we won't have suffered in vain.

FIRST SOLDIER: If we didn't have hope, we couldn't put up with all this.

Louis D'Avesnes enters. Gauthier goes toward him. The Captain leaves.

GAUTHIER: Master D'Avesnes! You can see I didn't delay.

LOUIS: It's true, you came quickly. What's the news?

GAUTHIER: The King of France will come to our aid. He said, "It's in my interest as much as it's in yours." But he won't come until spring.

LOUIS: Until spring!

GAUTHIER: First of all he has to hunt the Burgundians from his lands. And his army couldn't undertake this long journey in winter: they would find neither food for themselves, nor fodder for their animals.

LOUIS: Until spring!

The angelus bell rings. Two soldiers from the field-canteen[10] enter carrying a soup-kettle and a basket of bread. They start to serve the soldiers. The women come closer to them.

FIRST WOMAN: For pity's sake! A little soup for my child who is dying of hunger!

OLD WOMAN: A little morsel of bread, for pity's sake!

One of the soldiers from the field-canteen takes a loaf and hesitates.

THIRD WOMAN: I haven't eaten for three days.

The soldier from the field-canteen holds out the loaf to them. The other one seizes it.

SECOND SOLDIER: You're mad! It's *our* bread.

FIRST SOLDIER: Do you think our ration is too big?

The women begin to cry.

THIRD WOMAN: I'm hungry! I'm so hungry!

The soldiers eat with a stubborn air without looking at them.

GAUTHIER: Are you going to let them die of hunger? (*Silence. The soldiers continue to eat.*) Friends, have your hearts become so hard?

LOUIS, *approaching*: Leave them alone. They never have enough bread.

GAUTHIER: But what can we do for these women?

LOUIS: Nothing.

Second Tableau

In front of the belfry[11] *being built. A square with closed shops.*

The sound of hammering and sawing. Some laborers are at work. In a corner, in front of the Town Hall, women, children, old men, stand in line with food dishes in their hands.

OLD WOMAN: What is it you're eating?

ANOTHER: He's *eating*!

ANOTHER: Who is eating?

ANOTHER: What's up?

ANOTHER: Mathieu is eating!

MATHIEU: It's some straw.

OLD WOMAN: Where did you find the straw?[12]

Jeanne and Jean-Pierre pass by them.

JEANNE: Have you seen how the belfry has grown since you left?

JEAN-PIERRE: It's grown. And you're thin and pale, little sister.

JEANNE: Am I so pale? I don't feel ill. Did you eat white bread in Paris?

JEAN-PIERRE: Yes, white bread. What are these people waiting for?

JEANNE: Some food is distributed every day to the townspeople.

JEAN-PIERRE: Dried grass! And they wait for hours! (*A pause.*) When I left Vaucelles, there were still children playing in the streets and sometimes a woman singing.

JEANNE: Three months have gone by.

JEAN-PIERRE: Three centuries! I'd like to flee far from here! Since I crossed your walls, every breath of air that I breathe tastes of remorse. Even though none of it is my fault.[13]

JEANNE: Don't torment yourself.

JEAN-PIERRE: All the looks that I meet seem to be either reproaches or prayers. Everyone is a beggar in this town, but I've never asked anything from anyone. I want to be left alone at peace with myself.

JEANNE: Come on, you'll get used to it.

JEAN-PIERRE: Do you think so? It was good galloping by myself along the roads! (*A pause.*) How is Clarice?

JEANNE: She's fed up.

JEAN-PIERRE: And Georges?

JEANNE: You know him.

JEAN-PIERRE: Tell me frankly: do you love him?

JEANNE: Is it necessary[14] that I love him?

Clarice runs in, sees Jean-Pierre, stops, then comes forward with a show of indifference.

JEAN-PIERRE: Clarice!

CLARICE: Hello, Jean-Pierre.

JEAN-PIERRE: Were you looking for me?

CLARICE: No. I was out walking.

JEAN-PIERRE: I'm so happy to see you!

CLARICE: Really?

JEAN-PIERRE: Do you doubt it? Since I crossed the ramparts, I have wanted nothing else! (*He takes her hands. They look at each other.*)

CLARICE: Since you crossed the ramparts . . . Did you think about me during the previous three months?

JEAN-PIERRE: Often.

CLARICE: But did you miss me?

JEAN-PIERRE: What could I miss? It was enough to know that these blue eyes, this smile, were somewhere in the world.

CLARICE *(disengaging herself)*: Me, I didn't think of you. I never think about the dead, nor the absent. I don't like ghosts.

JEAN-PIERRE: I'm no longer a ghost. (*He makes a movement toward her. She pulls back.*) Why are you pulling away from me?

CLARICE: We have lived for three months like strangers and we haven't suffered because of it. What's the good of seeing each other again?

JEAN-PIERRE: It's good that we haven't suffered. If your absence hollowed out a void in me, if my image hid the world from you, then that would be a reason why we ought not to see each other again.

CLARICE: You're right. I hate suffering.

JEAN-PIERRE *(Taking her in his arms.)*: You are here; I see you; I smell you: there is nothing more to wish for. I'm glad that you haven't thought about me.

CLARICE: *Are* you happy about it?

JEAN-PIERRE: Oh, if I thought it was my fault that these eyes were sullied by tears . . .

CLARICE: What would you do?

JEAN-PIERRE: I would feel smothered at your side like I feel smothered in this town.

CLARICE, *after a pause*: Why have you come back?

JEAN-PIERRE: I left so I could come back.

CLARICE: I wouldn't have come back.

JEAN-PIERRE: You would have forgotten your home?

CLARICE: I would have forgotten everything. I would have lived alone and free. I would have *lived.*

JEAN-PIERRE: And you would never have thought about me?

CLARICE: Maybe I would have thought that somewhere in the world there were these green eyes, this smile. (*Jean-Pierre looks at her in silence with a smile.*) Why are you looking at me like that?

JEAN-PIERRE: You please me, Clarice, you are real, pure and alone.[15]

CLARICE, *appealing to him*: Jean-Pierre . . . !

JEAN-PIERRE, *perturbed and tender*: What do you want?

CLARICE: Don't worry. I'm not angry with you about anything. I had forgotten to tell you that my father wishes to speak to you as soon as possible. Perhaps he is still at the house. Go quickly.

JEAN-PIERRE: Won't you come with me?

CLARICE: It's better that he doesn't see us together.

JEAN-PIERRE: Until this evening, then, my beautiful black diamond.[16]

He leaves, she follows him with her eyes.

CLARICE: Fool! Blind fool!

She sits in a corner and stays still. Two masons enter carrying a stone.

FIRST MASON: We're not getting very far.

SECOND MASON: I feel weak as a woman.[17]

FIRST MASON: Give me a hand. I can't lift this stone, I no longer have enough strength.

SECOND MASON: How do they expect us to work, with just this paste of straw in our stomachs!

THE SITE FOREMAN:[18] You have only to say the word and the Council will stop the work.[19]

FIRST MASON: What would become of us, walking around empty-handed with hunger in our guts, in this town where there isn't a strand of wool left to weave?[20]

SECOND MASON: Wouldn't that be a nice thing, if the belfry wasn't finished by spring for when the King of France arrives!

THE SITE FOREMAN: Well then, stop complaining.

FIRST MASON: We're not complaining. We're saying we'd do better work if we were better fed.

FIRST WOMAN: They aren't in a hurry.

AN OLD MAN: They're never in a hurry.

CHILD: Mother, I'm bored. Can't I go and play?

SECOND WOMAN: No, my child. You must be here when the bread is given out.

THE CHILD:[21] I'm bored.

SECOND WOMAN: Be good. In a little while you're going to see the Deputies of the Three Arts[22] go past, with their beautiful embroidered banners.

OLD MAN: I'd really like to know what they're going to decide.

ANOTHER: They'll certainly cut down the rations again.

Jacques van der Welde enters. Clarice notices him and gets up to leave.

JACQUES: I'm making you run away?

CLARICE: I must go home.

JACQUES: Will you please listen to me for a moment?

CLARICE: If you like.

Silence.

JACQUES: Have you heard the news?

CLARICE: What news?

JACQUES: The King of France has promised to come to our aid in the spring.

CLARICE: Yes, I know that. (*She laughs brusquely.*) In the spring! We will all be dead a long time before then. I know there isn't even six weeks supplies left in the granaries.

JACQUES: In a while the Council is going to meet. We will take steps.

CLARICE: Can they make wheat grow in the streets? What are you going to decide?

JACQUES: How would I know?

CLARICE: You are a man without ambition, Jacques van der Welde. If I were in my father's place or in yours, I would not allow myself to be dictated to by thirty craftsmen.[23]

JACQUES: We overthrew the Duke so that Vaucelles would be free. (*A pause.*) We will soon have the most beautiful belfry in all Flanders.

CLARICE: These stones bore me.

JACQUES: I'm afraid of boring you too. (*A pause.*) Clarice, will you ever love me?

CLARICE: I don't believe in love.

JACQUES: If you would let me, I would know how to love you.

CLARICE: You would take me in your arms, you would press me to your heart while smiling at me with your big green eyes, and then you would go off on your own pleasures.

JACQUES: My eyes are grey.

CLARICE: They *are* grey! (*She laughs.*) That changes nothing.

JACQUES: I would never leave you. I don't like pleasures.

CLARICE: Well, I do. (*A pause.*) I'm not a suitable wife for a leading Alderman. I'm not like my mother.

Cries of horror. A commotion. A man runs past them.[24] *He is shouting, "A doctor, a doctor!" Men cross the building-site carrying a body.*

JACQUES: Don't look.

CLARICE: Why not?

JACQUES *stops two masons on their way past*: What has happened?

FIRST MASON: He fell from the scaffolding.

SECOND MASON: He fell from weakness. It's going to happen to us all.

They go out.

CLARICE: It serves them right.

JACQUES: What are you saying?

CLARICE: It serves them right; they are more obstinate than ants. Soon worms will eat their hearts and they're amusing themselves piling up stones.

Louis D'Avesnes and François Rosbourg enter.

LOUIS: What is this dress, Clarice? Aren't you ashamed? Two soldiers could be clothed with the material from your skirt. And I have forbidden you to wear your jewelry before the siege ends.

CLARICE: Must I wait until I'm dead in order to be allowed to live?

LOUIS: Go home. I will lock you in your room and you won't come out until after the Burgundians have gone. (*Clarice leaves.*) Have you spoken to her?

JACQUES: She doesn't want to listen to me.

LOUIS: I swear she will have no other husband but you. (*A pause.*) Why is the building-site empty?

JACQUES: A mason collapsed from weakness and fell from the top of the scaffolding.

LOUIS: It's the third accident since Sunday. The work is too hard for badly fed men.

FRANÇOIS: Hard and useless.[25] What do we need a belfry for?[26]

JACQUES: These men accept their suffering only because they have their eyes fixed on the future. Let's not force them to live in the present.

FRANÇOIS: This work must[27] be stopped. It is not the moment to waste our strength.

LOUIS: We cannot make so important a decision so lightly. I will convene a meeting with the Site Foreman and the Master Masons so we can deliberate with them.

They stop talking and listen to the voices.

VOICE: Are they coming? I can't see anyone.

A CHILD: It's been so long. I'm hungry.

THE MOTHER: Everybody is hungry.

ANOTHER WOMAN: They're not going to come.

ANOTHER: I can't stand it any longer!

JACQUES: Do you hear?

LOUIS: I hear.

JACQUES: What can we do?

LOUIS: I don't know.

FRANÇOIS: A decision must be made in the next two hours.

LOUIS: Yes, it must.

FRANÇOIS: In the next two hours a way must be found to hold out for another three months.

LOUIS: It must. (*Long silence.*) I don't see any way.

JACQUES: Nor I.

FRANÇOIS: Nor I.

JEAN-PIERRE, *entering*: Master D'Avesnes, they told me you want to see me.

LOUIS: Yes, we need to speak. You have rendered the town exceptional service. Because of this, we have decided to offer you an exceptional reward.

JEAN-PIERRE: A reward? I don't want anything.

LOUIS: We want you to govern this community with us.

JEAN-PIERRE: What, me, govern?

LOUIS: We will ask the Deputies to create the position of Prefect of Provisions for you. They will agree to it, for they know that your help can be useful to us. Come to the Council meeting with us.

JEAN-PIERRE: I can't accept.

LOUIS: I know that you have always refused political office, but today you must accept. Victory has never been more sure, nor more impossible. The siege will be relieved in the spring. But how to hold out for three months with only six weeks food left in our granaries? You can't refuse to join our deliberations with us.

JEAN-PIERRE: I don't know anything about public matters.

LOUIS: I know that we will gain from listening to your views. And then . . .

JEAN-PIERRE: And then?

LOUIS: I don't know what measures we will have to take; but they will be hard. People trust you, they like you; they will accept things getting worse from you better than from anyone else.

JEAN-PIERRE: Ask me to cross the Burgundy camp again. Ask me to swim the sea, or to walk back to Paris, but don't ask me to share power with you.

LOUIS: Why?

JEAN-PIERRE: If I had to think that I am the one who is condemning these old men and these women to beg for their bread, and that I'm responsible for their suffering, then my heart would break. I do not want to weigh out their rations each day. I will not be complicit in their fate of being crushed.

LOUIS: If I had folded my arms and bowed my head in front of the Duke's Bailiff, wouldn't the misfortunes of this town have been greater?

JEAN-PIERRE: How can suffering and joy be measured? Can one[28] compare the weight of a tear to the weight of a drop of blood? I wish that tomorrow the men of Vaucelles could be free and prosperous. But these children who are dead of hunger today, nothing will ever give them their lives back. I want to keep my hands clean.[29]

LOUIS: And what does the color of our hands and the peace of our hearts matter? Before our uprising, men were crawling about like animals in misery and pain. It's not too much, to sacrifice a few lives, so that henceforth life will have meaning.[30]

JEAN-PIERRE: I don't want to pay in blood for the tears and sweat of others.

LOUIS: So be it. We will do without you.

Jean-Pierre walks away. A procession, with banners, enters and climbs the steps of the Town Hall.

THE MOTHER: Look at the beautiful golden banners.

THE WOMAN: Here are the Master Weavers!

AN OLD MAN: What are they going to decide?

A WOMAN: Maybe they're going to give out the secret supplies to us.

ANOTHER WOMAN: There are no secret supplies.

ANOTHER: Well then, what can they do?

LOUIS: Let's go. The Deputies of the Three Arts have arrived.

JACQUES: May God direct us!

They go toward the Town Hall.

THE CHILD: Here they are, here they are!

VOICES: Here they are, here they are! They're bringing the bread! We're going to eat. At last! I couldn't hold out any longer!

Two men carrying bags of bread cross the stage.

A CHILD: Here they are!

FIRST MASON: What are they carrying?

SECOND MASON: It looks like bread.

FIRST MASON: What are you carrying there? (*The men continue on their way.*) Hey there! Do you hear us? What are you carrying there?

The masons surround the men and feel the bags.

THE PORTER: Let us pass. It's the bread for the townspeople.

A MASON: We're dying of hunger and the townspeople are being fed!

FIRST MASON: Give *us* this bread. Those who don't work don't need to eat.[31]

THE PORTER: Someone help! Help!

They start fighting.

LOUIS: Drop your hands. Would you steal the bread of old men, of children, of women?

FIRST MASON: *We* need to be strong. But what good are *they*?

Silence. François puts his hand on Louis' arm.

FRANÇOIS: Yes. What good *are* they?[32]

They look at each other in silence.

Third Tableau

In Louis D'Avesnes's house. In a big room on the ground floor are Catherine, Jeanne, Georges, Clarice. At the back of the room are large cauldrons. By the half-opened door, Catherine is ejecting an old woman.

CATHERINE: There is nothing to eat! I'm telling you, there is nothing more to eat!

She slams the door shut.

MANY VOICES OUTSIDE: Open up! Open up! We haven't eaten for two days; have pity on us. Open up! We can't last any longer. We're not animals. Open up! We're all going to die!

Fists are pounded against the door.

GEORGES: Let them die! Good riddance!

CATHERINE: Go away. I have nothing more to give you.

VOICES: Food. For pity's sake!

CATHERINE: Why isn't Louis coming back?

JEANNE: Aunt Kate, what are they going to decide?

CATHERINE: How should I know?

GEORGES: There has to be some action here!

CATHERINE: But what action?

GEORGES: *Any* action.

VOICES: Open up! We want to eat.

CLARICE: Shut them up! Can't they think of anything else but eating?[33]

JEANNE: Clarice!

CLARICE: Shut them up!

CATHERINE: What can I say to them? We have to wait until your father returns.

CLARICE: Waiting! More waiting!

CATHERINE: Waiting, that should be easy. Just stay there. Let the time just pass and give up on living. (*She makes a gesture of weariness, then she pulls herself together, goes toward the back of the room and takes hold of a cauldron.*) Help me, Clarice.

They leave carrying the cauldron.

GEORGES: Stupid wretches! Those cauldrons should have been put away before they were emptied.

JEANNE: Would you have those poor people die of hunger?

GEORGES: If I were in charge, I'd have got rid of those vermin a long time ago. (*A pause.*) Is it true that my father offered the post of Prefect of Provisions to your brother this morning?

JEANNE: It's true. Jean-Pierre refused it.

GEORGES: He's offered it to *him*! Aren't I his son?

JEANNE: Exactly. The two of you can't govern together.

GEORGES: Who'd dare complain about it?

JEANNE: Have patience. In a year the Council will name new Aldermen. Then you will succeed your father.

GEORGES: A year! My hour will have passed! By then, Vaucelles will be lost or saved. But today, in famine, in fear, it's for the taking. Oh, to feel all this strength in me and not *do* anything with it.[34] It will kill me!

JEANNE: Why aren't you doing anything?

GEORGES: I stand guard when it's my turn.

JEANNE: You can work on the belfry.

GEORGES: I don't have the soul of a mason. Building, weaving, is that action? I want to shake the world down to its foundations. (*A pause.*) Well then! Say something!

JEANNE: What could I say?

GEORGES: You don't love me, do you?

JEANNE: Are you concerned about my love?

GEORGES: Perhaps. (*A pause.*) Has Jean-Pierre seen my sister again?

JEANNE: Yes, this morning.

GEORGES: Were they alone together?

JEANNE: Why are you asking me these questions?

GEORGES: Clarice is very beautiful today. She has put on her finery and her eyes have never shone so brightly.

JEANNE: She is beautiful.

GEORGES: She loves Jean-Pierre, doesn't she?

JEANNE: Well, I don't know.

GEORGES: What's between them?

JEANNE: I don't know.

GEORGES: You're lying!

JEANNE: I won't tell you anything.

GEORGES: I will make you speak.

He grabs her wrists.

JEANNE: You're hurting me.

GEORGES: I'll *make* you speak.

JEANNE: I will tell you nothing. Aaaah!

She lets out a stifled scream. Someone knocks. Georges lets go of Jeanne.

JEAN-PIERRE: Open up! It's Jean-Pierre.

Jeanne goes and opens the door. Jean-Pierre enters and a few women try to come in as well.

THE WOMEN: Give us food!

GEORGES, *pulling out his sword and dashing forward*: Back! Everyone back! Empty the place or I'll empty it with the point of my sword! (*He re-closes the door and turns toward Jean-Pierre.*) What are you here for? An Alderman's robe?

JEAN-PIERRE: I was told that Aunt Kate wanted to see me.

JEANNE: I'll go and tell her.

She leaves.

GEORGES: You seem to be the savior of Vaucelles, then!

JEAN-PIERRE: I did what I had to.

GEORGES: It seems that no reward is good enough for you.

JEAN-PIERRE: You don't need to hate me: I'm not ambitious.

GEORGES: Be careful of becoming so.

A silence. Catherine enters.

CATHERINE, *to Georges*: Leave us alone, please. (*Georges leaves. To Jean-Pierre*): Sit down. Is it true that you refused the post of Prefect of Provisions this morning?

JEAN-PIERRE: It's true.

CATHERINE: Are you lazy, or a moral coward?

JEAN-PIERRE: I am not able to take things lightly enough, nor am I presumptuous enough to agree to govern men.

CATHERINE: Do you want always to remain uninvolved, an adventurer?[35] Was it for this that I raised you with so much care?

JEAN-PIERRE: I know what I owe you. You have been more than a mother to me and my sister. But now let me lead my life without your help.

CATHERINE: Who could look at you wasting your gifts without being impatient? You have a head, a heart, two hands, don't you want to do anything with them?

JEAN-PIERRE: I would prefer to cut off these hands, tear out this heart; I live, I breathe, and already this is enough to make me feel a criminal. If I could completely efface myself from the world . . .

CATHERINE: But you can't.

JEAN-PIERRE: I could at least try not to weigh upon the earth.

Catherine gets up and leads Jean-Pierre to the window.

CATHERINE: Look, what do you see?

JEAN-PIERRE: I see the belfry, a part of the Town Hall, roof-tops.

CATHERINE: I laid the first stone of this belfry. The flag which floats on the Town Hall, I sewed it with my own hands. Will you never know the joy of looking around you and thinking: this is my doing.

JEAN-PIERRE: I also see women and children wandering in the streets and crying with hunger.

CATHERINE: When the bells on the belfry ring for victory, they will quickly forget their troubles. (*A pause.*) Without us, this world would lack a face; it's up to us to shape it with our hands.

JEAN-PIERRE: I admire your attempt to tailor, to cut, to build in the material of living flesh.

CATHERINE: I want to build happiness.

JEAN-PIERRE: You want it. And do you know what you are doing? There are so many hidden threats in each of our gestures, in each of our words; our actions are going to explode far away from us with unknown consequence.[36] I would never have the audacity to throw the weight of my will over someone else's life. (*A pause.*) Jeanne doesn't love your son.

CATHERINE: She's a child. She will know later that I have acted for her own good. (*She sits down.*) You are so afraid of doing or saying something that you let happiness wither right next to you instead of picking it. Have they told you that Jacques van der Welde wants to marry Clarice?

JEAN-PIERRE: No.

CATHERINE: Her father wants this marriage. (*Silence.*) Why don't you want to occupy the place in the town that you deserve? You're the one that I would give Clarice to.

JEAN-PIERRE: Give her to me? Do you think that I would agree to lock her up and tell her that I alone am her portion of the world. I don't have the soul of a jailer.

CATHERINE: Love isn't a prison.

JEAN-PIERRE: All commitment is a prison.

CATHERINE: You believe yourself to be free, you who are capable neither of action nor of love.

JEAN-PIERRE: I do not want to lie to Clarice nor to myself. Everyone lives alone, and dies alone.[37]

CATHERINE: No. If a man and a woman propel [*élan*] themselves toward the same future, in what they have built together, in the children they have engendered, in this whole wide world that has shaped their common will, they would find themselves merged indissolubly.

JEAN-PIERRE: Clarice is not like you. She is a stranger to this world and expects nothing of the future. It is enough for her to be herself. There is nothing I could give her, nothing she could give me.

CATHERINE: Are you sure you know what Clarice thinks?

Clarice enters in a lively way.

CLARICE: Who's talking about me? What are you plotting? I forbid you to involve me in your arguments.

CATHERINE: I was warning Jean-Pierre that from now on I forbid you to see him or speak to him. He is not your fiancé, nor your brother, and you are no longer children.

Cries from outside.

VOICES: We don't want to die like dogs! Open up! Open up!

Jeanne and Georges come running in.

JEANNE: They're here again!

GEORGES: I'll shove their screams down their throats.

He takes out an arrow, opens the window and takes aim.

JEANNE: Don't shoot!

She rushes forward and pushes his arm aside.

GEORGES: Bitch! You made me miss my aim!

CATHERINE: Put down that bow.

GEORGES: Should they be allowed to break down the door and sack the house, then?

CATHERINE: Put down that bow.

Georges takes aim. Jeanne hides against Catherine's shoulder. Jean-Pierre takes a step toward Georges, but Clarice stops him.

CLARICE: A man who's afraid is very ugly.

GEORGES, *turning toward her*: You think I'm afraid?

CLARICE: You are afraid of a pack of women and old men.

GEORGES: All right, let them howl to their hearts content. (*He goes toward the door. Clarice laughs*). Why are you laughing?

CLARICE: I'm laughing because you have thrown down your bow.

GEORGES: You asked me to throw it down.

CLARICE: *I* asked you nothing.

GEORGES: I forbid you to laugh.

CLARICE: Don't shout. When you shout the veins in your forehead swell and you become red.

GEORGES: One day I'll strangle you!

He goes out slamming the door.

JEANNE: He would have killed them!

CATHERINE: Don't cry. He is still young. He will change, you will change him.

JEANNE: He doesn't love me.

CATHERINE: He needs a woman like you at his side.[38]

JEANNE: I'm not strong enough.

CATHERINE: You are strong; otherwise, do you think I would have chosen you to one day take my place, in this house and in this town?[39]

JEANNE: Aunt Kate, I wouldn't be happy with him.

CATHERINE: There are many kinds of happiness.

JEAN-PIERRE: It is not for you to choose hers for her. (*To Jeanne.*) Listen only to your heart, my little sister. You are not tied by any oath.

CATHERINE *(breaking away from Jeanne)*: An *oath*! (*Jeanne hesitates. A pause.*) You are free, Jeanne.

JEANNE: You know full well I will do what you expect of me.

CRIES: Bread! Open up, open up!

There is banging on the door. Catherine goes toward it.

JEANNE: What are you doing?

CATHERINE: They want to come in, so let them! (*She opens the door. Women, old men, children, come in.*) Come in, search the house from the cellar to the attic, you won't find a grain of wheat nor a handful of husks.

The people stop, intimidated.

A WOMAN: Are they going to let us die of hunger?

AN OLD MAN: Why don't they throw open the storehouses?

CATHERINE: Measures are going to be taken.

A WOMAN: What measures?

ANOTHER: To give us bread.

CATHERINE: You know what's in store for you if the Duke enters the town? (*Silence.*) Accept and suffer, then. Go to your homes. The Council is in the process of deciding. Await its decisions patiently.

AN OLD MAN: What are they going to decide?

CATHERINE: You will know soon.

A WOMAN: Are our misfortunes going to end?

CATHERINE: They will end. Patience. If you will wait, deliverance will come. (*She closes the door.*) More waiting! If only I could sleep . . .

She half-faints. Jeanne and Jean-Pierre rush forward and hold her up.

JEANNE: Aunt Kate, you are at the end of your strength. You have eaten nothing since yesterday.

The three of them go out. Clarice follows them with her eyes.

CLARICE: Food, more about food!

She goes to the mirror. She brings her face close to it and looks at herself for a long time. Jean-Pierre comes in. He approaches Clarice and kisses her.

JEAN-PIERRE: How beautiful you are! All the other women have become so ugly. How do you manage to stay as beautiful as ever?

CLARICE: They won't get the better of me.

JEAN-PIERRE: Wonderful Clarice. How I love it that you exist.

He takes her hand. She pulls it back. Georges enters without being seen, and hides in order to spy on them.

CLARICE: But don't you love me at all, Jean-Pierre?

JEAN-PIERRE: We agreed that this word doesn't have any meaning.

CLARICE, *sitting down*: Don't worry. I don't love you either. I was asking that question on principle. What do you think of Jacques van der Welde?

JEAN-PIERRE: Is it true that your father wants you to marry him?

CLARICE: It's true. And it's also true that I'm *going* to marry him.

JEAN-PIERRE: Jacques van der Welde. But he's a *weaver* by trade, he's not a *man*.[40]

CLARICE: He is a man who dares to love me.

JEAN-PIERRE: He dares, but such promises are lies. Since when do you believe his words? You used to press your hand against my mouth and look at me with that silent and vulnerable face that is so dear to me . . .

CLARICE: Don't.

JEAN-PIERRE: Have you forgotten our silences? Do you prefer the chatter of promises?

CLARICE: He will make me his wife and his life will be my life.

JEAN-PIERRE: He will put a ring on your finger and there will be only one roof over your heads. But it will still be your heart in your breast, and his thoughts in his head, the thoughts of a draper and an Alderman.

CLARICE: And you, what could I expect from you?

JEAN-PIERRE: Nothing.

CLARICE: So then, go.

JEAN-PIERRE: Goodbye, Clarice.

He leaves. She bursts into tears. Catherine enters, followed by Jeanne.

CATHERINE: You're crying? (*Silence.*) I had forbidden you to speak to him.

CLARICE: Let me be.

CATHERINE: Do you think I haven't heard you weeping all these nights? He leaves: you cry. He returns: you cry. Is this my daughter, this suffering flesh?

CLARICE: I'm not suffering. I'm not crying. I will never see him again. (*A pause.*) I am going to have a child by him.

GEORGES: Bitch! Whore!

CATHERINE: Clarice! Does he love you?

CLARICE: I detest him.

GEORGES: You will pay me for this.

He seizes her by the shoulders.

CLARICE: Don't touch me.

GEORGES: You weren't so fierce with *him*. He lifted up your dress, he ran his hands over your body and this arrogant face[41] laughed with pleasure.

CATHERINE: Stop it!

GEORGES: You closed your eyes, you slipped your tongue into his mouth, you moaned under his caresses. Whore!

CLARICE: Let go of me. You stink like a soldier. I can't stand that smell.

GEORGES: How long has he been your lover? How many nights have you spent in his arms? (*He shakes her.*) Answer.

CLARICE: I won't answer you.

CATHERINE: I order you to let her alone. She doesn't have to answer you.

A pause. He lets go of her.

GEORGES: You're right. It's up to my father to sort this out. He will know how to make her speak.

CATHERINE: Georges! Do not say anything to your father.

GEORGES: You won't hold your head up so high. We will hear you sing, my beautiful.

CATHERINE: I forbid you to say anything to him.

JEANNE: Georges! For pity's sake stop! He will kill her!

CLARICE: Let him beat me! Let him drive me away! Let him kill me! I don't care about any of you.

GEORGES: You're laughing, you whore. You won't feel like laughing when he's finished with you.

He shakes her violently.

JEANNE: Let go of her. You're hurting her! Let *go* of her.

The door opens. Louis D'Avesnes enters.

LOUIS: What noise!

CATHERINE: Here you are at last. How tired you look! (*She kisses him.*)

LOUIS: Why all this noise?

JEANNE: Georges, be quiet.

GEORGES: Your daughter is pregnant by Jean-Pierre Gauthier.

Silence.

LOUIS: Oh, well! They have only to marry.

He sits down.

CLARICE: I don't want to marry him; I will throw his child in the river.

LOUIS: Don't marry him, then. Why are you crying?

GEORGES: Father, whatever are you thinking? She must be locked up in a convent.

LOUIS: I do not want her bothered.

Silence.

CATHERINE: You're frightening me. (*She looks at him. A pause.*) What has the Council decided? (*Silence.*) You're not surrendering the town?

LOUIS: No.

CATHERINE: What will you do?

LOUIS: We will ask for help from Bruges.

CATHERINE: Bruges has always refused to help us.

LOUIS: I know.

CATHERINE: Well then?

LOUIS: What are you worrying about? And why is Clarice crying? Why do you look so sad?

CATHERINE, *to the three children*: Leave us. (*They go out.*) Tell me the truth. (*Silence.*) You know full well that no help will come before spring.

LOUIS: Do not ask me anything, Catherine.

CATHERINE: Has there ever been a secret between us? (*Silence.*) If all is lost, if we must die in a hopeless attempt to escape, don't be afraid to tell me: I'm ready.

LOUIS: It would be easy to die holding you in my arms.

CATHERINE: Why do you turn your eyes away? One[42] would think that you are afraid to look at me.

LOUIS: Leave me alone. Do not ask anything of me.

CATHERINE: Whatever the future will be, I want to face it with you. Speak to me.

LOUIS: As soon as I have spoken, we will be separated forever. (*Silence.*) The Council has decided to get rid of the useless mouths.[43] Tomorrow before sunset they will be driven into the ditches: the infirm, the old men, the children. The women.

CURTAIN

ACT II

Fourth Tableau

The three leading Aldermen. The Site Foreman. Three Masons.

LOUIS: So then, these men are grumbling because they are hungry, not because they don't want to work. Wouldn't they grumble even more if we condemned them to a fruitless wait?

THE SITE FOREMAN: That's so, that's exactly so.

LOUIS: Then do you agree to continue with the work?

FIRST MASTER MASON: It would be very hard to have labored so much, to have given our sweat and our blood, and the belfry not be ready for the King of France!

SECOND MASTER MASON: If you don't want the belfry completed, you shouldn't have asked us to start it in the first place.

LOUIS: It seems to me that the question has been settled, then.

JACQUES: Without any doubt.

FRANÇOIS: I beg your pardon! We need to know if these men are the best judges of what's good for them.

JACQUES: Who should judge it, then, if not they themselves?

FRANÇOIS: The people have put themselves in our hands. It's up to us to guide them, not follow them blindly.

JACQUES: They know the situation as well as we do, but even more so because they feel it in their flesh; we have nothing to do but to respect their decision.

FRANÇOIS: Are you telling me these men are infallible? *They* don't know what's good for them!

LOUIS: They know it. A mistake is impossible because their good is precisely what they will choose it to be; no other good exists.[44]

FRANÇOIS: Of what use is this belfry? We overthrew the Duke and took power in order to govern our town with wisdom and efficiency. We should no longer permit these men to waste their lives in worthless ventures. Markets, storehouses, workshops, that's what we have to build. From now on, every action should have purpose, every breath must have purpose and every heartbeat.

LOUIS: Vaucelles isn't made to serve. There is nothing higher than herself for her. If she wishes to build this belfry, then let her. It's her will that commands.[45]

Catherine enters.

CATHERINE: Is it true? You're worried about a pile of stones, on a day like today?

JACQUES: We would be happy to hear your opinion.

CATHERINE: What kind of men are you?

LOUIS: Leave. (*The masons leave.*) She knows.[46]

CATHERINE: I know. Don't lower your eyes; that would be too easy. It's me here and I know. (*Silence.*) I sat in this chair and you asked for my advice. You were looking for hope in my eyes. For you and me the same hope. We told each other: *our* suffering, *our* victory. We had one future between us.

And suddenly, here I am alone, in front of you; you will throw me in the ditches, where cold cinders, peelings, bones, old rags are thrown. But at least look me in the face!

LOUIS: I *am* looking at you, Catherine. This community is your achievement as much as ours, and you want its triumph, just as we do; we *can* ask you to lay down your life for her.

CATHERINE: You're not *asking* me. You have condemned me.

LOUIS: Why do you hate us? When it is necessary, we will agree to die.

CATHERINE: Am I free to agree? What would you do if I refused? (*Silence.*) I am no longer permitted to have a will. I was a woman and now I am no more than a useless mouth.[47] You have taken from me more than life itself. All that is left to me is my hate.

JACQUES: Should we have agreed to open our gates to the besiegers?

CATHERINE: We could have thrown ourselves at the Duke's army, set fire to our houses and all died together.

LOUIS: Vaucelles must live! (*A pause.*) Something has been accomplished here which hasn't yet happened anywhere else. A town has overthrown its prince; men[48] have chosen to become free and to determine their happiness for themselves. And the other towns of Flanders, of France and of Burgundy are looking at her intently with hope-filled eyes. We must have victory.

CATHERINE: Your wives, your fathers, your children will be dead, and Vaucelles will live! Were we not her flesh and blood too? Can we be cut off like a rotting hand? (*She calls.*) Jeanne, Clarice! (*Jeanne and Clarice enter.*) Come here. Look at these men. They have met with thirty other men[49] and they have said, "We are the present and the future, we are the entire town, only we exist. We decide that the women, the old men, the children of Vaucelles are no more than useless mouths. Tomorrow they will be driven outside the town and condemned to die of hunger and cold in the ditches."

Silence. Jeanne throws herself into Catherine's arms.

CLARICE: This is what you've come up with? You are going to murder us so that you can eat your fill! (*A pause. To Jacques*): Is this what you call love?

Silence.

LOUIS: It is true that we have become executioners. Certainly the points of spears, the flames of death, would be more merciful to us than the horror which from now on will be our lot.[50] But because it is necessary either to die as innocents or live as criminals, we choose crime because we choose life.

CATHERINE: You choose life for yourselves, but death for us.

LOUIS: It's not about you, or us: it's about our community and the future of the entire world.

CATHERINE: Won't the men who'll be left tomorrow be made of the same flesh as us? If in your eyes we are only hungry cattle, what are they? Why sacrifice us for them?

LOUIS: To choose life, is to always choose the future. Without this choice [*élan*] which carries us forward we would be nothing but vegetation on the face of the earth. Of what importance is it, then, whether our hearts beat or are silent. To reduce Vaucelles to ashes, to reduce the future to ashes, also reduces our past to ashes and denies all that we are.

A pause.

JEANNE: No! No! It's too unjust.

CATHERINE: We shall not beg for their pity.

She leads her out. Clarice follows slowly.

JACQUES: Clarice! (*Clarice stops.*) I want to speak to her.

LOUIS: All right. You may speak to her.

Louis and François go out. Jacques goes toward Clarice.

JACQUES: Tonight when everyone is asleep, slip out of your room; come and knock at the door of my house: the little door that leads out to the side-street. Knock twice. Tomorrow the guards will search the camp. But nobody will dare suspect me. You will be in safety until the end of the siege. (*Silence.*) I swear on the Virgin to respect you like a much-loved sister.[51] (*Silence.*) Well then! Why do you say nothing?

CLARICE: Do you expect me to fall at your feet while kissing your hands? Keep your presents.

JACQUES: Do you prefer to die of cold and hunger?

CLARICE: I can choose my death.[52] Go away.

Jacques moves away.

JACQUES: I will wait for you all night.

He goes out. She shuts the door after him, takes down a dagger from the wall, looks at it and quickly puts it back in its place on hearing footsteps.[53] *Georges comes in.*

GEORGES: Are you alone?

CLARICE: Yes.

GEORGES: Jeanne and Mother are praying. They told me about the Council's decision. Don't you want to pray?

CLARICE: No.

GEORGES: Aren't you afraid?

CLARICE: What are you worried about?

GEORGES (*approaching her*): It's cold at night in the ditches. There are slimy creatures slithering under the grass.

CLARICE, *recoiling a little*: I'm not frightened.

GEORGES: You are beautiful, Clarice. You are alive and warm. And soon you will rot under the earth. The worms will eat these sweet lips.

He embraces her.

CLARICE: Georges! You are my brother!

GEORGES: I am a man that desires you, Clarice.[54]

CLARICE: Stop it!

GEORGES: Why should I stop! I desire you, and you know it.

CLARICE: Yes, I know it. I have felt your troubled gaze linger on me and your dirty thoughts. I also know that hunger, thirst and death would be easier to put up with than this kiss that you have inflicted on me.

She wipes her mouth.

GEORGES: Insult me! Kill me with your hate-filled eyes! Until this morning I felt ashamed, but now you're going to die; your tongue is no more than a piece of red flesh which will become blackened and disintegrate. These eyes will dissolve, their look will no longer burn me.

CLARICE: Must I spit in your face?

She spits.

GEORGES: What's that? Nothing but a little saliva on my cheek. (*He seizes her.*) You are going to die, and all your thoughts will die with you. They are already dead. I am alone with your body, alone with my desire.

CLARICE: Georges!

Louis enters. Georges lets Clarice go and she runs off.

LOUIS: Get out of this house. You are no longer my son.

GEORGES: And so what! Aren't you going to kill her?

LOUIS: How dare you look me in the face! Get out or I will kill you like a dog!

GEORGES: Why these hypocritical accusations? You yourself have done something appalling. From now on there's neither good nor evil. Force rules.[55]

LOUIS: Be silent! (*A pause.*) I put force to the service of the good, the good of my town, the good of the world.

GEORGES: You've served your own desires.

LOUIS: My desires! I have sacrificed more than my life.

GEORGES: You've chosen your sacrifices yourself. I choose my pleasure.

LOUIS: What? Must I justify myself to *you*? Go away! (*Georges leaves. Louis paces up and down. He calls very quietly:*) Catherine! (*He calls more loudly, with anguish:*) Catherine!

Catherine enters.

CATHERINE: You called me?

They look at each other. A pause.

LOUIS: No!

Fifth Tableau

Scenery the same as in the second tableau. The building-site is empty. It's morning. People are going toward the Town Hall. Three old men are passing through.

FIRST OLD MAN: What do you think they've gone and invented again?

SECOND OLD MAN: Nothing good, nothing good.

THIRD OLD MAN: Walk more quickly. All the good places will be taken. We will hear nothing.

Two merchants are passing.

FIRST MERCHANT: We don't want to surrender the town; so we won't ever surrender her. And the Burgundians aren't able to take her, so they won't ever take her.[56]

A couple pass.

THE WOMAN: I'm frightened.

THE MAN: What are you frightened of?

THE WOMAN: What are they going to tell us? Why are the streets full of armed men?

Catherine has come in during the last exchange. She looks at the belfry, touches the stones.

CATHERINE: No, it's useless.[57] Things no longer have any voice, or perhaps it's me that no longer understands them. They have cut me off from the world; there is nothing left for me. (*She sits down.*) I'm tired. (*A pause.*) And for him, all this will continue to exist. The belfry will be completed, the rose trees will bloom again: for him.

JEAN-PIERRE *runs in*: I've been looking for you everywhere.

CATHERINE: Go away!

JEAN-PIERRE: Just a word.

CATHERINE: Go away. I can't stand the sight of a man.

JEAN-PIERRE: What are they going to do?

CATHERINE: You will know soon enough.

JEAN-PIERRE: It will be too late.

CATHERINE: Too late?

JEAN-PIERRE: Too late to save you. There are horrible rumors flying about.

CATHERINE: The most horrible is true.

A pause.

JEAN-PIERRE: The people will not permit this crime. I'm going to speak to them.

CATHERINE: You're wasting your time. The people are proud of the leaders they have chosen. They will obey them. (*A pause.*) Why are you worried about *us*?

JEAN-PIERRE: Am I worried about *you*? Or am I worried about *myself*? The smell in the air has changed and the saliva in my mouth has a bitter taste. I can't stand the color of this sky! Where are the three leaders?

CATHERINE: They will pass this way. But don't hope to influence them. They're blind and deaf.

JEAN-PIERRE: I will speak to the men of Vaucelles. I will know how to convince them.

CATHERINE: No, it's too late! *Yesterday* you should have taken the destiny of the town in your hands. *Yesterday* the members of the Council would have listened to you; you would have turned them away from this crime. But you wanted to keep yourself pure.

JEAN-PIERRE: How could I know that my silence would make a murderer of me?[58]

CATHERINE: A murderer, an executioner. From the moment you were silent, you accepted any outcome.

A pause.

JEAN-PIERRE: Where is Clarice?

CATHERINE: I don't know. (*She gets up.*) They are coming. May God be with you.

She goes out. The three leading Aldermen enter.

JEAN-PIERRE: Just a minute, please! I want to speak to you.

LOUIS: We can't listen to you now. The people are waiting for us.

JEAN-PIERRE: Let them wait. I know what you are going to tell them. Be careful. The men of Vaucelles will revolt against so barbaric a decision.

JACQUES: They love their town; they will obey the law.

FRANÇOIS: Get out of the way or I will have you seized by the guards.

JEAN-PIERRE: They will revolt! You have noticed that I have influence over them. Now I won't hesitate to use it. I will turn them against you.

JACQUES: You won't do that. You won't betray your town.

JEAN-PIERRE: This is no longer a town, there are only executioners and their victims here. I will not be your accomplice.[59]

FRANÇOIS: This man should be thrown into prison.

LOUIS: Go away!

JEAN-PIERRE: I will stop this crime from being accomplished.

They go out. People hurry across the stage. Bells ring.

FRANÇOIS: What, you're letting him go?

JACQUES: What crime has he committed? What law authorizes us to punish him?

FRANÇOIS: Is this the moment for us to worry about justice? Is what we are about to do *just*?

LOUIS: All decrees voted by the Council are just.[60] But we three don't have the right to take an arbitrary decision.

FRANÇOIS: Cowards! You will let Vaucelles be lost for fear that your mirrors will reflect you as tyrants.

JACQUES: I fear that Vaucelles is less dear to you than power. Under pretext of saving her, you would not hesitate to reduce her to slavery.

ONE WOMAN, *to another*: Hurry up! The bells are ringing.

ANOTHER WOMAN: Has it started?

AN OLD MAN: It's started?

A MAN: It has started.

VOICES: It's started! It has started!

They run out. Clarice and Jeanne had come in during the last exchange.

CLARICE, *leading Jeanne along:* Come this way.

JEANNE: Did you catch sight of Jean-Pierre? I'm sure that he was looking for you.

CLARICE: Exactly. I don't wish to see him.

JEANNE: If we stay here we won't hear anything.

CLARICE: You will know soon enough how the people react to what they say.

JEANNE: When going to the square, women were leaning on the arms of their husbands, and sons were holding up their old fathers. They *are* going to revolt.

CLARICE: Does our future depend on the capriciousness of their feelings?

JEANNE: They're speaking. Your father is speaking. They're listening to him. What is he saying? (*A pause.*) What silence! Not a word! Not a cry! (*A pause.*) They are saying *nothing*. They are saying nothing! How cold it will be tonight in the ditches!

CLARICE: There are slimy creatures slithering under the grass.

JEANNE: Clarice!

CLARICE: Don't be afraid, we can escape from them.

JEANNE: How? Where to flee to?

Clarice pulls a dagger from her belt.

CLARICE: I want my father to find me dead on these steps.[61]

JEANNE: I don't want to die.

Catherine enters.

CATHERINE: What are you doing? Are you going to let them see you praying and crying?

JEANNE: Is there no longer any hope?

CATHERINE: As soon the vespers bell rings, the children, the women and the old men will be assembled in the Town Hall square, and the police will herd them to the other side of the ramparts.

JEANNE: So the men of Vaucelles have accepted this judgment!

CATHERINE: First, they looked at their wives, they took hold of their hands; then they averted their eyes, and their fingers let go.

JEANNE: Oh, God!

CATHERINE: It won't be so easy for him to let go of *my* hand.

She goes out.

CLARICE, *taking the dagger*: Goodbye forever!

JEANNE: Stop! As long as we are alive, there is still hope.

CLARICE: What have I to hope for? There is nothing except this little life moving inside that tomorrow will tear itself from me.

JEANNE: Clarice, don't leave me alone!

CLARICE: You are alone and I am alone! Goodbye!

JEANNE: No, stay with me. The night will be less cold if I sleep in your arms. At least *that* is left to us; until our last breath, we can still smile at each other, love each other, cry together.[62]

CLARICE: I don't know how to smile, nor to cry. I don't know how to love. They haven't allowed me to live. But they will not rob me of my death.

She lifts the dagger. They struggle.

JEANNE: Jean-Pierre! Jean-Pierre!

They struggle.

CLARICE: Give it to me!

JEANNE: No. Jean-Pierre! Jean-Pierre!

Jean-Pierre runs in. Jeanne gives him the dagger. A pause.

CLARICE: Give it to me, or I will throw myself from the top of the belfry.

JEAN-PIERRE: Do you believe that I would let you die alone? (*Jeanne moves away and goes to sit among the stones on the site.*) I am going to speak to the men of Vaucelles. I am going to persuade them to try to break out.

CLARICE: The breakout will fail and we will all be massacred.

JEAN-PIERRE: At least we will all die together.

CLARICE: We will die together! (*A pause.*) I don't want your pity.

JEAN-PIERRE: Pity? Who would dare have pity for you? I can't bear to live if you are dead. I love you, Clarice.

CLARICE: Yesterday you said that that word had no meaning.

JEAN-PIERRE: Was it yesterday? It seems so far away to me now!

CLARICE: It *was* yesterday, and you didn't love me.

JEAN-PIERRE: I didn't dare to love you because I didn't dare to live. This earth seemed impure to me and I didn't want to sully myself. What stupid pride.

CLARICE: Does it seem purer to you today?

JEAN-PIERRE: We belong to the earth. Now I see it clearly; I was pretending to cut myself off from the world, but it's on earth that I was running away from my duties as a man, on earth I was a coward and I was condemning you to death by my silence. I love you on earth. Love me.

CLARICE: And how does one love on this earth?

JEAN-PIERRE: We struggle together.[63]

A pause.

CLARICE: You said that everyone is alone.

JEAN-PIERRE: This suffering in my heart is you, Clarice, and at the same time it's me.[64] You are my life because your death will kill me.

CLARICE: This joy that has just been born in me, is it you then?

JEAN-PIERRE *takes her in his arms*: Tell me that you love me.

CLARICE: My love! How I have suffered from not loving you!

They kiss. They go out. The crowd comes back into the Town Hall square. The women and the old men form one group, the men another.

A WOMAN: I will hide.

ANOTHER: *Where* will we hide? The police will search all the houses.

AN OLD MAN: My God, have pity on us! My God, have pity on us!

A WOMAN: Nobody will have pity on us. God is deaf!

THIRD WOMAN: Murderers, why don't you cut our throats and be done with it?

FOURTH WOMAN, *going toward one of the men*: You're my husband, and you're going to let me die. (*The two groups stop.*) Answer me! Speak to me! Have you become deaf?

FIRST MAN: The Council has decided, Maria. I have nothing to say to you.

JEAN-PIERRE *goes up to the men*: The *Council* has decided! I believed up to now that you were free men. The Duke would never have dared ask of you what these men are asking. And you bow your heads to their authority!

SECOND MAN: We want to save our town.

JEAN-PIERRE: You could try to break out. Are you afraid?

THIRD MAN: We aren't afraid.

JEAN-PIERRE: So then, let's arm ourselves and attack the Burgundian camp.

Silence.

FIRST MAN: It isn't what the Council has decided.

JEAN-PIERRE: Wake up! Aren't you fighting for your wives and your children?

THIRD MAN: We're fighting for our community.

JEAN-PIERRE: Are you going to turn your town into a den of murderers?

FIRST MAN: We will do what we are ordered to do.

JEAN-PIERRE: You speak like slaves!

François and Georges enter.

FRANÇOIS: No gathering in the streets. Disperse.

The crowd disperses.

JEAN-PIERRE *to Clarice*: This is not their last word on it. I will eventually shake their resolve.

They leave. Georges looks after them, then turns toward François.

GEORGES: What scruples are holding you back? My father and Jacques van der Welde have set us an example. They haven't hesitated to smite the weak and the useless. Are you more cowardly than they?

FRANÇOIS: I will be in control at last![65] Nothing could stand in my way!

GEORGES: Say the word, and I will slaughter them. Do you hesitate? We don't have another life to live: this is our only chance. If we let it go, we will never have the chance again. Vaucelles is for the taking. It must be taken.[66]

FRANÇOIS: Vaucelles will be mine! I will collect all these men who grow haphazardly like wayward plants into one straight and hard sheaf. I will not allow a gesture, a word, to be lost uselessly in the air. What great things I will be able to do!

GEORGES: No other law but our will shall exist. Nobody will dare call us to account: nobody will dare judge us. Each beat of our hearts will be inscribed on the face of the earth. I will be myself at last and the whole world will bear my stamp!

FRANÇOIS: We will send for women from the neighboring countries, child-bearing women who will give us sons capable of conquering Flanders and the world. I will build a new universe; I will make something so perfect and so fulfilling that it will no longer be possible for men to dream.

GEORGES: We must act quickly. I want to take advantage of the confusion after the women and children's exodus.

FRANÇOIS: Come and find me before vespers.

GEORGES *goes to leave from the other side of the stage and stops*: Who's there? (*Silence.*) There's someone here! (*Silence.*) You were spying on me!

He leaps forward and drags out Jeanne.

JEANNE: I'm glad! For all these years I dared not believe my heart, but now I know I was right to hate you.

GEORGES: Yes, my angel! And even more than you might have thought.

Sixth Tableau

In Louis D'Avesnes's house. Catherine comes in, followed by women who are hanging onto her.

THE WOMEN: Save us. Save our children! You are our last hope.

CATHERINE: I implore you, leave me. Leave me alone.

THE WOMEN: Master D'Avesnes has always listened to your voice. Beg him. Persuade him. He is good, he is just. He will listen to your prayers. Save me. Save us.

CATHERINE: I can't do anything more for you.

THE WOMEN: Don't abandon us.

CATHERINE: I can do nothing. Leave me alone.

A WOMAN: What was the use of giving us soup and bread each day? I would prefer to die of hunger in my house than be thrown to the Burgundians.

ANOTHER: Be quiet.

ANOTHER: She is right. Why not have let us die? It would have been done with.

CATHERINE: My God, you're blaming me for having wanted to help you!

ONE WOMAN, *to another*: Shut up. Aren't you ashamed?

A WOMAN, *to Catherine*: We're blaming you for nothing.

CATHERINE: I am going to be thrown to the Burgundians as well.

A pause.

A WOMAN: Forgive us.[67]

They begin to leave.

CATHERINE: All that I can do for you, I will. (*They leave.*) In truth, it *would* have been better to have let them die of hunger. (*She goes to the window and looks out.*) I can *do* nothing more, I *am* nothing now.[68]

A pause. Clarice enters.

CLARICE: Mother darling! (*Catherine looks at her.*) Mother, how sad you look, what's the matter with you?

CATHERINE: What is the matter with me, Clarice?

CLARICE: Yes, I know. But don't be sad, Jean-Pierre will save us.

CATHERINE: Has he spoken with the men of Vaucelles?

CLARICE: He has spoken to them, and they didn't listen to him. The Council has decided, that's enough for them. But we will escape them. Jean-Pierre knows a way through the Burgundian camp. Tonight he will slip down into the ditches and help us to flee. We will reach France.

CATHERINE: France!

CLARICE: And if we are caught, we will kill ourselves together! Now I am no longer afraid of either death or life!

CATHERINE: You love him then.

CLARICE: He loves me too.

CATHERINE: Leave with him for France, Clarice, and be happy.

CLARICE: Mother, you're frightening me. Aren't you going to escape with us?

CATHERINE: Nothing can save me now. For me, everything is finished.

CLARICE: Don't talk like that. Doesn't life begin anew each day? (*A pause.*) My child will be born. Don't you want to smile at it?[69]

CATHERINE: It will be *your* child, *your* future, *your* happiness.

CLARICE: I will share everything with you.

CATHERINE: No, I want *my* life, *my* future. *Our* life, *our* future. Or if nothing else is left to us, our death.

CLARICE: What are you trying to say?

CATHERINE: Don't worry about me. Think of Jean-Pierre, think of your child, think of yourself. Be happy and my life will not have been completely in vain. (*A pause.*) Now you must leave me. I need silence. (*Clarice leaves. Catherine takes her dagger from her belt.*) No. That will not be. There will not be this separation between us. It will not come to that.

A pause. Louis comes in a door at the back. A long silence. Louis and Catherine look at each other.

CATHERINE: Is it you? I must look at you. You and I were so intermingled that I could no longer distinguish your face from mine: and now here you are in front of me with those two creases at the corner of your mouth, and those frightened eyes.

LOUIS, *speaking in a low voice*: Catherine, my wife.

CATHERINE: No, not your wife. An instrument that one breaks and throws on the scrap-heap when one has finished with it.[70]

LOUIS: You are here, but I am alone.[71]

CATHERINE: You have betrayed me! To die is nothing, but you have erased me from the world. All the promises of the past, you have turned them into lies. A lie the day that I brought Clarice into the world, and that sunny morning when I laid the first stone of the belfry. A lie our kisses and our nights. Our love was only a lie.

LOUIS: You can save our love, Catherine. You can save the past and the future. Say one word only: accept!

CATHERINE: Can I repudiate my very self? (*A pause.*) You spoke to me, I answered, and I was a living and free woman in front of you. And I spoke to you and you freely replied to me; neither one of us ever accomplished an act in which the other didn't recognize their own separate will. And now, you have disposed of me as just one more stone; and you are no more than this blind force that is crushing me.

LOUIS: I ask you again and you answer me again. Accept our decree: recognize your own separate will in it: our common will is to save Vaucelles at any cost.

CATHERINE: It is too late. You have decided without me and all the words that I say will be no more than the words of a slave. I am your victim; you are my executioner. (*A pause and very sadly.*) We are two strangers. (*There is knocking. Jacques and Jean-Pierre enter carrying Jeanne.*) Jeanne! What has happened?

JACQUES: Our servants found her at the foot of the belfry swimming in blood. She is saying strange things.

Jean-Pierre goes out, carrying Jeanne. Catherine follows, but she stops near the door and listens.

LOUIS: What is she saying?

JACQUES: Your son is conspiring against us. He wants to kill us and take power. (*Silence. Louis sits down, stricken.*) But we mustn't lose a moment.

LOUIS: Georges wants to kill me! (*A pause.*) Is it our fault?

JACQUES: Our fault?

LOUIS: I don't know anymore.

JACQUES: Call the Captain of the Guard. Give the order to seize your son. He is the one who is going to strike against us.

LOUIS: There is no longer good or evil. Force rules.

JACQUES: What are you saying?

LOUIS: That is what *he* said; was he wrong?

JACQUES: Wake up! Summon the Captain.

LOUIS: Why?

JACQUES: Wake up. (*A pause.*) I know.[72] It's your son.

LOUIS: What does my son matter to me?

JACQUES: But it concerns your life.

LOUIS: What does my life matter to me!

JACQUES: It concerns Vaucelles.

LOUIS: Does Vaucelles still exist? We wanted to save her and it seems to me we have killed her soul.

JACQUES: This is not the time for questions and remorse. We must *act.*

LOUIS: Forgive me. I need to be alone for a while.

Jacques goes out. A pause.

CATHERINE: Why are you sad? You had already lost your daughter and your wife. You no longer have a son. The future is wide open before you!

LOUIS: You hate me, Catherine?

CATHERINE: No . . . come here.

He gets up.

LOUIS: Will you leave me without having forgiven me?

CATHERINE: Can I forgive you? Can I curse you? Aren't we a single flesh? Take my hand. (*She gives him her left hand and presses herself to him.*) A single flesh, a single destiny. Nothing will be able to part us. Neither death, nor life!

She tries to stab him. He seizes her wrist. The weapon falls to the ground.

LOUIS: My dear love! You still love me, then?[73]

CATHERINE: If you live, I have lost you!

LOUIS: You have been given back to me, my wife. No kiss or promise has bound us as tightly as this dagger blow. You love me and I can hold you in my arms.

He takes her in his arms.

CATHERINE: I have lost you.

LOUIS: No! Can't you feel my heart beating against your heart, like it used to. I am not your executioner; you are not my victim. For you and me, the same destiny; and its cruelty cannot destroy our love. We are now reunited forever.

CATHERINE: Why did you hold my hand back? (*Silence.*) There is still time.

A pause.

LOUIS: I do not have the right to run away.

CATHERINE: You love me and you will let me die alone!

Long silence. Clarice enters.

CLARICE: She is dead.

CATHERINE: Did she say who struck her?

CLARICE: It was Georges.

CATHERINE: Georges! It's all my fault! (*Silence.*) The love and the joy which I denied her, who will give them back to her? I'm a criminal! I thought: later, she will be happy. But her life has stopped now, in suffering and in hate; she died with this crushing weight on her heart: the weight of my stupid will. (*Silence. She turns toward Louis.*) You can sacrifice me without remorse. How could I ever have believed that this world was malleable clay [*pâte*] which I could shape and fashion by my will? Do what you want. I deserve to be thrown into the ditches, to die there alone and lost.[74]

LOUIS: No!

CATHERINE: What are you saying?

LOUIS: I have denied half of my people, and the whole town has turned into a horde without law and without love. How can we reach a higher life if we first of all kill all our reasons for living? (*He takes her in his arms.*) A single flesh, a single destiny! We will triumph together, or we will be buried together in the earth.

CATHERINE: What are you going to do?

LOUIS: I am going to call the Council together.

Seventh Tableau

The Council Chamber. The Deputies. The three leading Aldermen. Some guards.

LOUIS: Did you sleep last night?

VOICES: What is he saying? What a strange question! Why has he brought us together?

LOUIS: If you have slept, you are lucky. (*A pause.*) We made a mistake.

What we decided yesterday was wrong and should not be carried out [*s'accomplir*].

Murmurs of surprise.

FRANÇOIS: Be careful; there are things that cannot be said without courting death.

LOUIS: Do you think that I want you to surrender Vaucelles? I would sooner kill myself! (*A pause.*) We will not buy our victory with a crime. Let us arm the men, the old men, the women and even the children. Under the cover of night, let us storm the Burgundian camp. Together we will triumph or together we will die.

FRANÇOIS: We know that you are a good husband and a good father. But aren't you forgetting that you are first of all the leader of this town? You admitted yesterday that a successful breakout would need a miracle.

LOUIS: Ghent was at the end of its strength; the enemy promised to spare it if all the young people of the town were handed over to them.[75] But the inhabitants preferred death to shame; without hope they attacked the besiegers' army; and they swept them away.

JACQUES: Why should we run this senseless risk when we know that victory is secure if we hold out until spring?

FIRST DEPUTY: Ever since yesterday every one of us has heard a wife, a cherished mother, crying in his house; when our little children smiled, we turned our heads away and wiped our tears. We didn't sleep. But we don't have the right to lose Vaucelles in order to soothe our own feelings.

VOICES: We don't have the right.

LOUIS: The right? Then who decides, if we do not? Nobody before us has ever resolved this question that we have to answer, and nobody can answer it for us. It is for us alone to choose: what do we want?

JACQUES: We want victory.

VOICES: Victory. We want victory!

LOUIS: What victory? (*A pause.*) The people of Vaucelles were crawling about in misery and slavery. We said that we will turn these slaves into men; and as soon as these words were pronounced, poverty, hunger, death took on a different face. For eighteen months, we have struggled side by side, and, despite suffering, joy was ours. Ever since yesterday, joy is dead. From where do we draw the strength to be men, if not in those looks lifted toward us with trust? Now all eyes are averted. Each one is alone like an animal. What does our triumph or our ruin matter, if we are no more than a wild horde? No. We will not end this struggle by trampling under foot all our reasons for struggling. That would be the worst of all defeats.

FRANÇOIS: There is only one defeat and that is not reaching the goal we have chosen. We have not overthrown the Duke for death but life. And we *will* live.

LOUIS: We have overthrown the Duke to win liberty and justice.

FIRST DEPUTY: Today we dare to behave like tyrants for the love of freedom and justice,[76] otherwise we will be vanquished and we will lose them forever.

SECOND DEPUTY: What he's saying is true. We need strength first. The time for justice will come.

VOICES: No weakness. It's not the time for us to weigh ourselves down with scruples. It is useful to the community that these people die: they *will* die![77]

FRANÇOIS: What good is it to continue this chattering any longer? Our decisions are already taken. I ask the Council to vote.

VOICES: Yes, let's vote, let's finish it.

JEAN-PIERRE, *bursting into the room*: Wait!

VOICES (*together*): What does he want? What's he doing here? It's out of order! Who let him in? What a nerve! How dare he?

LOUIS: Don't you know that it is forbidden to cross this threshold during the Council meeting?

JEAN-PIERRE: For the love of Vaucelles, in the name of the service I've given to this community, listen to me. It will be time to punish me later if you judge that I've breached your laws lightly. The news that I bring cannot wait.

FRANÇOIS: You will be made an example of! (*To the guards.*) Take him away.

JACQUES: No. Let him speak. The things that he has to say to us must be important.

THE DEPUTIES: Let him speak! We want to hear him. He wouldn't run such a risk without having good reason.

FRANÇOIS: This is unlawful.

JACQUES: We make the law.

LOUIS: Speak then.

JEAN-PIERRE: First I will ask you a question: doesn't our constitution require that our laws be voted by the three leading Aldermen, assisted by the Council?

LOUIS: Without doubt.

JEAN-PIERRE: Well then! I tell you that none of the decisions you will make today will have the force of law, because here there are only two Aldermen and a traitor. (*He points at François.*)

VOICES: What? What is he saying? Is it possible? What is he trying to say? What treason does he speak of? He is accusing François Rosbourg?

FRANÇOIS: This is too much!

LOUIS: Explain yourself.

JEAN-PIERRE: My sister has just died, murdered. Do you know who murdered her?

LOUIS: I know, it is my son.[78]

Movements on the stage.

JEAN-PIERRE: And do you know why? He was conspiring against the community and she discovered his plans. He wasn't alone; before dying, Jeanne revealed to me the name of his accomplice: François Rosbourg.

FRANÇOIS: Are you allowing one of your leading Aldermen to be insulted with impunity in full Council? I demand that this man be thrown in prison!

JEAN-PIERRE: He wanted to get rid of Master Van der Welde and Master D'Avesnes and to rule alone. My sister heard his words!

FRANÇOIS: It is easy to invoke the witness of the dead. Once more, I ask you to put an end to this outrage.

JEAN-PIERRE: I have succeeded in finding another witness. (*To Louis.*) Will you allow him to enter?

LOUIS, *to the guards*: Let him enter.

The guards open the door. Georges enters surrounded by three youths holding him at spear-point.

JEAN-PIERRE: I won't ask you to repeat here the confession that we've taken from you. Tell us just this: this man accuses you of having attempted to corrupt him and he claims to have rejected your offer with horror. Is this true?

GEORGES: Corrupt him, really? He was very quick to listen to what I had to say. I even ask myself if he isn't the one who suggested it in the first place.

VOICES: Is it possible? François Rosbourg? What awful treason!

FRANÇOIS: He is lying!

GEORGES: Do you think I'd agree to take the blame for you? No, if I must hang from the gallows, I want you to keep me company. I know very well that if our plan had succeeded, you'd have tried to get rid of me.

FRANÇOIS: It's a plot! They have come up with these lies to get me out of power.

JEAN-PIERRE: We have obtained from Georges the name of your accomplices, and we have been able to seize many of them. Does the Council want to hear them?

Jean-Pierre's friends open the door and let some men in.

FIRST DEPUTY: You traitor! You took advantage of our misfortune to serve your ambition.

THIRD DEPUTY: And you dared speak to us of the good of Vaucelles, you hypocrite!

FRANÇOIS: It is true. I wanted power. But it's also true that it was for the good of Vaucelles. Your feeble hearts will never be capable of giving her the destiny that I dreamed for her. In my hands, she would have become the queen of Flanders and of the world.

JACQUES: She would have become the docile instrument of your pride: the good of this town is what she herself chooses as her good.[79] If she received the world as an empire from the hands of an outsider, she would be only a slave.[80]

LOUIS: His admission is enough! (*To a guard.*) Take him away.

François steps down from the rostrum; the guards take him away, as well as Georges and the witnesses.

JACQUES: You have saved Vaucelles. I propose that the Council call on Jean-Pierre Gauthier to occupy this vacant place at our sides.

VOICES: Yes! He deserves it! Let him be a leading Alderman!

VOICES: Let him be an Alderman!

LOUIS: Do any members of the Council oppose this decision? (*A pause.*) The responsibility of being an Alderman is offered to you, then: will you accept it?

JEAN-PIERRE: I accept it. (*He climbs the rostrum.*) As I am now permitted to take part in your debates, I want to ask you: this man that you have just expelled from your midst, is he not a criminal?

VOICES: Yes. Certainly. He *is* a criminal.

JEAN-PIERRE: Well then! All he did was to follow your example. (*Movements.*) You had decided that the old men and the infirm are useless mouths; why wouldn't a tyrant judge *your* liberties useless and your lives insignificant? If one man alone can be seen as disposable, a hundred thousand men together are merely so much waste.

Silence.

JACQUES: Must a whole town be condemned to die to save half of it?

LOUIS: We will condemn nobody! The men of Vaucelles are free and we will appeal to their liberty. They have agreed to obey you because they trust our wisdom. But tell them you will allow them to risk their lives to save that of their children and their wives, and they will risk it with joy.

FIRST DEPUTY: They will risk it and they will all perish.

LOUIS: A freely chosen death is not a bad thing. But these women and old men that you will throw in the ditches are not allowed to choose. And so you will rob them of both their deaths and their lives. We will not do that! On this night, united in a single will, a free people will confront its destiny.

SECOND DEPUTY: Vaucelles must live!

LOUIS: Who is Vaucelles? Between each of us and all the others there is a pact; if we break it, our community crumbles into dust.

SECOND DEPUTY: Vaucelles won't cease to exist because our women and children will be dead. We will find other wives who will give us other sons.

JEAN-PIERRE: Other wives? Other sons? But with what eyes will they look at us? And what words will we dare speak to them?

A pause.

FOURTH DEPUTY: What he says is true. Since yesterday I have not dared to lift my eyes for fear of meeting those of a victim or an accomplice. Our mouths will never be able to smile again.

THIRD DEPUTY: Imagine the King of France arriving. He will enter a town of assassins, so will the bells of our belfry ring for joy or instead as a death toll?

FIRST DEPUTY: And can you imagine our belfry razed to the ground, our walls reduced to rubble?

LOUIS: We are not fighting for stones.

SECOND DEPUTY: Vaucelles must live.

LOUIS: Is an accursed people eaten up by shame still living?

SECOND DEPUTY: Is it living when its bones nourish the earth?

LOUIS: It could live forever in our hearts. Yes, Vaucelles must live. Let us not kill her soul.

JEAN-PIERRE: Can you look this future in the face that you have built with crime and with treason? Some of you, eaten up by remorse, will run from the town; the others will be eaten away in solitude and silence. We will have sacrificed our flesh, our blood and all that will be left in the middle of the plain is an empty tomb. Will you be satisfied with such a victory? (*Silence.*) Reply!

THIRD DEPUTY: I don't know anymore.

FIFTH DEPUTY: I don't know anymore.

FOURTH DEPUTY: He is right, we will be cursed.

JEAN-PIERRE: What woman will cross our walls? What friend will touch our hands?

JACQUES: He is right. We will have killed trust and love. We will no longer be a town but a horde. We wanted to serve as an example to the world, and instead we will be an object of horror to it.

FIRST DEPUTY: Our goal is within our reach: will we renounce it?

LOUIS: What is the goal? We have overthrown the Duke to be free men. We have only to say one word, make one gesture, and this goal is attained. Failure is no longer to be feared. Whether we succeed in breaking out or are massacred, we will triumph. (*A pause.*) We will vote by raising hands.

In silence, they all raise their hands.

Eighth Tableau

At night, under the ramparts, in front of a gate. To the right, a Captain is giving out arms. To the left, Catherine and Clarice are giving out soup and bread.[81] *There is a large crowd of men, women, children and old men.*

CATHERINE: Who wants more soup?

A MAN: I'm not hungry anymore.

A MAN: Nor me.

ANOTHER: Nor me.

AN OLD MAN: I dreamed of eating my fill before I die!

A WOMAN: This is perhaps our last meal.

A MAN: Come on now! Tomorrow, we will drink the Burgundians' wine and slaughter their pigs!

ANOTHER: What a feast!

ANOTHER: We will make them pay for these months of famine.

CATHERINE: Tomorrow! There will be the same black sky around the earth, the same icy wind will sweep the plain. Will we still see this sky, or will our eyes be closed forever?

CLARICE: It doesn't matter, we will have lived.[82] I've had my share of life.

Louis and Jacques come in from the two sides of the stage.

LOUIS: Is everything ready?

JACQUES: We only need a spark to set fire to the belfry, the ramparts and the houses. The infirm and the old men are at their posts. Before the Burgundians could reach our gates, the town would be in flames.

LOUIS, *to the Captain*: Are they all armed?

THE CAPTAIN: Yes.

LOUIS: Have they eaten enough?

CATHERINE: We've given out two weeks rations to them. (*Jean-Pierre runs in.*) Well then?

JEAN-PIERRE: It's exactly like the other night. They are sleeping and, at this side of the camp, the sentries are playing dice. I came to within a hundred paces of them without being seen.

LOUIS: We will start when two o'clock strikes. (*A pause.*) The gate will close behind us.

VOICES: We will not go back.

Louis and Jacques move away.

THE CAPTAIN: In your places! Men in front. Women and children at the back.

They rush, bumping into each other.

CLARICE: Are these the same people as yesterday?

JEAN-PIERRE: Today, their future is in their hands. (*To Catherine.*) Vaucelles owes you her salutations.[83]

CATHERINE: Perhaps it would have been better to have let myself be thrown into the ditches without resisting. Have I saved these children and women? Have I condemned these men to death?

JEAN-PIERRE: Your silence would perhaps have saved these men. It would certainly have lost these women and children. Instead we will weigh upon the earth.[84]

CATHERINE: How can we know?

JEAN-PIERRE: We cannot know. Now I see it clearly: our lot is to take the risk and the anguish. But why should we hope to be at peace?

THE CAPTAIN: To your places.

Jean-Pierre kisses Clarice. The three of them go back to their places. Louis comes toward Catherine.

LOUIS: Farewell, Catherine!

CATHERINE: No, not farewell. Now we are together forever.

They kiss. Two o'clock strikes.

LOUIS: Let joy be ours! We are fighting for liberty, and liberty will triumph through our freely given sacrifice. Alive or dead, we are the victors.

Two o'clock strikes for the second time. Louis goes to his place at the head of the column.

LOUIS: Open the gate!

The gate starts to open.

THE END

NOTES

Our grateful thanks to Sylvie Le Bon de Beauvoir for permission to translate *Les bouches inutiles* for publication in the Illinois edition of Beauvoir's work. We would also like to thank Marybeth Timmermann for helpful suggestions on the specifics of our translation, Margaret Simons for general encouragement and support, and Joan Catapano and the University of Illinois Press for embarking on this major publishing project.

1. As a translation of the original publication of Beauvoir's play, we have followed the Gallimard edition in including the names of the actors who played each of the characters.

2. When this is said it is heard as "vaut-elle," which, in a play on words, implies the question "does she have worth?"

3. The stage directions are at points rather schematic. Our Introduction discusses Michel Vitold's directional style.

4. The original Gallimard text capitalizes all the dramatic personae. Some (names, and names taking the form of titles) start with capital letter of a larger size, and these have been capitalized here. However, the women and other "ordinary people" who speak are not individualized, to indicate that they are "the useless mouths" and do not have value, and so they have not been capitalized here. Even when the children or women or old speak, they are not accorded a name or title, which connotes individuality and worth.

5. The verb "se coller" here in the Gallimard text is the first use of a reflexive verb in the play. The frequent and "strong" use of reflexives in French is one of the marked differences between it and English, and it brings particular difficulties in translating. A reflexive verb is one that is preceded by a reflexive pronoun—a pronoun that refers to the self. In English, the word "self" preceded by the possessive pronoun comes after the verb; for example "she throws herself into the work" is translated as "elle se lance dans le travail," with the word "self" being included in the "se" here. This difference between the two languages means that the French rendering imparts much less of a sense of ownership, and as a result the self and the subject are more integrated.

6. The French "maître," used in the Gallimard text, contains a number of different meanings. A more literal translation as "mayor" or "magistrate" is not appropriate here, given that well-known terms existed for the various ruling groups in the Flanders city-states. In Ghent, the model for Vaucelles, the three leading Aldermen were known as the "Three Members." The appropriate title to indicate the status of Louis D'Avesnes, Jacques van der Welde and François Rosbourg as the "Three Members" of the Aldermanate of Vaucelles is the honorific "Master." What Beauvoir terms as the "Council," the historical Aldermanate, is in the case of Vaucelles composed of thirty representatives from the guilds and dominated by the weavers' guild, "top dogs" because of the supreme role of cloth in the creation of wealth. See our Introduction for more detail.

7. "Bourgeoisie" has a double meaning here. It was the term used at the time the play is set to describe the citizens of the city-states of Flanders; but when Beauvoir wrote *The Useless Mouths* and still now, it conveys a class characterized by complacency as well as prudence.

8. "Freedom" has central place within Sartrean existentialist thinking and Sartre, particularly in his earlier philosophy, held by this as an "absolute freedom." However, *The Useless Mouths* instead emphasizes that freedom of decision and choice is always conditional and

is often in fact determined by social situation and category-membership. This comment by Jean-Pierre Gauthier is the first time that Vaucelles is named as being composed by its men. Indeed, the "nous" in the original French—"nous serons," "nous travaillerons pour nous," and "nous vivrons"—is multiply repeated; and "des hommes" is explicitly used, rather than "un peuple" or "des gens," both appearing elsewhere in the play, so Beauvoir is making the point very clear here.

9. That is, the other city-states in Flanders, which included Bruges, Antwerp, Lille, and Oudenburg as well as Ghent.

10. Now associated with "a canteen of cutlery," in a military context a canteen is a traveling mess that serves food to frontline soldiers. There is no suitable English word for the kind of soldiers that do this: neither a "mess orderly" nor a "canteen orderly" sounds right, so we have opted to use a description—a "field-canteen"—as the occupational title.

11. This is the first mention of the immensely important belfry being built in Vaucelles. Its significance both in the real Flanders city-states and in the fictional Vaucelles is explored in the Introduction.

12. As this indicates, in the *in extremis* situation the town is in, even straw and husks have value as desirable foodstuffs.

13. This comment points up Jean-Pierre's disassociation, his disengagement or "désengagement" in French.

14. Here Jeanne is acting as a mouthpiece concerning the role of necessity in (Sartrean) existentialist ideas and in a way parroting Catherine's ideas, expressed later in the play, about there being different kinds of happiness, only one of which concerns love and with "higher" forms existing. Beauvoir's approach in the play is instead concerned with authenticity, with people coming to recognize the fundamental nature of the self as "self-and-other."

15. His statement positions Clarice as the principle of solipsism personified, and a direct parallel of how Jean-Pierre situates himself. Our Introduction discusses the role of characters in *The Useless Mouths* as embodying philosophical positions and changes to these.

16. This is a curious phrase, indicating "exceptionally rare." Most diamonds come in the form of a solitaire, a word also indicating being by itself, solitary and alone. The actor playing Clarice was Beauvoir's close friend Olga Dominique, a dark-haired woman; newspaper photographs of cast members suggest that her costume was a striking black and white.

17. This is literally what the mason says; the intimation is, women are useless.

18. The French "chef de chantier" is still used of someone who is a "site foreman." Although the present-day meaning of this loses the power and status of the role in the medieval hierarchy, Beauvoir quite explicitly does not term this person a "master" of a trade in the way she does some of the masons and weavers. Consequently, we have decided to translate it as "Site Foreman" rather than elevating it in a way that would disregard Beauvoir's choice.

19. He is being sarcastic, because the three leading Aldermen and the Council are not likely to do the heeding of two ordinary masons.

20. This is the first explicit intimation of the leading position of the weavers' guild in the traditional power structure of Vaucelles. Later in this tableau, these two masons attempt to take bread that is intended to feed the townspeople from a porter, showing that they do not accept some decisions made by the Council, all of whom are weavers. The power base of the weavers' guild no longer exists because there is no more cloth to weave or sell: what counts is the belfry, and thus what the masons do.

21. There is no indication that the child is male: the text says simply "enfant," so we treat the child as intentionally unsexed.

22. The "Three Arts" are painting, sculpture, music.

23. Thirty is symbolic here and again later in the play because thirty pieces of silver were paid to Judas to betray Jesus.

24. The stage direction does not indicate very clearly what is happening here. Clarice and Jacques are the center of the scene; the commotion breaks out at one corner where the belfry is being built. Then the man, followed by a group of masons, some of whom are carrying the body, pass in front of Clarice and Jacques. Jacques stops two of this group to question them about what has happened.

25. This is the first occurrence of the word "useless." Beauvoir is using it here to intimate that the only useless thing is actually the belfry, not the so-called useless mouths.

26. At this point, François sees the belfry as useless and the work on it as without value; over the course of this tableau, however, his philosophical position undergoes a complete volte face.

27. This is the first of some strong "musts" in the play, and these signal significant points in the developing events.

28. There are five highly significant uses of "one," the impersonal form, in *The Useless Mouths*, of which this is the first. They all indicate an important degree of distance and disengagement on the part of a character from something that is happening or that has been said to them.

29. This is another expression of being disengaged, or désengagement, on Jean-Pierre's part, and again gestures toward the betrayal of Jesus.

30. Louis says in French, and he means, "men" in the second sentence here. However, at this point he knows that the "few lives" would actually be all the women, as well as all the children and the old and infirm, but not the men. He is lying.

31. This, together with the fact that only men can work, as work is being defined in Vaucelles, is the crux of the decision about the useless mouths.

32. This is a strong remark and shows how much François' philosophical position has shifted and also how much the emphasis for him is on women's uselessness. It is omitted from the Francis and Gontier translation.

33. Clarice is behaving with childish petulance here, as Jeanne's response indicates—of course they cannot, they are starving.

34. For Georges, action entails doing anything. Catherine later points out that it matters in a fundamental sense what it is that action consists of.

35. The adventurer as a moral type, like the tyrant, is developed from Beauvoir's interest in Hegel and is commented on in Beauvoir's *The Ethics of Ambiguity* (New York: Citadel Press, 1976 [1948]), 58–62, 63. Solipsism is thus an element within the adventurer position.

36. At this point, Catherine fails to realize that she has been permitted to have this symbolic role, but that she has always been excluded from real power because she has never been seen to have the use and value that men have.

37. This is a stark expression of a solipsist stance.

38. Catherine's approach is a very instrumental one, of just using Jeanne to "change" and tame Georges.

39. Catherine's comment here is made in bad faith—she knows full well that Jeanne is not "strong" but has surrendered her will to another, that is, to Catherine herself.

40. Jean-Pierre here is expressing a patrician scorn for the weavers, who are seen by others as central to the economic and political life of Vaucelles.

41. Georges means that Clarice's face laughed with pleasure, perhaps indicated by touching it.

42. This is perhaps the strongest use of the impersonal pronoun in the play, indicating Catherine's attempt to gain emotional distance from the horrors happening.

43. This is the first time that the precise words "the useless mouths" are used, although the idea has been intimated before. It comes at a very dramatic point and is the culmination of the events unfolding in Act I. What Louis' saying this makes clear is that it encompasses "the women" as an absolute, the category membership in total, but that it is only certain kinds of men, those who are sick, old, and children, who are useless.

44. This tautological two-part "logic" appears a number of times in the play. Louis' false argument here is that the ends of the decision are by definition good, so any decision to produce these ends is also good.

45. There is immense irony here. Louis is emphasizing the femaleness of Vaucelles and that it must be saved, while in the play it is femaleness that has to be sacrificed. The fact that orally Vaucelles sounds like "vaut-elle" (see footnote 2) makes the irony resound. Beauvoir uses "elle" here three times for Vaucelles, so there can be no mistaking her meaning, which is to emphasize the absurdity of what is going on.

46. Louis' bald statement that "she knows," and then Catherine's "I know," involve a quantum leap kind of knowledge, knowledge that changes everything.

47. What Catherine does not yet appreciate is that, as a woman, she never had worth and that there has been no change concerning this, but rather the open recognition of where ethically this leads to in the *in extremis* situation Vaucelles is in.

48. That this is indeed men is shown by Catherine's response, contrasting it as she does with "the useless mouths."

49. This is the Aldermanate.

50. "Our" lot is used duplicitously here by Louis, for there has been no choice for Catherine or any others of "the useless mouths."

51. There is an immense irony here that the audience will be aware of at this point: Georges, for whom Clarice is a literal sister, does not respect her sexually at all.

52. Clarice has been denied the ability to make her own choices in life. By choosing her death, Clarice exercises her free will for the first time and in doing so comes to "grow up" and become an adult person or self.

53. There is probably a mistake in the stage directions, because Clarice is not alone from this point on, but in the next tableau takes a dagger from her belt to kill herself. It would be more appropriate if Clarice had hidden the dagger in her belt rather than replacing it on the wall, and it may well have been done like this in actual performance.

54. Georges' incestuous desire for Clarice is a Hegelian *in extremis* behavior, one of a number that Beauvoir makes use of in *The Useless Mouths*.

55. This statement from Georges does not have to be true, and later Louis comes to realize this.

56. The tenses of these two parallel statements of entirely faulty two-part logic are crucial—"if we don't want to, then we won't have to; and they haven't so far, so they never will."

57. The French is "non, c'est inutile" and involves a very deliberate use of "inutile" of

"useless" to describe the belfry, offering a direct contrast to the men's application of "useless" to women.

58. This is clearly intended as a universal statement, not only about the specific situation in Vaucelles. Silence always entails "accepting any outcome," as Catherine phrases it, and involves complicity, and only the exertion of will in contrary action does not.

59. This is the point at which Jean-Pierre refuses the complicity that comes from silence.

60. This is tautological. It is also patently untrue.

61. Clarice intends to kill herself, while a little later in this tableau Catherine intends to kill Louis. They both see Louis as responsible for the decision and therefore the person who is "going to be shown" through the consequences of their freely chosen actions. This is important for the development of the ethical ideas being developed about the relationship between self and others with regard to free will and wider notions of freedom.

62. While not a very developed character in the play, Jeanne is more than a cipher, for she is connected to others, committed to them, and she acts in concert with them; indeed, these things are her undoing, leading to bad faith through her relationships with Catherine and with Georges. Her commitment also leads her to be murdered off stage in the next tableau.

63. "On lutte ensemble" (we struggle together), is a major statement in the play of what it is to be what we term in our Introduction "self-and-other" and to live purposefully in the world.

64. This comment by Jean-Pierre is a key statement of Beauvoir's idea of self-and-other and an indissoluble interconnection rather than solipsism characterizing the human condition.

65. What François is clearly meaning is, "I will be dictator." When Beauvoir drafted *The Useless Mouths* she thought she would have to submit it to the German censor so that it might be licensed for performance, and presumably she does not use the word for this reason. François, however, is revealing himself as a kind of Hitler figure, intent on achieving a putsch, and is a tyrant and dictator in the terms she explored later in *The Ethics of Ambiguity* (62, 71).

66. This is the same faulty two-part tautological logic as the merchants earlier used: "this could be, therefore it must be."

67. For the women, Catherine has suddenly stopped being "one of them" and has become "one of us"; Beauvoir expands on this idea in her Introduction to *The Second Sex* (Paris: Gallimard, 1949), trans. Constance Borde and Sheila Malovany-Chevallier (New York: Vintage Books, 2010).

68. The Sartrean emphasis is on the movement from doing to being, while here Beauvoir is in a subtle way reversing this: unless Catherine has human worth and "being" in this sense, she is unable to "do," to act in the existentialist sense of the term. It is of course also reminiscent of Descartes' formulation, but his "je pense donc je suis" (I think, therefore I am) has been reworked by Beauvoir to become "je peux donc je suis" (I can, therefore I am).

69. The word for child in French is necessarily residually sexed (that is, it appears under the covering law of "il" and "ils"), whereas the English allows what is more likely here, which is that only the child's existence is being indicated.

70. The two uses of "one" by Catherine here again distances her, in this case from the terrible fact that it will be Louis doing this, killing her "like an instrument that you will break."

71. This is a statement about solipsism and it is a condition existing between him and Catherine that "the useless mouths" decision, and the wider notions of use and value underpinning it, have brought about. However, at this point in the play Louis cannot grasp that this is so.

72. This comment from Jacques parallels the even more portentous repetitions of "I know" earlier in the play.

73. There are echoes here of Françoise killing Xavière in *She Came to Stay*, as someone who was loved but who also threatened Françoise's very selfhood. It is another example of the Hegelian *in extremis* situation that Beauvoir was so much engaged by when she wrote *The Useless Mouths* and is discussed further in the Introduction.

74. This is a particularly "writerly" speech-act from Catherine, involving two colons and a semicolon which are highly consequential for the development of her thinking but which cannot be "heard" by the audience and can only be read.

75. Morally speaking, Louis is using this as a direct parallel to what he now thinks Vaucelles should do. Given the details of the play, and as noted in our Introduction, we think that Beauvoir saw it as such too. That is, she saw the intended genocidal banishment of the women as a product of the wider dynamics of power operating, and not as implying a different basis for the intended expulsion of women.

76. The First Deputy is assuming that it is possible to behave like a tyrant without actually being a tyrant, that doing and being are different things. The whole import of the play is to reject the means/end separation implicit in this.

77. This is the same false logic indicated earlier—"it is useful to us, so therefore they will die."

78. This is another resounding "I know" in the play.

79. This repeats once more the tautological false logic that underpins many of the men's decisions in Vaucelles.

80. These statements by François and then Jacques express aspects of the master/slave relationship in Hegelian thinking, which Beauvoir rejects.

81. As this stage direction indicates, the sexual division of labor in Vaucelles remains intact, but it now means something very different because different ideas about usefulness and worth underpin it.

82. That is, Clarice will have lived both in the specific sense of "being together forever" which is stated by Jean-Pierre immediately before everyone leaves Vaucelles, and in the more profound sense of "struggling together" that is fundamental to Beauvoir's ideas about self-and-other.

83. Elsewhere in the Series "salut" has been translated as salvation. This would be an inappropriate term at this juncture, when the inhabitants are possibly all about to be slaughtered—"salut" in the sense of a salutation which is owed is what Beauvoir intends in the text here and was the prevailing 1940s meaning of the word.

84. That is, they will have "lived" and "acted" in the sense of "struggling together" fundamental to Beauvoir's argument in *The Useless Mouths*.

2

Short Articles on Literature

INTRODUCTION

"It's Shakespeare They Don't Like," "The Novel and the Theater," "An American Renaissance in France," and "New Heroes for Old"

by Elizabeth Fallaize

"In the same week we have heard Sartre's lecture, been to the opening night of *Les bouches inutiles* (*The Useless Mouths*) and read the first issue of *Les temps modernes* (Modern Times)."[1] So wrote a mildly irritated critic, according to Beauvoir in *La force des choses* (*Force of Circumstance*). It is not difficult to understand this reaction to the "existentialist offensive" in which Beauvoir and Sartre found themselves unwittingly engaged in the autumn of 1945. Beauvoir's second novel *Le sang des autres* (*The Blood of Others*) was published in September, followed a few weeks later by the publication of the first two volumes of Sartre's novel *Les chemins de la liberté* (*The Roads to Freedom*). On October 15, she and Sartre launched *Les temps modernes*, a journal that would become an important forum for left-wing opinion and in which extracts of a number of Beauvoir's works were later published, and in November *Les bouches inutiles*, Beauvoir's first and only play, opened in Paris. In December Beauvoir gave a lecture entitled "Roman et métaphysique" ("The Novel and Metaphysics") defending the metaphysical novel, while Sartre gave a defense of existentialism in a lecture entitled "L'existentialisme est-il un humanisme?" ("Is Existentialism a Humanism?").[2] The whole issue of what literature could achieve, its relation to philosophy, and the techniques which different literary forms have at their disposal to create a fictional world consonant with a philosophical viewpoint were thus at the forefront of Beauvoir's preoccupations. The four articles that follow all address these questions, in a variety of ways.

The first of the articles, "C'est Shakespeare qu'ils n'aiment pas" ("It's Shakespeare They Don't Like") appeared in the spring of 1945, just before the autumn offensive, and is in essence a circumstantial piece. The theater director Charles Dullin had been a friend of Beauvoir since 1932 and had directed a number of Sartre's plays. Dullin was dismayed at the dismissive reaction of theater critics to his production of *King Lear*; fearing that he might lose his position as director of the Sarah Bernhardt theater in Paris he begged Beauvoir to write a piece in defense of it.[3] Beauvoir duly obliged, no doubt particularly conscious that she herself would be facing the theater critics shortly. The essence of her argument is that behind the critics' dislike of the production is a covert dislike of Shakespeare, whose popularity had never been high in France. Beauvoir accuses the critics of using their articles to indulge in witticisms designed to showcase their own polemical talents, instead of educating the public into appreciating Shakespeare. She strikes a heartfelt note when she points to the disparity between Dullin's creative ambition in rethinking Shakespeare's play and the triviality of the critical response.

Commenting on the piece in her memoirs, Beauvoir writes somewhat ruefully that the value of her defense was undermined by the violence of her tone, and that the principal practical result was to make her some unfortunate enemies. One other aspect of the piece deserves comment however. In *L'invitée* (*She Came to Stay*), which Beauvoir completed in the summer of 1941, the central male figure, Pierre, an actor and theater director, is partly based on Dullin.[4] In the novel, Pierre directs *Julius Caesar* and attempts a balance between realism and stylization that attracts criticism.[5] One of the characters, Gerbert, remarks of the critics: "they daren't admit that it's Shakespeare they can't stand."[6] Beauvoir is thus drawing in 1945 on ideas about the theater in which she had been interested for some time.

"Roman et Théatre" ("The Novel and the Theater") is a much more substantial piece, published in October 1945, only weeks before the first night of *Les bouches inutiles* in November. Although it does not refer specifically to the play it clearly draws on Beauvoir's experience of writing it and sets out in some detail her thinking about the difference between technique in the novel and technique in the theater. The question of technique in the novel had preoccupied Beauvoir since her first attempts at writing fiction. In her memoirs she describes the influence on her writing of the American novelists of the

1930s—especially Dos Passos, Hemingway, and Faulkner—and their use of new narrative techniques influenced by the cinema and by behaviorism. All her writing on literature emphasizes her desire to communicate a meaning to the reader based on the real world, and, in this piece, she argues that the fictional universe, while not merely a copy of reality in the way some of the nineteenth century realists assumed, has to be credible in the eyes of the reader and must therefore be rooted in the real world. Within this constraint the novelist nevertheless has considerable freedom to manipulate time, space and place, to base the plot on an individual or a group, to describe the characters from the outside or from the inside, and to make considerable demands on the reader. The reader also has considerable freedom, since she can go at her own speed, stop when she feels like it, and reread anything she has not understood. In the novel, the issue of whether characters are seen from the inside or the outside was one which particularly interested Beauvoir since it mirrors her concept of the ambiguity of our existence. Seen from the outside we are captured in our being-for-others. Seen from the inside, the reader follows the movements of being-for-itself, freely constituting its own meaning in the world. Both points of view are possible in the novel, and Beauvoir had used both in the two novels she had already published.

In the theater, however, as she goes on to explain, we can only know the characters in their being-for-others. We have nothing but their words and actions to guide us. This restriction means, in Beauvoir's view, that the choice of subject in the theater is limited to a conflict of some kind between different characters—interior drama will not work on the stage.[7] There are also limits on space, time, place, and number of characters. Spectators must be given more help than a reader, since they are captive in a way that a reader is not. However, the great advantage of the theater over the novel is that the illusion of the real world, so crucial to Beauvoir, does not depend merely on the novelist's skill and the reader's imagination. In the theater, the physical presence of the actors, the décor, the costumes, and the stage itself bring an imaginary universe to life. If the playwright succeeds, he will have the immense privilege of communicating an important and dramatic truth to a community of spectators.

Such were Beauvoir's hopes when she attended the opening night of *Les bouches inutiles*. They were almost immediately dashed by the reaction of the playwright Jean Genet, seated beside her, who muttered to her "That's not what the theater is at all, not at all."[8] Most of the critics agreed, and the play closed after a limited run. A new critical climate is however bringing about a more positive reading of the play.[9]

The second group of articles presented here, "An American Renaissance in France" and "New Heroes for Old," returns to the subject of the novel and the questions of what it can achieve and by what means. However, a new dimension is added to the discussion by Beauvoir's firsthand experience of America, gained during the lecture tour she undertook in the United States between January and May 1947. Both articles appeared in English in the American press and are directly addressed to an American audience. The first one sets out to explain the reception recent American literature has received in France, and its influence on French novelists, and the second turns more specifically to French writing and the aims of postwar French writers. Beauvoir's desire to clarify these issues would seem to have arisen directly from her conversations with American intellectuals and, in particular, from a number of heated discussions that she had had with the editorial board of the *Partisan Review*. As she describes in *L'Amérique au jour le jour* (*America Day by Day*), the account of her visit that she published in 1948, the members of the board told her that the French enjoyed only second-rate realist American writing, devouring it in much the same way as they might thrill to an account of the exotic habits of a barbarous tribe. In the editorial board's view, this accounted for the French preference for the works of writers like Hemingway and Wright, Steinbeck and Dos Passos, over the writings of Faulkner, or the writers of the American tradition—Thoreau, Whitman, Melville, Henry James, and Stephen Crane.[10]

Stung by these accusations, Beauvoir rehearses in "An American Renaissance in France" some of the arguments that she later gives in *L'Amérique au jour le jour*. First of all, she is careful to underline the standing of American authors including Faulkner in France since the interwar period, when the discovery of the work of Dos Passos, Hemingway and Faulkner came as a revelation to French readers. Forbidden in France during the Occupation, American literature was welcomed all the more enthusiastically at the Liberation—perhaps too enthusiastically and uncritically, Beauvoir concedes. Her key concern, however, is to explain what the French novel has been able to gain from the realism of American literature in the postwar period. In Beauvoir's view, the tradition of French writing to be found in writers like Gide, Valéry, and Giraudoux in which analysis and style are all important, did not correspond to the needs of a new generation of French writers returning from the trenches or from concentration camps. They required a different language and an array of new techniques with which to describe their experiences. The narrative of action that they found in Dashiell Hammett, and the realism that they found in Steinbeck and Wright served as models not of an objective pretence of realism, of the sort found in the nineteenth-century French novel, but of a committed realism—an account of individual freedoms struggling with the contingencies of the real world.

Here we again note Beauvoir's concern with introducing elements of realism into the novel in such a way as to permit the development of the philosophical novel. A focus on action rather than analysis might seem to be mere behaviorism, but, properly handled, permitted just the kind of metaphysical dimension that she sought. Both Beauvoir and Sartre had been directly influenced in their own writing by their reading of American novels, and she was determined to show that this was not a question of poor literary judgment on their part, or, even worse, of a patronizing dismissal of the best in American writing. She defends the idea of influence and exchange between the two cultures as enriching to both.

"New Heroes for Old," published two months later, takes up some of the same themes in greater detail and with more of a focus on the French tradition. The various schools of French writing from the French revolution onward are described by Beauvoir as corresponding to their own era and in particular to the historical pressures of their times. The exaltation of the individual hero in the novels of Stendhal or Balzac reflected the triumph of the French revolution and of Napoleon's rise to power; the Naturalist novel shifted the emphasis to the social group as people lost faith in the agency of the individual. At the turn of the century, with the bourgeoisie securely in power, the psychological novel turned attention inward, toward the complex emotions and ambitions of heroes considered purely in their individual psychology, isolated from class, context, and history.[11] The French novel, writes Beauvoir, has come to be considered as synonymous with this tradition of psychological analysis. But this tradition cannot serve a generation who have "felt the hard pressure of history."[12] New circumstances demand new forms of writing and, returning to the theme of the young men who have experienced the trenches and camps, Beauvoir defends the use of behaviorist techniques by a number of contemporary writers who focus above all on an extreme situation and on the acts which link an individual to it, rather than their emotional response to it.

Despite this defense, it is nevertheless clear that Beauvoir's own preference is for novels that go one step further and that depict the individual in these extreme situations as faced with an ethical choice. In making a difficult choice, the individual "gives proof of his liberty," reveals a metaphysical attitude that even the most humble among us takes up to life. In the philosophical novel, exemplified here by Sartre's *Les chemins de la liberté*, the author has a philosophical view of the world, which does not illustrate a ready-made conclusion but which aims to reveal the basic metaphysical attitude underlying the characters' response to "the great realities: death, the existence of others, suffering, life." Although Beauvoir modestly does not cite her own novels here, this is precisely what she seeks to do herself. The culmination of her argument comes in the claim that, far from being an impoverishment of the psychological tradition, the philosophical novelist's emphasis on metaphysical and moral choice in fact deepens the psychological analysis of the novel, a claim that not only poses a strong challenge to an earlier generation of writers but foreshadows the interest that she and Sartre were later to show in "existentialist psychoanalysis," a form of analysis focusing on individual choice.

The last section of the article turns to a more unusual topic for Beauvoir: the role of the body in contemporary literature. "The human condition is carnal," she writes, and moral dramas are often also physical dramas. One has only to think of episodes such as the abortion that Hélène undergoes in *Le sang des autres* to see that the embodied nature of consciousness and choice is a strong feature of Beauvoir's own novelistic practice.

Both the articles written for an American audience bear witness to a strong desire on Beauvoir's part to communicate to her readers the urgency and importance of the writing that she and her contemporaries were engaged in, and the nature of the experience that the war had forced upon them. Taken overall, these four articles reveal the very developed nature of Beauvoir's thinking about the role and function of literature at this early stage of her writing career. They argue for a concept of the metaphysical novel and an awareness of the techniques that it could deploy, which had been enriched by her reading of the American novel, but which she and her contemporaries were deploying to deal with the rather different and pressing realities of postwar France.

NOTES

1. See *La force des choses*, Folio ed., 2 Vols. (Paris: Gallimard, 1963), I, 60–61.

2. "Roman and métaphysique" was later revised by Beauvoir for publication in the April 1946 issue of *Les temps modernes* as "Littérature et métaphysique" and appears in English translation in Beauvoir's *Philosophical Writings*, ed. M. A. Simons, M. Timmermann, and M. B. Mader (Urbana: University of Illinois Press, 2004), 270–71.

3. *La force des choses*, I, 49.

4. See *La force de l'âge* (*The Prime of Life*), Folio ed., (Paris: Gallimard, 1960), 391.

5. See the conversation between Elisabeth and Claude, *L'invitée* (Paris: Gallimard, 1943), 95–97.

6. See *L'invitée*, 112.

7. Dramatists such as Marguerite Duras or Nathalie Sarraute would disagree.

8. See *La force des choses*, I, 77. By an odd coincidence Genet was to die on the same day as Beauvoir, and many newspapers carried a joint report of their deaths with photographs of them together.

9. See the Introduction to *The Useless Mouths* above.

10. *L'Amérique au jour le jour* (Paris: Morihien, 1948), 59–60, 78–81.

11. Beauvoir seems to be thinking here of Proust and Gide.

12. This phrase recalls a well-known phrase from Beauvoir's memoirs: "History took hold of me, and never let go thereafter" (*La force de l'âge*, 410).

IT'S SHAKESPEARE THEY DON'T LIKE

by Simone de Beauvoir

TRANSLATION BY MARYBETH TIMMERMANN

NOTES BY JANELLA D. MOY AND MARYBETH TIMMERMANN

For a year now there have been some rather considerable changes in the French press. It is truly regrettable that in glancing through the newspaper columns devoted to theatrical critiques, one might think one has been transported back to the time when Alain Laubreaux and the like systematically strove to muddle values, destroying any strong and great work with their insults.[1] It seems they have, alas, created a tradition. This outrage is what one discovers when reading the articles written in reaction to the presentation of *King Lear*.[2]

For the first time in years, one of Shakespeare's most remarkable masterpieces is put on in France by one of our greatest directors, who is also one of our greatest actors. However, with disconcerting frivolity, most of the critics, Mr. Augagneux in particular, talk to us only about the shape of the helmets and the style of the warriors' garments. They have every right to not like these costumes, but it is inconceivable that they allow themselves to be fascinated by the shape of a shield or a hairstyle to the point that they

---

"C'est Shakespeare qu'ils n'aiment pas," *Action* (May 11, 1945); reprinted in *Les écrits de Simone de Beauvoir*, ed. Claude Francis and Fernande Gontier (Paris: Gallimard, 1979), 324–26.

become blind to all the rest. If they exercised their profession seriously, they would have the basic scruple to speak to their readers about the show of which they are claiming to give an account. But that is the least of their concerns. They speak only of themselves; an article for them is an exercise of style; they try to be witty, brilliant, biting. They have no other goal than to manifest their polemicist qualities. It's an understatement to say that they prefer themselves to the object before which they should eclipse themselves. The object doesn't exist for them. And this excessive complacency with themselves explains why they come off as totally devoid of any sense of hierarchies. Whether they are speaking of *Moumou* or of *King Lear*, they make no distinction.[3] It is never anything but a pretext for them. Such insolence is dishonest. Even if Dullin is totally mistaken, the importance of his attempt must be taken into consideration.[4]

This stubborn frivolity does not exclude an extreme arrogance. Many of these gentlemen imagine that, by who knows what supernatural grace, they hold the secrets of the "Great Will" (which is what they readily call Shakespeare, sparing us no cliché). Mr. Paul Bizos declares with aplomb, "In Lear, there is no physical degradation!" And Mr. Robert Kemp laments, "Where is the old stricken giant of our dreams, and the dreams of the Great Will?" They refuse to consider for one instant that Dullin must have also pondered over Lear somewhat, and that his interpretation might be as valid as theirs. Of course, they have the right to their own opinion; only it is a bit impudent to attribute it to Shakespeare himself. There is doubtless no more of a "veritable Lear" than there is a "veritable Hamlet." But strengthened by what they tranquilly see as supremely obvious, our critics are astonished that Dullin could have questioned and searched further. The ignorant public readily resents artists' desire for searching out something new, without understanding that art is essentially invention and novelty, but it is astonishing to find such reproaches written by better informed men. "It is always perilous," writes Mr. Robert Daniel, "under the pretext of wanting to break with the routine, to allow oneself to be led into unknown spheres where originality skirts nonsense." I am not sure that the originality of Mr. Daniel's style doesn't skirt nonsense in this sentence, and I wonder what routine Simone Jollivet should follow when faced with a new question that demands new solutions.[5] For putting on *King Lear* is a question, and one of the most difficult.

In truth, the French public has little taste for Shakespeare and our critics are no exception. They pretend to attack Dullin, but actually, they bear a grudge against Shakespeare. Mr. J. J. Gautier naively admits, "This presentation of *King Lear* will not make it acceptable to those who dare to admit that they find it boring." What did they hope for, then? Acrobatic intermissions? Naked dancers? If they find *Lear* boring, they should not hold it against the director. Mr. Treich, for his part, seems to praise Ducis for having hesitated to show *Lear* because of the hero's madness, while Ms. Jollivet, on the contrary, is unleashed, he tells us. But that is precisely the thing; one cannot perform *King Lear* without being unleashed, and that is what Ducis understood.[6] Do we conclude that this great work must not be presented in France? Here Dullin is the one being reproached for everything that is shocking in Shakespeare. They declare that the show is a "nightmare that ends as a *Grand Guignol*,"[7] but it is Shakespeare, not Ms. Jollivet, who has Lear, his three daughters and Edmond killed in the last scene for everyone to see. Mr. Robert Kemp complains that "at a certain point, when Edgar, King Lear, and his jester exchange their crazy dialogue, it's like being in the yard of the mad house of "Plume et Goudron" [Tarr and Fether]."[8] Does he think that Dullin is the one who wrote this scene?

One could multiply such citations, but that is enough. The critics have the right not to like Shakespeare, or Dullin's aesthetic, but not the right to shy away from their duty as critics, which is to first understand, and then make [others] understand. They apparently do not suspect that such responsibilities rest upon their shoulders. The artist needs a public, and the public needs reliable guides. Their clumsy frivolity, their complacency, ingenuous in itself, their disdain for quality, and their arrogant bad faith are the detestable heritage of a past that should be swept away.

NOTES

1. Alain Laubreaux (1899–1968) was a theatrical critic for the Collaborationist paper *Je suis partout*.

2. *King Lear*, a tragic play written by William Shakespeare (1564–1616), is the story of an old king who decides to split his kingdom between his three daughters, but not before they have each verbalized to what extent they love their father. The two older daughters regale their father with accounts of great love and are granted large portions of the kingdom in return. The youngest daughter, Cordelia, refuses to put her love into words and is disowned by her father. Cordelia marries the king of France and leaves the kingdom, while King Lear places himself in the care of his two eldest daughters, Goneril and Regan. Lear soon realizes he has made a very bad mistake. The older two daughters rule over their father with cruelty and he begins to show signs of insanity after spending a night out in a storm. He is rescued by Cordelia and realizes her true love for him, but tragedy strikes as the play comes to a close. A parallel story about the Duke of Gloucester and his two sons is being told alongside

the Lear tale and Gloucester's painful awakening mimics that experienced by King Lear. The presentation that Beauvoir is referring to here is Simone Jollivet's adaptation of the play, directed by Charles Dullin at the Théâtre de la Ville (also called the Théâtre Sarah Bernhardt) in 1945.

3. *Moumou* was a French comedy written by Jean de Letraz; it was made into a film directed by René Jayet in 1951.

4. Charles Dullin (1885–1949), French actor, producer, and director, was an outstanding member of Copeau's Théâtre du Vieux Colombier. He organized and toured with his own group before opening the Théâtre de l'Atelier in Paris in 1921 (www.bartleby.com). A friend of both Sartre and Beauvoir, Dullin figures prominently in Beauvoir's *Wartime Diary*, trans. Anne Deing Cordero, ed. Sylvie Le Bon de Beauvoir and Margaret Simons (Urbana: University of Illinois Press, 2008).

5. Simone Jollivet, a French dramatist and friend of Simone de Beauvoir, wrote this adaptation of King Lear that Dullin directed, and also wrote *The Princess of Ursins*. She is referred to as "Camille" in Beauvoir's autobiographies.

6. Jean-François Ducis (1733–1816) was a French poet as well as a dramatist. He adapted and produced several of Shakespeare's plays and wrote two tragedies, *Œdipe chez Admète* (1778) and *Abufar* (1795).

7. As used today, the term "Grand Guignol" refers to any dramatic entertainment that deals with macabre subject matter and features "over-the-top" graphic violence. It is derived from *Le Théâtre du Grand Guignol*, the name of the Parisian theatre that horrified audiences for over sixty years (www.grandguignol.com).

8. "The System of Doctor Tarr and Professor Fether," a short story by Edgar Allan Poe, was published in the November 1845 issue of *Graham's Magazine*. A French translation by Charles Baudelaire, "Le Système du docteur Goudron et du professeur Plume," was published in 1865 in a collection of Poe's short stories, *Histoires grotesques et sérieuses* (Paris: Michel Lévy). The story was adapted for the French stage by André de Lorde, and it was performed at the Théâtre du Grand Guignol in Paris in 1903 before being made into a film in 1912 by Maurice Tourneur.

THE NOVEL AND THE THEATER

by Simone de Beauvoir

TRANSLATION BY MARYBETH TIMMERMANN

NOTES BY JANELLA D. MOY AND JOE FEIGL

The novel and the theater are two forms of fiction: in both cases, it is a matter of creating an imaginary world, and making characters, whose story constitutes what is called the plot, enter into this world. In order for the impact of the work to surpass that of simple entertainment, the story must also have a signification. Through carefully constructed lies, the book, like the play, strives to communicate a general human truth, but they do not rely on the same devices, and they do not seek the same type of truth.

The novelist has a varied and supple technique at his disposal: he describes, he narrates, he comments, or at the very least suggests commentaries; he gives speech to his heroes, he enters into their consciousnesses, he adopts different points of view, he is the master of space and time, he moves around as he pleases, he speeds up the course of events, or reverses it, or

"Roman et théâtre," *Opéra* 24 (October 24, 1945); reprinted in *Les écrits de Simone de Beauvoir*, ed. Claude Francis and Fernande Gontier (Paris: Gallimard, 1979), 327–31. The article is preceded by the following introduction: "In a few days, Simone de Beauvoir, author of the novels *L'invitée* [*She Came to Stay*] and *Le sang des autres* [*The Blood of Others*] is going to make her debut as a playwright with *Les bouches inutiles* [*The Useless Mouths*], which is to be performed at 'Carrefours.' Today she shares her conception of these two literary genres with the readers of *Opéra*."

stops it; he can skip over an hour or a century if he so pleases. Moreover, the relations he maintains with the public allow him a great deal of freedom. Each reader is alone before the book, deciphering it as slowly as it suits him, leaving it, and taking it up again. One can expect a great deal of patience and concentration from him. Also, the author has full license to treat any subject he wants and fit it into the plot of his choice. There are hardly any restrictions imposed on him by the novelistic form. He can tell the story of a collectivity, a family, an era, or paint a character, a passion, a situation, or evoke a drama. He can be interested in singular cases because he has the means and the time to develop them thoroughly enough to bring out the general truth from them.

Things are completely otherwise in the theater. The entire story must be expressed through the language of the characters: their words, gestures, and facial expressions. Their consciousnesses are closed; we only know the relationships they maintain with each other. The action must therefore be founded on language, and the language must itself be action. The characters must be entirely engaged in this exchange of appeals and responses, since there exists no means of endowing them with an interior dimension. This is why a true play is almost necessarily the exposé of a conflict. Since verbal expression doesn't last long as a simple impassioned reaction and since each phrase immediately tends toward the universal, the fact that the characters "speak" this conflict makes it into an opposition of rights, principles, life attitudes, or points of view on the human condition. This limits the choice of subjects. Individual adventures and interior dramas are not suited to the theater, and neither are studies of singular cases. Because theatrical techniques are incompatible with deeper character development, the singular would not be able to coincide with the general here; it would remain anecdotal and ludicrous. From the outset, the playwright must place himself on the plane of generality. His characters must be typical, either by their personalities, or by their passions or the ideas they express, or by their situation. Moreover, plot construction is limited by numerous constraints. The author must give his work the dimensions of a show, and must overcome the resistances of space and time, for even dividing his play into scenes allows him to situate it in only a limited number of places and moments. He must restrict the number of characters and keep in mind the problems raised by their flesh-and-blood existence: their entrances and exits, their least gestures are so visible that they must be regulated with a great deal of economy. In order to inform the public about what is useful for them to know, there is no other means than dialogue. Here one runs into the great difficulty of expositions. All this leads to seeking out a plot as simple and compact as possible. But simplicity does not mean poverty; the stripped-down quality of the plot must not harm the grandeur of the subject, or else the theater would only be a minor art. And the conditions under which the play is presented to the public require that this grandeur be immediately perceptible. Indeed, the public here is a community of spectators; men endowed with a social existence have more demands and less patience than an isolated individual. Moreover, those watching a play being performed do not have the freedom enjoyed by a reader. They are not satisfied unless each moment of the show is fully and clearly expressive. The slow parts, digressions, and nuances that so often give novels their charm are banished from the stage. A play must continually reach out to grasp and subjugate. As you know, the theatrical perspective calls for an exaggeration of intonations, gestures, costumes, make-up, and lights. This exaggeration authorizes and requires the exaggeration of the plot itself. The problem that the playwright must resolve is how to present an inter-human conflict of universal reach to men gathered together in society, and to present it through a simple and striking critique. There is but one solution: to place the heroes in extreme situations and drive them to extreme choices. The extreme situation has universal signification; the conflict that pits Antigone against Creon is revived each day between the political realist and the intransigent moralist.[1] And this signification is disclosed in a gripping manner.

Death plays such an important role in the theater because it is one of the natural results of these kinds of situations. And since there is something exceptional about such extreme situations in that they are hardly encountered in the everyday world, it is therefore understandable that the playwright might be led to seek historical or mystical justifications for them. Stage adaptations, which are so often criticized, are imposed upon the theater by its very essence.

Theater draws its grandeur from these constraints weighing it down. To express lofty truths in a simple, direct, and evident manner is a success for the theater, but at the same time, it is a precious privilege not shared by the novelist.

In a novel, indeed, there are no perceptible givens other than the form of words printed in black on white paper. Nothing limits the inventiveness of the author, but nothing supports the imagination of the reader either. The author is free to recount whatever he pleases as he pleases; but will anyone believe him? If he wants to be convincing, he must not copy the real world like the naturalists wanted to, but rely upon it for support. Its presence must be suggested in such a way that the fiction, be it heroic, poetic, or even fantastic, unfolds against the backdrop of a world. This is why the plot will seek to imitate the contingence of lived events; the language will imitate the hesitations and incoherencies of the spoken language, and the behaviors and feelings of the heroes will be based in psychology. This concern for the natural can be found in Kafka, as well as in Stendhal, in Poe as in Dostoevsky.[2] Even during the most exceptional stories, we must still feel immersed in this everyday world. If not, they seem gratuitous to us and do not move us.

The theater, on the contrary, offers a tangible point of support for the spectator's imagination: the physical presence of the actors, whose reality radiates to the sets and costumes. The stage itself is a world foreign to the real world, possessing its own dimensions, light, and simple, striking forms. It takes an effort to penetrate into it; the moment the curtain rises, the spectator hesitates for an instant before accepting all the conventions that are being imposed upon him. But once he enters, it is quite possible for him to remain enclosed within it until the end of the play. The playwright can therefore transport us to China, the Middle Ages, heaven or hell, and we are ready to follow him. Only there must be no clumsy realism in the stage sets, props, or text to recall the existence of another universe. The universe of the stage must faultlessly affirm its own existence through its perfect coherence and the rigorous logic that ties together all of its diverse elements.

It follows that, among other things, theatrical dialogue must submit to other laws than those that govern dialogues in novels. In neither case is it a matter of making the characters speak as they would in life. But in the novel, the naturalness of spoken language is imitated. For example it is good when the protagonists do not answer each other exactly because they must follow the unfolding of their own thoughts at the same time as following that of the conversation. Theatrical dialogue can not and should not aim for naturalness. In a world where every bit of knowledge, every feeling, and every event exists only through verbal expression, the text not only represents the characters' conversations but the totality of their beings and their situations. Their responses are a sequence of reactions and provocations that must fit together exactly (unless an effect of incoherence is precisely being sought). They must be compact, direct and immediately expressive like the plot itself. Besides, adapting the plot for a stage production requires an adaptation of the language, which can even take on the conventional form of verse. Made to be spoken and not read, the lines must also be easy to articulate, and the meaning must flow with a certain verbal rhythm, acting as a point of support for the reactions of the protagonists. If it responds to all of these demands, it will seem right. Here, as with directing and acting, a rigorous approach makes it possible to attain an aesthetic truth that dispenses with all realism.

Thus in the theater as in the novel, different types of freedom are born of different constraints. There is no reason to choose between these two modes of expression. One must simply strive to use each one according to its own demands.

NOTES

1. The conflict between Antigone and Creon, which pits moral right against political right, comes from the Greek tragedy, *Antigone*. Written by Sophocles around 450 B.C., *Antigone* is a tale of a young woman's defense of her moral right to bury her dead brother, Polyneices, who led the rebel forces against Creon's forces in the Theban civil war. Creon, King of Thebes, in accordance with civil laws, refuses to allow Antigone the right to bury her brother's body. Antigone buries Polyneices against Creon's decree. Sealed in a cave to die as punishment for defying Creon's edict, Antigone hangs herself. It is Antigone's great love for her brother that prompts her defiance of Creon, and she is said to be maintaining the moral right of a sister against the political right of Creon.

2. Franz Kafka (1883–1924), born in Prague (then part of Austria), was the son of a Jewish shopkeeper. Prior to World War I, Kafka published several short stories. However, his novel *Der Prozess* (*The Trial*) written in 1914, was one of the three unfinished novels, including *Das Schloss* (*The Castle*) and *Der Verschollene* (retitled *Amerika*), that were considered Kafka's finest works and were published posthumously by his friend and biographer, Max Brod; Stendhal (1783–1842) (pseudonym of Marie-Henri Beyle) was a French writer who helped develop the modern novel. Considered his literary masterpieces, *Le Rouge et le Noir* (*The Red and the Black*) (1830) and *La chartreuse de Parme* (*The Charterhouse of Parma*) (1839) chronicle the French moral and intellectual climate following Napoleon's defeat. His writing was rediscovered in the 1870s and proved influential on young writers like Joseph Conrad and Henry James; Edgar Allan Poe (1809–49) was an American poet and short story writer acclaimed for his beautiful poetry, horror stories, and detective tales. His most famous poem is *The Raven* (1845), and many of his well-known horror stories and detective stories, such as *The Pit and the Pendulum* (1843) and *The Murders in the Rue Morgue* (1841), were also made into films; Fyodor Mikhaylovich Dostoevsky (1821–81), born in Moscow, was educated as a military engineer. After his father's death in 1839, Dostoevsky quit his job and devoted the remainder of his life to writing. He became a famous Russian novelist, journalist, and short story writer, whose psychologically penetrating novels—*Notes from Underground* (1864), *Crime and Punishment* (1866), and *The Idiot* (1868–69)—present probing questions about human nature, morality, and religion.

AN AMERICAN RENAISSANCE IN FRANCE

by Simone de Beauvoir

NOTES BY JANELLA D. MOY

One of the significant events in French literature during the period between the two wars was the discovery of American literature.[1] I remember with what fervor the initiated, those who could read English, passed along the first books of Dos Passos, Hemingway and Faulkner.[2] The appearance in French translation of *Manhattan Transfer*, *Farewell to Arms*, and *Sanctuary* was a revelation to the entire French reading public.[3]

During the occupation, when American books were forbidden, they became all the more precious.[4] On the morning after the liberation, there were wonderful opportunities for the booksellers. Copies of *God's Little Acre* and *Of Mice and Men* were sold for fabulous sums.[5] Since then, books in the hundreds of thousands of copies, by Faulkner, Hemingway, Dos Passos, Steinbeck, and Caldwell, have been printed.[6] Each review has made it a point of honor to discover unknown young authors; in almost every magazine one finds some short story or extract of a novel by an American.

"An American Renaissance in France," *New York Times Book Review* (June 22, 1947), pp. 7, 29; reprinted in French translation in *Les écrits de Simone de Beauvoir*, ed. Claude Francis and Fernande Gontier (Paris: Gallimard, 1979), 353–57.

The infatuation became so strong that certain French writers, who at first had welcomed with the greatest warmth the message from America, began to find the whole thing a bore. The newspaper *Combat* featured a series of discussions on the influence of American literature. In it, the contributions of Camus, and of many others, expressed a certain amount of fatigue, and even of antagonism.[7]

Even here, I have met many writers and critics who are scandalized by the interest we take in the books coming from this country: they find it suspect; they accuse the French public of uncritically talking up second-rate or third-rate works with an enthusiasm appropriate only to masterpieces; and this excessive admiration seems to them a subtle form of scorn. The fact is that in the current fad there are many confusions and perils.

First of all, the French reader's understanding of American culture is jeopardized. The American article sells too well, anything and everything indiscriminately appears on the market, and there is no care for real values. The public, which has already a developed taste for mediocre and easily read books, is only too happy to welcome as masterpieces works whose poverty would leap to the eye were they stripped of the seductive colors of exoticism; the public takes brutality for force, obscenity for psychological depth, the superficial picturesqueness of local color for imaginative riches. To fall in with this lack of discrimination means to prevent oneself from understanding the efforts of exacting writers to achieve real force, true profundity or inventiveness.

The second-rate novels, so easy to read, are also easily imitated: the brutal, the obscene, the picturesque are facilely come by. In France, any young man of 18 who has a little talent can successfully bring off an American-inspired short story; this flatters him, he believes he has found his bent. He does another of the same sort; instead of reflecting before writing, deciding what he has to say and how he should say it, he merely writes. He thinks he knows what writing is; this false facility is dangerous. To tell a story well, one must first have something to relate; the taking over of a technique borrowed from others is not the same thing as serving a true literary apprenticeship. It is really frivolous and harmful to speak of Dashiell Hammett with as much enthusiasm as Faulkner, for the lazy reader and the hasty beginner tend to stop with Dashiell Hammett and dispense with Faulkner.[8]

However, the confusion I have singled out is no worse than another one into which we are also in danger of falling: that of French writers rejecting utterly the influence of the American novel; this would be stupid and, moreover, impossible. We have already assimilated the influence, and it has served us well; one consequence is that new problems have appeared, but we can scarcely think of rejecting what has been acquired.

For my part, I am convinced that the American influence has been extremely fruitful. There has been a very happy accord between the internal needs of the contemporary French writers and the new possibilities which came to them from outside. It is a great privilege and also a great danger for a literature to have at its disposal a language which is many centuries old: the result of purifying and subtilizing its vocabulary, of rendering its syntax flexible, is that the language comes to be regarded as an end in itself and becomes cut off from daily life. For writers like Gide, Valéry, Giraudoux,[9] literature had become a purely abstract domain; nothing could be integrated with it that had not first been reduced to concepts by analysis or poetry. Academicism and preciosity are the dead-ends along this road.

What is one to do if one wants to express the truth of life in its crude materiality, if one wants to present life to the reader as it appears in the words and acts of men before having been altered by their consciousness? Italian writers tell me they have felt the same difficulty, insofar as they have no alternative but to write in Tuscan (in which one must refer to water as "the waves" and to a horse as "a steed").[10] What struck us in the great American novelists was their effort to bring into their books life that was still throbbing; to describe it, they employed a living language, and they invented daring and flexible techniques to preserve the freshness of the events they described.

We, also, before the war, but even more since then, have felt the need to express the immediate truth of human adventures. The young people who came back from the war, from the Maquis, from prison and concentration camps, like to express their experiences nakedly.[11] The tradition of *Princesse de Clèves* and of Valéry is not of much help to them.[12] Dashiell Hammett serves them better. For in his books, as in the "hardboiled" novels which we are rash enough to enjoy, there is an art of narration adapted to the vicissitudes of action. One of the most difficult tasks one can set oneself in literature is that of depicting an action: this requires much technical skill.

The detective story by definition is the depiction of an action; if it is good of its kind, one can learn many useful lessons from it. This, of course, does not warrant putting the detective story on the same plane as *Moby Dick*;[13] but it explains why the young French writers have been led to attach so much importance to works of this kind. They are of course even more interested in those writers who can depict not only external action, but human drama charged with significance.

Now, the merit of the great American novelists consists in the fact that they were able to deal with life in its dramatic aspect. In a sense, one can call Steinbeck and Richard Wright "realists"; but the distinctive trait of French realism is its refusal to take a position: the world is described with a wholly abstract objectivity, and the author does not adopt any point of view toward it. In Steinbeck's *In Dubious Battle*, as in Richard Wright's *Black Boy*, reality is invested with the concreteness of an experience in which an individual consciousness and an individual liberty have been staked; the struggle of a man against the resistances of the world is depicted.[14]

And it is just this which today in France appears to us to be the true mission of the writer: to describe in dramatic form the relationship of the individual to the world in which he stakes his freedom. What we found in the great contemporary American writers was not so much riches of language or even skilled technique, as this authentic sense of the function of literature. The mistake would be to believe that the admiration we have conceived for them ought to deflect us from our own heritage. The attempt to grasp the very movement of life does not involve the giving up of thought. To describe acts and words is not to forbid oneself depth in the knowledge of man. Neither philosophy nor psychology has anything to lose here; on the contrary: it is thanks to precisely this technical tool borrowed from America that we could undertake to give philosophy itself a novelistic form. Any vein may be badly worked; this does not mean that there is not real gold to be found. It was Gide who said very justly that fear of influence is a sign of weakness.

French culture is strong enough not to fear what comes to it from the outside; it can renew itself without loss. Perhaps only by such exposure will it be able, in its turn, to aid American literature in that transcendence of itself which every literature must achieve.[15]

NOTES

1. World War I, also called The Great War, took place between 1914 and 1918. World War II was fought from 1939 through 1945.

2. John Dos Passos (1896–1970) was born in Chicago, Illinois. He received a Harvard education and became a prominent writer, commenting on what he saw as the corrupting influence of capitalism in government and on American society. Dos Passos is best known for his three novels, *The 42nd Parallel*, *1919*, and *The Big Money*, which were published together in 1938 as the trilogy *U.S.A.* (1996); Ernest Hemingway (1899–1961) was an American author born in Chicago, Illinois; he became a newspaper writer at age seventeen. In the 1920s, he lived in France and associated with other famous American (expatriate) authors such as F. Scott Fitzgerald and Gertrude Stein. Hemingway's novels were published in America and abroad in the 1930s and '40s. Some of Hemingway's most famous novels were *The Sun Also*

Rises (1924), *A Farewell to Arms* (1929), and *For Whom the Bell Tolls* (1939); William Faulkner (1897–1962), an American short story writer born in Mississippi, often wrote about the South. Although he never completed high school, Faulkner's novels are considered some of the greatest and most remarkable works of the twentieth century. A few of his works are *The Sound and the Fury* (1929), *Absalom, Absalom!* (1936), and *Go Down Moses* (1942).

3. *Manhattan Transfer* (New York: Harper and Brothers, 1925), written by Dos Passos, describes the alienation and corruption of the city; *Farewell to Arms* was first serialized in *Scribner's Magazine* from May–August of 1929, and also published as a book by Charles Scribner's Sons (New York) in September of that year. It was written by Ernest Hemingway and is thought to confront many of Hemingway's personal experiences during World War I; *Sanctuary* (New York: Vintage, 1993), written by William Faulkner in 1931, is a commentary on social and legal injustice, moral corruption, and the sordid effects of the Prohibition.

4. The four-year German occupation of France began in June 1940 and ended with the liberation of Paris in August and Strasbourg in November of 1944.

5. Erskine Caldwell's *God's Little Acre* (New York: Viking Press, 1933), reflects his outrage over the persistence of poor health, squalid living conditions, and inadequate education endured by small-time Southern farmers and sharecroppers; *Of Mice and Men* (New York: Covici Friede, 1937), written by John Steinbeck, looks at the lives and dilemmas of two migrant workers.

6. John Steinbeck (1902–68), born in Salinas, California, is best known for his novel *The Grapes of Wrath*, written in 1939. This story examines the hardships and poverty of the 1930s migrant workers and their families; Erskine Caldwell (1903–87), born in White Oaks, Georgia, wrote about poverty, racism, and ignorance in novels such as *Tobacco Road* (1932) and *God's Little Acre*. His writing often included ribald humor and twisting plots.

7. *Combat*, a French clandestine newspaper, was first published in 1941 in support of the French Resistance. It was edited by Albert Camus (1913–60), who was born in Mondovi, Algeria. Camus worked as a schoolmaster, playwright, and journalist and is best known for his novels, *L'étranger* (*The Stranger*) (1942) and *La peste* (*The Plague*) (1947).

8. Dashiell Hammett (1894–1961), born in St. Mary's County, Maryland, was a novelist and screenwriter. He is best known for his detective novels and more specifically his novel *The Maltese Falcon* (1930).

9. André Gide (1869–1951) was a French writer, psychological novelist, and literary critic, as well as a homosexual and social activist. His most famous work, *Nourritures terrestres* (*Fruits of the Earth*), begun in 1893 but not completed until 1896–97, influenced younger French writers; Paul Valéry (1871–1945) was a French poet, writer, and literary critic. One of his best-known works is *La jeune parque* (The Youngest of the Fates) (1917); Jean Giraudoux (1882–1944) was a French playwright, novelist, and French politician. He is known internationally for plays like *Amphitryon 38* (1929) and *Ondine* (1939). He also wrote powerful essays and literary studies such as *Racine* (1930).

10. The language spoken and written in Tuscany in Italy.

11. *Maquis* is a name for groups of the French Resistance that fought against the Germans in World War II.

12. *La Princesse de Clèves* (*The Princess of Cleves* [New York: New Directions, 1988]) was a novel written anonymously in 1678 and attributed to Madame de La Fayette. A serious attempt at depicting the sixteenth century French court, the novel is celebrated in France as a "roman d'analyse classique" (classic psychological novel).

13. *Moby Dick* (Oxford, UK: Oxford University, 2002) is Herman Melville's most famous novel. Published in 1851, this novel about the enormous white whale, Moby Dick, and Captain Ahab, who pursues the whale, is much more than a tale of the nineteenth-century whaling industry. Melville's novel, unappreciated at the time of its publication, is now considered a master critique of the world, religion, morals, and prominent political figures of his day.

14. *In Dubious Battle* (New York: Covici Friede, 1936), by John Steinbeck, tells the story of a group of migrant workers rising up against the landowners in their fight against injustice; Richard Wright (1908–60) was born in Natchez, Mississippi. He was one of the first African-American novelists to gain success as a novelist. He is most noted for his novels about African-American life such as *Native Son* (New York: Harper and Brothers, 1940) and his autobiography *Black Boy* (New York: Harper and Brothers, 1945), which was published in French in *Les temps modernes*, the journal edited by Beauvoir and Sartre and others.

15. The following editor's note appears at the end of the published article: "Simone de Beauvoir is the author of the novel *L'invitée* [She Came to Stay], and one of the leaders of the Existentialist movement in France."

NEW HEROES FOR OLD

by Simone de Beauvoir

NOTES BY MARGARET SIMONS AND OTHERS

Today in France they frequently say that the novel is dying, that the novel is dead. That is one of the leitmotivs of postwar criticism. Nevertheless, if you loiter by the bookshop windows, or prowl among the editors' offices, you cannot help being struck by the great number of books and manuscripts that flaunt the label "novel." Nor are they dead works, for many of them are received by the public with enthusiasm. The critics cannot ignore this fact, but they nevertheless shake their heads and mutter, "These are not true novels. The novel is dead." You might be tempted to regard this argument as a mere quibble; but even quibbles have some meaning, and the meaning of this one is clear: the modern French novel has so far departed from tradition that for those souls who respect outmoded forms it no longer deserves the name.

Like all other artistic forms, the novel has always reflected the social, economic and political structure of its epoch. The triumph of the French revo-

Reprinted from *Town & Country*, July, 1947; Vol. 101, No. 4298, pp. 53, 121, 123, 124; © Sylvie Le Bon de Beauvoir. The article is preceded by the following introduction: "The characters in modern French novels, precisely as they differ from their forerunners, follow tradition in reflecting their epoch."

lution and the Napoleonic epic were accompanied by the exaltation of the individual in fiction. The novels of Stendhal, and many of Balzac's, paint the passions and ambitions of heroes who, though they most assuredly pit themselves against the resistance of the world, are not dominated by it. Rastignac, surveying the city stretched at his feet and impetuously crying, "Paris for us two!" or Julien Sorel, perched in his tree and proudly dreaming of his destiny, incarnate in the most thrilling way the hopes of the young men of their time.[1]

But by the end of the nineteenth century such hopes were dead, and with the coming of the naturalistic school the hero in the romantic sense was dead too. The individual no longer appeared to have much efficacy in this world, nor much importance; it was social groups, and positions defined by the intersection of social groups, that the novelist set about describing. If any hope remained for the individual, it was in his awareness of his own position in the bosom of this coagulated society. Thus, along with the novel of manners, we saw budding the so-called psychological novel, in which the hero, instead of turning toward the world to conquer it, turned inward in order to know himself. He studied his own heart.

But even his manner of studying himself was symptomatic. The writers of this period, as almost always in France, belonged to the bourgeoisie, a class which enjoyed such economic and moral security that it had hardly any feeling of its relations with the rest of the world, or of its historic destiny. It confused its own image with the eternal image of humanity. Accordingly a novel of manners, when it described a social group, did not do so in general historical perspective, but rather analyzed the elements in a whole which appeared to have been established once for all in eternity. Nor did even the psychological novel assign a definite place to its heroes: in studying the loves, jealousies, deceptions, ambitions, and nostalgias of a young bourgeois of the twenties it considered itself studying mankind in general. Psychology was confounded with analysis. Novelists believed they could isolate the hero from the rest of the world, cutting him free from any concrete links with his country, his class, and his epoch, and at the same time untangle his inward, clashing emotions and leanings. They thought they could understand him merely by displaying, side by side, the various motives of his acts. It is well known that the words "French novels," "psychological novels," and "analytical novels" have long been synonymous.

The profound change that has disconcerted the traditional critics appears precisely here. The novelists of today, like those of yesterday, belong to the liberal bourgeoisie, but to the extent that they are French, and bourgeois, they have lost the false feeling of security that drew their fathers into a blind retreat upon themselves. They have felt the hard pressure of history. They have learned that the universe is not made up of separate cells which can be separately described, as a naturalist describes first an anthill and then a beehive. They know that their substance is not distinct from that of the world that surrounds them. They cannot speak of themselves without first speaking of this world in which they have their roots. Pure inner analysis seems vain to them, for they no longer believe that the limits of a man are within his own heart, but that a man is a human destiny and as such is bound up with the whole universe.

The deportee returning from a concentration camp will not attempt the analytical methods of a Proust in recounting his experience.[2] He must describe the situation into which he and his companions were thrown before he can describe their courage or cowardice, greed or generosity, diffidence or arrogance. Psychological differences draw their meaning and authenticity only from the context of the concrete situation.

This explains an important tendency of the imaginative literature of today: the tendency to accent the situation rather than the man, to describe the exterior conditions of experience rather than the individual's interior awareness of them. In this sense it is true that certain works which have appeared since the liberation—David Rousset's *L'univers concentrationaire* [*A World Apart*] [1947], Roger Vailland's *Drôle de jeu* [A Funny Sort of Game] [1945], Jacques Laurent Bost's *Le dernier des métiers* [*The Last Profession*] [1946], and Jules Roy's *La vallée heureuse* [*The Happy Valley*] [1946]—are more like newspaper correspondence than novels, for it is the *life* of the deportee, resister, foot soldier, or aviator that the authors try to set forth, and the character himself is nothing except for that life of his. Nevertheless, it is striking that after *L'univers concentrationaire* which is an objective study, David Rousset wrote a more imaginative version of his experience in *Les jours de notre mort* [The Days of Our Death], which seems concerned with a single individual rather than a merely collective one.[3] Vailland, Bost, and Roy also choose a privileged consciousness—a hero. The stories they tell are human stories, with a past, a present, a future, and a development—with hopes, fears, disgusts, and joys; and these cannot be made real to the reader unless he is able to embrace the living movement, unless he can so identify himself with the consciousness that has actually lived it that this consciousness is evoked before him. All experience is *somebody's* experience, and it is necessary that this somebody be present.

Obviously the presence of such a modern hero is different from the presence of Fabrice watching the Battle of Waterloo in *Chartreuse de Parme* [*The*

Charterhouse of Parma].[4] It is the lesson that Fabrice draws from the battle, rather than the spectacle of the battle itself, that interests Stendhal and his readers; whereas with the young writers I have mentioned it is the war itself, the camp, the bombardment, and the resistance that are of primary importance. The hero is hardly more than a witness; and the difficulty is that he must be at once real enough to engage the reader's sympathy and anonymous enough to reflect his experience without deforming it. He must be present yet invisible.

This desire for effacement manifests itself in the use of a type of psychology and a technical style that are interdependent. In place of an inner analysis that individualizes the subject, the author employs a kind of behaviorism that links the situation to the reaction without having any *particular* person react. The thoughts of the hero are not revealed to us, nor is there any attempt to communicate his impressions from within; only his acts are described. He appears to the reader, and to himself, as but one simple element of the reality that surrounds him, an object neither more nor less important than the obstacles he encounters. To the extent that it is revealed to us at all, his interior life is revealed under an *exterior* form, by speech.

By a curious paradox, that instrument invented by James Joyce and widely used in France today, the interior monologue, is in fact a means of exteriorization.[5] Phrases stammered by the hero are given as reactions among other reactions, communications as direct as the trajectory of a bullet. In order to be understood they do not require of the reader the participation that is required by as simple a phrase as "he experienced a sharp pain." Doubtless, in writing "he went to throw up in the basin," instead of "he had a feeling of disgust," you are approaching a new kind of triteness; but it is a significant triteness, because it indicates a fear of deforming the experience, of obscuring it through the mysterious intervention of a purely interior reality.

More deeply still, this very fear betrays how little faith the individual as such has in himself today. For the young French who were influenced by Barrès, Proust, or Gide,[6] nothing seemed more passionately interesting than the feverish, amused, wild, unusual savor of their lives. Through experience these young men sought knowledge of their own emotions. But now, as the price of what they have encountered in the exterior world, their own emotions seem to them insignificant, their personal judgments futile. Of what value are the feelings of a young correspondent confronted with the infirmary at Dachau? The color of his personal confusion interests nobody—not even himself. He knows that he must try to tell what he has seen, and the rest is silence.

It is a proof of the gap between the horrible and marvelous wealth of the experience and the poverty of language and even emotion that the young writers have accorded such importance to silence. It isn't that they choose heroes devoid of complexity, or that they deny their heroes any inner life; the point is that that life can be described only in terms of what it embraces outside itself. The complexity lies in things and events which must be faithfully reproduced. To a superficial reader it might seem that all the heroes of this generation of writers are poured in the same mold: detached, cold, almost cynical by force of indifference. It is hard to understand these writers; you find in them no great movements of revolts, no cries of enthusiasm, no emotional outbursts, no cerebral subtleties. They try to look a difficult world in the face, to decipher it, and to find their own place in it; they have no time to waste in long discourses. They are not complacent, and they invite the reader to understand their modesty. Between the printed lines they write all the expectations, pains, and joys that they do not wish to detach from their object.

Perhaps the critics are right in deciding that their silent, impartial heroes are not precisely novelistic; for a novel is not a pure description even when it concerns an outward experience, since it implies an active human presence. Still, despite his wish for effacement and his lack of faith in himself, it often happens that the hero finds himself on his proper path, no longer as one object among others but, in the utter necessity of performing an act, as a subject obliged to be aware of himself in relation to problems that must be solved and that he alone can solve because there is no solution outside himself. At this point he appears as a moral agent and assumes a measure of liberty.

One of the characteristics of the novel and the theater today is that it is the ethical content of choice, rather than the psychological motivation, that seems important. In the old days of material and spiritual security, moral values were regarded as absolute and no one dreamed of putting them to the question. Whether in certain circumstances a certain individual would respect them or not was a purely psychological problem: an attempt was made to describe his heredity, his infancy, his temperament, and his manner of accounting for his choice; but the norms were established in advance.

In recent years, however, men have been thrown into a world in which none of the old criteria any longer served, and traditions no longer guided their choice. Circumstances were horribly new, and everything had to be improvised. Now, when they reflect on their experiences, the question that arises is not Why did I do it? but What should I have done? Here again, interest in subjective description is effaced by the desire for objective truth. In the concentration camps the S.S. gave certain duties, such as supervising barracks, to responsible prisoners. Ordinary civil-lawbreakers had shown themselves incapable of performing them, and so they were confided to political deportees. Should the deportees have accepted the duties? In accepting they were able to help their comrades, to bring a bit of order to chaos, and to work for the future; but also they were obliged to make atrocious decisions like picking from their own number the victims the S.S. demanded for its furnaces. In such a dilemma none of the values of peacetime or of liberty could be of the least help; and the decision should not be regarded as dictated by subjective caprice rather than by an inner psychological determinant.

In agony and doubt, the man who strives honestly to decide questions so urgent gives proof of his liberty. And if, later, he tries to communicate his experience, he must revive for the reader that doubt and that agony, and begin again with the reader the difficult quest for truth. Ethical problems so urgent and so new compel us to a more general and more profound investigation of the whole problem of human conditions.

An ethic is not created in a void; it presupposes a metaphysic. As soon as a man asks himself How should I act? he is led also to ask Why thus rather than otherwise? In whose name? Who am I? What is this world into which I thrust my decision? He feels free because he must choose; but he also feels his freedom limited precisely because the necessity of choice has been forced upon him. What, precisely, is liberty?

We see that it is not simply by chance, or by fashion, that philosophy has taken such an important place in French literature and the French theater. The desire to recreate upon an artistic plane a complete human experience leads to a desire to comprehend this experience. That is why, alongside the novels of observation of which I have spoken, we encounter philosophical novels like those of Jean-Paul Sartre. Such novels are profoundly different from the philosophical tales of the classic French tradition. The traditional philosophic tale is an allegory: it makes no pretense of creating an imaginary world or of evoking characters endowed with living weight. On the other hand, a book like Sartre's *Les chemins de la liberté* [*Roads to Freedom*] is a true novel, in which men of flesh and bone confront one another.[7] Nor is there here any question of what is called the "thesis novel," in which the whole plot serves merely to illustrate a conclusion that has been determined in advance; the reader demands a story as complex as the real events of this world, a story whose fluctuating verity cannot be fitted into a formula.

To describe a novel as "metaphysical" is not to define it as the pure exemplification of a theory; it is only to indicate that the author has a certain philosophical view of the world and that he gives his heroes a metaphysical dimension—defines them, that is, not simply according to social position, temperament, or character, but primarily according to their attitude in the presence of the great realities: death, the existence of others, suffering, life. Still, they are no more the prisoners of the necessity of making decisions than were Julien Sorel and Rastignac the prisoners of their ambition. To grasp a character from a metaphysical rather than a psychological angle is not to rob him of his living reality, for he may, on the contrary, remain quite as unpredictable and complex as any character of the classical novel—perhaps more so. Nor is it necessary to believe that we must put upon the scene only intellectuals who are aware of the great philosophical problems. In all men there is a metaphysical attitude that transcends any explicit knowledge they may have gained. Even the most ignorant, the most thoughtless, has his own feeling of relationship with life and death and his own manner of sensing his own existence and his ties with the world about him. In the background of his decisions, his behavior, his feelings, and even his emotions, there is not only the affective social history from tenderest infancy that the psychoanalysts have taught us about: there is also an experience and a truly metaphysical power of choice in his reaction to the pure fact of existence—astonishment, horror, disgust, anguish, indifference, or joy.

It is upon this background that the philosophical novel will attempt to throw light. Naturally, the author will often find it interesting to create a hero who is explicitly aware of his problems. Beside the hero-witness I have mentioned we find also heroes who question themselves, and discuss and absorb their experiences as deeply as possible. But the greatest diversity is permissible here. Beside a Mathieu or a Daniel, who are lucid, restless intellectuals, Sartre gives us, for example, in the same perspective, a shepherd of the Cévennes, a dark-souled young Slav, laborers, peasants—types as different as possible considering their social standing, culture, aspirations, and horizons. Every novelist must always choose a perspective; but the unity of his vision does not injure the diversity of the world he evokes. On the contrary, the choice of a metaphysical and moral point of view constitutes a deepening, rather than an impoverishment, of the traditional psychology.

Far from presenting characters who are pure abstractions, or pure spirits, the metaphysical novel, like the novel of reportage of former times, strives to give them a fleshly dimension. This importance accorded to the body, even in its humblest functions, is one of the most characteristic features of the French novel of today. Some persons claim that this indicates a desire to debase mankind; but in truth any genuine humanism, whether that of

Socrates or Rabelais, has always given the body an important place, not out of contempt for man but out of respect for his true integrity.[8] The human condition is carnal, and we have learned through blinding evidence during the terrible years of the war that it was in terms of the body that human dramas were played: in terms of hunger, fatigue, disease, and pain. The moral dramas that interest us so passionately today are at the same time physical dramas. And if the young novelists apply themselves with a kind of cruelty to evoking the fleshly misery of man, it is because the most authentic witnesses of human grandeur shine in the bosom of this misery.

It would certainly be futile to try to fit into a single formula the so-varied tendencies of the contemporary French novels and the type of hero they present to us. Nevertheless, despite their diversity, nearly all try to express the same concept of man—the one we encounter in Pascal, who describes man as a "thinking reed."[9] Never have the forces of the universe, united to crush mankind, seemed to us heavier; but never, just the same, has the fact of our power to hold the universe at a distance through conscience [consciousness] and moral liberty seemed more important.[10] There are these two aspects of truth that it is important to set forth together: the conditioning of the individual by his organism, his period, his country, the economic, social, and political structure of the society to which he belongs; and at the same time the autonomy of his thought and the singularity and importance of his personal destiny. You cannot define an individual without defining his relationship to the world, for it is only in the midst of the world that he realizes himself. But still, the world is not an indistinct mass; it is inhabited by individual consciences [consciousnesses].

That is why, along with the sciences—sociology, economics, and history—which study the collective avatars of humanity, there is a place for the novel which sets forth the adventure of men considered one by one in their individuality.

For this reason, the novel in France is not dead. There is a novel so long as, upon the basis of an imaginary world, imaginary characters are presented in their moment of liberty. It is the presence of this liberty that gives dramatic and romantic character to such diverse works as *La Princesse de Clèves* [*The Princess of Cleves*], *The Charterhouse of Parma*, *The Brothers Karamazov*, *The Egoist*, *Moby Dick*, and *Light in August*.[11] For it is this moment of liberty that seems also the main point of the books of Malraux, Sartre, Camus, and most of the young novelists.[12] That their notion of liberty and their measure of a man are different from those of their fathers, and that they express themselves with new techniques, does not mean that the novel is dying.

Only things that are dead and embalmed remain identical with themselves. The newness, the restlessness, the investigations of the novel today are, on the contrary, signs of vitality.[13]

NOTES

Margaret Simons would like to thank Courtney Crockarell, Margaret Doucette, Laura Elam, Briana English, Josh Haegele, Sarah Jansen, Yuk-Emmanuelle Kaïj a Kamb, Elizabeth Killingbeck, J. Debbie Mann, Jessica Martin, Jessica Perkins, Danielle Robinson, Michael Robinson, Meagan Saale, and Nathalie Woloszyn for their contributions to the endnotes.

1. Stendhal was the pen name of Marie-Henri Beyle (1783–1842). Originally from Grenoble, France, Beyle traveled throughout Germany as part of Napoleon's army. An innovator of the "realistic style" in literature, he is especially known for two works: *Le rouge et le noir* (*The Red and the Black*) (1830) and *La chartreuse de Parme* (*The Charterhouse of Parma*) (1839). Julien Sorel, the flawed hero of Stendhal's *Le rouge et le noir*, attempts to rise above his plebeian birth through a combination of talent, hard work, deception, and hypocrisy, only to find himself betrayed by his own passions; Honoré de Balzac (1799–1850), French journalist and writer best known for a collection of stories and plays entitled *La comédie humaine* (*The Human Comedy*) depicting French life in the years after the fall of Napoléon Bonaparte in 1815. Regarded as one of the founders of literary realism, Balzac is known for his complex, morally ambiguous human characters and for imbuing inanimate objects, including the city of Paris, with human qualities. Eugène de Rastignac, a fictional character in Balzac's *La comédie humaine*, uses his charm and wit to move up the social ladder in post-Revolutionary France.

2. Marcel Proust (1871–1922), French modernist author best known for his monumental work, *À la recherche du temps perdu* (*Remembrance of Things Past* or *In Search of Lost Time*), characterized by an exploration of memories through free association reflecting Proust's interest in Freud's analytic method.

3. David Rousset (1912–97), French writer and political activist, was a survivor of the Buchenwald concentration camp; he recounted the Nazi's destruction of the human spirit in his award-winning book, *L'univers concentrationaire* (Paris: Hachette, 1947) and in *Les jours de notre mort* (Paris: Hachette, 1947). In 1949 he led the condemnation of the Soviet Union's forced labor camps; Roger Vailland (1907–65) was a French novelist, essayist, and screenwriter. His involvements in surrealism and the Resistance are evidence in his prize-winning novel, *Drôle de jeu* (Paris: Éditions Corrêa, 1945), the story of Resistance fighter with the soul of a seducer hiding from the Nazis in a village in the south of France; Jacques-Laurent Bost (1916–90) was a journalist, writer, and member of *Les temps modernes* editorial team with Beauvoir and Sartre. Wounded in June 1940 during the German invasion of France, Bost later worked as a war correspondent for Albert Camus' underground newspaper, *Combat*, reporting in 1944 on the liberation of the Dachau concentration camp. *Le dernier des métiers* (Paris: Gallimard, 1946) is his war diary; Jules Roy (1907–2000) was born to French colonists, the *pied noir*, in Algeria. He commanded a Royal Air Force squadron that bombed the Ruhr Basin in Germany during World War II, missions described in *La vallée heureuse* (Paris: Charlot, 1946). In June 1953, he resigned from the French army in protest against the French government's policies in the First Indochina War.

4. Fabrice Del Dongo, the young Italian protagonist of Stendhal's *La chartreuse de Parme*, the story of Del Dongo's misadventures during the age of Napoleon.

5. James Joyce (1882–1941), Irish writer and poet, was a key figure in the development of the modernist novel, best known for his novel, *Ulysses* (1922).

6. Maurice Barrès (1862–1923), a French novelist, journalist, and conservative politician whose "cult of the self" as in his 1888 novel, *Le culte de moi*, was an important early influence on Beauvoir (see her *Diary of a Philosophy Student: 1926–27*, ed. and trans. by Barbara Klaw et al. [Urbana: University of Illinois, 2006], p. 201, n.18 and p. 212, n.142); André Gide was a French novelist and essayist, winner of the 1947 Nobel Prize in Literature, whose work pursues the ideas of self, morality, social equality, and intellectual honesty. Much of his work is autobiographical, exemplifying his own struggle with the human conflict between desire and conventional morality, as in his 1897 novel, *Les nourritures terrestres* (*Fruits of the Earth*). Gide was also an important early influence on Beauvoir (see her *Diary of a Philosophy Student: 1926–27*, p.154).

7. Jean-Paul Sartre (1905–1980) was a French philosopher and author; by 1947, there were two published volumes of Sartre's *Les chemins de la liberté*: Vol. I, *L'âge de raison* (Paris: Gallimard, 1945), translated by Eric Sutton as *The Age of Reason* (New York: Knopf, 1947); and Vol. II, *Le sursis* (Paris: Gallimard, 1945), translated by Eric Sutton as *The Reprieve* (New York: Knopf, 1947).

8. Socrates (c. 469 B.C.–399 B.C.) was a classical Greek philosopher, considered one of the founders of Western philosophy, whose teaching method is featured in the dialogues of his student, Plato; François Rabelais (1494?–1553), a French Renaissance satirist who stressed the importance of individual liberty and thought.

9. Blaise Pascal (1623–62) was a French philosopher, physicist, and mathematician. A child prodigy educated by his father, at eighteen he constructed a mechanical calculator, called *Pascal's calculator* or the *Pascaline*. He wrote treatises on projective geometry and later on probability theory. In 1654 he abandoned his scientific work to devote himself to theology and philosophy. The famous phrase, "Man is but a reed, the most feeble thing in nature, but he is a thinking reed," is from his *Pensée* 347; see *Pascal's Pensées*, trans. A. J. Krailsheimer (1966; London: Penguin, 1995).

10. In this paragraph, the word "conscience" is surely a translation of the French word *conscience*, which can mean either "conscience" or "consciousness," depending on the context. Assuming Beauvoir originally wrote "conscience" in French, the meaning in this context should more appropriately be translated as "consciousness" (and "consciousnesses" near the end of this paragraph).

11. *La Princesse de Clèves*, considered the first French novel and an early prototype of the psychological novel, was published anonymously in 1678. The novel, which is set in the 16th century French royal court, is generally attributed to Madame de La Fayette; *The Brothers Karamazov*, a profound philosophical novel exploring questions of faith, free will, and morality, is the final novel by the Russian author, Fyodor Dostoevsky; *The Egoist*, a tragicomical novel by the British novelist, George Meredith, was published in 1879; *Moby Dick*, by the American author, Herman Melville, was first published in 1852. An example of American Romanticism, the novel tells the story of the adventures of a sailor Ishmael on a whaling ship commanded by Captain Ahab. "Call me Ishmael," is the novel's famous opening line; *Light in August* is by the American author, William Faulkner. Like most of Faulkner's novels, this work revolves around racial conflict in the South.

12. André Malraux (1901–76) was a French author, adventurer, and politician. He was a critic of government policy in French Indochina in the 1920s, supported the Republicans in the Spanish Civil War in the 1930s, and fought with the Resistance and French Army in World War II. His best known novels include *La condition humaine*, (*Man's Fate*) (1933) and *L'espoir* (*Man's Hope*) (1937); Albert Camus (1913–60) was a French Algerian author, philosopher, journalist, and winner of the 1957 Nobel Prize for Literature. His most famous work may be *L'étranger* (*The Stranger*) (1942).

13. The article is followed by this note on "the author": "Sartre's Existentialist executive officer and one of the movement's ablest proponents through her own three novels (the latest, '*L'invitée*,' [*She Came to Stay*] is to be translated and published here this year), Simone de Beauvoir was born in 1908 in Paris and educated at the Sorbonne, where she took second place (Sartre took first) in the "agrégation" in Philosophy in 1929. Both taught in various lycées in France before establishing Existentialist HQ in the Hotel Louisiana. Now she is back on the Left Bank, after an extensive lecture tour in the United States."

3

Existentialist Theater

INTRODUCTION

by Dennis A. Gilbert

One must admire today the extent to which the terrain of Simone de Beauvoir scholarship has changed over these last decades: the Beauvoir whose centennial we celebrated in 2008 is a very different public and private figure from the one whose death we mourned in 1986. Still, little critical attention continues to be paid to Beauvoir's relationship to theater, admittedly a small portion of her creative activity with *Les bouches inutiles* (*The Useless Mouths*) as her only play, and even less to her ideas on theater.[1] Until recently, Beauvoir's theoretical interest in the genre as both a written and a performed activity had been evident only in two texts from 1945, "C'est Shakespeare qu'ils n'aiment pas" ("It's Shakespeare They Don't Like") and "Roman et théâtre" ("The Novel and the Theater"). Through the Shakespeare article, Beauvoir engaged with French theatrical polemics toward the end of the war. With the longer article on the novel and the theater, she was able to elaborate upon the processes of creation and reception armed with the comparative techniques of each genre in her mind. These overlooked texts reveal a Beauvoir immersed in the issues of dramatic history and theatrical aesthetics and preoccupied by the debate surrounding the classical unities of time, place, and action and the interaction of the real and the imaginary on stage.[2] The present volume in the Beauvoir Series provides a good opportunity to return to this neglected aspect of her work and to reexamine the nature of her remarks both on theater in general and on the state of postwar French theater in particular.

For fifty years, then, access of a substantive nature to Beauvoir's relationship to theater had been limited to a single play, an intervention in a war of words over Parisian theatrical taste, and a foray into generic criticism or "genre theory."[3] In 1996, Ingrid Galster published an important article resulting from exhaustive research conducted at the Bibliothèque de l'Arsenal in Paris. Her focus was on a series of radio plays written and produced by Beauvoir for Radio-Vichy during the Occupation.[4] Their existence had been known for some time, Beauvoir discusses them in her autobiography, but the scripts themselves had never before been located. Beauvoir's critics, over the decade since her death, used the few references in secondary-source material concerning these fictional works of performance to suggest that she had somehow collaborated with the German cultural authorities through this project and that the predominant themes of those texts, escape and distraction, could be interpreted as being favorable to the Nazis.[5] While not totally dismissing this interpretation, Galster offers another one based upon a close reading of Beauvoir's actual writing: certain of the characters do indeed function as representative of an idea of refusal. They oppose the established order, find themselves socially marginalized, or push gender limits to the extreme. In these ways, their actions can also be viewed as being supportive of a notion of resistance. Galster concludes that the stark opposition between collaboration and resistance no longer remains a useful tool to understand the behavior of the French under Nazi rule and that the inherent ambiguity of all fictional writing, as in these radio plays, actually works against such a facile determination. Galster's contribution to first-hand knowledge of these performance texts by Beauvoir serves then as pertinent background for our purposes here. Her discovery sheds additional light on Beauvoir's conception of the impact that the spoken word can have on an audience; she places these scenarios in a thematic context resembling the treatment of gender marginalization and resistance to established order that Beauvoir was pursuing at that same time in her writing of *The Useless Mouths*; and her emphasis on Beauvoir's practical involvement with theatrical production, in advance of any theoretical reflection on the genre, suggests a dramatic methodology in which concrete representation takes precedence over abstract formulation.

These themes play a major role in a previously unknown text by Beauvoir that also came to light in 1996. The Jean-Paul Sartre scholar, Michel Rybalka, found a curious reference to a text entitled *Le théâtre existentialiste* (*Existentialist Theater*) in an online search and graciously told me about it. Since no direct mention of this text had ever appeared in any other biographical or bibliographical documentation, this reference was indeed in need of examination. I soon discovered it to be a lengthy sound recording made by Beauvoir, complemented by the voices of unidentified professional actors. The recording, which was apparently made during one of her stays in New York City, was housed solely at Wellesley College. Thanks to the generous cooperation of that university's library staff, I was granted access to it: six 78 rpm records, in French, recorded on both sides. Although a possible copyright date of 1947 coincides with Beauvoir's presence in New York and seems justified by the context of her oral remarks, it must be noted that nothing contained on the phonographic documents themselves verifies this assumption. One can only guess that the circumstances surrounding the recording had something to do with the New York premiere of Sartre's play, *The Flies*, which was brought to the stage by Erwin Piscator in April of 1947 and which Beauvoir mentions briefly in *America Day by Day*: "This evening they're giving the first performance of *The Flies*. For the last few days I have attended final rehearsals and found the same excitement as in Paris in similar circumstances."[6] In her *Letters to Sartre* Beauvoir alludes also to a talk on the play that she gave in English around the same time: "On Saturday [April 19] I *spoke in English* on *The Flies* at the New School: it was a debate, and I think people admired my courage more than my accent."[7] Perhaps the closest to a direct reference that we have is contained in a slightly later letter to Sartre where she summarizes her activities in New York from the previous week: "On Thursday [May 1] I made a recording and worked on some articles" (*LS* 454). It is therefore the transcription and the English translation of this recording that we proudly publish here for the first time.[8]

In the spring of 1947 the vogue of existentialism was everywhere, and the United States was no exception. During Beauvoir's first trip to America, she lectured on this intellectual phenomenon at various colleges, universities, and events sponsored by the French Cultural Services. In this regard Sartre had preceded her a year earlier. His lecture at Carnegie Hall in March of 1946, "Forgers of Myths" in the published version, had been by all accounts a major success. In it he had introduced the names and recent dramatic works of Jean Anouilh, Albert Camus, and Beauvoir to his audience, while also focusing on more general themes regarding the development of French theater since the Occupation: the return of mythology, the importance of aesthetic distance, and the rejection of a fixed human nature on stage.[9] Beauvoir's technique in *Existentialist Theater* is at once more analytical and more pedagogical. In what will become the central theme throughout the text, she concentrates on the three principal plays by Sartre and Camus to this time—*The Flies* (1943), *No Exit* (1944), and *Caligula* (1944)—in order to arrive only afterward at a working definition of existentialist theater.[10]

Beauvoir's own introduction to what will become the most controversial of Sartre's dramatic works considers *The Flies* as both a complex fictional vehicle and an ethical discourse that brought a message of hope to the French during the Occupation. She sees Sartre's use of myth, Greek mythology in this instance, as a way to replace a theater of fatality, i.e., tragedy, which remains completely loyal to its ancient story line, with a theater of freedom, i.e., tragedy, which now deviates from the apparent meaning of the classical fable for a contemporary audience.[11] This move changes a possible interpretation of the play to focus on current events and Orestes' specific fictional role in calling attention to them. Since Beauvoir anticipates the unfamiliarity of her American audience with these aspects of *The Flies*, she introduces the recitation by professional actors of the last part of act 3 involving Orestes, Zeus, and Electra. Her choice of scene underscores then the significance of Orestes' final refutation of Zeus's authority and the optimistic meaning that this subversive act confers on the ending of the play: "The folk of Argos are my folk. I must open their eyes. [. . .] They're free; and human life begins on the far side of despair."[12]

Beauvoir's reference to Sartre's recourse to mythology in *The Flies* sheds important light on the problem of tragedy and the representation of myths in French theater of the 1930s and 1940s. This problem can best be understood as the persistence of a certain tragic tradition and the insertion of this tradition into a dramatic text as its actual subject matter, also known as theatrical metatextuality. Therefore, dramatists of the interwar period in France who sought to address serious issues, such as Jean Cocteau, Jean Giraudoux, and Jean Anouilh, placed on the page and on stage characters who were conscious of their roles in a performed drama and whose remarks stressed the impossibility of escape from a prefigured ending.[13] As Beauvoir suggests in *Existentialist Theater*, however, *The Flies* is Sartre's response to previous and contemporary essentialist and predetermined drama. While it is true that he does insert himself into this mythological tradition by virtue of a respect for the classical unities, a plot that begins at the point of moral conflict, and a rejection of realism in the name of aesthetic distance, he dismisses completely the fundamental bases of a theater of fatality in his overall program for the renovation of French literature during the postwar era as outlined in "Qu'est-ce que la littérature?" ("What Is Literature?"), also from 1947. In place of this theater Sartre proposes a theater of freedom, where the primacy of free will enables his heroes to break the power of destiny and ancient heritage with regard to the meaning of their actions: "[T]he heroes are freedoms caught in a trap like all of us. What are the ways out? Each character will be nothing but the choice of a way out and will equal no more than the chosen way out. [. . .] A way out is invented. And each one, by inventing his own way out, invents himself."[14] As such, the Sartrian Orestes creates his own self throughout the course of this play and proves that, in existentialist theater, the chips are never down, that is, until death or until the curtain falls.[15]

However, the echo of Beauvoir's assertion in *Existentialist Theater* that *The Flies* represented an ethical discourse that brought a message of hope to the French during the Occupation has provoked a significant controversy surrounding the play. For over forty years Sartre's active role with regard to resistance/the Resistance went relatively unquestioned. Over the last two decades, though, certain writers and intellectuals, most notably Sartre and Beauvoir, have been taken to task for, according to some historians, their lack of action and resistance during the German Occupation of France. In 1986 Ingrid Galster published her first major study, *Le théâtre de Jean-Paul Sartre devant ses premiers critiques* (The Theater of Jean-Paul Sartre in the Eyes of His First Critics), in which she addresses these accusations. Her main concern is to examine whether or not Sartre's avowed intentions for the plays in question, *Bariona*, *The Flies*, and *No Exit*, were understood at the time of their creation and representation, as Beauvoir maintains here. In addition, she is interested in determining the extent to which the fictional vehicle of theater modified the reception of these messages and made ambiguous the true intent of the dramatist. With specific regard to *The Flies*, her analysis of its reception in both the authorized press and the clandestine press places in doubt whether it could indeed be considered a resistance play. She concludes that a fundamental discrepancy existed between intention and reception due to the literary nature of the text and the mythological staging by Charles Dullin. So, despite Sartre's claim of presenting a tragedy of freedom and Beauvoir's support of such a claim, the inherent and unavoidable ambiguity of the theatrical event became "the main obstacle which prevented his intentions from reaching the audience."[16]

Beauvoir next discusses Sartre's play from the following year, *No Exit*. If, over time, *The Flies* has proven to be Sartre's most controversial play, then *No Exit* has certainly become his most widely performed dramatic work; it has never failed to provoke a debate surrounding the famous line spoken by Garcin: "Hell is—other people!" Beauvoir's goal in 1947 is to reconsider and ultimately to refute the various misinterpretations of this line that were already prevalent during the postwar period in France and abroad. To this end she emphasizes Sartre's relocation of the torment experienced by Garcin, Inez, and Estelle from the anticipation of imposed, external torture to the realization of personal, internal conflict. From an existentialist perspective, in life an individual can indeed prove to be an obstacle to the freedom of someone else. This situation must be overcome or else life becomes hell, like the fictional predicament of the deceased characters in *No Exit*. Yet, this bleak picture need not serve to represent the totality of one's relations with others provided that one realizes the possibility of friendship, confidence, and respect among people and strives to achieve these goals while still alive and free to act. In this way, Beauvoir suggests an optimistic yet cautionary interpretation of the play to her postwar American audience and once again complements her analysis with the recitation by the same actors of one of its important scenes. This time it is the opening interaction between Garcin and the Valet. At first, this choice appears curious given Beauvoir's thematic concern for the internal torment of the characters, while the beginning of the play deals rather with the external description of hell as Garcin comes to understand it. Yet as the scene develops, one realizes Beauvoir's intention to privilege the mythological aspect of the play and the discrepancy at work between hell as a received notion or Christian belief and hell as a theatrical fabrication or existentialist construct. The reader/spectator is thus introduced to Sartre's existential vision of hell and the objects associated with it: a Second Empire drawing room, the absence of the usual methods of torture, no mirrors or windows, just "existence," which simply continues and which forms the worst part of Garcin's situation: "Ah, I see; it's life without a break."[17]

The themes of existence and mythology enable Beauvoir then to introduce Albert Camus, known primarily at this time in France for his novel, *The Stranger* (1942), and for his most recent play, *Caligula* (1944). Camus' thinking in these early works can best be summarized as the objective presentation of the notion of the absurd: man's free existence as disengaged from others remains empty and never achieves justification in the world. This estrangement results primarily from the failure of rational man's search for meaning in an irrational world. Short of finding that meaning, one is forced to act at the expense of other people. Beauvoir's understanding in *Existentialist Theater* of the Camusian definition of the absurd can be traced back to *Le mythe de Sisyphe* (*The Myth of Sisyphus*), his important theoretical work on the subject from 1942; but, as in the previous discussions, she illustrates this abstract metaphysical problem through a specific theatrical text. Beauvoir shows how Camus' choice of the Roman emperor, a character steeped this time in historical mythology, can carry with it certain preconceived notions for a contemporary audience. Caligula looks not to improve the world, as was the case with Orestes, but to revolt against it and against others, to make the absurd even more evident by his brutal crimes in a vain attempt to justify his life. His predicament can certainly be understood then as a reflection of the dark days and events of the Occupation. From a postwar perspective, Beauvoir's analysis reconfirms as well the importance of a negative portrayal of the human condition in existentialist theater, such as we saw in *No Exit*, as a means of awakening the reader to positive action and shocking the theatergoing public out of any possible return to prewar complacency. As if realizing that her own American audience might have some difficulty with a number of these Camusian notions, Beauvoir closes with a familiar pedagogical strategy: to have excerpts from the play, in this case of multiple scenes from the first act, performed by the actors working with her. In each instance Caligula is presented as wanting, as unsatisfied, as betrayed by the events of his life, and therefore as unable to be positively engaged in the affairs of his Roman empire. In a reply that suggests more resignation than revolt, he says to Helicon, "Really, this world of ours, the scheme of things as they call it, is quite intolerable. That's why I want the moon, or happiness, or eternal life—something, in fact, that may sound crazy, but which isn't of this world."[18]

Beauvoir's concluding remarks in this text synthesize her previous discussions into a working definition of what might properly be called existentialist theater. As was mentioned at the outset, critical appreciation of Beauvoir's work has considerably changed since her death in 1986, and at the forefront of such a revision lies an emphasis on her innovative contribution to the development of existentialism. Her own creative method displays the need to work in the concrete world of literature and not just in the abstract domain of philosophy.[19] In fact, nowhere is this intervention any more apparent than in the application of her ideas to theater. Claude Francis and Fernande Gontier, in their biography of Beauvoir, quote a conversation with her in which she emphasizes an early philosophical disagreement with Sartre:

> We argued quite a bit about *Being and Nothingness*. I was opposed to some of his ideas. . . . In the first version [. . .] he spoke about freedom as though it were equally complete for everybody. Or at least that it was always possible to exercise one's freedom. I, on the other hand, insisted

> that there exist situations in which freedom cannot be exercised or is nothing more than a hoax. He agreed with that. As a result, he gave a lot of weight to the situation in which the human being finds himself.[20]

This understanding of the concept of situation coincides then with the predicament of the main characters in existentialist drama and leads Beauvoir to refer to the postwar French stage as a theater of situations. No longer concerned with the depiction of character types, as in Molière's plays, or the reduction of man to a psychological determinism, as in the realist and naturalist schools of the nineteenth century, this theater maintains a belief rooted in the demonstration of man's freedom as his primary dimension. But, as Beauvoir reminds us, in the theater of Sartre and Camus this freedom must be given content by one's concrete action in the world. At the heart of each of the plays discussed is the realization that the actions of the characters are only able to meet with limited degrees of success.[21]

Finally, Sylvie Le Bon de Beauvoir's preface to the *Letters to Sartre* contains a notable reference to Simone de Beauvoir's appreciation for the spoken text. While meant to establish a metaphorical relationship between the letters and Beauvoir's continued, vocal presence, these lines could easily be understood with regard to the original, oral nature of the theatrical text just introduced:

> Simone de Beauvoir used to say that one of her most enduring fantasies involved the conviction that her singular existence, [. . .] her entire existence was recorded somewhere on a giant tape-recorder. These letters, in their own way, form part of that dream of a complete recording. At all events, you can certainly hear her voice in them, its most fleeting along with its most constant tones: her true, living voice. (*LS* xii)

It would indeed be reasonable then to acknowledge an interest in *Existentialist Theater* based solely on our own scholarly curiosity about it as a previously unknown text on a hitherto neglected subject within the Beauvoirian canon. However, this estimation would certainly undervalue its real worth. At a distance of over sixty years now, Beauvoir's "true, living voice" provides us with a unique glimpse at a moment in dramatic, literary, and cultural history, which Jacques Guicharnaud simply but aptly refers to as "those existentialist years."[22]

NOTES

1. For notable exceptions, see, on the one hand, Virginia M. Fichera, "Simone de Beauvoir and 'the Woman Question': *Les bouches inutiles*," in *Simone de Beauvoir: Witness to a Cen-*

tury, ed. Hélène V. Wenzel, spec. issue of *Yale French Studies* 72 (1986): 51–64, and Teresa L. Myintoo, "*Les bouches inutiles* et *L'Eden cinéma: Le théâtre du manque*" ("*The Useless Mouths* and *The Eden Cinema*: The Theater of Lack"), *Simone de Beauvoir Studies* 12 (1995): 100–05, who concentrate their analyses of Beauvoir's play on the dramatic presentation of the construction of women as marginalized subjects, and, on the other hand, Ted Freeman, "Simone de Beauvoir: *Les bouches inutiles*," in *Theatres of War: French Committed Theatre from the Second World War to the Cold War* (Exeter: University of Exeter Press, 1998), 73–87, and Catherine Léglu, introduction, in *Les bouches inutiles*, by Simone de Beauvoir, ed. Léglu, French Texts (London: Bristol Classical Press, 2001), vii–xxxvii, for whom the play must also be understood as a reflection of the political climate in France under the Nazi Occupation. See as well the introduction by Liz Stanley to a new translation of *Les bouches inutiles* contained in this volume.

2. Cf. Simone de Beauvoir, "C'est Shakespeare qu'ils n'aiment pas" and "Roman et théâtre," in *Les écrits de Simone de Beauvoir: La vie, l'écriture*, and in appendix, "Textes inédits ou retrouvés," by Claude Francis and Fernande Gontier (Paris: Gallimard, 1979), 324–26 and 327–31. For a closer look at Beauvoir's arguments and a comparison with Jean-Paul Sartre's reflections on the same subjects, see Dennis A. Gilbert, "Sartre and Beauvoir on Theater: Force of Circumstance?" *Simone de Beauvoir Studies* 8 (1991): 137–51. Elizabeth Fallaize comments on a new translation of these two texts as part of her introduction to short articles on literature also contained in this volume.

3. Beauvoir does relate anecdotal information on this relationship in her autobiographical writings and in the Josée Dayan and Malka Ribowska movie on her from 1978.

4. Ingrid Galster, "Simone de Beauvoir et Radio-Vichy: A propos de quelques scénarios retrouvés," *Romanische Forschungen* 108 (1996): 112–32; "Simone de Beauvoir and Radio-Vichy: About Some Rediscovered Radio Scripts," *Simone de Beauvoir Studies* 13 (1996): 103–13.

5. These accusations first surfaced in Deirdre Bair, *Simone de Beauvoir: A Biography* (New York: Summit, 1990).

6. Simone de Beauvoir, *America Day by Day*, trans. Carol Cosman, fwd. Douglas Brinkley (Berkeley: University of California Press, 1999), 257.

7. Simone de Beauvoir, *Letters to Sartre*, trans. and ed. Quintin Hoare, pref. Sylvie Le Bon de Beauvoir (New York: Arcade, 1992), 451; translation slightly modified; hereafter cited *LS*.

8. A preliminary look at its contents can be found in Dennis A. Gilbert, "Forging New Myths: Beauvoir's Recorded Comments on Existentialist Theater," *Simone de Beauvoir Studies* 14 (1997): 114–23. At this time I would like to express my gratitude to Michel Rybalka and in particular to Barbara Flaherty, reserve room supervisor, Margaret Clapp Library, Wellesley College, for having provided me with the audio components necessary to tape Beauvoir's remarks. A more recent online search indicates that these remarks have also been placed on audiocassette for greater access. My thanks go as well to Sabine Crespo for her excellent transcription and Marybeth Timmermann for her faithful translation.

9. Cf. Jean-Paul Sartre, *Sartre on Theater*, ed. Michel Contat and Michel Rybalka, trans. Frank Jellinek (New York: Pantheon, 1976), 33–43; hereafter cited *ST*. Sartre's theoretical remarks mirror Beauvoir's own themes in "The Novel and the Theater."

10. Beauvoir does not proceed directly though to a discussion of Sartre and *The Flies* but rather concedes that in fact this play was not the first one written by him and that his initial theatrical experience had actually occurred some years earlier within the confines of the

prison camp where he had been held during the war. She does not name the earlier play in question, which we know now to be *Bariona*, and in this way her account follows Sartre's own revelation in "Forgers of Myths": "My first experience in the theater was especially fortunate. When I was a prisoner in Germany in 1940, I wrote, staged, and acted in a Christmas play which, while pulling wool over the eyes of the German censor by means of simple symbols, was addressed to my fellow prisoners" (*ST* 39). By augmenting this basic information with thematic details, however, Beauvoir makes *Existentialist Theater* the first in a series of invaluable contributions to our knowledge of Sartre's theatrical activity prior to 1943; it is as much thanks to Beauvoir as through Sartre himself that we have come to understand the context of his entry into the practice of writing for the stage.

11. As Sartre wrote in 1943, "Tragedy is the mirror of Fatality. I did not believe that a tragedy of freedom could not be written, since the ancient Fatum is simply an inverted freedom" (*ST* 186).

12. Jean-Paul Sartre, *"No Exit" and Three Other Plays*, trans. Stuart Gilbert and Lionel Abel (New York: Vintage International, 1989), 119.

13. Specific examples can be found in Cocteau's *La machine infernale* (*The Infernal Machine*) from 1934, Giraudoux's *La guerre de Troie n'aura pas lieu* (*Tiger at the Gates*) from 1935, and Anouilh's *Antigone* from 1944.

14. Jean-Paul Sartre, *"What Is Literature?" and Other Essays*, intro. Steven Ungar (Cambridge: Harvard University Press, 1988), 235; translation slightly modified.

15. For a more complete analysis of Sartre's subversive relationship to mythological theater, see Dennis A. Gilbert, "'Enfin Sartre vint': D'un théâtre de la fatalité à un théâtre de la liberté" ("'Finally Sartre Came': From a Theater of Fatality to a Theater of Freedom"), *Chimères, Vol. 26* (Lawrence: University of Kansas, 2002): 15–26.

16. Ingrid Galster, *Le théâtre de Jean-Paul Sartre devant ses premiers critiques*, Oeuvres et Critiques (Tübingen: Gunter Narr; Paris: Jean-Michel Place, 1986), 337; my translation. Many studies have followed in Galster's wake, including Gilbert Joseph, *Une si douce Occupation: Simone de Beauvoir et Jean-Paul Sartre, 1940–1944* (Such a Sweet Occupation: Simone de Beauvoir and Jean-Paul Sartre, 1940–1944) (Paris: Albin Michel, 1991), whose virulent personal polemic against both Beauvoir and Sartre derives mainly from incomplete archival research and overused private sources.

17. Sartre, *No Exit*, 5.

18. Albert Camus, *"Caligula" and Three Other Plays*, trans. Stuart Gilbert (New York: Vintage-Random House, 1958), 8.

19. Examples of this important theme can be found in many of her essays that comprise *Philosophical Writings*, ed. Margaret A. Simons, with Marybeth Timmermann and Mary Beth Mader, fwd. Sylvie Le Bon de Beauvoir (Urbana: University of Illinois Press, 2004), especially "Literature and Metaphysics" and "What Is Existentialism?"

20. Claude Francis and Fernande Gontier, *Simone de Beauvoir: A Life, a Love Story*, trans. Lisa Nesselson (New York: St. Martin's, 1987), 210.

21. These same points are recalled in Sartre's own 1947 article, "For a Theater of Situations" (*ST* 3–5).

22. Jacques Guicharnaud, "Those Years: Existentialism 1943–1945," trans. Kevin Neilson, in *Sartre: A Collection of Critical Essays*, ed. Edith Kern, Twentieth-Century Views (Englewood Cliffs, N.J.: Prentice-Hall, 1962), 15–20.

EXISTENTIALIST THEATER

by Simone de Beauvoir

TRANSCRIBED BY SABINE CRESPO

TRANSLATION BY MARYBETH TIMMERMANN

NOTES BY DENNIS A. GILBERT

Today I intend to speak to you about French theater such as it has developed and affirmed itself since the war. But, as it is a subject that would be much too long for a short talk, I think it would be best to limit ourselves to a few plays and a few authors.

I have chosen the two authors that seem to be the most representative: Jean-Paul Sartre and Camus, who had never published theatrical works before the war, and who are very indicative of the tendencies of modern theater.[1] And among their plays, I chose *The Flies* and *No Exit* for Jean-Paul Sartre and *Caligula* for Camus. I think that by studying these works rather attentively, we will have a more accurate and worthwhile idea of the modern tendencies of French theater than by a long and superficial enumeration of all the riches, for there are indeed many, that have appeared during this period.

I will first speak to you about *The Flies* by Jean-Paul Sartre. This is the first play by an author who, until then, was only known for philosophical works and novels. To be more precise, this was not exactly his first play, for in the

Le théâtre existentialiste, a lecture by Simone de Beauvoir with readings by others of scenes from plays by Sartre and Camus, sound recording, six records, FG 1034–45, 78 rpm, Apex Recording Studios, New York, (May 1, 1947), © Sylvie Le Bon de Beauvoir.

camp where he was a prisoner of war for nine months,[2] Jean-Paul Sartre had his first theatrical experience, which made a big impression on him and certainly influenced him a great deal. Around Christmastime he was asked to write a play, and he tried to communicate a bit of hope and some of his ideas to his comrades, in spite of the surveillance and the censures that surrounded any attempt. The subject that he put forth was the subject of the nativity, since it was for Christmas. But this allowed him to represent the drama of the Occupation in France in a very transparent manner since he had conceived his subject in the following way: he described Judea occupied by the Romans, the temptations of despair and collaboration that there were in this little country crushed by an immense power, and yet a part of the population had the will to affirm their resistance. And this play was very inferior to those that Sartre has written since, but it was very interesting to him and was a great experience for him because he felt the possibility of a direct and very significant relationship with the public.

In a theater, the public is oftentimes a group of people who come simply to be entertained, to kill time, to criticize, or to do what everyone else is doing, with no real ties of situation or interest binding them together, whereas the public in this case were all prisoners united by the same situation, coming to listen to what one of their own had to say to them. And there was something in this communication that was very exalting and also very instructive for Sartre because he understood for the first time, and very clearly, what the true function of literature was: that it was not simply a distraction, an escape or even a contemplation of certain eternal truths, but that it was truly an action and must be situated in time, in space and in concrete situations.

So when he returned to Paris, he again made the decision, along with many other writers, that in spite of everything and in spite of the Occupation, French intellectuals must try to write and express themselves. When he found himself in these circumstances, he remembered his experience in the prison camp, and the play he then wrote, *The Flies*, was an effort to communicate with all French people in spite of the censures and in spite of all the difficulties. And the first thing that must be understood if one wants to clearly read *The Flies*, is that this play was written in 1943, performed in 1943, and intended to bring a message of hope to oppressed people who were reduced to silence and for whom action was only clandestine and very difficult.

For this reason Sartre chose to take shelter behind an historical myth. Personally, he would have preferred to situate this drama, which is a drama about freedom, in contemporary circumstances since he wanted precisely to write a drama that was actively engaged in the present moment. But this engagement could not be revealed or the play would never have escaped censure, so it was a matter of masking the intention. Sartre therefore borrowed an old story from Greece. And to all appearances, he tells the story of Orestes who returns to Argos, and, encouraged by Electra, as in the ancient story and in order to take his revenge, kills his father's murderer, Aegisthus, and Clytemnestra, his mother who incited the murder.[3]

But from this drama, Sartre makes not only a classic story, but, as I was saying, truly the drama of freedom. And this is a very important point for him, because this idea of freedom is at the center of existentialist doctrine, which is, as you know, under its current form in France, the philosophical doctrine founded by Sartre. It is also interesting to note that Sartre had not yet developed this idea of freedom in its theoretical form when he gave it concrete expression in *The Flies*. This is important because it shows us what is possible in this kind of collaboration between philosophy and literature found in France today—that the concrete meditation on a particular individual side of the human drama might very well lead the philosopher to clarify his thought even on a theoretical plane.

One mustn't believe that when an author like Sartre writes a play or a novel, he first starts with the theory and then tries to illustrate it by a play or story. This would be a very bad method that would make the novel or play something abstract or dry. He simply situates himself in a certain philosophical universe which is his own, and he gives his characters the metaphysical dimension that is, according to him, the real dimension, and he makes their story into a kind of interior experiment as all playwrights and novelists are led to do. In other words, with this philosophical background, he writes the play or novel for himself, so that the play can teach him something just as it can also teach something to the reader that he would have never found in theoretical treatises.

This was the case for *The Flies*, which is so far the most clear and gripping expression of Sartre's theory of freedom, that is to say his ethics of engagement. The hero Orestes appears in the beginning as a young man blessed with the sort of freedom that was thought to be true freedom for a long time in France, namely a pure lack of restraint [*disponibilité*]. Gide, for example, spoke of this lack of restraint.[4] And this is an interesting fact to note, because this is exactly the type of freedom that was enjoyed before the last war by many young French intellectuals and many young bourgeois in general whose own lives were not strongly affected by the pressure of history, or the pressure of economic, social, or political conditions. And they believed that they were free because they saw a great many possibilities opening up before them and nothing was putting pressure on them.

This is the freedom enjoyed by Orestes who, for years, has traveled across the world with his preceptor, having no ties, no attachments, and no precise tasks to accomplish either. But this freedom is not sufficient for him; he feels that it is an abstract, empty, dead freedom, and that a man is only truly free if he has something to do and has roots, and he wants to give himself these roots. And it is not by chance or by simple curiosity that he arrives in Argos, breathes in the atmosphere of that city, and discovers that there is something for him to do in that city. He discovers that the people of Argos, who are his people, live in terrible oppression. First of all, they live in remorse because Aegisthus thinks that in order to appease the gods whom he has offended, the entire people must repent for the crime that he, Aegisthus, committed. Or, to better express it, he doesn't even exactly believe in the anger of the gods, but he thinks that maintaining the people in the abjection of remorse and repentance is the easiest way to smother their freedom and, consequently, to force them to accept servitude and a dictatorship.

And indeed the people live in terror and remorse, which is contrary to every kind of human dignity and freedom. So Orestes understands two things. He understands that, in his own interest, one could say for his subjective salvation, he must accomplish an act that truly roots him in this world and particularly in his city. On the other hand, he understands that, in order to be saved, the people need to be liberated from the yoke of Aegisthus. And his decision to rid the people of Aegisthus and Clytemnestra is born of this double motive. He is pushed into it by Electra because, of course, there must be psychological motives for any decision, even a metaphysical and moral one. In reality, the decision is always embodied in very concrete situations, and the pressure put on him by Electra, as well as Orestes' affection for Electra, play a very important role in Orestes' determination.

But, essentially, and on the moral plane, his intention [*volonté*] was to find himself by saving his people. And to me, this link between subjective salvation and the objective motivation of an act seems to be the most important thing in the play, as well as in Sartre's general theory of freedom, which consists not in positing a purely individual freedom detached from any content, and detached from its ties with the rest of the world, but what he calls an engaged freedom, in other words a freedom that gives itself content by employing itself for the utility of others. One cannot say that Orestes simply acted for himself, as if he were animated by that sort of will to power about which a Nietzsche, for example, speaks.[5] Nor can one say that he acted for the people, with a total abnegation of himself as if he were not important in his own eyes. He acted at the same time for himself and for others, which is, according to Sartre, the only really valid way to act, for a man must not totally lose himself or forget himself in his action; he is the one who acts and his action has repercussions for him. But he must not accomplish it in a purely gratuitous way either, for a gratuitous action would have no content and would not truly be an action.

So Orestes accomplishes this murder, and he accomplishes it against the will of the gods, which is also a very important point. In Sartre's eyes, the gods represent the established ethics and the established order, the entire ensemble of conventions to which man, too often, submits simply out of a kind of laziness and fear. And Orestes' act is free in that on the one hand it has a content and, on the other hand, it is truly assumed by the hero; in other words Orestes does not ask anyone to judge if his act is good or bad [*mauvais*]. Instead, he takes only the testimony of his own conscience[6] and his own judgment, which leads him to a rather tragic solitude. He does not accomplish this act happily, but accomplishes it with a kind of anguish which, according to Sartre, and based on Kierkegaard, must always accompany the truly moral act—not with the self-certainty of a Pharisee, but with the turmoil, disquietude, and kind of suffering of a truly moral soul.[7] Yet, by accomplishing his act in this way, without joy but with firm decision, he also has no regrets; he is going to escape from the terrible Furies, the flies that were devastating the city of Argos and would devastate even Electra's heart, because he knows that he did what he willed to do and that man's will is precisely what determines what is right and wrong, and illuminates the truth of good and evil.

You will now hear one of the principal scenes in *The Flies*: Orestes has killed Clytemnestra and Aegisthus, and has taken refuge in Apollo's temple. The Furies are surrounding him, and Zeus in person comes to demand that he repent of his error and to ask him to declare that the act he has committed was wrong. And Orestes refuses and opposes Zeus's will with his own human affirmation of a freedom that nothing outside of itself can determine, condemn, or justify.

[Scene from *The Flies*, Act III. Actors read through the entire scene beginning with "Zeus: 'Orestes, return to your saner self; the universe refutes you, you are a mite in the scheme of things'" and concluding with Zeus's final exchange with Orestes: "Zeus: 'Good-by, Orestes. As for you, Electra, bear this in mind. My reign is not yet over—far from it!—and I shall not give up the struggle. So choose if you are with me or against me. Farewell.' Orestes: 'Farewell.'"][8]

During the Occupation, Jean-Paul Sartre wrote another, very different play called *No Exit*. In this work, he wanted to point out a truth that is also very dear to him; that good or evil [*mal*] can only exist for men through men. This is the meaning of one of the most famous lines in *No Exit*, when one of the characters says: "Hell is—other people!"[9] What Sartre means is that hell, like paradise, in his way of thinking, can only come to men through men. The world's obstacles [*résistances*]—sickness, poverty, captivity, and even death—inasmuch as they appear to be natural, are neither good nor bad [*mauvaises*], but are made to be overcome, as the Stoics once said. On the contrary, there is a veritable and absolute evil [*mal*], and that is the bad will of a man who wants to harm another. And human nature is such that each man, in a sense, is an enemy to other men due to the very fact that he coexists with them and wants to posit himself as consciousness and as freedom, seeing the others only as objects. This state of things can be overcome by friendship and trust. But the moment men refuse friendship and trust, they truly become torturers for each other, and their coexistence becomes hell.

Sartre wanted to illustrate this dark aspect of the human condition in *No Exit*. Once again he resorted to a myth for the same reason as in the preceding play. He would have liked to show the interactions between men locked up together in a cell in Fresnes,[10] for example, or in another prison, in real, concrete and historical conditions, but this was impossible, so he transposed this coexistence in hell. He supposes that three individuals find themselves together in hell, each guilty for one reason or another, but all three having consciences [*conscience*] weighed down by serious crimes. And because of their bad will, because of the fear they have of each other and the fact that they retreat behind their selfish interests, they become torturers for each other. And this is the torment awaiting them—not exterior torments of fire or iron grills, etc., but the torment that any man of bad will can be for other men.

And to give you an idea of this play, which is very different in tone than the one from which you just heard a scene, you will now hear the first scene of *No Exit*, the one that introduces the whole play, when the journalist Garcin arrives in this strange place. He does not know which one it is yet when he is welcomed by a valet who is like any valet in a hotel. Here is the dialogue between Garcin and the valet.

[Scene from *No Exit*. Actors read from this scene beginning with "Garcin: 'Hm! So here we are?' Valet: 'Yes, Mr. Garcin.' Garcin: 'And this is what it looks like?' Valet: 'Yes.'" The scene ends with the following exchange between Garcin and the valet. "Garcin: 'What's this?' Valet: 'Can't you see? An ordinary paper-knife.' Garcin: 'Are there books here?' Valet: 'No.' Garcin: 'Then what's the use of this? Very well. You can go'" (*No Exit*, 3–7).]

Albert Camus was, as you no doubt know, one of the great discoveries in French literature over the last few years. He first became known for his novel, *L'étranger* [*The Stranger*], and then two of his plays were performed in Paris: *Le malentendu* [*The Misunderstanding*] and *Caligula*.[11]

One of the themes that haunts Camus' way of thinking is the theme of the absurd. It seems to him that existence in general and human existence in particular deserve to be called absurd, unless they have found their justification in the way that, say, an Orestes found justification for his life. There is a brute fact in existence, something gratuitous which satisfies the requirements of neither reason nor ethics. And clearly, for Camus, there is the possibility of escaping this absurdity, in precisely the same way that Sartre thinks it possible: by engaging and applying this freedom in some kind of work. Yet as long as freedom remains something empty [*vide*] and as long as existence has not found a way to establish its connection with the world and with action, it is something that is unjustified like a rock or any sort of natural object that is simply there, without really having a raison d'être.

This is the theme he treats in his novel, and that he takes up again in a very gripping way in the more interesting, I think, of these two plays, namely *Caligula*. Here he also has used a myth, the myth of the emperor Caligula who made terror reign in the Roman Empire for many years.[12] He imagines that a young man, whom he calls Caligula, is blessed with the fortune of immense power, that is to say that his freedom of action, in the abstract sense of the word, has an almost unlimited reach. He can give orders that will be obeyed. He can kill and no one will revolt against him. He can pillage and give in to all his impulses. And on the other hand, he finds within himself and around him no requirement to undertake any kind of action and he hasn't the slightest sense of human solidarity or any kind of ethics that could help him to use the power at his disposal. He thus has a power for absolutely no reason, and one could say, with absolutely no point of application. This power and the idea of the absurdity of all action give him a sort of vertigo. And that is what Camus wants to illustrate: the extreme limit of absurdity, the point at which a freedom that has no use for itself could arrive. Caligula is haunted, like the author of the play, by the feeling of absurdity. It seems to him that this world is not a possible world or a world in which life has a signification. And precisely because he is irritated with this world, he is going to try not to improve it, but, out of a kind of youthful and rebellious exasperation, to make it even more horrible and to make absurdity into a sort of law.

Camus, also, seeks to give a psychological motivation to such a decision. At the beginning of the play, we see Caligula, who has just lost a woman whom he loved very much, who is quite distressed by this death, and who escapes from the palace without letting anyone know what has become of him. We later learn that he was searching for the moon, that is to say he was searching for the impossible. He did not find it. And so, in revenge for this sort of disappointment, he decides to rule the world with not only terror, but a strange and particular terror that will be arbitrary and capricious. And in the beginning of the play, we see him deploy this capricious will without meeting any real resistance around him, because the men whom he treats contemptuously are not capable of undoing or renouncing this contempt by having something of a really honest or moral attitude, except one among them whom Caligula respects, incidentally, and who is the young Scipion. All the others are in a period of moral, intellectual, and you could say general decadence, which prevents them from having the burst of dignity that might have led Caligula to other feelings. So, the very servility of those who surround him lead him to new crimes and new caprices until at the end, out of necessity and in spite of everything (one could almost say dialectically), the forces he has unleashed turn against him, resulting in his assassination by a conspiracy. And he dies understanding that, as he says exactly, his freedom was not the right kind, that is to say that the purely empty freedom that he used and abused was not, actually, the true way to resolve the great problem of life. This problem is not resolved in the play; Camus does not claim to resolve it. He simply claims to describe it, to posit it, as it were, and to show one of its solutions: a false yet interesting one by the very fact of his exasperation, and by the fact that it reaches certain limits.

You are going to hear a few of the most important scenes from the first act, when Caligula returns to the palace after they have been searching for him for several days, and when he starts to resolve to make arbitrary and absurd terror reign around him.

[Scenes from Act 1 of *Caligula*. Actors read beginning with scene 4: "Helicon: 'Good morning, Caius.' Caligula: 'Good morning, Helicon'" and ending with "Helicon: 'In what way can I help you?' Caligula: 'In the way of . . . impossible.' Helicon: 'I'll do my best.' [Helicon leaves, the Intendant enters with several patricians]." Excerpts from scenes 7, 8, and 9 follow, beginning with: "Intendant: 'We . . . we've been looking for you, Caesar, high and low'" and concluding with "Caesonia: 'I doubt if this discovery of yours will make us any happier.' Caligula: 'So do I. But, I suppose, we'll have to live it through.'"][13]

I think that, through these summaries and texts, you can grasp a completely new orientation of French theater, one that is parallel to that which we see in literature, incidentally. For a very long time in France, theater mostly sought to describe, in a rather definitive way, either society as it was, which was called theater of manners [*le théâtre de moeurs*], or character types, also as they were thought to be, which was called psychological theater. And, it was essentially these social descriptions or this kind of psychological analysis that appeared as the substance of theater and as the moving force for the dramas that were presented to the spectator.

Our playwrights today have another conception of what a play is because they also have another conception of man and his relationship to the world. You have seen that in the plays by Sartre and Camus, the first dimension of man is his freedom, a freedom that succeeds in giving itself content and saving itself only if it engages itself in the world through action. But the very fact of using or not using one's freedom is an extremely dramatic choice [*alternative*]. And our playwrights are going to present and embody this choice more particularly in very concrete and very human stories that can speak to the imagination and the emotions, yet have very important metaphysical and moral implications. In other words, instead of being as interested in sociological or psychological descriptions as they used to be, today they are especially interested in moral conflicts. But the very word conflict indicates to us that ethics could provide an extremely interesting basis for theater since theater has always tried, above all, to be the presentation of human wills in opposition to one another, or passion in opposition to ethics; in other words, conflicts.

And another consequence resulting from this is the idea that the situation in which a man finds himself, much more than his own character, is what defines him. Instead of being psychological theater, today's theater will essentially be a theater of situations. The examples I have given can help to illustrate this assertion: when Orestes arrives in Argos, he is not a young man having such and such type of character. We are not told that he is either generous or avaricious or courageous or cowardly or lazy or hardworking. What we are told is that he is a young man who has always been free with an empty freedom, and who suffers from the anguish of this freedom. He is in a certain situation, and the choice that he is going to make of himself in this situation will, on the contrary, define his character. This is based upon one of the fundamental ideas of existentialism, namely that man is not given once and for all, and the qualities that can be attributed to him, such as being avaricious, generous, cowardly or courageous, are not qualities analogous to the fact of having blond or black hair. They are actually the result of certain choices. He chooses himself and he finds himself afterward to be such as he chooses himself. Nothing is given ahead of time to Orestes or to Caligula, for example. They are simply conscious of the situation in which they find themselves. But they can react to this situation, in so many very diverse ways, and according to their reactions, they will then define themselves as heroic, as in the case of Orestes, or on the contrary as cruel, demented and mean as in the case of Caligula. The definition of themselves follows, rather than precedes, their choice.

Naturally in this effort to describe the most interesting situations, and present men who find themselves in these situations and react to them, the concern for social and psychological truth must not be lost, so these plays will have that complexity. For example, as I have indicated, when Orestes resolves to commit the crime, it is not merely for abstract reasons, but also because of the affection he feels for Electra. In other words, his moral choice must fit into his psychological circumstances; the moment he decides what he will be, he also succumbs to motivations, which can indeed be very compelling, such as the tenderness and pity he has for his sister. Likewise with Caligula, it is not at all without importance that he discovers the absurdity of the world after the death of a woman whom he loved. But these psychological truths become secondary, giving a concrete and one could say carnal background to the personages who are presented; they do not constitute the veritable core of the drama.

The core of the drama in these plays and in others of the same type is really man who is faced with his freedom in specific, concrete circumstances, and who has to make valid use of this freedom or who fails to make valid use of this freedom. The author can put forth some very different illustrations, but the same theme will always haunt him.

This trend in theater, which can be called moral and at the same time philosophical, has at times been worrisome. Both morality and philosophy are involved because the veritable moral problem is what a man has to make of himself, or what he can make of himself. And to respond to this question, one must also know what man is, what the world is, and what the connections between man and the world are, which presupposes a whole metaphysical background.

So this simultaneously moral and metaphysical characteristic of theater has at times been worrisome because the playwrights who were trained in the old school and also certain critics thought that the human, concrete, and living truth of theater would be killed by giving this ideological content to theater. They thought that theater would be made into a demonstration [of a thesis]. I have already tried to respond to this objection when I told you that in writing *The Flies*, Sartre had truly discovered his thought. He did not limit himself to illustrating a preformed theoretical thought.

In truth, every author, whether playwright or novelist, has a singular vision of the world; the very singularity of this vision is what interests the reader or the spectator since one writes because one has something to say. To have something to say is to have one's own grasp on, one's own conception of the universe that surrounds us. That the author has a more particularly metaphysical vision and is more especially interested in moral questions does not prevent him from attaining completely universal truths, nor does it prevent him from being able to be concerned about art and aesthetics, which are naturally necessary in order to write a play. For although today's theater is in part an ideological theater and at the same time a theater that is concerned with engaging itself, as I was telling you at the beginning—a theater that is concerned with being an action and not simply a diversion, for example, and even not simply an abstract instruction but truly an action—the author also knows perfectly well that theater can not be realized as an action and as an engagement unless it succeeds in being a communication. That is the first condition of any work of art, and whatever purpose is put forth by theater or literature, it does not intend to escape from this foremost condition, which is to succeed as a communication.

Consequently, we will not have an aesthetic debacle in plays like *The Flies* and *Caligula*; to the contrary, all the problems of communication, that is to say aesthetics, will be posed for these new authors as they were posed for the old ones. In any case, it is a question of making what one has to say into something living and gripping for the public that is being addressed. And so, that's where we find absolutely all the problems of what is sometimes called form. On the other hand, these inventions of content are what will allow form to become something really interesting again, and not something academic and dead. I mean to say that if one form is always used to envelop the same preoccupations and the same material, it is not renewed and cannot renew itself. And it will easily end up becoming something frozen. Along with modifying the content itself, theater must at the same time modify its form. In fact, this is the only valid modification that can be found. Introducing new material, new concerns, and new problems into theater will bring a general renovation which would never be reached if one were limited to a kind of artificial rejuvenation from the outside, as directors between the two wars were for a long time.

People have talked for a long time, and rightly so, about a theater crisis in France, because theater did not truly have a rejuvenation that came from the interior. Despite the increase in theater schools, the efforts to change the way actors performed, the increase in certain types of productions, and the efforts to change the way plays are presented, all of that remained exterior and could not succeed in truly giving theater the life it was lacking. I think that, on the contrary, this kind of renewal from the inside and from the things that playwrights are trying to express has repercussions for the whole of theater, namely in the very manner of expression, therefore in the manner of acting as well as directing, and today's theater must truly seek itself along this path. That is to say, by taking the task it has to accomplish seriously, which is the feat of communicating with the public and addressing the public in order to transmit certain truths and messages, and by becoming aware of this role, theater will at the same time be able to succeed in becoming fully aware of itself. And this resurrection, as one could really call it, of concerns and interests that are going to be manifested in theater, will resound throughout the entire production process and the very language of everything that could be called theatrical aesthetics.

In truth, the playwrights who are engaged on these paths have much to do because, of course, the pitfalls that are talked about—such as making theater too abstract, too ideological, too purely philosophical, or not human enough—these pitfalls exist. Certainly by defining the situation and moral problems of the characters first, one might risk making them into abstract entities lacking their living and carnal depth. But precisely, the very existence of these problems and the new questions that will be posed, will serve to stimulate authors to create new plays in order to respond to these problems and invent diverse solutions. So I think that this path in which theater is engaged is extremely fertile.

There is another reproach that is sometimes addressed to modern theater, and to all of literature in general, which is its preference for presenting dramas that are extremely dark dramas and for bearing a message of despair. Orestes kills Aegisthus and Clytemnestra, and Caligula has patricians put to death by the thousands. One critic had fun counting up the number of murders that were seen carried out on French stages during the last three years. And, clearly, if you count all the people massacred by Caligula, you arrive at a very considerable figure. You might wonder why. Well, it is not from a pure taste for violence, but it is, I think, because our playwrights, like our writers in general, have a very sharp sense of the tragedy of the modern world. And of course, theater, even more than novels, demands an exaggeration of the problems of the world. If one wants to bring the violence of the modern world to the stage, one will be led to describe situations and conflicts where violence is exacerbated.

Yet, I do not think it necessary to see in the blackness and tragedy of these descriptions, any more than in literature in general, a will to debase man or a will to describe him in absolutely dark and despairing colors. I think that really, for theater as for literature, one can always say what Sartre just wrote in the article he is now in the process of publishing in *Les temps modernes* about the very general subject of literature.[14] One can say that there is never any literature or theater that is truly black, because to make theater is always to address human freedoms with the intention of bringing them a message. In other words, it is always to think that there is something to say, that something is worth being said, and that something, therefore, has a value. And furthermore, there are men to whom it can be said, men who are capable of hearing, therefore men who are free and also capable of responding. So it is to say that there is something to express, and something to do, and something to hope for.

Our playwrights give us dark visions of the world because they are convinced that the world initially presents a dark aspect, and the worst defeat would be to hide it from oneself and willingly resort to lies. Yet, they strive to present it in its truth, even if this truth is black, precisely because they trust this truth and because they think that, beyond all the tragedies that they describe and present, to which they try to bring solutions or upon which they at least try to meditate, beyond all these tragedies, there is the possibility of a hope.

And I think that this is one thing, among others, that must be understood if one wants to grasp to some extent the true meaning of today's literature and theater. One could say that with all their violence and cruelties, and in the intention of not masking any of the reality of either the world or men, even in their most disturbing and dark aspects, there is however, a very certain hope in the possibilities of man and the world. I think that you could even feel it in the texts that were presented to you today, and I think that it is one of the points that must essentially be retained if one wants to grasp to some extent what the inspiration is for today's theater.

NOTES

1. Jean-Paul Sartre (1905–80), who may be best known for his philosophical essay *Being and Nothingness*, was also a prolific dramatist, novelist, and cofounder of the postwar journal, *Les temps modernes*; Albert Camus (1913–60), born in Mondovi, Algeria, was a play-

wright and journalist, member of the French Resistance, and editor of the French underground newspaper, *Combat.*

2. Sartre was taken prisoner during the German invasion of France in June of 1940; the German Occupation ended in 1944.

3. Orestes, in Greek mythology, is the son of Clytemnestra and Agamemnon and heir to the throne of the House of Atreus. After Clytemnestra and her lover, Aegisthus, murder Agamemnon, Orestes is sent into exile. According to *The Oresteia*, the trilogy written by Aeschylus in 458 B.C., Orestes returns to his homeland of Argos and, with the instigation of his sister, Electra, kills their mother and her lover to avenge his father's death. Orestes is pursued by the Furies, the three Greek goddesses who hunt down and punish wrongdoers. In the final play he is acquitted at trial in Athens, and the cycle of violence is replaced by a system of justice. Between 1942 and 1943 Sartre lectured on Greek theater at Charles Dullin's Ecole d'Art Dramatique in Paris. His familiarity with this trilogy provided the mythological background for *The Flies.*

4. André Gide (1869–1951), influential French writer and literary critic, was best known for *Les nourritures terrestres* (*The Fruits of the Earth*) (1897); see his *L'immoraliste* (*The Immoralist*) (Paris: Mercure de France, 1902) for the theme of lack of restraint.

5. Friedrich Nietzsche (1844–1900), German philosopher, discusses the will to power in several works, including the second essay of *On the Genealogy of Morals* (1887), section 12.

6. In French the word "conscience" can mean either "conscience" or "consciousness." Although Beauvoir often uses "conscience" to mean "consciousness," the translator has translated it as "conscience" in this context because it concerns judging one's own actions within oneself.

7. Søren Kierkegaard (1813–55), Danish religious philosopher, existentialist, and critic of rationalism, describes the anguish of the biblical Abraham in *Fear and Trembling*, trans. Walter Lowrie (Princeton: Princeton University Press, [1843] 1968); on Kierkegaard, see Beauvoir's "Pyrrhus and Cineas," in *Philosophical Writings*, ed. M. Simons, M. Timmermann, and M. B. Mader (Urbana: University of Illinois Press, 2004), 105.

8. Jean-Paul Sartre, *No Exit and Three Other Plays*, trans. Stuart Gilbert and Lionel Abel (New York: Vintage International, 1989), 117–20.

9. Sartre, "No Exit," 45.

10. Fresnes Prison, located near Paris, is the largest prison in France and was used by the Germans during World War II to house members of the French Resistance and the British Special Operations Executive agents.

11. Albert Camus, *L'étranger* (*The Stranger*) (Paris: Gallimard, 1942); *Le malentendu* (*The Misunderstanding*) (Paris: Gallimard, 1944), also published as *Cross Purpose.*

12. Caligula or Gaius Caesar Augustus Germanicus (A.D. 12–A.D. 41), a cruel, despotic Roman emperor, ruled from A.D. 37 until A.D. 41 when he was assassinated by his guards.

13. Albert Camus, *Caligula* (Paris: Gallimard, 1944), translated as "Caligula," by Stuart Gilbert, in *Caligula and Three Other Plays* (New York: Vintage Books/Random House, 1958), 7–9, 11–14.

14. *Les temps modernes* is a monthly French literary and political review founded by Jean-Paul Sartre, Simone de Beauvoir, and others in October 1945. Sartre's "Qu'est-ce que la littérature?" a manifesto of "littérature engagée" originally published in *Les temps modernes* in 1947, is translated by Bernard Frechtman in *What Is Literature? and Other Essays*, intro. Steven Ungar (Cambridge: Harvard University Press, 1988).

4

A Story I Used to Tell Myself

INTRODUCTION

by Ursula Tidd

In the following short radio broadcast, in which Simone de Beauvoir reflects upon her engagement with the autobiographical genre and its relation to fiction, a meta-narrative of her autobiographical project is briefly emplotted. Beauvoir echoes here certain of her "in-flight" observations on autobiography in *The Prime of Life* and *Force of Circumstance* and anticipates the lengthier and later analyses of the roles of fiction and autobiography of her 1966 lecture, "My Experience as a Writer," delivered in Japan.

As the title, "A Story I Used to Tell Myself," and certain of her comments in this broadcast suggest, there is an evolution in Beauvoir's conceptualization of her autobiographical project from life-writing as personal "story" to life-writing as "history," both stages of which mobilize the productive tensions of the French term "histoire." The narrating self as contingent narcissus, seeking ontological reassurance, swiftly abandons the solipsistic universe of *Memoirs of a Dutiful Daughter* to become the narrating, situated self who assumes a necessary commitment to others and to history in the production of autobiographical testimony. Throughout her extensive engagement with the genre of autobiography, however, Beauvoir will always—as she tells the reader of *The Prime of Life*—use her privilege as a writer, philosopher, and intellectual to prioritize self-narration over self-knowledge, firm in her conviction that her life story, if told with sincerity and clarity, can bridge the alienation between selves and others and facilitate a dialectical relationship between personal and collective "histories." In this way, Beauvoir rejects the Husserlian notion that there exists an unmediated consciousness transparent to itself and, in a move which anticipates Paul Ricoeur's notion of "narrative identity" (first adumbrated in his *Time and Narrative*), pursues a narrative quest for self and Other as they are mediated by language, literature and history.[1] In so doing, Beauvoir dismantles the Sartrean dichotomy of *Nausea*—that we must choose either to live or to narrate. For her, the concept of the "true story" is not an oxymoron but a necessity because the production of "true stories" is how we make sense of the world around us, even if these stories are more "*véridiques*" ("truthful," "corresponding to reality") than "*vraies*" ("true"). Indeed, Beauvoir's phenomenologically grounded choice is to live to narrate, to describe her lived experience in detail. Of paramount importance to her own engagement with autobiography are the stories of others—one thinks, for example, of her citing of George Eliot's *The Mill on the Floss* in *Memoirs of a Dutiful Daughter*, which suggests that, by a process of narrative identification, Eliot and Maggie Tulliver, the novel's protagonist, constituted significant precedents that shaped Beauvoir's own aspirations to become, respectively, a writer and an intellectual.[2]

In this radio broadcast, Beauvoir focuses on four main areas relating to her engagement with autobiography: her motives for writing autobiography; the impact of her wartime experience on the writing of her autobiography; the differences that she perceives between writing autobiography and fiction; and the relationship between time and narrative.

From Beauvoir's various statements on autobiography during the course of her writing career, one can distinguish, as already suggested, two stages in her engagement with the genre: the first encompassing the period until she begins writing *The Prime of Life*, marked by a somewhat solipsistic retreat into her childhood and early adult life, exiled as she felt at that time from the contemporary France of the 1950s in the grips of the Algerian War; the second, from *The Prime of Life* onward, inflected by her heightened political and historical consciousness, in which she effectively abandons her rather classical autobiographical approach in favor of a memorial encounter with history. As she explains here and elsewhere, from *The Prime of Life* onward, she refuses to avoid what she perceives as a responsibility to history in her ongoing project of autobiographical self-representation. In this, Beauvoir is always conscious of her privilege as one of the most prominent intellectuals of the postwar period and, as such, one who is also subjected to the myth-making of celebrity. One of her motives for continuing to write her memoirs is consequently to dispel misunderstandings about her life and choices. In conceptualizing autobiographical writing in this way, she constructs herself as the most authoritative witness to her life. This may seem, at surface level, rather grandiose; however, in so doing, Beauvoir deliberately assumes autobiographical agency and writes herself into an autobiographical tradition constructed, until relatively recently, as a predominantly male preserve by practitioners and literary critics alike. Beauvoir's self-construction as a testimonial figure can be interpreted, then, as a gender political strategy to inscribe a woman's life and presence into the traditionally patriarchal arenas of autobiographical literature and history.

If one cannot tell all in autobiography and never achieve a desired self-coincidence, one can aim, as Beauvoir explains here, to seize life in its contingent detail. When all is (not) said and done, this is one of the advantages of autobiographical writing—that it seems closer, in her view, to the contingent chaos of life, unlike fiction, which must be driven by the structuring of signification and the elimination of the merely gratuitous. In short, she recognizes a different set of reader(ly) expectations in the case of fiction, which allow its umbilical cord to the real to be severed on condition that life's loose ends are tidied up and art is allowed to exist beyond life.

Beauvoir's conceptualization of autobiography and fiction has certain implications for the organization of time and narrative, as she explains here. Unlike many of her contemporaries who wrote autobiographies, she adopts a largely chronological textual presentation until the final volume, *All Said and Done*. This choice is closely related to her own perception of time and aging—that as one ages, one's future shrinks and with that perception of abbreviated time comes a propensity to live in past and present moments. Although the life is lived in extension, it is de facto more usually remembered in narrative fragments. Consequently, autobiography cannot capture the temporal enchainment and depth of our lived experience, how each present moment is necessarily and deeply imbued with the past and yet portends the future. In fiction, however, the depth of that lived experience can sometimes be communicated to the reader by the manipulation of text-time and story-time, for example, in the use of "scene" in which story-duration and text-duration are considered identical. As Beauvoir observes here, in fiction, the narrator can linger on the representation of a few minutes in a character's life, thereby conveying the rich detail of lived experience. In autobiography, because of its referential relationship to the real and its traditional investment in verisimilitude, extensive use of detailed descriptions in "scene" is nevertheless restricted because of the impossibility of being able to "tell all." Beauvoir's judicious approach to autobiography is to opt for a relative balance between representing the contingent detail of "scene" in which, as Jeanson has argued, certain moments are represented as being definitive in the shaping of her "becoming," and the inevitable textual summary and condensation of life events.[3] Inevitably, such choices of narrative presentation can lead to accusations of "unnecessary" ellipsis and, perhaps, of falsification, as if "the whole truth and nothing but the truth" were somehow possible to represent. The autobiographical task is further complicated in Beauvoir's case because of the extent and generic diversity of her published corpus, so that episodes such as her 1947 trip to the United States are not related in detail in *Force of Circumstance*, as she explains here, but rather elsewhere in the alternative genres of travel diary in *America Day by Day* and of fiction in *The Mandarins.* Autobiographical material is, thus, necessarily reworked and re-presented in different textual forms.

In summary, this short broadcast provides the reader/listener with a valuable, if inevitably elliptical, reflection on the art of autobiography and fiction as practiced by Simone de Beauvoir.

NOTES

1. Paul Ricoeur, *Time and Narrative*, Vol. 3, trans. Kathleen Blamey and David Pellauer (Chicago: University of Chicago Press, 1988).

2. Simone de Beauvoir, *Memoirs of a Dutiful Daughter* (Harmondsworth: Penguin, 1963), 140; George Eliot, *The Mill on the Floss* (London: Blackwood, 1860).

3. Francis Jeanson, *Simone de Beauvoir ou l'entreprise de vivre* (Paris: Seuil, 1966), 108–109.

A STORY I USED TO TELL MYSELF

by Simone de Beauvoir

A SOUND RECORDING PRESENTED BY MARC BLANCPAIN

TRANSCRIPTION BY JULIEN BREINING AND SYLVIE LE BON DE BEAUVOIR

TRANSLATION AND NOTES BY

VERONIQUE ZAYTZEFF AND FREDERICK MORRISON

Side One

Marc Blancpain:[1]

We know about Simone de Beauvoir's life, because for the last seven years, she has devoted her efforts and talents to making it known to us. *Mémoires d'une jeune fille rangée* [*Memoirs of a Dutiful Daughter*], *La force de l'âge* [*The Prime of Life*], and *La force des choses* [*Force of Circumstance*], make up three volumes of autobiography that follow *Les Mandarins* [*The Mandarins*], which already was a harbinger of the memoirs.[2]

Simone de Beauvoir does not repudiate the novel. She knows that it goes further than the raw document, which always only skims, as she says so well, the surface of the moments. However, she states firmly, and I think with rea-

"Une histoire que je me racontais," a sound recording, was produced under the aegis of the Alliance Française and presented by Marc Blancpain. *Collection Français de notre temps, No. 24* (French of Our Time Collection, Number 24) (Paris): *Disques Culturels Français* (1963?), (French Cultural Records) 1 sound disc: 33 1/3 rpm, microgroove; 7 in. Manufacturer's number: 24 FT 63 Dunod.

son, that one cannot mix both genres in one without scrambling the cards. Usually, the memoirs of great writers are the work of their old age, a work that is supposed to be detached and endeavors to attain the serenity of a judge's decree, a work from beyond the tomb, as the greatest one of them said.[3]

Simone de Beauvoir is writing her memoirs on the brink of her maturity, at the time of *The Prime of Life* and *Force of Circumstance*, where she is wrestling every day with her private affairs as well as the harsh realities of her public life. And, she has naturally discovered the repercussion that a public life has on an engaged writer's private life and that she can no longer separate her own adventure from the collective one.

Simone de Beauvoir:

Sometimes I have been asked why I spent seven years writing my autobiography. For, as a matter of fact, it does represent an important part of my œuvre, in that there are three volumes: *Memoirs of a Dutiful Daughter*, *The Prime of Life*, and *Force of Circumstance*. I entitled the last volume *Force of Circumstance* because it covers the period from 1945 to 1962, and at the time, after the war, I became aware of the importance that circumstances have in the course of an existence, while previously, I had thought that my life was a story that I used to tell myself.

Therefore, this story is the continuation of the preceding one. To be quite honest, as soon as I began *The Prime of Life*, after *Memoirs of a Dutiful Daughter*, I had decided to relate my life more or less up to the moment where I found myself in the actual process of writing it. However, I stopped at the Liberation of Paris because I felt the need, as it were, to get my wind back, considering that *The Prime of Life* was already a very long volume and I also wanted to know what kind of reception the public would give it.[4] Because, in a certain way, it seemed rather arrogant of me to talk about myself so much. And I saw that, on the whole, my account had created a great deal of interest, and that, consequently, there were valid reasons to pursue it. There were certainly also reasons for not doing it. Many people told me, "After all, you say a lot more in your *Memoirs* than in your autobiography and since one cannot say absolutely everything, in a way, one falsifies reality. It would be better to wait and do it when you can be more detached and write it at a much later date." However, for all that, I disregarded those comments, because I wanted to tell about something that, for me, was still a totally live experience. And the recollections that one writes at age seventy or seventy-five can be charming, but they in no way have, in spite of everything else, the same sharp characteristics, as the recollections one has when almost still on the spot.

And specifically, in order to relate the transition from one age to the other, which is generally what happens during one's fifties, well, it is better to be within them than to have already left them behind completely. Moreover, I was also told that it was interesting to relate my youth when I was utterly unknown, so that basically, ever since I entered public life, the story of my life would be a sort of copy [*doublé*] of what was already known. In my opinion, the public dimension of an author's life is precisely nothing more than one single dimension, and I think that everything having a relation to my literary career is but one aspect of my private life. And that is exactly why I was trying to figure out, for myself as well as for the readers, what having a certain public existence means from a private point of view. I was also told that it was going to intersect with *The Mandarins*, but this statement was based on a considerable error made regarding *The Mandarins*, an error that, by the way, often annoyed me. They absolutely insisted in calling it an autobiography, while, in reality, it was truly a novel. A novel inspired by circumstances, inspired by the postwar era, by people I knew, by my own life, etc., but really transposed on a totally imaginary plane widely straying from reality. Incidentally, if one reads *Force of Circumstance*, one realizes that *The Mandarins* has absolutely none of the traits of a chronicle. Therefore, these objections did not seem valid to me—quite the contrary—perhaps because I indeed had had a public life that had given rise to many a misunderstanding—I mean my writings themselves and then the details of everything that publicity can tell about an author and has told about me. On the contrary, because of that, I wanted to put the record straight and show the reader my true face, whether he likes it or not, so that, in any case, he might detest me or like me for true reasons and not because of some legends that one could hawk about me and not because of some bad interpretations of my books. And I took this last volume as a sort of clarification regarding my attitude, whether private or public, as well as my own books, some of which, as I have already pointed out regarding *The Mandarins*, have been very badly misunderstood. I was particularly interested in revisiting *Le deuxième sexe* [*The Second Sex*] to know in what circumstances I had written it, and to show that it was not, as it had been said too often, a book of resentment, rancor, and discontent at being a woman, but that it was a totally impartial book.[5] In a word, this last volume gave me the opportunity to talk things over with my readers about my œuvre itself, much better than I had been able to do throughout the œuvre itself.

There is also another reason why I have written these books, this reason being that personally I really enjoy reading autobiographies and everything that is essentially a raw document, such as memoirs, recollections, newspapers, etc. There is a certain quality in the precise and factual truth that cannot be found in even the best, even the most inspired, even the most profound of novels.

Side Two

In the first place, in a novel there is an issue that always bothers me: the fact that nothing is ever gratuitous. Or, if it is gratuitous, then it is a waste. Without it, the story is always crafted so that a certain—I would not say a certain message, because I do not like this word very much—but at any rate, a certain signification can be derived from it. And even if one tries to conceal this signification, in this effort there is still something organized, well thought-out and intentional: never gratuitous. But in recollections, one retells events as they happened and simply because they happened that way. There is another advantage: due to the fact that one provides details rooted in the reality of the world, the world is, in brief, their guarantee; it lends them weight. If I say in a true story "I cried," that is enough for it to be moving. While in a novel, one will be forced, since everything is imaginary, to reconstruct the heroine's tears, to really convince the reader that the tears were shed, and one will be led into an entirely different style, to a tenor that is utterly different from the direct tone that can be so very lively and that can be had in an autobiography. It does not mean, incidentally, that I do not find disadvantages in autobiography as well. Especially as after having practiced it for almost seven years, I found myself rather sated with it and wanted to begin doing something completely different. There is, actually, a defect, which is that in the end, one is compelled to follow the chronology of the events and hardly has the opportunity to pause—naturally one is free, but the genre takes hold of you and carries you away almost despite yourself. Of course, one can make pauses, delve into certain details, meditate, reflect, and dream from time to time. Nevertheless, in the end, unless one truly wants to write an œuvre with no end in sight, unless one interrupts the rhythm of the story, one is led to heed the chronology and to skim, so to speak, the surface of the moments. While, in truth, both dimensions are present in an existence: at the same time these very instants follow each other, are linked together, and in this very minute each one has its own depth since it refers to the entire past and since, at the same time, it is pregnant with the whole future. And a novel can suggest this much more readily than an autobiography. One can linger on a morning, an hour, or several minutes and so give them a quite considerable depth. So, in other words, there are advantages with each of the two genres and I would not like to be exclusively confined to one or the other. Besides, I believe that one cannot mix them together. Because if the reader is placed in the situation of belief, of perception so to speak, he cannot, by the same token, ramble and dream. And sometimes there are writers who have tried to do both at the same time, but I find that they are then blurring the reader's sight because one does not focus in the same way on the realm of truth as on the realm of fancy. If need be one can put under one cover two different books, but this makes it truly two books. Personally, I prefer, on the one hand, to write autobiographies and, on the other hand, to write novels, without combining them.

The third volume of my memoirs spans a period of time which was extremely rich in historical events, in public events and also rich for me in private events, for, due precisely to the fact that I was a writer, I was able to make many trips, have numerous encounters and a great many opportunities that I did not have in my former existence. From the point of view of the book's composition, it had, of course, advantages, since it allowed me to make the reader a participant in a rich experience. It also had its disadvantages because there were so many things that I could not conjure everything up, and incidentally, some of these things had been mentioned already in other books. Consequently, there is a certain imbalance in this last work. For example, I speak very little of the [1947] trip to America, which was very important to me, since I had already told about it in *L'Amérique au jour le jour* [*America Day by Day*];[6] neither did I speak about the [1955] trip to China—which was also very important—while at the same time I devote some sixty pages to the [1960] trip to Brazil, a trip that was very interesting, but did not amount to such an exceptional experience.[7] It simply amused me to talk about it, because I had not previously mentioned it. Likewise, I am far from having talked about all the books, all the movies—I made a choice, at times, rather capricious, and somewhat arbitrary, considering the fact that now the things I encountered no longer had the same formative power they might have had in my youth or in what I called "the prime of life" [*la force de l'âge*]. It is quite obvious that things appealed to me and interested me; however, nothing fundamentally modified my way of thinking or my way of being. What certainly had more importance than the people encountered, the books read, the movies seen, were the historical events. It was mainly history which has truly been the cause of the great changes, even inner ones, that I might have undergone because I lived history much more closely than I did prior to the war, having learned during the war precisely how much I was linked to history, being unable now to separate my own adventure from the collective adventure. History was, predictably enough, extremely rich, but at times also extremely painful. We began with the great joys of the Liberation, in short with all the celebrations that followed and which were translated into the warmest friendships with all those who had been on our side. After that, there was what was called the failure of the Resistance, that is to say, those who temporarily had found themselves united by their refusal of the Occupation were once again actually split into two camps; the class struggle was once again rediscovered, and it was necessary to make choices. That was not always very easy since during the Stalinist era, one could not choose the USSR with a light heart, even if one was, as I was, entirely opposed to the Western Alliance. Later, throughout the world a total evolution took place, which turned out to be much more fortunate, since after the Twentieth Congress, we were able frankly to join forces with the East and to see in the USSR, an unconditional ally.[8] However, this joy was spoiled by the events taking place in France itself. There was the War in Indochina, and there was the War in Algeria, which was much closer and much more painful, because it was closer to home and because we were engaged. This war was for me a very painful experience, because I lived it mostly as a part of a small group of friends, utterly on the sidelines of my own country, against it, something that one cannot enjoy doing, and it was at that moment that I felt like a kind of exile in my own country. Now the war is over. A new era is opening, but the war was obviously an experience that profoundly affected me and that I will certainly never forget.

NOTES

1. Marc Blancpain (1909–2001) was born in Nouvion and was a prisoner of war between 1940 and 1943. In 1944, he was named secretary-general of the Alliance Française and then was its president from 1976–94. He was a historian, novelist, essayist, and author of short novels.

2. *Mémoires d'une jeune fille rangée* (Paris: Gallimard, 1958), translated as *Memoirs of a Dutiful Daughter*, trans. James Kirkup (New York: Harper and Row, 1959); *La force de l'âge* (Paris: Gallimard, 1960), translated as *The Prime of Life*, trans. Peter Green (New York: World Publishing, 1962); *La force des choses*, 2 Vols. (Paris: Gallimard, 1963), translated as *Force of Circumstance*, 2 Vols., trans. Richard Howard (New York: G. P. Putnam's, 1964, 1965); *Les Mandarins* (Paris: Gallimard, 1954), translated as *The Mandarins*, trans. Leonard Friedman (New York: World Publishing, 1956).

3. Blancpain refers to François-René de Chateaubriand's (1768–1848) *Les mémoires d'outre-tombe* (1847), translated by Robert Baldick as *Memoirs from beyond the Tomb* (New York: Knopf, 1961).

4. Paris was liberated from German occupation on August 25, 1944.

5. *Le deuxième sexe*, 2 Vols. (Paris: Gallimard, 1949); *The Second Sex*, trans. H. M. Parshley (New York: Knopf, 1952), and more recently translated by Constance Borde and Sheila Malovany-Chevallier (New York: Vintage Books, 2010).

6. *L'Amérique au jour le jour* (Paris: Gallimard, 1948), translated by Carol Cosman as *America Day by Day* (Berkeley: University of California, 1999).

7. Beauvoir chronicled her 1955 trip to China in *La longue marche: Essai sur la Chine* (Paris: Gallimard, 1957); translated by Austryn Wainhouse, as *The Long March: An Account of Modern China* (London: Phoenix, 2001).

8. The Twentieth Congress of the Communist Party of the Soviet Union, which took place February 14–25, 1956, marked the beginning of First Secretary Nikita S. Khrushchev's program to repudiate Stalinism in the Soviet Union.

5

Preface to *La Bâtarde* by Violette Leduc

INTRODUCTION

by Alison S. Fell

"I took great pleasure in writing a preface for Violette Leduc's *La bâtarde* [The Bastard]. I liked all her books, and this one more than the rest. I read them again, trying to make out just what it was that gave them their value and trying to pass on that understanding" comments Beauvoir in *Tout compte fait* (*All Said and Done*) as she reviews and reflects on her 1960s literary output.[1] Beauvoir's preface to Violette Leduc's sixth published work and first volume of autobiography was published in 1964. *La bâtarde* tells the story of Leduc's life from her birth in 1907 until the end of the Second World War. It focuses on her difficult relationship with her mother, her various intense and doomed love affairs (with both men and women), and her increasing contentment during the Occupation as she begins to write and make money by trafficking goods on the black market.[2] Beauvoir's preface constituted not only the first comprehensive analysis of Leduc's writing, but also the culmination of a collaboration that had begun more than twenty years earlier. When Beauvoir agreed to read the manuscript of Leduc's first novel, *L'asphyxie* (*In the Prison of Her Skin*) in 1945, she imagined initially it would contain nothing more than the "confessions of a woman of the world."[3] Instead, she was immediately impressed by Leduc's writing, stating in a later interview that "she had a tone, a style, a manner that appealed to me right away."[4]

Convinced of Leduc's worth as a novelist, Beauvoir became her most important mentor and literary advisor, meeting her every two weeks to comment on what she had produced. That Beauvoir's editorial influence on Leduc's oeuvre was enormous is not in doubt, but her support of Leduc's work went much further than the numerous cuts and corrections she made to her manuscripts. Beauvoir introduced her to many of her own acquaintances, including writers such as Nathalie Sarraute and Colette Audry, and it was through Beauvoir that Albert Camus became interested in *L'asphyxie*, which he published in his *Espoir* series for Gallimard in 1946. When Leduc's novels failed to sell, Beauvoir also offered financial support, arranging in 1948 for a small monthly stipend to be paid to Leduc (ostensibly by Gaston Gallimard, who happily went along with the deception) and paying for psychiatric treatment in a clinic when she became concerned about Leduc's deteriorating mental health in 1956. Beauvoir's input into *La Bâtarde* was particularly significant. It was Beauvoir who first suggested to Leduc in the late 1950s that she begin work on an autobiography, and who came up with the striking title (Leduc had originally thought of *La cage* [The Cage] as a possibility).[5] Her long preface to the work, moreover, provided the author with an enthusiastic endorsement from "la grande sartreuse" that, as Elizabeth Locey comments, "helped [. . .] to deliver Violette Leduc from obscurity by boosting her from the Parisian literary scene into the public eye."[6] The preface functioned as an excellent marketing tool, and *La bâtarde* sold 170,000 copies in a few months. Beauvoir was delighted that her faith in Leduc's talent had finally been justified by high sales figures and widespread critical acclaim.

But perhaps Beauvoir's most important role for Leduc was not that of patron, editor, or financial support, but that of muse. On a personal level, relations between the two women were often fraught. Leduc was sexually attracted to Beauvoir, who was also for Leduc a mythical mother-figure or idol to be worshipped.[7] In a letter written in 1950, for example, Leduc relates how she erected a kind of shrine to Beauvoir: "I had written a short note to the Gallimard press office, asking for your photograph. They sent it to me straight away. It arrived this morning, and is on my table, against a jar that I've filled with some tall flowers. [. . .] It's the Harcourt photograph, the one I often saw in bookshop windows."[8] As a successful author and, in Leduc's eyes, beautiful and desirable woman, Beauvoir appeared to embody everything Leduc wished to be and yet felt she would never become. In contrast,

Beauvoir's letters to Nelson Algren reveal a despairing exasperation in relation to the excesses of Leduc's devotion to her. In one letter, for example, she comments: "I don't really care for her and she knows it. What is strange is she can talk very freely about her love for me and discuss it as if it were a disease. Nevertheless, you can guess that to spend an evening with her is not a very easy thing [. . .] I hate leaving her in the streets, alone and hopeless and thinking of death. But what may I do? Too much kindness would be the worst of all. Anyhow, I could never kiss her and that is the question."[9] Beauvoir's reservations led to a desire to set up clear boundaries between them. She admits in an interview with Isabelle de Courtivron, for instance, that she "established a certain distance from the very beginning" and "blocked [her] self," considering Leduc's writing "exclusively as literature."[10] Leduc's obsessive desire, on the other hand, led to insecurities and despair, which she never ceases to express in her almost daily letters to her inaccessible beloved.[11]

But despite the emotional difficulties Leduc's adoration of Beauvoir provoked, she was able productively to transform her passion into writing. Beauvoir plays a central role in nearly all of Leduc's works, not only in her volumes of autobiography, but also in *L'affamée* (The Starveling), an account in diary form of Leduc's passion for "Madame," a thinly disguised version of Beauvoir, and *Trésors à prendre* (Treasures for the Taking) a travel journal that describes Leduc's retracing of a trip taken by Beauvoir and Sartre. Isabelle de Courtivron persuasively argues that these texts exploit the language and conventions of mysticism as Leduc transforms Beauvoir into a saintly icon. While the first meeting with Beauvoir is narrated in *L'affamée* as a "conversion," the first stage of the mystical experience, *Trésors à prendre* is a mystic's tale of a pilgrimage. Leduc's writing can be read as a quest mediated by the sanctification of Beauvoir, who functions as "the primary catalyst, the marker who traces the road figuratively, (and literally in the case of *Trésors à prendre*), that leads Leduc from the mortification of the sinner-bastard to the discipline of the writer-novice."[12] At the end of the quest Leduc's narrator is "re-born" in the mold of Beauvoir, her goddess-muse. Her new identity is that of a woman writer, a vocation she consistently evokes in quasireligious terms.

The relationship of influence between the two writers was not as unidirectional, however, as it may first appear. Beauvoir derived great satisfaction from editing and exploring the works of other writers, as she confirms in *Tout compte fait* when discussing the preface she wrote for *La bâtarde*: "Immersing oneself in another writer's work, turning it into your whole world, trying to discover their cohesion and their diversity, to plumb the writer's intentions and to display his methods—all this means traveling outside oneself; and I have always delighted in changing my surroundings."[13] And she was particularly fascinated by the writings of Leduc. This is evident, for example, in her use of Leduc's works as examples to illustrate her arguments in the second volume of *Le deuxième sexe* (*The Second Sex*). *L'asphyxie* is cited on four occasions in order to provide the reader with a case of damaging maternal behavior, and *Ravages* (Ravages) is also referred to as an example of the possessive tendencies displayed by the "amoureuse" (woman in love).[14] Like the many other extracts from diaries, letters, and literature to which Beauvoir refers in *Le deuxième sexe*, Leduc's literary portraits (either of her mother or of herself) function as case studies that support Beauvoir's philosophical conclusions about the maternal and amorous behavior of women trapped in a state of bad faith. To some extent, the preface to *La bâtarde* also depicts Leduc as a "case"—albeit an unusual one—to be considered and analyzed. Beauvoir picks up on Leduc's ironic reversal of Rousseau in her opening sentence: "My case is not unique." She then sets out the terms in which we can make sense of the case study of a woman who begins her autobiography by defiantly proclaiming her status as illegitimate and ugly. In this light, Beauvoir's preface can be considered to have much in common with Sartre's *Saint Genet, comédien et martyr* (*Saint Genet, Actor and Martyr*), revealing an individual's emancipation through art from the role of social outcast. For Sartre and Beauvoir, Genet and Leduc are both seen to have rejected moral absolutes, to have renounced the names of "thief" or "bastard" in favor of that of "writer."

Beauvoir's preface thus functions not only to elucidate *La bâtarde* and its author, but also to illustrate and corroborate some of her philosophical beliefs. Hélène Jaccomard suggests, for example, that Beauvoir's preface "serves the book and makes use of it: the existentialist framework of her reading [. . .] is coupled with feminist beliefs, the theory elucidating the text, and the text endorsing the theory."[15] The heroine of *La bâtarde* is presented as an individual dominated by guilt and shame, negative emotions that are reinforced by the accusing gaze of the other, primarily embodied for the protagonist in her mother, Berthe. Beauvoir then analyzes the series of damaging self-other relationships in which the heroine becomes embroiled according to an existential understanding of intersubjectivity. She argues that the love affairs depicted in *La bâtarde* follow the same pattern as the oppressive mother-daughter relationship.[16] In Leduc's literary universe, in other words, lovers are masters or slaves, and no real exchange or reciprocity is possible: "either the other is an object for her, or she becomes an object for the other." But while an inattentive reader will see "only a series of chance happenings" in Leduc's unhappy story, Beauvoir unearths a very different narrative: "In reality, it is about a choice that is maintained and renewed over fifteen years before culminating in a literary work." Beauvoir concludes that Leduc's narratively transcribed life demonstrates, despite its apparently chaotic nature, an individual's lucid choice of her own destiny. In the case of Leduc, the choice was to become a writer. In effect, Beauvoir defines Leduc's life-choices according to an existentialist and feminist framework; her decision to write is read as a woman's willingness to take responsibility for her own destiny and so free herself from the shackles of a life lived in bad faith. For Beauvoir, in short, writing represents a salvation for Leduc that she needed in order to escape from the "infernal machine" of her tyrannical relationships: "The failure to connect with others has resulted in that privileged form of communication—a work of art."

Beauvoir's reading of *La bâtarde* has been enormously influential for literary critics considering Leduc's oeuvre.[17] Certain commentators, however, have pointed to some limitations of her reading of Leduc's autobiography. Her assertion that it is possible to consider the structure of *La bâtarde* as goal-oriented rather than "a series of chance happenings," for example, arguably does not explain the cyclical patterning and lyrical digressions that disrupt the chronology of Leduc's life-story. Indeed, the narrator's description in the opening paragraph of her vainly chewing over the past as if chewing on a wilted lettuce leaf from which she will gain no nourishment scarcely implies the kind of triumphant advancement toward a self-created destiny and liberation through art suggested by Beauvoir. In effect, the structure, tenor, and implications of Leduc's and Beauvoir's autobiographical practice differ greatly, and it is possible to argue that Beauvoir does not take these differences sufficiently into account. Mireille Brioude notes that "[in Leduc's autobiography] anything intellectual is deliberately devalued. The autobiography does not tell the story of the development of a way of thinking, an approach which is radically opposed to that of Simone de Beauvoir."[18] De Courtivron concurs that unlike Beauvoir's *Mémoires d'une jeune fille rangée* (*Memoirs of a Dutiful Daughter*), "the retrospective view of life communicated in Leduc's autobiographies does not, in any way, impose a rational and distanced perspective on this disordered life experience."[19] Other critics have quibbled over Beauvoir's praise of Leduc's "intrepid sincerity," suggesting that this overlooks the subtle interplay between art and reality, and between the "I" of the narrator and "she" of the fictionalized former self, that characterizes Leduc's work. Leduc's narrator freely admits in later volumes of autobiography to distorting facts for literary ends, which goes against Beauvoir's insistence on the importance of autobiographical "truth" and contradicts her emphasis on the frankness and refreshing honesty of the narrator of *La bâtarde*.

If later analyses of Leduc's writing have productively foregrounded aspects other than those focused upon by Beauvoir, however, her essay remains an impressive piece of literary criticism. Her shrewd observations on the role of objects and the erotic in the work, and her careful and detailed examination of Leduc's style serve to defend her from accusations of an overly dogmatic philosophical interpretation. The attraction of Leduc's writing for Beauvoir lies, perhaps, in the very differences that oppose their styles and approaches. If we turn the tables, we can attempt to read between the lines of Beauvoir's analysis of Leduc in order to investigate Beauvoir's own motivations and concerns. It can be argued, for example, that Beauvoir in her own autobiography "disciplined herself not to express her anxiety and rage for fear of shattering her carefully constructed image" and thus in Leduc's work "found relief in splitting herself off to merge with the passionate and chaotic Violette, her other, darker side."[20] From this perspective, Beauvoir's immersion in Leduc's literary world allowed her to experience vicariously areas of her emotional life (sexual passion, lesbian desire, jealousy, depression, insecurity, madness, etc.) that remained relatively taboo in her own autobiographical writing. But whatever the personal and psychological reasons for Beauvoir's readerly seduction, it is clear that her preface to Leduc's best-known work has played a crucial role in introducing, promoting and shedding light on Leduc's writing for countless readers. It stands, therefore, as a fitting tribute to what was an important and unique relationship for both women.

NOTES

1. Simone de Beauvoir, *Tout compte fait* (Paris: Gallimard, Folio, 1972), 170; trans. P. O'Brian *All Said and Done* (London: Deutsch, Weidenfeld and Nicolson, 1974), 134.

2. For discussions of *La bâtarde* as an Occupation narrative, see Alison S. Fell, "Literary Trafficking: Performing Identity in Violette Leduc's *La bâtarde*," *Modern Language Review* 98:4 (2003): 870–80; Elizabeth A. Houlding, " 'L'envers de la guerre': The Occupation of Violette Leduc," in *Gender and Fascism in Modern France*, ed. Melanie Hawthorn and Richard J. Golston (Hanover, N.H.: University Press of New England, 1997), 83–100.

3. Simone de Beauvoir, *La force des choses*, Folio ed., 2 Vols. (Paris: Gallimard, 1963), I, 35; *Force of Circumstance*, trans. R. Howard, 2 Vols. (New York: Harper and Row, 1963), I, 19.

4. Unpublished interview with Isabelle de Courtivron, June 1983, cited in Isabelle de Courtivron, "From Bastard to Pilgrim: Rites and Writing for Madame," *Yale French Studies* 72 (1986): 145.

5. Leduc writes in a letter of June 18, 1963 to Beauvoir that "the book will be called *The Cage*." Cited in Carlo Jansiti, *Violette Leduc* (Paris: Grasset, 1999), 361.

6. Elizabeth Locey, *The Pleasures of the Text: Violette Leduc and Reader Seduction* (Lanham, Md: Rowman and Littlefield, 2002), 4.

7. For discussions of Beauvoir as Leduc's "mythical mother" see Mireille Brioude, *Violette Leduc: la mise en scène du "je"* (Violette Leduc: the Theatrical "I") (Amsterdam and Atlanta: Rodopi, 2000), 113–15; Colette Trout Hall, *Violette Leduc la mal-aimée* (Violette Leduc, Unloved) (Amsterdam and Atlanta: Rodopi, 1999), 66–68. Critics have also argued that Leduc's obsessive passion for Beauvoir stems from the latter's embodiment of both the masculine, or the father (in her authorship) and the feminine, or the mother (in her beauty/feminine allure).

8. Violette Leduc, "Lettres à Simone de Beauvoir," ("Letters to Simone de Beauvoir") *Les temps modernes* 495 (1987), 33. [my translation]

9. Simone de Beauvoir, *Beloved Chicago Man: Letters to Nelson Algren 1947–64* (London: Phoenix Giant, 1999), 27.

10. Unpublished interview with Isabelle de Courtivron, June 1983, cited in de Courtivron, "From Bastard to Pilgrim," 143–48.

11. See Leduc, "Lettres" and Jansiti, *Violette Leduc* for numerous examples.

12. de Courtivron, "From Bastard to Pilgrim," 143. See also Nina Bouraoui, "Violette Leduc: l'écriture comme pratique amoureuse," ("Violette Leduc: Writing as an Exercise in Love") *Magazine Littéraire* 426 (2003): 47.

13. Beauvoir, *Tout compte fait*, 170; *All Said and Done*, 134.

14. See Simone de Beauvoir, *Le deuxième sexe*, Folio ed., 2 Vols (Paris: Gallimard, 1949), II, 48, 79, 373, 380, 565–66.

15. Hélène Jaccomard, *Lecteur et lecture dans l'autobiographie française contemporaine* (Reader and Reading in Contemporary French Autobiography) (Geneva: Droz, 1993), 165. [my translation]

16. For further discussion of mother-daughter relationships in Beauvoir and Leduc, see Alison S. Fell, *Liberty, Equality, Maternity in Beauvoir, Leduc and Ernaux* (Oxford: Legenda, 2003).

17. Beauvoir's preface is referred to in every major critical study of Leduc, many of which concur with her existential analysis. Alex Hughes notes, for example, that Beauvoir's analysis "led the authors of several works dealing with modern French literature to suggest that Leduc's writing might have Existential implications." Alex Hughes, *Violette Leduc: Mothers, Lovers and Language* (London: W. S.Maney and Sons, 1994), 6.

18. Brioude, *Violette Leduc*, 87. [my translation]

19. Isabelle de Courtivron, *Violette Leduc* (Boston: Twayne, 1985), 54.

20. de Courtivron, "From Bastard to Pilgrim," 146.

PREFACE TO *LA BÂTARDE* BY VIOLETTE LEDUC

by Simone de Beauvoir

TRANSLATION BY MARYBETH TIMMERMANN

NOTES BY JANELLA D. MOY

When, early in 1945, I began to read Violette Leduc's manuscript—"My mother never gave me her hand"—I was immediately taken by her temperament and her style.[1] Camus welcomed *L'asphyxie* [*In the Prison of Her Skin*] right away into his *Espoir* [Hope] series.[2] Genet, Jouhandeau, and Sartre hailed the arrival of a writer.[3] In the books that followed, her talent was confirmed. Exacting critics openly praised it. But the public did not respond. Despite a considerable *succès d'estime*, Violette Leduc has remained obscure.

They say that there are no longer any unknown authors; anyone, or almost anyone can get published. But that is exactly why mediocrity flourishes. The good seed is choked out by the weeds. Success depends most of the time on a stroke of luck. Yet even bad luck has its reasons. Violette Leduc does not try to please; she does not please and what's more, she frightens. The titles of her books—*L'asphyxie*, *L'affamée* [The Starveling], *Ravages* [Ravages]—are not pleasant. Paging through them, one glimpses a world full of noise and fury, where love often bears the name of hate, where a passion for living cries out in howls of despair; a world devastated by loneliness that seems arid from

Simone de Beauvoir, "Préface" to *La bâtarde*, by Violette Leduc (Paris: Gallimard, 1964). Translated by Derek Coltman as *La Bâtarde* (London: Virago, [1965] 1985).

afar. It is not. "I am a desert talking to myself," Violette Leduc wrote to me one day. I have encountered innumerable beauties in deserts. And whoever speaks to us from the depths of loneliness speaks to us about ourselves. The most worldly or the most militant man has his undergrowth where no one ventures, not even himself, but which is there: the darkness of childhood, the failures, the renunciations, the sudden distress at a cloud in the sky. We have all cherished the impossible dream of catching a scene or a being as it exists in our absence. If we read *La bâtarde*, this dream is almost realized. A woman delves into the most secret parts of herself, and she tells us about it with an unflinching sincerity, as if there were no one listening to her.

"My case is not unique," says Violette Leduc as she begins her narrative. No, but it is singular and significant. It shows with exceptional clarity that a life is the reworking of one's destiny by one's freedom.

Right from the first page, the author overwhelms us with the heavy misfortunes that shaped her. During her entire childhood, her mother instilled an irreparable feeling of guilt in her: guilty for having been born, for having fragile health, for costing money, for being a woman doomed to the hardships of the feminine condition. She saw her own reflection in two hard, blue eyes: a living offense. By her tenderness, her grandmother preserved her from total destruction. Violette Leduc owes her grandmother for having safeguarded her vitality and sense of equilibrium that, in the worst moments of her life, prevented her from going under. But the role of "the angelic Fidéline" was only secondary, and she died early. The Other was embodied in her steely-eyed mother. Dominated and humiliated by her, the child wanted to annihilate herself completely. She idolized her mother; she engraved her mother's law within herself: flee from men. She dedicated herself to serving her mother and made her a gift of her future. When her mother got married, the little girl was shattered by this betrayal. From then on she was scared of all other consciousnesses because they held the power of turning her into a monster, and of any presence because it risked fading away into absence. She curled up within herself. Anguished, disappointed, resentful, she chose narcissism, egocentrism, and solitude.

"My ugliness will isolate me until my death," writes Violette Leduc.* This interpretation does not satisfy me. The woman depicted in *La bâtarde* interests fashion designers—Lelong, Fath—so much that they are happy to give her their most daring creations. She inspires a passion in Isabelle; in Hermine, an ardent love that lasts for years; in Gabriel, feelings violent enough

**L'affamée.*

for him to marry her; in Maurice Sachs a decided affinity. Her "big nose" discourages neither companionship nor friendship. Though she sometimes makes others laugh, it is not because of her nose. There is something provocative and unusual in her clothes, her hairstyle, her facial features. They tease her in order to reassure themselves. Her ugliness did not control her destiny but symbolized it; she searched in her mirror for reasons to pity herself.

For, after adolescence, she found herself stuck in an infernal machine. She has made her lot out of this loneliness which she detests, and because she detests it, she plunges deeper into it. Neither hermit nor exile, her misfortune is to never experience a reciprocal relationship with anyone. Either the other is an object for her, or she makes herself an object for the other. Her inability to communicate is apparent in the dialogues that she writes; the speakers are side by side, but do not respond to each other. They each have their own language; they do not understand each other. Even in love, especially in love, any exchange is impossible, because Violette Leduc will not accept a state of duality in which the risk of separation is always lurking. Every breakup intolerably revives the trauma she experienced at the age of fourteen: her mother's marriage. "I don't want anyone to leave me" is the leitmotiv of *Ravages*. So the couple must be only one single being. At times, Violette Leduc claims to annihilate herself, playing the game of masochism. But she has too much energy and lucidity to continue for long. It is she who will devour the beloved being.

Jealous and possessive, she finds it hard to tolerate Hermine's affection for her family, Gabriel's relationships with his mother and his sister, and his friendships with men. She demands that her girlfriend devote every second to her after the workday is finished; Hermine cooks and sews for her, listens to her grievances, drowns with her in pleasure and gives in to her every whim. Hermine demands nothing in return, except to sleep at night. Violette, who has insomnia, rebels against this desertion. Later, she also forbids Gabriel to sleep. "I hate sleepers." She shakes them, wakes them up, and, by tears or caresses, makes them keep their eyes open. Less docile than Hermine, Gabriel intends to keep his job and spend his time as he pleases. Each morning, when he wants to leave, Violette tries everything to bring him back into their bed. She attributes this tyranny to her "insatiable loins." In fact, what she desires is something quite different than sensual pleasure; it is possession. When she gives Gabriel pleasure, when she receives him within her, he belongs to her; their union is realized. As soon as he leaves her arms, he again becomes the enemy: an other.

"Identical mirages of presence and absence."* Absence is torture: the anguished wait for a presence, and presence is an interval between two absences: a torment. Violette Leduc detests her torturers. Each of them—and everyone—has a complicity with himself that excludes her, and they also possess certain qualities of which she is deprived. She feels wronged. She envies Hermine's good health, her stability, her activity, her cheerfulness. She envies Gabriel because he is a man. The only way she can ruin their privileges is by destroying their entire person, which is what she tries to do.

"You want to destroy me," says Gabriel. Yes, she does, in order to eliminate that which differentiates them, and in order to take her revenge. "I was taking revenge for her too-perfect presence," she says with regards to Hermine. When, one after the other, they leave her forever, she despairs, and yet she has reached her goal. Secretly she wanted to shatter each relationship and marriage, because she craves failure and because she aims at her own destruction. She is "the praying mantis devouring herself." But she is too healthy to work only for her ruin. The truth is, she loses in order to both lose and win. Her break-ups are recoveries of her self.

Through storms and lulls, she always makes the effort to protect herself, and this is her strength. She never gives herself entirely. After a few ardent weeks, she quickly arranges to avoid Isabelle's passion. When she first starts living with Hermine, she fights to continue working and providing for her own needs. Defeated by the doctor, her mother, and Hermine, dependence weighs her down. She escapes from it thanks to her ambiguous friendship with Gabriel which remains secret for a long time. Once married to him, she contests that bond by developing a burning desire for Maurice Sachs. When Sachs, who left to work in Hamburg, wants to return to the village where they spent a few months together, she refuses to help him. Transporting suitcases full of black-market butter and meat with her own two hands, amassing a fortune, exhausted and triumphant, she experiences the intoxication of surpassing herself. Sachs would disturb the universe over which she reigns, straight and proud as a cypress tree. "If he returns, the earth will swallow me up again."

Others always frustrate her, hurt her, humiliate her. When she grapples with the world, without help, when she has a job and is successful, she is uplifted with joy. This sniveling girl is also the traveler who, in *Trésors à prendre* [Treasures for the Taking] backpacks across France, intoxicated by

L'affamée

her discoveries and by her own energy. A self-sufficient woman: this is the role that pleases Violette Leduc. "I was going all the way in my efforts; finally I was existing."

Yet she needs to love. She needs someone to whom she can dedicate her joyous élans, her sorrows, her enthusiasms. The ideal would be to devote herself to a being who does not encumber her with his presence, to whom she could give everything without anything being taken from her. This is why she cherishes Fidéline—"My little pippin who never grows old"—marvelously embalmed in her memory, and Isabelle, who became a dazzling idol in the depths of the past. She invokes these figures, caresses herself as she imagines them, prostrates herself at their feet. Her heart beats wildly for an absent and already lost Hermine. She falls in love at first sight with Maurice Sachs, and later with two other homosexuals. The obstacle that separates her from them is as insurmountable as a light-year; in their company she "burns in the fires of the impossible." There is sensual pleasure in an unquenched desire when it contains no hope. The woman whom Violette Leduc calls Madame in *L'affamée* is no less inaccessible. In *La vieille fille et le mort* [The Old Maid and the Dead Man], the fantasy of an unreciprocated love, in which the other has been reduced to the passivity of a thing, is pushed to the extreme by the author. One evening Miss Clarisse, an old maid at the age of fifty—not because men have neglected her, but because she has been disdainful of them—finds the dead body of a stranger in the café adjacent to her grocery store. She lavishes her attention and tenderness upon him, and he does not disturb her effusions. She talks to him and invents his responses. But the illusion fades; since he has received nothing, she has given nothing. He has not given her new warmth, and she finds herself alone in front of a corpse. For Violette Leduc, love from a distance is as destructive as shared love.

"You will never be satisfied," Hermine tells her. Hermine destroys her by overwhelming her with her gifts, and Gabriel does the same by withholding himself. Presence drives her to madness; absence devastates her. She gives us the key to this malediction: "I came into the world, and I vowed to have a passion for the impossible." This passion took possession of her on the day when, betrayed by her mother, she took refuge in the phantom of her unknown father. This father had existed, and he was a myth. By entering into his universe, she entered into a legend. She chose the imaginary, which is one of the forms assumed by the impossible. He had been rich and refined; she brought his tastes back to life, without hoping to satisfy them. In her twenties, she coveted the luxuries of Paris to a dizzying extent: furniture, clothes, jewels, beautiful cars. But she did not make the slightest effort to attain them. "What did I want? To do nothing and possess everything." The dream of grandeur counted more that the grandeur itself. She lives off symbols. She transfigures the moments of her life by performing rites: the apéritif shared in the basement with Hermine and the champagne with her mother belong to a fictitious life. She disguises herself when, to the sound of unreal drums, she slips on the eel-colored Schiaparelli suit, and her walk along the Paris boulevards is a parody.

However, these delusions do not satisfy her. From her rural childhood, she has retained the need to hold something solid in her hands, to feel the weight of her feet on the ground, to accomplish true acts. To fabricate reality with the imaginary is the distinction of artists and writers, and she gradually moves toward this answer to her dilemma.

In her relationships with others, she had simply assumed her destiny. She invents an unexpected meaning for it when she turns to literature. Everything started the day she entered a bookstore to ask for a book by Jules Romains.[4] In her narrative, she does not emphasize the importance of this fact whose consequences she obviously did not suspect at the time. An inattentive reader will only see a series of chance happenings in her story. In reality, it is about a choice that is maintained and renewed over fifteen years before culminating in a literary work.

As long as she lived in the shadow of her mother, Violette Leduc scorned books. She preferred to steal a cabbage from the back of a cart, pick grass for the rabbits, chat, live. From the day that she turned to her father, books—something he had loved—fascinated her. Solid and shiny, they held worlds where the impossible becomes possible under their beautiful, glossy covers. She bought and devoured *Mort de quelqu'un* [*The Death of a Nobody*].[5] Romains. Duhamel. Gide.[6] She was never to let them out of her life again. When she decides to start a career, she puts an ad in the *Bibliographie de la France* [Bibliography of France]. She starts at a publishing house where she writes gossip columns. She doesn't yet dare to think of writing books, but she revels in famous names and faces. After her break-up with Hermine, she arranges to work for a film producer; reading synopses, and making suggestions for changes to them. As such she alters the course of her existence and brings about her fortunate encounter with Maurice Sachs. She interests him; he appreciates her letters; he advises her to write. She begins with short stories and articles that she writes for a woman's magazine. Later, tired of her dwelling upon her childhood memories, he tells her: write them down, then! The result would be *L'asphyxie*.

She immediately understood that literary creation could be a salvation for her. "I will write; I will open up my arms; I will embrace the fruit trees; I will give them to my piece of paper." It is a sardonic game to speak to the dead, to the deaf, to things. The reader provides the impossible synthesis of absence and presence. "Today, Reader, the month of August is a rosette glowing with heat. I offer it to you; I give it to you." He receives this gift without disturbing the author's solitude. He listens to her monologue; he doesn't respond to it, but he justifies it.

Still, it is necessary to have something to tell him. Violette Leduc is in love with the impossible, yet she has not lost contact with the world. On the contrary, she clutches it to her in order to fill her loneliness. Her unique [*singulière*] situation protects her against prefabricated visions. Ricocheting from failure to nostalgia, she takes nothing for granted. She tirelessly questions and recreates with words what she has discovered. It is because she had so much to say that her weary listener put a pen in her hands.

Since she is obsessed with herself, all her works—except *Les boutons dorés* [The Golden Buttons]—are more or less autobiographical: memoirs, a love affair, or rather an absence of one, a travel diary, a novel which transposes a period of her life, a lengthy novella that plays out her fantasies, and finally *La bâtarde*, which revisits and surpasses her previous books.

The wealth of her narratives comes less from circumstances than from the burning intensity of her memory: at every moment she is there in entirety piercing through the thick layers of time. Every woman she loves brings Isabelle back to life, herself the reincarnation of a young and idolized mother. The blue of Fidéline's apron lights up every summer sky. Sometimes the author leaps into the present, inviting us to sit down next to her on the pine needles, and in doing so, abolishing time. The past takes on the colors of the present moment. A fifty-five year old schoolgirl writes in her notebook. And sometimes, when her memories are not sufficient to clarify her emotions, she carries us away into her strange flights of fancy. She wards off absence by lyrical and violent phantasmagorias. Lived life envelops the dream life which shines through between the lines of the simplest narratives.

She is her principal heroine, but her protagonists exist intensely. "Excruciating pointillism of emotions." A tone of voice, a frown, a silence, a sigh: everything is promise or rebuff; everything takes on dramatic highs and lows for a woman who is passionately engaged in her relationship with others. The "excruciating" attention that she pays to their least movements is her good fortune as a writer. She makes them live for us in their disturbing opacity and their minute details. The mother, who is flirtatious and violent, imperious as well as an accomplice; Fidéline; Isabelle; Hermine; Gabriel; Sachs, as shocking as in his own books: it is impossible to forget them.

Because she is "never satisfied," she remains available [*disponible*]. Every encounter can assuage her hunger or at least distract her from it. She pays sharp attention to everyone she meets. She uncovers the tragedies and farces that are hidden beneath ordinary appearances. In a few pages or a few lines, she animates characters who held her curiosity or her friendship: the old seamstress from Albi who made dresses for Toulouse-Lautrec's mother, the one-eyed hermit from Beaumes-de-Venise, Fernand the "slaughterman" who furtively poaches cattle and sheep, with a top hat upon his head and a rose between his teeth.[7] Moving and unusual, they captivate us as they captivated her.

She is interested in people. She cherishes things. Sartre tells in *Les mots* [*Words*] how, brought up on Littré, things appeared to him as precarious embodiments of their names.[8] For Violette Leduc, on the contrary, language is within things, and the writer runs the risk of betraying them. "Don't murder that warmth at the top of a tree. Things talk without your help; remember that your voice will muffle them." "The rose-bush buckles under the intoxication of its roses: what is it you want to make it say?" She decides nevertheless to write and to capture their murmurs. "I will bring the heart of each thing up to the surface." When absence devastates her, she takes refuge among things; they are solid, real, and they have a voice. Sometimes she becomes enamored of strange and beautiful objects; one year she brought back from the south of France one hundred and twenty kilograms of dawn-colored stones with the imprints of fossils in them; another time she brought back pieces of wood, in delicate shades of gray and shaped as if by inspiration. But her favorite companions are familiar objects: a box of matches, a kitchen range. She captures the warmth and the softness of a child's slipper. She tenderly inhales the odor of her poverty from her old rabbit fur coat. She finds solace in a church pew, in a clock. "I took the back of it into my arms; I touched the polished wood. It feels friendly against my cheek." "Clocks console me. The pendulum swings back and forth, outside happiness, outside unhappiness." The night after her abortion she thought she was dying and lovingly hugged the little electric bulb hanging over her bed. "Don't leave me, dear little bulb. You have chubby cheeks; I am being extinguished with a cheek in the hollow of my hand, a shiny cheek that I am keeping warm."*Because she knows how to love them, she makes us see them. No one before her had ever shown us those tarnished, glittering flecks incrusted in the stairs of the Metro stations.

All Violette Leduc's books could be called *L'asphyxie*. She feels stifled with Hermine in their suburban house, and later in Gabriel's wretched little apartment. This is the symbol of a deeper confinement; she withers away inside the prison of her skin. But every now and then her robust health bursts forth. She tears down the barriers; she clears the horizon and escapes, opening herself up to nature, and the roads unfold beneath her feet. Aimless excursions, wanderings. Neither the grandiose nor the extraordinary have any attraction for her. She likes being in Ile-de-France and Normandy where there are meadows, gardens, and furrows; the land there is worked by man with his farms, orchards, houses, and animals.[9] Often the wind, a storm, the night or a fiery sky bring drama to this tranquillity. Violette Leduc paints tortured landscapes which resemble those of Van Gogh.[10] "The trees have their crisis of despair." But she also knows how to describe a peaceful autumn, a timid spring, the silence of a sunken lane. Sometimes her somewhat precious simplicity reminds one of Jules Renard.[11] "The sow is too naked, the ewe is overdressed." But it is with a completely personal art that she colors sounds, or makes "the sparkling cry of the lark" visible. In her writing, the abstract becomes tangible when she evokes "the playfulness of the cow parsnips . . . the distressed scent of fresh sawdust . . . the mystical vapor of flowering lavender." There is nothing forced in her notations; the countryside spontaneously talks about the men who cultivate and inhabit it. Through this countryside Violette Leduc is reconciled to those who live in it. She gladly wanders through their villages, open as well as closed, shut in on themselves but where each inhabitant knows the warmth of a connection with everyone else. In the bistros, the peasants and the carters do not frighten her off; she toasts, confident and gay, winning their friendship. "What do I love with all my heart? The country. The woods, the forests . . . My place is there, with them."

All writers who tell us about themselves aspire to sincerity; each has his own, which resembles no other. I know of none more honest than Violette Leduc's. Guilty, guilty, guilty: her mother's voice still reverberates within her; a mysterious judge stalks her. In spite of that, because of that, no one intimidates her. The faults that we impute to her will never be as serious as those of which she is charged by her invisible tormentors. She openly dis-

***Ravages*.

plays every piece of evidence in the case before us so that we can deliver her from the evil she has not committed.

Eroticism is an important part of her books; it is neither gratuitous nor meant to shock. She was not born from a couple, but from two sexes. Through her mother's constant harping, she first knew herself as a cursed sex, threatened by all males. As a sequestered adolescent, she was stagnating in sullen narcissism when Isabelle introduced her to sensual pleasure. She was stunned by this transfiguration of her body into a garden of delights. Destined for what is called abnormal love, she was not ashamed of it. Furthermore, even though among the names she gives to her solitude she sometimes uses that of God, she is a solid materialist. She does not seek to impose her ideas or her self-image upon others. Her connection with others is carnal. Presence, for her, is corporeal; communication takes place between bodies. To cherish Fidèline means to bury herself in her skirts; to be rejected by Sachs means to endure his "abstract" kisses; narcissism leads to onanism. Sensations are the truth of emotions. Violette Leduc weeps, exults, and trembles with her ovaries. She would tell us nothing about herself if she did not talk about them. She sees others through her desires: Hermine and her tranquil ardor; Gabriel's ironic masochism; the pederasty of Maurice Sachs. Wherever she happens to meet them, she is interested in all those who have reinvented sexuality for themselves, people like Cataplame, at the beginning of *La bâtarde*. Eroticism for her leads to no mysteries and is never cluttered up with nonsense, yet is the master key to the world. It is by its light that she discovers the city and the countryside, the density of the night, the fragility of the dawn, the cruelty of ringing bells. In order to speak of it, she has forged for herself a language devoid of sentimentality and vulgarity which I find to be a remarkable success. It alarmed her publishers however. They would not allow the account of her nights with Isabelle to appear in *Ravages*.* There were suspension points, here and there, replacing the omitted passages. They accepted *La bâtarde* in its entirety. The most daring episode depicts Violette and Hermine in bed together before the eyes of a voyeur. It is narrated with a simplicity that disarms all censure. Violette Leduc's discreet audacity is one of her most striking qualities, but one which has certainly done her a disservice. It scandalizes the Puritans, and the dirty-minded are left dissatisfied.

These days, there is an abundance of sexual confessions. It is much rarer

*A part of which appears in *La bâtarde*. The complete account appeared in a limited edition entitled *Thérèse and Isabelle*.

for a writer to speak frankly about money. Violette Leduc does not hide its importance for her; it too is a materialization of her relationships with others. As a child, she dreamed of working in order to give some to her mother, but once rejected, she insolently defies her by filching her money here and there. Gabriel places her on a pedestal when he empties his wallet for her; he pulls her down from it as soon as he becomes thrifty. One of the things that fascinates her about Sachs is his prodigality. She likes to beg; it is taking revenge on those who have it all. Above all, she loves to earn money; it is an affirmation of herself; she exists. She hoards with passion. The fear of going without has dwelt within her since childhood, and she measures her own importance by the thickness of the bundles she pins under her skirt. Sometimes, in the camaraderie of village bistros, she happily pays for rounds of drinks. But she does not hide the fact that she is miserly, out of prudence, egocentricity, and bitterness. "Help my neighbor. Did anyone help me when I was dying of unhappiness?" She acknowledges her hardness and rapacity with amazing honesty [*bonne foi*].

She admits to other petty traits that one is usually careful to conceal. There were many embittered people who angrily profited from France's defeat, and their first thought, after the Liberation, was to have it forgotten. Violette Leduc calmly admits that the Occupation gave her her chance and that she took advantage of it; she was not upset to see misfortune falling on heads other than her own for once. Hired by a woman's magazine but convinced that she was worthless, she dreaded the end of the war which would mean that the "valued" people would return and she would be fired. She neither excuses nor accuses herself; that is how it was. She understands why and makes us understand.

Yet she softens nothing. Most writers, when they confess to their faults, manage to remove the sting from them by the very frankness of their admissions. She forces us to grasp them within her and within ourselves in all their corrosive bitterness. She remains an accomplice to her desires, her rancor, and her petty traits. In this way she takes responsibility for ours and delivers us from shame: no one is monstrous if we are all so.

This audacity is a result of her moral candor. It is extremely rare for her to blame herself for anything or to produce any sort of defense. She doesn't judge herself; she judges no one. She complains; she flies into rages against her mother, against Hermine, Gabriel, Sachs, but she does not condemn them. She is often tender, sometimes admiring, but never indignant. Her guilt came to her from the outside, without her being any more responsible for it than for the color of her hair, and so good and bad are empty words to her. The things from which she suffered most—her "unforgivable" face, her mother's marriage—are not listed as faults. Inversely, what does not touch her personally leaves her indifferent. She calls the Germans "the enemy" to indicate that this borrowed notion remains exterior to her. She does not owe allegiance to any camp. She has no sense of the universal, nor of simultaneity; she is where she is, with the weight of her past upon her shoulders. She never cheats, never yields to pretensions or bows to conventions. Her scrupulous honesty has the value of challenging the status quo.

In a world swept clear of moral categories, her sensibility is her only guide. Cured of her taste for luxury and worldliness, she takes her stand with determination on the side of the poor and the neglected. So she is still faithful to the meager circumstances and modest joys of her childhood, and also to her present life, for after the triumphant black-market years she once again found herself penniless. She holds the destitution of Van Gogh and the Curé d'Ars in veneration.[12] All forms of distress find an echo inside her: the distress of those who are abandoned, lost, orphaned, childless old people, vagrants, the homeless, washerwomen with chapped hands, little fifteen-year-old housemaids. She is disconsolate when—in *Trésors à prendre*, before the Algerian war[13]—she sees the owner of a restaurant refusing to serve an Algerian carpet-seller. When in the presence of injustice, she immediately takes sides with the oppressed and the exploited. They are her brothers; she recognizes herself in them. And the people situated on the fringes of society seem more real to her than the settled citizens who adapt to their allotted roles. She prefers country pubs to elegant bars, a third-class railway compartment smelling of garlic and lilacs to the comfort of traveling first class. Her settings and her characters belong to this world of ordinary people whom literature today usually passes over in silence.

Despite "the tears and the cries," Violette Leduc's books are "invigorating"—a word she loves—because of what I shall call her innocence in evil, and because they wrest so much richness from the shadows. Stifling rooms; grieving hearts; the little gasping phrases take us by the throat; then suddenly a great wind carries us away beneath an endless sky, and gaiety beats in our veins. The cry of the lark sparkles over the bare plain. In the depths of despair we encounter a passion for living, and hate is only one of the names for love.

La bâtarde ends at the moment when the author has concluded the account of her childhood with which she also began the book. Thus we have come full circle. The failure to connect with others has resulted in that privileged form of communication—a work of art. I hope I have convinced the reader to enter within: he will find in it even more, much more, than I have promised.

NOTES

1. Violette Leduc (1907–72), a French author born to an unmarried servant girl, attended the Collège de Douai as well as the Lycée Racine. She began writing in 1932, and her first novel, *L'asphyxie* (*In the Prison of Her Skin*), was published by Albert Camus in 1945. Leduc wrote several novels including *L'affamée* (The Starveling) (1948) and *Ravages* (Ravages) (1955); however, she is best remembered for her first memoir, *La bâtarde* (The Bastard) (1964) and its sequel, *La Folie en tête* (*Mad in Pursuit*) (1970).

2. Albert Camus (1913–60), born in Algeria, worked as a schoolmaster, playwright, and journalist. Some of his best known works include the novel *L'étranger* (*The Stranger*) (1942), *La peste* (*The Plague*) (1947), and *La chute* (*The Fall*) (1956). Active in the French Resistance during World War II, Camus edited the underground newspaper *Combat*.

3. Jean Genet (1910–86), an illegitimate child brought up in state institutions, spent much of his life in and out of European prisons for homosexual behavior, stealing, and smuggling stolen goods. He began writing in 1939 and published several books detailing his life of crime—*Our Lady of the Flowers* (1944), *Querelle of Brest* (1947), and his autobiography, *The Thief's Journal* (1949). In the 1940s Genet began writing drama for the theater—*Deathwatch* (1947), *The Balcony* (1957), and *The Screens* (1961); Marcel Jouhandeau (1888–1979) was a French writer whose work reflected the conflict he experienced between his Catholic beliefs and his homosexual life. He published numerous novels between the 1920s and 1960s. A few of his works include *The Youth of Theophilus* (1921), *Intimate Mr. Godeau* (1926), and *Chronicle of Passion* (1949); Jean-Paul Sartre (1905–80), a famous philosopher, writer, playwright, and literary critic, was the long-time companion of Simone de Beauvoir. He may be best known for his philosophical treatise, *L'être et le néant* (*Being and Nothingness*) and *Qu'est ce que la Littérature?* (*What Is Literature?*), a book of literary criticism.

4. Jules Romains (1885–1972), also known as Louis Farigoule, was a French novelist, poet, and dramatist. He is best know for *Knock* (1923), a farcical comedy, and *Les Hommes de bonne volonté* (*Men of Good Will*) (1932–46), a novel written in several cycles that gives an overview of French life between 1908 and 1933.

5. *Mort de quelqu'un* (*The Death of a Nobody*), a novel written by Jules Romains and published in 1911.

6. Georges Duhamel (1884–1966), a French novelist and playwright who used his experiences as a World War I surgeon as material for his novels—*Vie des martyrs* (*The New Book of Martyrs*) (1918) and *Civilisation* (1918). Duhamel's later fiction included two cycle novels—*Vie et aventures de Salavin* (The Life and Adventures of Salavin) (1920–32) and *Chronique des Pasquiers* (The Pasquier Chronicles) (1933–45); Andre Gide (1869–1951) was a French writer, psychological novelist, and literary critic, as well as a homosexual and social activist. His most famous work, *Fruits of the Earth*, influenced younger French writers.

7. In *La bâtarde*, Fernand illegally poaches meat that Violette sells to wealthy Parisians on the black market.

8. Emile Littré (1801–81) was a great French lexicographer who wrote *Dictionnaire de la Langue Française* (Dictionary of the French Language).

9. Ile de France is a region in north central France, which includes Paris. Normandy is an agricultural region in northern France located along the English Channel.

10. Vincent van Gogh (1853–90), an historically important Dutch painter whose work influenced expressionism and abstract painting. Van Gogh's paintings span only a five-year

period, 1885–90, before he succumbed to mental illness and committed suicide. Some of his most famous paintings include *The Starry Night* and *Irises*.

11. Jules Renard (1864–1910) was a French writer, who wrote plays, essays, and an autobiographical novel. His best-known works are *Poil de Carotte* (Carrot Top) (1894) and *Les Histoires Naturelles* (*Nature Stories*) (1896).

12. Curé d'Ars (1786–1859), also known as Jean-Marie Vianney, was ordained as a priest at the age of thirty. He became the Curé of Ars in 1818 and following his death, was canonized by the Catholic Church as the patron saint of parish priests.

13. The Algerian War of Independence (1954–62) was fought between the French army and the Algerian independence movements.

6

What Can Literature Do?

INTRODUCTION

by Laura Hengehold

"To will that there be being," Simone de Beauvoir wrote in *The Ethics of Ambiguity*, "is also to will that there be men by and for whom the world is endowed with human significations. . . . To make being 'be' is to communicate with others by means of being."[1] However, for most of her intellectual career, literature was Beauvoir's preferred means for carrying out the philosophical task of disclosing being in a communicable, communicative way. As she argued in a series of essays and public lectures between the 1940s and 1960s, literature is better equipped to present the qualitative complexity, ambiguity, and multisidedness of being than many kinds of philosophical argumentation, especially the categorical, systematic, and idealistic approaches in which she was trained as a student in the 1920s. According to *The Prime of Life*, part of the multivolume memoir that both revealed and concealed Beauvoir's changing attitudes toward her relationships and intellectual projects, she was initially anxious that her desire to produce a "work" would require her to bracket the intensity of the lived experience that gave it value.[2] But Beauvoir's early diaries reveal that she regarded the novel as an ideal *philosophical* form, not as an alternative to philosophy.[3] During the first years of her companionship with Sartre, who seemed to have no compunction about such detachment in either discipline, Beauvoir regarded literature as sublimation—that is, isolated from worldly experience while bearing all the spiritual intensity of existence in concentrated form. As her novelistic technique developed, however, so too did her explicitly philosophical conviction that literature could provoke a reader's awareness of his or her responsibility for freely creating significations in the face of an ambiguous human condition—and, as such, be a form of action sustaining that same world.[4]

"What Can Literature Do?" was Beauvoir's contribution to a 1964 roundtable sponsored by *Clarté*, a communist youth journal seeking dialogue on cultural topics among socialists, anticolonial activists, and progressive Catholics.[5] The year was 1964, and the left had been severely shaken by de-Stalinization and the Algerian war of independence. The most experimental and prominent new voices in literature were advocates of the "new novel" (*nouveau roman*), which challenged the notion of the "real" in literary realism by interfering with readers' expectations that narrative, characterization, and anthropomorphic figures should enable a novel to reinforce a certain understanding of humanity.[6] Structuralism, as exemplified in the critical writings of Roland Barthes and a militant new journal, *Tel Quel* (whose contributors eventually included Foucault, Kristeva, Derrida, and Todorov), had challenged the intellectual hegemony of *Les temps modernes* (*TM*) and the ethos of "committed literature" (*littérature engagée*) TM shared with other postwar literary and political reviews.[7] Where Sartre, Beauvoir, Merleau-Ponty, and the other editors of *TM* promoted a conception of writing as a challenge to contemporary historical conditions and a provocation to the reader's freedom, the younger generation of critics argued that literature could have a political impact without self-consciously addressing the contemporary world.[8] By focusing on literary form and the materiality of language (an attitude Sartre characterized as "poetic" and devoid of any intention to sustain the reader's freedom), *Tel Quel* hoped to unmask linguistic conventions rendering literature complicit with a society of class and colonial divisions, as well as the crimes of Stalinism.[9] But the relative inaccessibility ("unreadability") of its literary products seemed only to reinforce waning commercial and public interest in literature by contrast to entertainment or information media. By bringing together supporters of committed literature (Semprun, Sartre, Beauvoir) with members of *Tel Quel*'s editorial board (Ricardou, Faye, Berger), the planners of the *Clarté* debate hoped to demonstrate the continuing political relevance of French literature and critical theory. To ask "What Can Literature Do?" was to ask whether writing should be a tool of liberation, explore language for its own sake, or, in Beauvoir's case, establish emotionally significant *communication* between readers and writers rendering freedom supportable and morally worthwhile.

As can be surmised from the foregoing sketch, the speakers in this debate had more in common as authors and critics than they would have liked to admit, despite real philosophical disagreements as to the relationship between literary creation and other forms of imaginative, existential, or material "reality." During the 1960s, Beauvoir and Sartre traveled extensively in the Soviet Union and the communist world, participating in numerous literary conferences where they spoke on behalf of dissident authors. Beauvoir's characters are hardly unfamiliar with the difficulty of balancing commitment and pure literary experimentation: Henri's first important crisis of conscience (in *The Mandarins*) involves reporting on the Gulag despite his friends' official refusal to support anticommunism in their literary review.[10] Although *engagement* was sometimes described in terms disconcertingly reminiscent of socialist realism, Sartre proclaimed the independence of literature from specific political goals in the opening issue of *Les temps modernes* and promoted Nathalie Sarraute and Raymond Queneau, "new novelists" praised by *Tel Quel*. In *Ethics of Ambiguity*, moreover, Beauvoir drew favorably on Francis Ponge and George Bataille, two writers favored by the younger critics, and argued that political commitment must never lose sight of the individuality and plurality of the people at whose liberation the militant aims. Finally, Beauvoir shared *Tel Quel*'s distaste for the nineteenth-century omniscient narrator who claimed only to reproduce a complete and self-justified reality and modeled her own work on modernists like Woolf, Kafka, and Hemingway. However, she parted company with fellow panelists decisively on the question of character development; without characterization, according to Beauvoir, readers could not experience the novel as a *world*, and their freedom could not be engaged on behalf of conflicting points of view, detotalizing a presumed totality.[11]

Sartre's notion of human experience as a "detotalized totality," projected as a whole by the same consciousness whose freedom disrupts its coherence as a whole, was cited in *Ethics of Ambiguity*,[12] and reappears here in Beauvoir's defense of literature as *communication* rather than solitary celebration of language's capacity to produce subjectivity as rhetorical effect. However, she develops this theme in terms of Leibniz—the thinker whose philosophy she explicated to Sartre and his friends on the occasion of their first encounter. The phenomena that relate humans to a common world and express their intervention into that world, she suggests in "What Can Literature Do?" are ironically those that also render their experience irrevocably singular—death, language, and historical/material situation. Against suggestions that *littérature engagée* merely informs and persuades, employing language instrumentally, Beauvoir insists that the creation of commonality in and through the media of our social and bodily individuation is the distinctive *ontological* function of literature. By acknowledging the transindividual status of language as a material reality that is associated with the mortal singularity of each existence, Beauvoir shares certain thematic concerns with the newer generation of critics. However, *contra* the Leibnizian and structuralist focus on discontinuous and synchronic sign systems, Beauvoir's totality is constantly evolving and changing *in itself* through the participation and interaction of individual consciousnesses.

"Literature and Metaphysics," Beauvoir's earliest published essay on the subject of writing, argues that the "original grasp" of reality by every human consciousness is temporal and has a qualitative, subjective tone betrayed and belied by the universal and systematic pretensions of most philosophical writing.[13] In "My Experience as a Writer," a 1966 lecture from Japan (included in this volume) revisiting many of the themes from her *Clarté* contribution, Beauvoir further characterized literature as inviting readers to enter *into* the phenomenological syntheses through which the writer lived experimentally with his or her characters, extending and developing the writer's own imaginative and historical reality by means of their own. The term "situation," she noted in "What Can Literature Do?" emphasizes the mobility and individuality of readers' interventions into the world of a novel—whether by Balzac or Robbe-Grillet—better than the familiar phrase "point of view" on the world. To say that we have a "view" on a common world implies a systematic idealism à la Leibniz or Hegel, whereby individuals are deprived of any real impact on one another or the nature of the whole that they contemplate. Since writers no less than readers must discover, interpret, and choose among situations in constructing and undergoing literary experience, Beauvoir regards literature as a search for community and the "privileged place of intersubjectivity."

Beauvoir had good reason to be concerned about the possibility of community in 1964. During the preceding decade, satisfaction with her identity as a French national had been destroyed by the Algerian war. The previous year, her mother had also died, provoking serious reflection on the scandal and solitude of human mortality. At the same time, Beauvoir's friendship with Sylvie le Bon was deepening and she had discovered a new role as interlocutor and spokesperson for women's concerns during her frequent international travels. Beauvoir was dismayed by the social changes brought about by television, advertising, and scientific management, which seemed to have displaced the novel and its characteristic subjectivity from a central place in French culture and which she associated with structuralism's aversion to the social and emotional (if not the political) functions of literary writing. A year after the *Clarté* debate she began work on *Les belles images*, a novel that grappled with these cultural changes and their impact on women using a new and ironically "contemporary" style.[14] Beauvoir's contribution to "What Can Literature Do?" concludes by rejecting both the dispassionate theorists of *Tel Quel* and communist critics who found political fault with the pessimism of her memoir on the Algerian war years. Literature's capacity to provoke psychological reflection and liberating "detotalization" of the reader's personal experience is an intrinsic source of relevance, she insists, doubtless with reference to her own recent history. No political movement or critical strategy can demand that novelists or memoirists deprive the public of opportunities to infuse their solitary experiences of joy, sadness, outrage, or anxiety with meaning that carries beyond a transitory situation, for the irreplaceable task of literature is to guard what is human in us against technocracies, bureaucracies, and their temptation to deny ambiguity.

NOTES

1. Simone de Beauvoir, *The Ethics of Ambiguity*, trans. Bernard Frechtman (1948; New York: Citadel Press, 1976), 71.

2. Simone de Beauvoir, *The Prime of Life*, trans. Peter Green (1962; New York: Paragon House, 1992), 37–38.

3. Simone de Beauvoir, *Diary of a Philosophy Student: 1926–27*, trans. Barbara Klaw and ed. Barbara Klaw, Sylvie le Bon de Beauvoir, and Margaret A. Simons (Urbana: University of Illinois Press, 2006), 66–67, 258, 277; Margaret Simons, "Bergson's Influence on Beauvoir's Philosophical Methodology," in *The Cambridge Companion to Simone de Beauvoir*, ed. Claudia Card (Cambridge: Cambridge University Press, 2003), 109–12.

4. For a detailed analysis of Beauvoir's novels as exemplars of phenomenological description, see Eleanore Holveck, *Simone de Beauvoir's Philosophy of Lived Experience: Literature and Metaphysics* (Lanham, Md.: Rowman and Littlefield, 2002), esp. pp. 4–5 and 15–41. On the "mechanics" of Beauvoir's notion of literary intersubjectivity, see also Toril Moi, "What Can Literature Do? Simone de Beauvoir as a Literary Theorist," *PMLA* 124.1(January) 2009: 189–98.

5. In *Que Peut la Littérature?* ed. Jean-Edern Hallier and Michel-Claude Jalard; intro. by Yves Buin, Coll. L'inédit 10/18 (Paris: Union Générale d'Éditions, 1965), 73–92.

6. Stephen Heath, *The Nouveau Roman: A Study in the Practice of Writing* (London: Elek Books, 1972).

7. For a discussion of the self-understanding of French intellectual reviews in the postwar period, see Anna Boschetti, *The Intellectual Enterprise: Sartre and "Les Temps Modernes."* trans. Richard C. McCleary (Evanston, Ill.: Northwestern University Press, 1988).

8. For discussions of the *Clarté* debate, see Danielle Marx-Scouras, *The Cultural Politics of "Tel Quel": Literature and the Left in the Wake of Engagement* (University Park: Penn State University Press, 1996), 63 and Moi (2009), 190–191.

9. For Sartre's views on poetry and prose, see "What Is Writing?" in *"What Is Literature?" and Other Essays*, trans. Bernard Frechtman (Cambridge: Harvard University Press, 1988), 25–47. Barthes' response can be found in "Écrivains et écrivants," translated by Richard Howard as "Writers and Authors," in *Critical Essays* (Evanston, Ill.: Northwestern University Press, 1972). *Le degré zéro de l'écriture* (Paris: Seuil, 1953) presents Barthes' general views on literature as a tool for the production of bourgeois class consciousness.

10. *The Mandarins*, trans. Leonard Friedman (1954; Cleveland: World Publishing Co, 1956).

11. For a discussion of Beauvoir's literary method and its blending of character and narrator points of view to indicate a situation's ambiguity, see Mary Sirridge, "Philosophy in Beauvoir's Fiction," in *The Cambridge Companion to Simone de Beauvoir*, ed. Claudia Card (Cambridge: Cambridge University Press, 2003), 129–48.

12. *The Ethics of Ambiguity*, 122.

13. "Literature and Metaphysics" (1946) In *Philosophical Writings*, ed. M. Simons, M. Timmermann, and M. B. Mader (Urbana: University of Illinois, 2004), 261–77.

14. *Les belles images*, trans. Patrick O'Brian (1966; London: Collins, 1968).

WHAT CAN LITERATURE DO?

by Simone de Beauvoir

TRANSLATION BY MARYBETH TIMMERMANN

NOTES BY JANELLA D. MOY AND MARGARET SIMONS

Well, I do not need to tell you that my conception of literature is not that of Ricardou.[1] For me, literature is an activity carried out by men, for men, in order to disclose the world to them, this disclosure being an action.[2]

However, my colleague touched upon an issue that I find very interesting, one that I wanted to talk to you about anyway; namely the relationship between literature and information. This is a pressing issue of our day, now that there are all these types of information to which Semprun just alluded and which are so very successful.[3]

I would even say that he too quickly considered them to be negligible because after all, there could be—I am not saying that there are, but there could be—a use of television and radio that would be valid and that would greatly inform people.

And in any case, there already is an entire sector of works in sociology, psychology and comparative history, documents that greatly inform the public about the world in which we live. And the fact is, as Semprun also

Contribution to *Que peut la littérature?* edited by Yves Buin (Paris: 10/18 Union Générale d'Éditions, 1965), 73–90.

said, that today we see the public very much favoring that type of book. People are more or less turning away from purely literary works.

Is this the fault of literary works such as they are today, or does literature no longer have a place in our world? This is the question that I would like to consider with you. It will be a manner of responding, overall, to the question posed: "What can literature do?"

I had some doubts, last year in particular, when I read a book that many of you have perhaps read, and that I find very remarkable, called *The Children of Sanchez*.[4]

It is about an investigation that was done by an American sociologist in the slums of Mexico.

This sociologist, over a period of eight years, at different and rather long intervals, lived with a family and tape recorded the stories that the father and four children told about their existence. These stories confirmed and contradicted each other. It was not at all a simple story, but a multi-dimensional story, like certain novelists have tried and even succeeded in doing. Also, this information far surpassed the majority of sociological works which ordinarily give only one point of view. Here, there was an enormous amount of material for the psychoanalyst as well as for the sociologist and the ethnologist, and for any person who is interested in the world and in men.

I therefore asked myself, "If there were more and more works of this genre—which is technically possible—and if there were a very large number of them, thus providing us with the secrets of cities, environments, and different sections of the world, would literature still have a role to play?"

And I answered myself, "yes." If the world were a given totality, if it were a being, something immutable that we could examine or survey as we do a world map, if this were the case and we saw the totality of the world in its unity, then what indeed would be important? Only to increase more and more our objective knowledge of the world and to discover it more and more extensively.

But in the philosophy called existentialism, to which I adhere, the world is, as Sartre said, a detotalized totality.[5]

What does that mean? It means that, on the one hand, there is a world that is indeed the same for us all, but on the other hand we are all in situation in relation to it.[6] This situation involves our past, our class, our condition, our projects, basically the entire ensemble of what makes up our individuality.

And each situation envelops the entire world in one way or another. It can envelop it as ignorance: I am unaware of what is happening, for example, in a certain city in India today, and that is part of my condition as a Frenchwoman living in Paris in the condition in which I live.

So implicitly enveloping the world does not mean that one knows it, but that one reflects it, typifies it, or *expresses* it in the way that Leibniz spoke of *expressing* the world.[7]

And what is most essential in the human condition and in man's relation to the world is precisely what is defined by this unity of the world that we express and yet at the same time this singularity, this detotalization of the points of view that we take on it, or rather—since the term "point of view" is a little idealistic—the situations in which we find ourselves in relation to it.

Here is where literature is going to find its justification and its meaning because these situations are not closed to each other. We are not monads.[8] Each situation is open onto all the others and it is open onto the world, which is nothing other than the swirling [*tournoiement*] of all these situations which envelop each other.

So we can communicate; we can communicate across this world which is a totality, although detotalized, this world which exists for us all and which allows us to agree upon what is green and what is red, for example.

We can understand one another, and we communicate. I am not one of those who believe that there is no communication, even in everyday life. I think that we communicate when we act together with certain ends in view or when we speak.

I think that at this moment we are communicating. I think that I say what I say, and that is what you hear. That is a true relationship created through language, which is opacity but is also a signifying vehicle common to all and accessible to all.

Nevertheless, at the heart of this communication there is a separation that remains irreducible.[9] I who am speaking to you am not in the same situation as you who are listening, and none of those who are listening to me is in the same situation as his neighbor. He did not come here with the same past, nor with the same intentions, nor the same culture. Everything is different; all these situations which, in a way, open onto one another and communicate with each other, have, all the same, something that can not be communicated through the means taken at this moment: lecture, discussion, or debate.

The singularity of our situation is an irreducible fact. But at the same time there is a communication in this very separation. I mean that I am a subject who says "I," I am the only subject for myself who says "I," and it's the same thing for each one of you.

I will die a death that is absolutely unique for myself, but that is the same thing for each of you. Each person's life has a unique flavor that, in a sense, no one else can know. But it's the same thing for each of us.[10]

And I think that literature's good fortune is that it can surpass the other modes of communication and allow us to communicate in what separates us.

Literature—if it is authentic—is a way of surpassing the separation by affirming it.[11] It affirms the separation because when I read a book—a book that counts for me—someone is speaking to me; the author is part of his book. Literature only starts at that moment, the moment when I hear a singular voice.

In fact, we accord much more importance to language than we sometimes admit. There is no literature if there is not a voice, and therefore a language that carries the mark of someone. There must be a language that carries the mark of someone. There must be a style, a tone, a technique, an art, an invention. It can be something completely different depending on the author, but the author must impose his presence upon me. And when he imposes his presence upon me, he imposes his world upon me at the same time.

There has been much written in the last few years about the relationship between the writer and reality. It was discussed at the Leningrad meeting which was mentioned a little while ago.[12] And people wondered, for example, if Robbe-Grillet, who distances himself from reality, is closer to or farther from it than Balzac, who believes he is revealing it to us in its objectivity.[13]

I find that the question is posed very poorly; put this way it does not allow for a response because reality is not a fixed being; it is a becoming.[14] It is, I repeat, a swirling of singular experiences that envelop each other while remaining separate.

So it is impossible for a writer to reduce reality to a fixed and completed spectacle that he might show in its totality. Each of us grasps but a moment of it: a partial truth. A partial truth is a mystification only if it is taken for the whole truth. But if it is taken for what it is, well, then it is a truth, and it enriches the one to whom it is communicated.

In the past, people spoke of a vision of the world. Okay, that is an idealistic expression, and therefore irritating, as if man's relationship to the world were simply a reflecting of it in his consciousness, seeing it from one angle or another.

But if we speak of situations, we can again take up the idea of this singularity of the world proposed to every writer, and by every writer. He obviously manifests the world such as he envelops it, such as he implicitly typifies it; his world.

And in my opinion there are hardly any readers, except the very naive, or children, who believe that in a book, they enter straight into reality. As for me, when I read *Le Père Goriot* [*Père Goriot*], I know very well that I am not walking through Paris such as it was in Balzac's time; I am walking through a novel by Balzac, in the universe of Balzac.[15]

And likewise, when I read Stendhal, I do not see Fabrice's Italy, but Stendhal's Italy.[16]

Really, it is not very important whether the author imagines that he is revealing reality in itself, or whether he is more critical and understands that he is in situation in the world, and that he reveals the world to us such as the world is revealed to him. In any case, for me, the reader, what is important is to be fascinated by a singular world that intersects with mine and yet is other.

This poses the question of identification. In today's literature, there is a tendency to reject identification with the character, and more radically, to reject the whole idea of characters.

But I also find that this discussion [is] irrelevant because, in any case, whether or not there is a character, in order for the reading to be gripping, I must identify with someone: the author. I must enter into his world and his world must become mine.

This is the essential difference with information. When I read *The Children of Sanchez*, I remain at home, in my room, in the time when I live, with my age, with Paris all around me; and Mexico is far away with its slums and with the children who live there. And I am interested in them; I annex them to my universe, but I do not change universes.

Whereas Kafka, Balzac, and Robbe-Grillet invite me and convince me to settle down, at least for a moment, in the heart of another world.[17] And that is the miracle of literature and what distinguishes it from information. A truth that is *other* becomes mine without ceasing to be an other. I abdicate my "I" in favor of he who is speaking, and yet I remain myself.

This confusion is continually initiated and continually undone, and is the only form of communication capable of giving me the incommunicable—capable of giving me the taste of another life. I am thrown into a world that has its own values, its own colors. I do not annex it to myself; it remains separated from mine and yet it exists for me. And it exists for others who are also separated from it and with whom I communicate, through books, in their deepest intimacy.

This is why Proust was right to think that literature is the privileged place of intersubjectivity.[18]

In my opinion, it is a literary work as long as the writer is capable of manifesting and imposing a truth—that of his relationship to the world, that of his world. But one must understand what these words signify: to have something to say is not to possess an object that one could carry around in a bag and then display on a table, searching afterward for the words to describe it.

The relationship is not given because the world is not given. And the writer is not given either. He is not a being, but an existant, who surpasses himself, has a praxis, and lives in time. In this world that is not given, facing a man who is not given, the relationship is obviously not given either. It must be discovered. Before revealing [*découvrir*] it to others, it is a matter of the writer discovering it, and that is why all literary works are essentially a search.[19]

On this point, Lukacs and Robbe-Grillet agree.[20] Lukacs said that the fictional hero was a problematic being in search of his values, and Robbe-Grillet—to come back to him—said last year in Leningrad, "I write in order to know why I write."

Novel, autobiography, essay: no valid literary work is without this search. Critics who believe they are more clever than the writer whose book they are reading are quick to say, "Mr. So and So or Mrs. So and So is completely wrong. He completely failed. He intended to write book A, but he wrote book B."

Well, the critic is really fortunate to have known ahead of time what the writer intended to write, because the writer himself didn't intend to write either book A or book B. He didn't know what book he was going to write. He simply had a line of research whose result, for him, is always something unexpected. And that is why the distinction between the ground [*fond*] and the figure [*forme*] is outdated. They are inseparable.

On this, I do not agree with Semprun when he says that the search is only for the form [*forme*], and that the content imposes itself.[21] If a definite content existed that could be packaged in words as chocolates are packaged in a box, then the search for the form would be of no interest.

In scientific works, the author has his content given ahead of time. He has files, he has notes, and he writes a book of history or mathematics, and well, he is not searching for anything other than a clear and simple layout of the things he has to say and that are already there, on his paper, simply as a rough draft that must be tidied up, and that's all.

There are also hack writers, of fake literature, who have a ready-made story at hand and then choose a fashionable packaging that they apply to this story. But that is not literature either.

When there is an authentic work where the author is searching for himself, the search is global. What is told and the manner of telling can not be separated, because the manner of telling is the very rhythm of the search; it is the way of defining it and the way of living it.

The Metamorphosis by Kafka and *The Trial* are not tacked-on symbols, but the very manner in which Kafka strives to realize the truth of his experience for himself and for the reader.[22]

And on this point, I would like to address a remark to Mr. Ricardou. You are very precise in your terms, but when you quote Kafka as saying "literature," we don't know, according to your quote, if he was speaking of literature in the sense that you take it to mean or in the sense we take it to mean.[23] He says that he lives for literature; but Sartre would say the same thing, and for Sartre literature is not the exercise of language that you have defined.[24] Nothing authorizes you to invoke Kafka on your behalf. I personally think that he was aiming at something completely different than you.

In any case, when it comes to Kafka's manner of telling a story, or Proust's phrasing, or Joyce's interior monologue, well, in all of those cases, these things are absolutely inseparable: the material they use, the manner in which they use it, and the search that they conduct and which constitutes (Proust says it very explicitly but it is also very clear for all the others) their literary work.[25]

Very well. Once there is search and discovery, there is a truth manifested and there is a literary work.

That said, this does not signify that every search and every discovery are of equal interest. Each of us expresses the entire world, agreed, but he expresses it implicitly. It can be in the mode of ignorance, or through mystifications—he can be mystified-mystifying—or it can be in the mode of alienation. There are so many ways of expressing the world, some of which can not be made explicit to reveal a truth to us.

And here I come back to the idea of engaged literature. The individual who is engaged in his time period, who tries to have a hold upon history by an action, or by an indignation, or by revolt, has much richer and much more profound ties with the world than the one who withdraws from the world in an ivory tower.

A writer can only be interested in what really interests him. If the field of his interests is narrow and petty, then he reveals a petty universe to us. He establishes a communication with us in an extremely restricted mode and in a very poor manner.

I am not going to linger on engaged literature; we have spoken enough about it, and I agree almost entirely with what Semprun said about it just a little while ago.[26]

For my conclusion, I would prefer to talk to you about what interests me today, what literature can do for me as a writer. This is also a way of responding to the question, "What can literature do?"

I mentioned a little while ago that the world was detotalized, but our own experience is also de-totalized. There is a totalization always in process but which is never achieved and which escapes us. Since consciousness is always surpassing and negation, we fail to live any moment in its plenitude. We always fall short of sorrow and fall short of joy.

An emotion, a feeling, a sadness or a joy lasts a long or short amount of time, but either way it dies, and we are incapable of perpetuating it forever.

And on the other hand—and what's even more radical—no emotion and no thought can encompass the whole of our experience: the sorrow as well as the joy, the ambiguity, and the contradictions that are the truth of our human condition. *That* escapes our lived experience.

And it must not be thought that memory performs miracles. Even it fails to revive the instant and give it a plenitude. And it also fails to unify the diversity of the instants.

There is only one way to push these things to their apogee: either the anguish of death, for example, or of abandonment, or the joy of a success, or the exultation that a young man can feel before flowering hawthorn; only literature can do justice to this absolute presence of the instant, to this eternity of the instant that will have been forever.

And literature alone can also make those hawthorn flowers and the death of a grandmother exist together, in a work that is a totality. It alone can succeed in reconciling all the irreconcilable moments of a human experience.

Words struggle, therefore, against time and against death, but they also struggle against separation, since they have the power to restore generality to what we have that is most singular: the passage of time, the taste of our life, death, solitude. And I think this is precisely one of the most obvious and most necessary functions of words.

Each writer was brought to literature by very different paths, but I think that none would write if he hadn't, in one way or another, suffered from separation, and if he wasn't searching, in one way or another, to shatter it.

I personally know very well that for me, in moments of collective joy, in moments of happy communication—for example what I felt during the days of the Liberation[27]—I have absolutely no desire to write. Literature, at that moment, seems totally useless to me.

Literature is impossible, not useless, but impossible, when one falls into an absolute despair since to despair is to no longer believe that there is any recourse. It is a truism, but the opposite of this truism is not one, or at least it is not recognized as such.

If one can never write in absolute despair, one can reciprocally say that there can not be despairing literature. But that is much less widely recognized.

In fact, if one expresses an anguish, it is because one thinks that through that expression it takes on meaning and a certain reason to be. It means that one still believes in communication, and therefore in men, and their fraternity.

And I mention this because the ending of *La force des choses* [*Force of Circumstance*] and the theme of my latest book, *Une mort très douce* [*A Very Easy Death*], have been much criticized in the name of socialistic optimism.[28] I have been told, "The anguish of passing time and the horror of death—that's all well and fine, you have every right to have those feelings, that's very honorable, but that's your business . . . and don't talk to us about it!" I have received letters, from the left, that have told me that.

I, myself, do not see why, under the pretext of having confidence in the future and believing that one day there will be a socialist society, they should silence the failure and hardship that play a part in every life. I, on the other hand, find that socialistic optimism resembles very much the technocratic optimism that currently reigns and calls misery abundance and uses the future as a pretext.

If literature seeks to surpass separation at the point where it seems most unsurpassable, it must speak of anguish, solitude, and death, because those are precisely the situations that enclose us most radically in our singularity. We need to know and to feel that these experiences are also those of all other men.

Language reintegrates us into the human community; a hardship that finds words to express itself is no longer a radical exclusion and becomes less intolerable. We must speak of failure, abomination, and death, not to drive our readers to despair, but on the contrary, to try to save them from despair.

Each man is made of all men, and he only understands himself through them. He only understands them through what they reveal of themselves, and through himself clarified by them.

And I think that that is what literature can and should give. It should render us transparent to one another in what is most opaque about us. There are other tasks and other undertakings: action, technology, politics, etc. but these are destined for men anyway, and they become absurd, even odious, if they take themselves as ends, and if they cut themselves off from the human.

I believe that literature's task is to safeguard what is human in man from technocrats and bureaucrats, and to reveal the world in its human dimension, that is to say as it is disclosed to individuals at once connected and separated. And I believe that this is the task of literature and what makes literature irreplaceable.

NOTES

1. See Beauvoir's *Tout compte fait* (Paris: Gallimard, 1972), 137–38, translated by Patrick O'Brian as *All Said and Done* (New York: Warner, 1975), 130–31, for her discussion of the political intrigues involved in this 1964 public debate between "engaged" writers and proponents of the "new novel." Organized by the Union of Communist Students in France (UECF) to bring about a "thaw" in relations among leftist intellectuals and to raise funds for their publication, *Clarté*, the round-table discussion attracted an audience of six thousand people to the amphitheatre of the Mutualité. Yves Buin, editor of *Clarté*, introduced the debate. Participants included: Jorge Semprun, Jean Ricardou, Jean-Pierre Faye, Simone de Beauvoir, Yves Berger, and Jean-Paul Sartre; Jean Ricardou (1932–) is a French novelist and theorist of the "new novel" (*nouveau roman*). His novel, *L'observatoire de Cannes* (The Cannes Observatory) (Paris: Minuit) was published in 1961. See also his *Problèmes du nouveau roman* (Problems of the New Novel) (Paris: Seuil, 1967), *Le nouveau roman* (The New Novel) (Paris: Seuil, 1973), and "Composition Discomposed," published in *Critical Inquiry* in 1976. In his contribution to the roundtable discussion, Ricardou attacks Sartre's concept of literature as communication, arguing that such a concept reduces literature to a means, "a pure vehicle for information," rather than an end in itself. For Ricardou, and other proponents of the "new novel," language is not an instrument but "a sort of material" to be worked with great care. Writing "is not some will to communicate prior information, but this project of *exploring language* understood as particular space" (*Que peut la litterature?* 51–52; my translation). See also Toril Moi, "What Can Literature Do? Simone de Beauvoir as a Literary Theorist," (*PMLA* 124:1(January)2009: 189–98.

2. On Beauvoir's concept of disclosure, see "Pyrrhus and Cineas," (1944) in *Philosophical Writings* (PW), ed. M. Simons, M. Timmermann, and M. B. Mader (Urbana: University of Illinois, 2004): "To seek to be is to seek *being*, because *there is no* being except through the presence of a subjectivity that discloses it" (136); and "Introduction to an Ethics of Ambiguity" (1946): "There is therefore an original type of attachment to being that is not the relationship 'wanting to be' but rather, 'wanting to disclose being.' And here there is not failure, but on the contrary, there is success" (PW 292); and "Literature and Metaphysics" (1946): "A metaphysical novel that is honestly read, and honestly written, provides a disclosure of existence in a way unequaled by any other mode of expression" (PW 276). On Beauvoir's appropriation of Bergson's concept of unveiling or disclosing reality, see Beauvoir's *Diary of a Philosophy Student: 1926–27*, ed. B. Klaw, S. Le Bon de Beauvoir, and M. Simons (Urbana: University of Illinois, 2006), 34, 58–61, 66–67, 87; and Margaret A. Simons, "Bergson's Influence on Beauvoir's Philosophical Methodology," in *The Cambridge Companion to Simone de Beauvoir*, ed. Claudia Card (Cambridge: Cambridge University, 2003), 110.

3. Jorge Semprun (1923–), a Spanish born militant and writer, studied philosophy at the Sorbonne, was active in the Communist Party in France during the Nazi Occupation and

later in Spain under Franco. Expelled from the Party in 1964, Semprun concentrated on his politically engaged writing, later winning an Oscar for his screenplay for the 1969 Costa-Gavras film, "Z." On information, Semprun remarks : "It seems to me, furthermore, that this question about the power of literature must be included in a more radical question: Will there still be literature in twenty or so years, in our neo-capitalistic societies? Sociological research seems to show the appearance of a trend that will lead to the replacement—or at least the displacement—of the book by audio-visual methods of diffusion of ideological consumer goods. I don't dare say cultural, for culture is an activity, not a consumption or a passive reception of ready-made ideas and images chosen more and more each day by State-controlled means" (*Que peut la littérature?* 45; my translation).

4. *The Children of Sánchez* (New York: Random House, 1961), the biography of a Mexican family written by American author and anthropologist Oscar Lewis (1914–70); published in French as *Les enfants de Sánchez: autobiographie d'une famille mexicaine*, trans. Céline Zins (Paris: Gallimard, 1963).

5. On "detotalized totality," see Jean-Paul Sartre, *Being and Nothingness*, trans. Hazel E. Barnes, (New York: Philosophical Library, 1953), where Sartre refers to the for-itself as: "a detotalized totality which temporalizes itself in a perpetual incompleteness" (180).

6. On Beauvoir's 1939 concept of being "in situation" and Sartre's rejection of it, see Margaret A. Simons, "Introduction," in Simone de Beauvoir, *Wartime Diary*, trans. Anne Deing Cordero, ed. M. A. Simons and S. Le Bon de Beauvoir (Urbana: University of Illinois, 2009), 9, 20–21.

7 Gottfried Wilhelm Leibniz (1646 1716), German philosopher and mathematician, the subject of Beauvoir's 1929 *diplôme* (graduate thesis) in philosophy. For Leibniz, the simple substances of the universe (called "monads") envelop and represent the whole world although often without awareness of it. A thing "expresses" another when there are relations in it that correspond to those in the thing expressed. For example, a model of a machine expresses the machine, or an equation expresses a curve in Cartesian geometry, or an idea expresses the thing of which it is the idea. See, for example, G. W. Leibniz. *Philosophical Papers and Letters*, ed. and trans. L. L. Loemker (Dordrecht: D. Reidel, 1976), 207–208.

8. *Monad*, Leibniz's term for the simple substances that compose the universe, substances that are closed to outside influence, as Leibniz explains in *Monadology* (7): "There is no way of explaining how a monad can be altered or changed internally by some other creature, since one cannot transpose anything in it, nor can one conceive of any internal motion that can be excited, directed, augmented, or diminished within it, as can be done in composites, where there can be change among the parts. The monads have no windows through which something can enter or leave," L. E. Loemker (trans. and ed.), *Gottfried Wilhelm Leibniz: Philosophical Papers and Letters*, 2 Vols. (Chicago: University of Chicago, 1956); II, 1044–45.

9. On Beauvoir's concept of separation, see "Pyrrhus and Cineas" (1944): "Freedoms are neither unified nor opposed but separated" (PW 108).

10. On what Beauvoir has called this "tragic ambiguity" of our human condition, see Beauvoir's "Introduction to an Ethics of Ambiguity" (1946): "[Man] alone holds this privilege of being a sovereign and unique subject in the middle of a universe of objects, yet he shares it with all those like him" (PW 289–90).

11. On the "authentic" novel establishing a "genuine communication with the reader"

and "surpass[ing] on the imaginary level the always too narrow limits of actual lived experience," see "Literature and Metaphysics," (1946) PW 272, 271.

12. The Leningrad meeting was the West-East Colloquium on the Contemporary Novel, held in Leningrad in August 1963; see Harry R. Grubs, "Review of Reviews July–December, 1964," *The French Review*, Vol. 38, No. 6 (May, 1965), 818.

13. Alain Robbe-Grillet (1922–2008) was a French writer, filmmaker, and founder of the "new novel" movement in the 1950s; Honoré de Balzac (1799–1850) was a French journalist and writer whose collection of novels and short stories are compiled under the title *La Comédie humaine* (*The Human Comedy*) (1842).

14. On *becoming*, see Henri Bergson, *Creative Evolution*, trans. Arthur Mitchell (New York: Modern Library, 1944): "Matter or mind, reality has appeared to us as a perpetual becoming" (296). See also Margaret A. Simons, "Bergson's Influence on Beauvoir's Philosophical Methodology," in *The Cambridge Companion to Simone de Beauvoir*, ed. Claudia Card (Cambridge: Cambridge University Press, 2003), 109–10.

15. *Le Père Goriot*, a novel, by Honoré de Balzac, translated as *Père Goriot*, by Burton Raffel, ed. Peter Brook (New York: Norton, [1835] 1994). Sharing many similarities to Shakespeare's *King Lear*, the main character, Goriot, has given all of his material wealth to his daughters only to be treated contemptuously by them and left to die alone.

16. Stendhal (1783–1842) (pseudonym of Marie-Henri Beyle) was a French writer who helped develop the modern novel. Fabrice del Dongo is the protagonist of Stendhal's novel, *La chartreuse de Parme* (1839), translated as *The Charterhouse of Parma*, by Richard Howard (New York: Random House, 1999). Considered one of Stendhal's literary masterpieces, *The charterhouse of Parma* chronicles the French moral and intellectual climate following Napoleon's defeat. His writing was rediscovered in the 1870s and proved influential on young writers like Joseph Conrad and Henry James.

17. Franz Kafka (1883–1924) was born in Prague (then part of Austria). His 1925 novel *The Trial*, trans. Breon Mitchell (New York: Random House, 1998), was one of three posthumously published novels considered his finest works; the other two are *The Castle*, trans. Anthea Bell (Oxford, UK: Oxford University, [1926], 2009) and *Amerika*, trans. Willa Muir and Edwin Muir (New York: Schocken, [1927] 1974).

18. Marcel Proust (1871–1922) was a French writer best remembered for his massive work *À la recherche du temps perdu* (*Remembrance of Things Past*) comprised of seven books, which he began in 1909 and finished just before his death in 1922. The reference is probably to *Time Regained*, in Vol. 3 of *Remembrance of Things Past*, trans. C. K. Scott Montcrieff and Terence Kilmartin (New York: Random House, 1981), 931–32.

19. See "Literature and Metaphysics" (1946) where Beauvoir describes the author as participating in a "search" and the novel as "endowed with value and dignity only if it constitutes a living discovery for the author as for the reader" (PW 271).

20. Georg Lukács (1885–1971) was a Hungarian Marxist philosopher and literary critic. He defended literary realism, opposing the formal innovations of modernist writers in essays such as his 1938, "Realism in the Balance," in *The Norton Anthology of Theory and Criticism*, ed. Vincent B. Leitch (New York: Norton, 2001), 1033–58.

21. Semprun's remarks on content: "Content is not an object of research; it is imposed upon us. Either by the world, or by our ideas or personal obsessions about the world" (*Que peut la littérature?* 31).

22. Kafka's 1915 novella, *The Metamorphosis*, in *The Metamorphosis and Other Stories*, trans. Donna Freed (New York: Barnes and Noble, 1996). Both *The Metamorphosis* and *The Trial* exhibit individuals experiencing loneliness, frustration, external threats, and circumstances beyond their control.

23. Ricardou on Kafka: "I note that no one more than him, perhaps, wanted to be a writer in every respect. This is made clear in the letter recently revealed to us by Marthe Robert: 'My job as a government worker is intolerable to me because it thwarts my unique desire and my unique vocation which is literature. . . . I am nothing but literature . . . I cannot and do not want to be anything else . . ." (*Que peut la littérature?* 58; my translation).

24. Jean-Paul Sartre (1905–80), philosopher and writer, may be best known for his philosophical treatise, *L'étre et le néant*, (translated by Hazel E. Barnes, as *Being and Nothingness*, (New York : Philosophical Library, [1943] 1953) and *Critique de la raison dialectique* (translated by Alan Sheridan-Smith as *Critique of Dialectical Reason*, (London: NLB, [1960] 1976). "Qu'est-ce que la Littérature?" a manifesto of "littérature engagée" was originally published in *Les temps modernes* in 1947, trans. Bernard Frechtman, in *What Is Literature? and Other Essays* (Cambridge: Harvard University Press, 1988).

25. James Joyce (1882–1941), born in Dublin, Ireland, was a poet and novelist. His inventive use of language and the interior monologue made his writing both innovative and fresh. Works like *Dubliners* (1914), The *Portrait of the Artist as a Young Man* (1916), *Ulysses* (1922), and *Finnegan's Wake* (1939) are considered Joyce's greatest works.

26. Semprun remarks, on "engaged literature": "[Engagement] first describes a situation of fact: the intellectual is never disengaged from the world, no matter how extremely formalist his research is. Secondly, this situation is tied to (or rather elicits) an awareness [*prise de conscience*] through which the situation of fact ceases to be passive and submissive, and becomes the source of a creative activity. By his engagement, the writer ceases to be *held* by the world—he has a *hold* over it. Thirdly, engagement is inscribed in a problematic that belongs exclusively to the social milieu of intellectuals; it is not a concept that can be applied indifferently to the situation or the exigencies of any other milieu or class of society. The laborer [. . .] can also become aware of his class situation and thereby become involved in a global revolutionary project—and become a proletarian and an activist. But his engagement as an activist will not translate to the level of his creative activity or his productive work [. . .] The writer, on the contrary, sees his engagement immediately affect his creative work. For it is as a writer and because he is a writer that he engages himself. He is putting his only *raison d'être* on the line, in other words, his existence . . . Finally, the notion of engagement includes and discloses an exigency that is objectively founded in a certain historical context; it is dated and corresponds to a specific era. In other societies and in other circumstances, the core of universal rationality contained within this notion has found and will find different ways of manifesting itself" (*Que peut la litterature?* 33–35; my translation).

27. "The days of the Liberation" refers to France's liberation from German occupation in 1944.

28. *La force des choses* (Paris: Gallimard, 1963), translated by Richard Howard as *Force of Circumstance* (New York: Harper, 1964), is the third volume of Simone de Beauvoir's autobiography; *Une mort très douce* (Paris: Gallimard, 1964), translated by Patrick O'Brian as *A Very Easy Death* (New York: Putnam, 1966), is Beauvoir's account of her mother's death.

7

Misunderstanding in Moscow

INTRODUCTION

by Terry Keefe

In 1992 the French journal *Roman 20–50. Revue d'étude du roman du XXe siècle* printed a previously unpublished story of some 21,000 words by Simone de Beauvoir, which receives no explicit mention in her memoirs.[1] The editor of the journal issue and of Beauvoir's text, Jacques Deguy, suggests that "Malentendu à Moscou" ("Misunderstanding in Moscow") was due to be included in the collection of short stories *La femme rompue* (*The Woman Destroyed*), but that Beauvoir rejected it—for unspecified reasons—"around 1967." Because whole textual sequences in the story are identical with sequences in one of the stories finally published in that collection, "L'age de discrétion" ("The Age of Discretion"), we may assume that this *replaced* "Misunderstanding in Moscow" (hereafter MaM).

The ninety-six-page typescript of MaM, deposited in the Bibliothèque Nationale, bears the title "Malentendu à Moscou - = 1965" in Beauvoir's handwriting. Although somewhat puzzling (since the story is set in 1966), the date seems to confirm that MaM was written very early in the process of composing *La femme rompue*. Deguy describes the typescript of MaM as "clearly ready for publication," without variants or significant erasures.[2]

The current state of public knowledge is such that answering the obvious question of *why* Beauvoir replaced MaM by another story is largely a matter of speculation; provided, that is, that one agrees with Deguy—as I am sure most readers will—that it is incomprehensible that this should have been on grounds of literary quality. Two lines of inquiry in particular may be pursued, even if they do not provide conclusive results. One might be described as "personal" and the other as "political."[3]

The elderly married couple André and Nicole in MaM bear evident resemblances to André and his unnamed wife in "L'age de discrétion," but Nicole's stepdaughter Macha has no counterpart in the latter. Contat and Rybalka hypothesize that Beauvoir may have put aside MaM because her transposition of Sartre's relationship with the interpreter, Lena Zonina, was "too transparent,"[4] and some will believe that the fact that Zonina's daughter is named Macha strengthens this suggestion. It would, however, raise further problems, since some transpositions in Beauvoir's other fictions are even more transparent.

Political considerations, therefore, could also have been a major factor. During their many trips to the Soviet Union, and especially between 1962 and 1966, Sartre and Beauvoir followed political developments there very closely. But by 1967 they seem to have become sufficiently disillusioned with the state of the country to refuse to go back. It is quite possible that Beauvoir's portrayal of the Soviet Union in MaM came to seem too favorable to her, so that she felt the need to replace it with a story centered on a similar couple, but set in Paris, hence excluding the Moscow-based character of Macha and turning André into a scientist.

In any case, the social and political dimension of MaM is far more prominent than that of "L'age de discrétion," constituting one of its most distinctive features. André's general political disillusionment is entirely recognizable as that of his counterpart, but MaM extends it in a different direction by examining the state and future of the Soviet Union, as well as Western attitudes toward the country—not least through heated discussions between André and Macha. Equally, just as—in *Les Mandarins* (*The Mandarins*)—it was through Anne (less involved in politics than her husband) that Beauvoir chose to show us America, so here it is largely through the observations of Nicole that we learn about day-to-day life in Moscow and other Soviet towns, in a detail that is not always dictated by the needs of the plot in the strictest sense. Looking back from the 21st century, we may see MaM as the story by Beauvoir that most clearly reflects the Cold War, with its insights into the Soviet Union being in some measure complementary to the treatment of Western society in *Les belles images*.[5]

Another—related—dimension of MaM strikingly lacking in the story that replaced it is a male viewpoint. While everything is seen through the eyes of the woman protagonist in "L'age de discrétion," Beauvoir chose in MaM to revert to a narrative strategy adopted in both *Les sang des autres* (*The Blood of Others*) and *Les Mandarins*, having the focus of the narration alternate regularly between one female and one male character. Here, of course, we do not have the separate chapters that we find in the novels, but the changes of focalizer are almost always marked by gaps in the text, with twelve sections written from the point of view of Nicole and twelve from that of André.

It would be difficult to overestimate the importance of this feature of MaM. Without the particular narrative technique involved, Beauvoir simply could not have brought out with the same impact and sharpness the specific "misunderstanding" that is part of the significance of the title. Again, the whole story is framed by references to the difficulties of communicating with others, with Nicole asserting at the beginning that these are unreal—at least with regard to a few people we love—but acknowledging such difficulties at the end. The resonance of this motif would have been greatly diminished if the narrative had been exclusively from Nicole's viewpoint. More generally still, Beauvoir's narrative strategy allows the story to incorporate the most detailed and perceptive portrayal of both sides of a couple's relationship in the whole of her fiction.

There can be little doubt, moreover, that the treatment of what is probably the major theme of the story—that of aging—loses breadth and depth when confined to the viewpoint of only one of the sexes. As it is, Beauvoir is able to show both the man and the woman—once they resolve their differences—as eventually drawing consolation from the fact that they will at least face the distressing process of aging together. More importantly, in the course of the events she reveals in subtle stages to what extent each partner misinterprets the distinctive sensitivities of the other, even while attempting to protect him/her from the worst psychological effects of aging. Having seen both Nicole's illusions and André's similar illusions concerning his wife, the reader's reaction is a satisfying one of recognition when they both come to acknowledge and articulate their mistakes at the end. Hence the "misunderstanding" of the title is seen to involve much more than disagreement over what was or was not said at a particular moment—a moment that Beauvoir is obliged to situate when both characters are too sleepy or drunk to remember accurately! In short, it is of great interest, both thematically and technically, that in MaM Beauvoir wishes to preserve a balance in her story, showing husband and wife as equally blameworthy—or equally blameless—for misunderstandings and disagreements that occur between them.

Yet this is achieved without any loss of insight into the mentality of her central woman character as such. In fact, Beauvoir breaks new ground here in the delineation of Nicole herself. Yet another female figure in Beauvoir's fiction formed by her mother and in some way neglected by her father, Nicole felt wounded by being a woman and was revolted at the thought of lying down beneath a man. It seems that, although she has recently become frigid, she enjoyed sex for much of her married life, but this is presented as something that André delicately helped her to accept, like motherhood, and Nicole suggests that her later attitudes may constitute a return to her natural reserve, even that she has never fully accepted womanhood at all. At the same time, she recognizes the loss of sexuality as a real and significant one. In short, in MaM we have—rather surprisingly—more of an outline of the whole complex sexual development of a woman character than anywhere else in Beauvoir's fiction.

It may also be the case that Nicole comes *closer* than any of Beauvoir's other fictional figures to being a feminist heroine. We know, after all, that she rejected male dominance and the image of femininity that her mother tried to force upon her, embracing ambitious projects and being determined to show that a girl *can* do certain things. The story also records, however, that in spite of her militant feminism (unique in Beauvoir's fiction) she was eventually swallowed up by husband, home, and son. It is not even entirely clear that she does not still regard André's earlier efforts to reconcile her to womanhood as a kind of trap. Perhaps any uncertainty that Nicole experiences on these matters parallels André's current agonizing over his political commitment, for it is intriguing to see that they each nurse a slight grudge against the other for having stifled their personal ambitions. Yet, unlike many of Beauvoir's women characters, Nicole accepts some responsibility herself for what she has become. She has no significant regrets or reservations at all about her long relationship with André, and her continuing confusion manifests itself, rather, in her reactions to women around her. She is aware of women's social status in a way uncommon in Beauvoir's characters, approving of working women's awareness of their rights, but feeling somehow uncomfortable in their presence. And while she admires the ease with which Macha accepts her femininity, she disapproves of the way in which her son's fiancée sets out to succeed "on all levels." These ambivalences, together with a significant degree of dependence on André prevent her from being the clear role model that some feminists might have had Beauvoir create in her stories, but they do enrich the characterization greatly, given the dimensions of the tale.

If Nicole is still in some measure a victim of male-dominated society, she is also largely free of the self-deception to which so many of Beauvoir's female figures are, at least temporarily, subject. It is true that her relations with her son have a great deal in common with those of the central female figure of "L'age de discrétion," but this relationship is kept rather in the background in MaM, where more complex patterns are created by the existence and presence of Nicole's stepdaughter Macha. There is no hostility between the two women, but André's own relationship with Macha has some bearing on his relations with Nicole. He sees his "new" relationship with Macha—she suddenly expressed a desire to get to know him six years earlier—as something especially exciting, akin to a sexual adventure, and a comparison and contrast is made at a number of points between his feelings for Nicole and his feelings for Macha. Even Nicole herself sometimes speculates that she has failed to maintain the tenderness and freshness of her relationship with André. There is nothing unhealthy about either André's affection for Macha or Nicole's strong bond with Philippe, but the general suggestion is that, with sexual activity between husband and wife ended, some of the intensity of their earlier relationship has been diverted into relations with their offspring—willingly on Nicole's part, but perhaps more unexpectedly for André. In both cases, however, the process is now in reverse—Nicole is alienated by Philippe's marriage, André not quite so excited at seeing Macha as on previous occasions—and the couple are genuinely turning back to each other at the end of the story.

For all its differences and additional dimensions, therefore, MaM remains, like "L'age de discrétion," the story of an elderly married couple who overcome temporary estrangement, to draw even closer together for the final difficult stages of their lives. Yet it is still useful to consider what would have been the broad effect of its inclusion in *La femme rompue* instead of "L'age de discrétion." The strong unity of the collection as published springs partly from the very fact that all three stories are written only from the viewpoint of the central woman figure. Each fascinatingly explores the way in which women who are overdependent on men deceive themselves about their situation, asking the reader to act as a kind of detective, tracking down the different degrees and varieties of self-deception involved.[6] Had MaM figured in the collection in place of "L'age de discrétion," very different processes of comparison and contrast would have been required of the reader. And the whole issue of blame for problems in relationships would have raised itself in another perspective, since it is much easier for the reader to abstain from judgment when only one side of the story is available. In the story "La femme rompue," a friend of Monique points out that "You would have to know how *he* sees things. You can never understand anything in these stories of a relationship breaking down when they are told only by the woman."[7] Beauvoir herself acknowledged that in the collection as it stands she scarcely sought to elucidate the roles of the men characters.[8]

For a number of reasons, then, it must remain an open question how greatly the inclusion of MaM in *La femme rompue* would have altered that collection. Would the book, for instance, thereby have become a more or a less feminist work? But what is unquestionable is that this "new" story has some features—and some merits—unique in Beauvoir's fiction, so that to regard it henceforth as an integral part of the corpus is to enrich and enhance the reputation of her writings considerably.

NOTES

1. "Malentendu à Moscou," *Roman 20–50. Revue d'étude du roman du XXe siècle* (*Novel 20–50: Review of 20th Century Novel Studies*) (Université de Lille III), no. 13, June 1992, 137–88. It is possible, though perhaps unlikely, that Beauvoir's comments in the second chapter of *All Said and Done* (on her abandoned draft of a "novel" about aging) refer to "Misunderstanding in Moscow"; see *Tout compte fait* (Paris: Gallimard, 1972), 137–39; translated by Patrick O'Brian as *All Said and Done* (New York: Warner Books, 1975), 129–31.

2. Deguy claims to have scrupulously observed Beauvoir's own punctuation in the published French text, doing no more than correcting some definite typing errors. (Which is not to say that it is now free of such slips—there are a dozen or so. I have drawn attention to them in notes only where they might bear on the translation process in some way.) Although—plainly—punctuation has frequently had to be changed, in the interests of good English, my own translation is made in the same spirit, with the layout of the text, Beauvoir's paragraphing, etc. being strictly followed.

3. I developed both—as well as a number of the other arguments in this Introduction—in rather more detail in my "Malentendu à Moscou." *Simone de Beauvoir Studies*, Vol. 11 (1994): 30–41.

4. Michel Contat and Michel Rybalka, *Sartre. Bibliographie 1980–1992* (Paris: C.N.R.S. Editions, 1993), 200.

5. Some relevant points here are brought out in my "Commitment, re-commitment and puzzlement: aspects of the Cold War in the fiction of Simone de Beauvoir." *French Cultural Studies*, VIII (1997): 127–36.

6. I have discussed these issues in *Simone de Beauvoir. "Les belles images" and "La femme rompue"* (University of Glasgow: French and German Publications, 1998).

7. *La femme rompue*, Folio ed. (1967; reprint, Paris: Gallimard, 1986), 197.

8. In Anne Ophir, *Regards féminins* (Paris: Denoël/Gonthier, 1976), 12.

MISUNDERSTANDING IN MOSCOW

by Simone de Beauvoir

TRANSLATION AND NOTES BY TERRY KEEFE

She looked up from her book. How irritating all these old refrains on non-communication were! If we really want to communicate, we manage to do so more or less successfully. Not with everyone, of course, but with two or three people. André was sitting in the seat next to her, reading a thriller. She kept from him certain moods, some regrets, some little worries; doubtless he, too, had his own little secrets. But, by and large, there was nothing that they did not know about each other. She glanced through the plane window: dark forests and pale grassland stretching as far as one could see. How many times had they forged forward together, by train, by plane, by boat, sitting side by side, with books in their hands? There would still be many occasions when they would glide silently side by side over the sea, the earth and the air. This moment had the sweetness of a memory and the brightness of a promise. Were they thirty, or sixty? André's hair had turned white quite early, and at one time the snowy white color that enhanced his fresh but matte complexion seemed stylish. It was still stylish. His skin had hardened and become lined, rather like old leather, but the smile at his mouth

"Malentendu à Moscou," *Roman 20/50*, no.13, June 1992, 137–88.

and in his eyes had kept its sparkle. His face today was preferable to that of his youth, despite what the photograph album might show. Nicole did not see him as having any particular age; probably because he himself seemed not to either. Although, in the past, he was so fond of running, swimming, climbing, and looking at himself in the mirror, he bore his sixty-four years nonchalantly. It was a long life behind them, with laughter, tears, moments of anger, caresses, confessions, silences, surges of affection [*élans*], and it sometimes seems that time has not passed by at all. The future still stretches out ahead, to infinity.

"Thank you."

Nicole took a sweet from the basket, intimidated by the plumpness of the air hostess, and by the severity of her stare, just as she had been three years earlier by the restaurant waitresses and hotel chambermaids. You could only approve of their refusal to affect friendliness, and their keen awareness of their rights, but you felt yourself at fault in their presence, or at least suspect.

"We're landing," she said.

She looked rather nervously at the ground coming up to meet them. An infinite future. But one that could be shattered from one minute to the next. She was very familiar with these sudden swings of mood, from smug security to pangs of fear: a Third World War was going to break out; André had contracted lung cancer—two packets of cigarettes a day was too many, far too many; or the plane was about to smash into the ground. That would've been a good way for it all to end: no complications, and with the two of them together. But not so soon, not now. "We made it safely again," she said to herself once the wheels hit the runway, albeit rather violently. The travelers put on their coats, gathered their hand luggage. They were standing around waiting, standing around for some time.

"Can you smell the birch trees?" André asked.

It was very cool, almost cold: 61°F according to the air hostess's announcement. How close Paris was, at three and a half hours of flight time, and yet how far away. This morning Paris had been sweltering under the first great heat wave of the summer, with the smell of asphalt and a storm in the air. How close Philippe was, and yet how far away. . . . A bus took them—across an aerodrome that was much more extensive than the one at which they had landed in 1963—to a glazed building in the shape of a mushroom, where the passports were checked. Macha was waiting for them at the exit. Once again Nicole was surprised to see, harmoniously blended in her face, the very dissimilar features of Claire and André. She was slim and elegant: only her over-permed hairstyle marked her as a Muscovite.

"How was the flight? Are you [*vous*] well? And how are you [*tu*]?"

She addressed her father informally, Nicole formally.[1] It was to be expected, and yet at the same time peculiar.

"Hand me your bag."

That was to be expected, too. But when a man carries your bags, it's because you are a woman: when a woman does, it's because she is younger than you, and you feel old.

"Give me the luggage slips and sit there," Macha said authoritatively. Nicole obeyed. She was old. With André she often forgot the fact, but dozens of little irritations periodically reminded her of it. "An attractive young woman!" she had thought, on spotting Macha. She remembered having smiled at the age of thirty when her father-in-law had used those very words to describe a forty-year-old. She, too, now found that most people seemed young. She was old. And she wasn't accepting the fact very easily (the combination of astonishment and distress that she felt was one of the rare things that she kept from André). She told herself: "In any case, there are some advantages." Being retired sounded a little like being on the scrap heap, but it was pleasant to take your vacation whenever you wanted; or, more precisely, to be on vacation all the time. Sweltering in their classrooms, her ex-colleagues would be beginning to dream of getting away. And she herself had already left. She looked around for André, who was standing in the crowd, next to Macha. In Paris, he allowed himself to be put upon by too many people. As much as he possibly could, he was always ready to come to the aid of Spanish political prisoners; Portuguese detainees; persecuted Israelis; rebels in the Congo, in Angola, in Cameroon; Venezuelan, Peruvian, Colombian partisans. And there were others she was forgetting. Meetings, manifestos, rallies, tracts, delegations—he took on all kinds of tasks. He belonged to a great many groups and committees. But here no one would be asking anything of him. Macha was the only person they knew. They would have nothing to do but look at things together: she loved discovering things with him and finding that time, usually static in the well-established routine of their happiness, could again become an outpouring of new experiences. She stood up. She would have liked to be out in the streets already, under the walls of the Kremlin. She had forgotten how long the waiting could be in this country.

"Is our luggage coming?"

"It'll come eventually," said André.[2]

Three and a half hours, he thought. How close Moscow was, yet at the same time so far! Why, at just three and a half hours away, did he see

Macha so rarely? (But there were so many obstacles, not least the cost of the journey.)

"It's a long time, three years," he said. "I must look older."

"Not at all. You haven't changed."

"You look even more beautiful than ever."

He looked at her with great delight. You think that nothing can happen to you any more; you have even resigned yourself to the fact (and that hadn't been easy, although he hadn't let it show). And then along comes a wholly new major affection, which lights up your life. He had scarcely taken any interest in the frightened little girl—she was called Maria at the time—whom Claire used to bring to see him for a few hours from Japan, Brazil, or Moscow. And the young woman who had come to Paris after the war to introduce her husband had remained a stranger to him. But during Macha's second trip, in 1960, something had happened between them. He didn't quite understand why she had become attached to him in such an extreme way, but it had moved him. Nicole's love for him remained alive, attentive, joyous, but they were too used to each other for André to be able to awaken in her the sparkling happiness that, at this very moment, was transforming the rather severe features of Macha.

"Is our luggage coming?" asked Nicole.

"It'll come eventually," said André.

What was the point of being impatient? They had plenty of time at their disposal here. In Paris, André was tortured by how fast the hours flew by, torn between appointments; especially since his retirement, for he had overestimated how much leisure time he would have. Out of curiosity, and because he had not thought things through, he had allowed himself to take on a raft of obligations from which he could not manage to free himself. He was going to escape from them for a month; he would be able to live in the carefree way that he liked so much; that he liked *too* much, since it was exactly what caused most of his worries.

"Here are our bags," he said.

They put them into Macha's car and she got into the driver's seat. She drove slowly, like everyone here. There was the smell of fresh greenery during their drive; whole fleets of tree-trunks were drifting down the Moscova; and André felt welling up inside him the emotion without which life for him would have been completely lacking in spice. He was at the beginning of an adventure which excited and frightened him, an adventure of discovery. He had never been concerned with succeeding, or being someone. (If his mother had not imperiously devoted herself to ensuring that he pursued his studies, he would have been perfectly content with the same status as his parents, that of primary-school teachers in the sunshine of Provence.) It seemed to him that the truth of his existence and what he was did not rest with him: it was mysteriously scattered across the whole world. To know it, he had to find out about the past and different places: that was why he loved history and traveling. But while he could serenely study the past as refracted in books, approaching an unknown country—which, in its living profusion, would go beyond everything that he could know about it—always made him giddy. And this one was of more concern to him than any other. He had been brought up in the cult of Lenin: his mother, at 83, was still a militant in the ranks of the Communist Party. He himself had not become a member, but he had always thought, through the turmoils of both hope and despair, that the USSR held the key to the future, and hence to the present era and his own destiny. Yet never, even in the dark years of Stalinism, had he had the impression of being so far from understanding the country. Was this stay going to cast any light on it? In 1963, they had traveled as tourists—to the Crimea and Sotchi—looking at things superficially. This time he would ask questions, he would have the newspapers read to him, he would mix with crowds. The car turned into Gorky Street. There were people, shops. Would he manage to feel at home here? The thought of failing threw him into a panic. "I should have studied Russian more seriously!" he said to himself. Another of the things that he had promised himself he would do, but hadn't done: he hadn't got beyond the sixth lesson of the Assimil course. Nicole was right to call him a lazy old thing. He always felt up to reading, talking, going walking, but he had no stomach for unrewarding tasks like learning vocabulary, or taking systematic notes. In that case, he shouldn't be taking the world so much to heart. He was too serious *and* too frivolous: "That's the contradiction in me," he cheerfully told himself. (He had been delighted to hear the expression from the lips of an Italian colleague, who was a convinced Marxist and yet oppressed his wife.) In truth, he didn't feel at all bad about himself.

The railway station, painted in a garish green: Muscovite green. ("If you don't like that, you don't like Moscow" André had said, three years earlier.) Gorky Street. The Peking Hotel: a modest, tiered wedding cake when you compared it with the gigantic, ornate buildings allegedly inspired by the Kremlin, with which the city was bristling. Nicole remembered everything. And as soon as she got out of the car she recognized the smell of Moscow, an even stronger smell of diesel fumes than in 1963, doubtless because there were far more vehicles, especially trucks and vans. "Was it three years ago already?" she asked herself as she went into the large, bare entrance lobby. (There was a greyish sheet over the newspaper-seller's stall; people were lining up at the door of the restaurant, with its extravagant Chinese décor.) How quickly the three years had gone by. It was frightening. How many more three years were there left in her life? Nothing had changed, except that for foreigners—Macha had forewarned them—the formerly derisory charges for rooms had tripled. The woman attendant on the fourth floor gave them a key. All along the long corridor Nicole sensed her stare on the back of her neck. They were lucky to have curtains at the windows of their room: often it was just bare window-panes in the hotels. (Macha didn't have proper curtains at home, just light net curtains. She said that you get used to it, and that she would even have found it difficult to sleep in complete darkness.) Down below, work on the broad avenue was complete and the cars were surging down into a tunnel under Mayakovsky Square. The crowds on the pavements were wearing summer colors: it was June and they imagined it was hot!

"Here are some things for you," Nicole said to Macha as she began to unpack her suitcase.

Some recent novels, some Pléiade volumes, some records. And also some cardigans, stockings, blouses: Macha loved clothes. She found it a joy to touch and feel the wool and the silk; she compared one shade of color with another. Nicole went into the bathroom. Another stroke of luck: the two taps and the flushing toilet all worked. She changed her dress and touched up her make-up.

"What a pretty dress!" Macha said.

"I'm very fond of it."

At the age of 50, her outfits always seemed either too sad or too gay for her. But now she knew what she ought and ought not to wear; what she wore was no problem to her. But it gave her no pleasure either. The intimate, almost tender relationship that she formerly had with her clothes no longer existed. She hung up her suit in the wardrobe; although she had been wearing it for two years, it was an ordinary, impersonal object that carried nothing of herself within it. Meanwhile, Macha was smiling into the mirror, not at the pretty blouse that she had just put on, but at an unexpected and attractive incarnation of herself. "Yes, I can remember that," Nicole said to herself.

"I've reserved a table at the Praga," Macha said.

She had remembered that it was Nicole's favorite restaurant: she's so considerate, and has a memory as well organized as mine. Nicole could understand the affection that André had for her. All the more so as he had always wanted a daughter; he bore something of a grudge against Philippe for being a boy.

It took Macha only ten minutes to drive them to the Praga. They left their coats in the cloakroom, which was a compulsory ritual: you were forbidden to go into a restaurant with a coat on your back or over your arm. They sat down in a dining room with a flagstone floor, full of palm trees and greenery, with a large purplish landscape painting covering the whole of one wall.

"How much vodka?" Macha asked. "I'm driving, so I won't drink."

"Order three hundred grams in any case," André said.

He looked toward Nicole. "Since it's our first evening?"

"All right. Since it's our first evening," she said, with a smile.

He tended to drink in the way that he smoked, to excess. As far as tobacco was concerned, she had given up the struggle, but she managed to moderate his drinking habits.

"Since it's our first evening, I'll forget my diet," she said. "I'll have caviar and chicken julienne."

"Are you on a diet?"

"Yes, for the last six months. I was putting on weight."

Perhaps she ate more than before she retired; in any case, she was getting less exercise. Philippe had said to her one day, "Well, fancy that: you're filling out." (Since then, he had scarcely seemed to notice that she had become thinner.) And, to make matters worse, all that people could talk about in Paris this year was keeping one's figure, or getting it back: low calories, carbohydrates, miracle drugs.

"You look fine," said Macha.

"I've lost five kilos. And I'm making sure that I don't put them back on. I weigh myself every day."

Some years ago, she had never imagined that she would ever worry about her weight. But now that's what it had come to! The less easily she was able to identify with her body, the more she felt obliged to pay attention to it. She was responsible for it and she looked after it with a kind of worried devotion, in the way she might have looked after an old friend who had become slightly unattractive, diminished, and who needed her.

"Well, Philippe is getting married then?" Macha said. "What's his fiancée like?"

"Pretty, and intelligent," André said.

"I don't like her at all," said Nicole.

Macha started to laugh. "You certainly said that with feeling! I've never known a mother-in-law who liked her daughter-in-law."

"She's the 'super woman' type," said Nicole. "There are a lot like that in Paris. They have some sort of career, they claim to dress well, to engage in sports, look after their house perfectly, bring up their children very well. They want to prove to themselves that they can be successful at all levels. And, in fact, they spread themselves too thinly, they succeed in nothing. Young women of that kind make my blood run cold."

"You're being a little unfair," said André.

"Maybe."

Once again she asked herself: Why Irène? I thought that when he got married . . . I thought that he wouldn't get married, that he would remain the little boy who had said to me, like all little boys: "When I'm grown up, I'll marry you." Then one evening he had said, "I've got some great news for you!" in the over-excited manner of a child who, on some public holiday, has been playing for too long, laughing too much, shouting too much. And Nicole had experienced that heaviness in her chest, that flushing of her cheeks, the straining of all her muscles to prevent her lips from trembling. One February evening, with the curtains drawn, and the lights picking out the rainbow colors of the cushions, suddenly his impending absence had opened up an abyss: "He will be living with another woman, somewhere else." Well, yes, it's true! I'll have to resign myself to it, she told herself. The vodka was iced, the caviar a velvety grey in color, she liked Macha, and she was going to have André all to herself for a month. She felt very happy.

He felt very happy sitting in an armchair between the two beds, with Macha propped up on one side and Nicole on the other. (In 1963, Youri was away on an archaeological trip; he had taken Vassili with him and Macha's apartment was empty. This year, for them to spend the evening alone with her, they had no alternative but to use their hotel bedroom.)

"I've arranged things so that I can be free for the whole month," Macha said.

She worked for a publisher who published Russian classics in French, in Moscow, and contemporary texts in a journal that went out to various foreign countries. She translated, but she also acted as a reader, choosing and recommending.

"We could leave for Vladimir at the end of the week," she continued. "It's three hours away by car."

She talked about places with Nicole: Novgorod, Pskoff, Rostov the Great, Leningrad. Nicole wanted to be on the move and that was fine: it was largely to please him that she had come to the USSR and he wanted it to be a pleasant trip for her. He looked at them, and felt a glow of warmth. Macha had much more in common with Nicole than with Claire, who was pretty but empty-headed, and, fortunately, had been as anxious as he was to get divorced once their child had been made legitimate. He was pleased that they got along so well together, the two people he loved most in the world. (As far as Philippe was concerned, he had never been able to rid himself of a certain jealousy. Too often he found himself as the third person, coming between Nicole and her son.) Nicole counted much more to him than Macha, but when he was with Macha he had this feeling that he would never again have experienced without her: a kind of romantic feeling. Nothing was stopping him from having new affairs. One fine day Nicole had announced that she considered herself too old for sexual pleasures. (It was absurd: he loved her just as fully today as he used to.) Accordingly, she had granted him his freedom. In fact, she would still have been quite capable of fits of jealousy; and they no longer had enough time left to live to waste it in quarreling. Then again, in spite of gymnastic exercises and severe self-restraint, he no longer liked his body: it was no gift to give to a woman. His chastity didn't torment him (except upon reflection, when he recognized his indifference as a mark of his age). But neither was there any pleasure in the thought: "It's all over. Life holds nothing unexpected for me any more." Then Macha had come along, and was still there.

"Isn't your husband going to be angry that we're taking you away from him?" he asked.

"Youri's never angry," Macha said cheerfully.

According to their conversation in the Praga, it seemed that her feelings for Youri were more a matter of friendship than of love. But, all in all, it was lucky that he more or less suited her: she had married him on impulse, in order to be able to stay in the USSR, since she was sickened by the circles that her mother and step-father mixed in, and by the capitalist world in general. This had become *her* country: that was part of what gave her such prestige in André's eyes.

"What's the situation like culturally this year?"

"The same as ever. We're struggling on."

She was in what she called the liberal camp, which was fighting against academicism, dogmatism, the vestiges of Stalinism.

"And are you winning?"

"Sometimes. There's a rumor that certain scholars are getting ready to shatter the sacrosanct idea of a dialectic of nature. That would be a great victory."

"It's good to have something to fight for," he said.

"You fight for things, too," Nicole said sharply.

"No. Not since the Algerian War. I try to be of some help; it's not the same thing. What's more, it's almost always futile."

Since 1962, he had lost all hold on the world. That was perhaps why he was so restless, because he was not acting any more. His powerlessness—that of the French Left as a whole—sometimes depressed him. Especially first thing in the morning, when, instead of getting up, he would bury himself in the bedclothes, pulling the sheet over his head until the moment when he remembered an urgent meeting and leapt out of bed.

"Then why do you do it?" said Macha.

"I can see no reason for *not* doing it."

"You could do your own work. Those articles that you were talking about three years ago . . ."

"I didn't write them. Nicole will tell you that I'm a lazy old thing."

"Not at all!" said Nicole. "You live in the way that you want to. Why force yourself?"

Is that what she thought? She didn't press him in the way that she used to, but that was probably because she had given up the struggle. She wouldn't have attached so much importance to her son's thesis if she hadn't been a little disappointed with her husband. Too bad.

"In any case, it's a pity," said Macha.

In his head, he kept hearing the same thing: it's a pity. He had resigned himself to Nicole's regrets, but he would have liked to present to Macha an image of himself other than that of an old retiree who has done nothing. He had had some ideas on the subject of certain contemporary events that Nicole found interesting. Several times he had promised himself that he would look into them more deeply. But it was the present that consumed him: he didn't want to turn back toward the past before he had finished understanding the world of today. And what time it took to keep up to date with things! Still, he had thought that the day would come when this investigation would be complete, and then he would be able to follow through the projects that he had enthusiastically outlined and—provisionally—abandoned. That day had not come, and would not come. He realized that now: the task was an infinite one. Year by year he became better informed, yet found himself to be more ignorant. The obscurities, difficulties and contradictions were multiplying around him. China seemed much more impenetrable to him than in 1950. The foreign policy of the USSR disconcerted him.

"It's not too late," Macha went on, in an encouraging tone, as if she were afraid of having upset him.[3]

"No, it's not too late," he said brightly.

It was too late; he would not change. In fact, if, like Philippe, he had been able to discipline himself, he would have been able at one and the same time to gather information about the present and go more deeply into a particular historical question. But any constraint made him bristle, perhaps because he had been subject to too many during his childhood. He had retained a taste for playing truant, and seeking adventures—something that was so severely punished and all the more delicious as a result. He had never sincerely reproached himself for his laziness: it arose out of his openness to the world, out of his determination to remain available. Suddenly, seen through the eyes of Macha, it looked like something quite different: an oddity, a habit, a flaw that marked him indelibly. He had given in to it; it sprang from within himself. And now, even if he wanted to, he could not overcome it.

"It's touching, the way Macha is fond of you," said Nicole, when they were alone together again.

"I wonder why," he said. "I think Youri is more of a comrade than a support to her. She wanted a father. When she came to Paris in 1960 she had decided to love me."

"Don't be so modest," said Nicole, laughing. "I loved you without having decided to do so."

"I was young."

"You haven't aged."

He did not protest. Nicole seemed not to be conscious of her age. He did not talk about his own age, but he thought about it often, being horrified by it. For a long time—in bad faith, thoughtlessly, by pulling the wool over his own eyes—he had refused to consider himself an adult. The teacher, the father, the fifty-year-old, he wasn't *really* any of these things. Now here he was with his life closing in around him; neither the past nor the future could offer him excuses any more. He was a sixty-year-old, an old retiree who had done nothing. Well, he might as well be that as anything else. The regrets that he had begun to entertain had already vanished. Had he been a lecturer at the Sorbonne and a well-known historian, he would have found himself with the weight of that other destiny behind him and it would not have been any lighter to bear. What was horrifying was to find himself defined, static, formed; to find that the ephemeral moments accumulate and form a matrix around you in which you are trapped. He kissed Nicole and climbed into bed. At least there was still dreaming. He put his cheek on the pillow. He liked to feel himself slipping away into sleep. His dreams involved more radical changes of scenery than any book or film. Their very gratuitousness delighted him. Except in those dreadful nightmares when all his teeth crumbled in his mouth, he did not have a particular age in his dreams; he escaped from time. His dreams doubtless were situated in his own history; they flourished on his past. But in a way that was mysterious to him, and they did not go on into the future. They constituted a pure present and he could forget them. From one night to the next they vanished; they sprang up without accumulating: a source of eternal novelty.

* * *

"I would still like to understand why they ban foreigners from going to Vladimir by car," said André.

The train was traveling fast, and smoothly; but all the seats in the coach were facing backward and Nicole was unable to travel backward without her stomach protesting. (How humiliating that had been at the stage when she was trying to rival boys in matters of health, strength and endurance!) She had her knees under her on the seat and was trying to face André and Macha: this eventually became grueling.

"What you must understand is that there is nothing to understand," said Macha. "It's a good road, and the villages that you go through are thriving. It's just bureaucratic absurdity, against the old background of mistrust of foreigners."

"Kindness and mistrust: it's a strange mixture," said Nicole.

That was what had disconcerted them in 1963. Standing in line—in front of the Mausoleum, at the Goum, or at the door of a restaurant—Macha had only to say a word for people to step aside to let them through. Yet in the Crimea they had come across prohibitions everywhere: the east coast and Sebastopol were prohibited areas for foreigners. Intourist had claimed that the mountain road linking Yalta and Simferopol was being repaired, but Macha had been told in confidence that it was, in fact, closed only to foreigners.

"You're not too tired?" André asked.

"I can manage."

She was rather worn out, but she forgot her tiredness as she watched the countryside race by, vast and quiet, softened by the light from a sunset that was never-ending. She had just had four splendid days. Moscow had changed a little, was somewhat uglier. (What a pity that changes are almost always for the worse, for places as well as for people.) They had discovered some avenues for the first time, gone all over ancient quarters of the city. Red Square, closed to motor vehicles, seemed bigger and more solemn: a holy place. Unfortunately, whereas Saint Basil's Church used to rise up into the sky, a huge hotel behind it now blocked off the horizon. Nevertheless, Nicole had been delighted to see the churches of the Kremlin again, as well as the icons there and in the museums. There were still a great many old houses that she found charming, especially in the evening, when you could glimpse through the windows and a screen of green plants the warm light from an old-fashioned lampshade, made of orange or pink silk, with fringes.

"Here we are at Vladimir," said Macha.

They left their luggage at the hotel. It was too late to dine there: Macha had decided that they would picnic outside. The sky was still pink and a full round moon had risen. They followed a path that ran alongside the Kremlin ramparts: beneath them was a river, the train station, flickering lights. There was a church in the garden that they crossed, with its scent of phlox and petunias; lovers were embracing on benches.

"We could stop here," Nicole said.

"A little further on is better," said Macha.

She gave orders, they obeyed. It amused Nicole, because she was not used to taking orders.

They kept walking and went into another garden surrounding another church.

"Let's sit here," said Macha. "This is the most beautiful church in Vladimir."

The church was slim and slender in a white dress covered with embroidery half way up, and crowned by a single, golden onion-shaped dome. Its simplicity shone out brightly. They sat down and Macha unpacked their food.

"I'll have just two hard-boiled eggs," said Nicole.

"Aren't you hungry?"

"Yes, but I don't want to put on weight."

"Oh, don't be obsessive!" said Macha. "You must eat a little more than that!"

Macha's indignant, gruff voice made Nicole smile: no one spoke to her in that tone. She bit into a *pirozhok*.

"Are Youri and Vassili as docile as I am?"

"They're quite docile," said Macha cheerfully.

"Try to intimidate your father then. Tell him that he risks lung cancer by smoking forty cigarettes a day."

"Get lost, both of you," said André in a polite tone.

"It's true that you smoke too much," Macha said.

"Pass me the vodka then."

Macha filled the paper cups and for a while they ate and drank in silence.

"The church is beautiful," said André with a tinge of regret in his voice. "I'm looking at it as hard as I can, and I know that in a week's time I won't remember it any more."

"Neither will I," said Nicole.

Yes, she would forget the golden and white church; she had forgotten so much! Her curiosity, which was still virtually intact, often seemed to her no more than a crazy relic: what was the point of it when memories crumble into dust? The moon was shining, as was the little star which faithfully accompanies it, and Nicole repeated to herself the lovely lines from *Aucassin and Nicolette*: "I see you tiny star. Drawn closely to the moon."[4] That's the advantage of literature, she told herself: you can take words around with you. Images fade, become distorted, disappear. But she could still find the old words in her throat, precisely as they had been written. They linked her to former centuries, when the stars shone in exactly the way they do today. And this rebirth, this permanence gave her an impression of eternity. The earth was worn down, yet there were moments like this, when it seemed as fresh as in primordial times, and when the present was self-sufficient. Nicole was here, she was looking at the church: for no reason, simply in order to see it. Warmed by a few mouthfuls of vodka, she found this very disinterestedness poignant and charming.

They went back to the hotel. There were no curtains, but Nicole tied a scarf around her head and quickly fell asleep. Tender waking moments. In the bedroom, now flooded with light, André was curled up on the bed, blindfolded like a condemned man, with his hand pressed against the wall in an infantile way, as if, during a disturbed sleep, he had needed to experience the solidity of the world. How many times had she sat—how many times would she sit in the future—on the edge of the bed, putting her hand on his shoulder, shaking him gently? Sometimes he murmured, "Good morning, mommy," and then he shook himself and smiled in a dazed manner. She put her hand on his shoulder.

"I want to show you something," said Macha, pushing open the door of a church. She led them through the semi-darkness. "Look at the fate reserved for foreigners."

The fresco represented the Last Judgment. On the right, angels and some of the chosen few in ageless long robes; on the left, condemned to hell, French people in period costumes, with black doublets, breeches tied above the calf, lace ruffles, little pointed beards, and behind them, Muslims in turbans.

"It really is an old tradition," said Nicole.

"Actually," said Macha, "except for a few rare periods, Russia has been broadly open to the West. But in certain quarters there has always been hostility, particularly in the Church. Notice that they are damned as infidels, not because of their nationality."

"In practice, it amounts to the same thing," said André.

He was in a bad mood this morning. The previous day had been delightful. He liked Vladimir, with its churches and the Roublov frescoes. And eating badly did not matter to him: his mother had brought him up well. But the discussion that he had started with Macha irritated him. Until then, he had been firmly convinced that she shared his views.

"Your nationalism won't be easily dislodged," he continued, as they came out of the church. "The gist of what you have just explained is that you are no longer a revolutionary country and that that's fine."

"Not at all. We have had the revolution and it is not in question. But in France you don't know what war is. We do. We don't want it."

Macha had spoken angrily and André, too, felt annoyed.

"No one wants it. What I'm saying is that if you give America a free hand, if you don't stop the escalation, that's when America is to be feared. Munich prevented nothing at all."

"Do you think that if we bomb the American bases, the USA won't retaliate? We won't take that risk."

"If they attack China, will you still not make a move?"

"Oh, you're not going to start again!" said Nicole. "You've been arguing for two hours: neither of you is going to persuade the other."

They walked on for a moment in silence. The streets were full of people. It was the Birch-Tree Festival; doubtless a substitute for Corpus Christi. People had danced until midnight in a huge open-air enclosure (there were neither tables, nor chairs, just a dance-floor surrounded by a fence). Early in the morning there had been a procession on the central avenue: trucks with girls in white dresses and boys in red ties, holding birch branches in their hands. They were singing. In the park, a pavilion had been turned into a buffet: there were little tables outside, large ones inside, and on them piles of cakes and rolls.

"Let's sit down and eat something," Macha suggested.

"Oh, yes! If we can eat, let's eat," said Nicole.

On the previous day, in Vladimir, there was a food shortage. The restaurant was not serving fish, or mutton, or poultry, or vegetables, or fruit: just stews that Nicole and Macha found inedible. The bread, which was neither white nor black, tasted like glue. In front of the hotel, people were lining up to buy pancakes hard enough to break your teeth. And there they were this morning, with women coming out of the pavilion loaded with garlands of pretzels and their shopping bags stuffed full of food. They ordered cakes and egg and cheese sandwiches, which were excellent.

"Nothing to eat in the towns, and here as much as one wants. How has that come about?" asked André.

"I've told you that you mustn't try to understand," said Macha.

According to her, they were not to be surprised by any incoherence, any absurdity. The country was still hampered by a fossilized bureaucratic machine, which was responsible for enormous wastage and paralyzing decisions. The government was doing its best by all possible means to combat this inertia, but it would take time to win the battle.

"Remember the story of the school chairs," she continued.

The previous morning, she had come out of the hotel doubled up with laughter, because of the program that she had just heard on Vladimir radio station. One factory made chair backs, another the seats, and a third assembled them. But, for one thing, there was always a shortage of either seats or backs; and, for another, whenever an attempt was made to fit the two pieces together, one of them broke. After a series of steps and measures, inquiries, checks, reports, it had been concluded that the assembly procedure was faulty. But they had to go around a vast administrative circuit before authorization to modify it could be given. "It's pure absurdity," Macha had said, pointing out at the same time that in putting out this story the radio was contributing to the struggle against bureaucracy. She was very free in her judgments of the régime, being critical and discriminating. If she approved of its foreign policy, therefore, it was not out of blind compliance, and this disturbed André all the more. But he did not want to talk about it again, for the moment. He looked at the crowd all around him: people's faces were shining with gaiety, as if they had participated willingly in the processions, the ceremonies, the whole of this festival. And yet they seemed firmly supervised; they were obeying instructions. Gaiety and discipline: there is no contradiction. But he would have liked to know how the two things were reconciled. Probably in different ways according to people's ages and circumstances. If only he had been able to understand what they were saying!

"You ought to give us Russian lessons," he said to Macha.

"Oh, no!" said Nicole. "I don't even know the alphabet. How much do you expect me to learn in a month? But you take lessons if you'd like to," she added.

"You'll be bored while I'm doing so."

"Of course not. I'll read."

"Fine! Tomorrow, in Moscow, we'll make a start," André said. "Perhaps I shall feel a little less lost."

"Because you feel lost?"

"Completely."

"Those will be your first words when you get to heaven—or hell: 'I feel completely lost,'" Nicole said, smiling at him affectionately.

She had always smiled at his confusion. When they were traveling, she accepted things as they were presented to her. "Well, what do you expect! It's Africa and this is a colony!" she said to him at Gardhaia. (André was still quite young, and it was his first encounter with the Maghreb. There were camels and veiled women, but also canned food and hardware in the shops. It was both distant Arabia and a French village: he could not manage to grasp what it was like for the men he came across to belong to both.) The reasons for his present confusion were much more serious. What did it feel like to be someone from the Soviet Union? To what extent did the singing young people on these avenues resemble French young people; in what respects were they different? In their minds, how did the will to construct, socialism, and national self-interest blend together? Much depended on the answers that could be given to these questions.

"You're wrong to talk of self-interest," Macha said to him a few hours later. In the room where they were drinking tea, resting after a long walk, she had taken up the morning's conversation again, but in a more relaxed tone. "Atomic war doesn't involve just us, but the whole world. You must understand that we are torn between two imperatives: helping socialism across the world and preserving the peace. We don't want to abandon either."

"Oh! I'm well aware that the situation isn't a simple one."

"Then why don't you leave it at that?" Nicole said quickly. "Macha wants me to look at her translation with her. It we don't do it immediately, we won't have time."

"Yes, we must get down to it," said Macha.

They sat side by side at the table. He opened a guide to the USSR that he had brought from Paris and pretended to be absorbed in it, but his thoughts continued to go around in circles. It was true that one could not rule out the possibility of a terrifying American retaliation for any attempt to counter their escalation. What followed from this?

In 1945, the atomic bomb was only a fairly abstract threat: now it had become an anguishing possibility. There were people who were not worried by it: "If I have to die, whether the world survives or not is all the same to me." One of André's friends had even said, "If it comes to it, I shall have fewer regrets if I can think that I'm leaving nothing behind." He himself would have killed himself at once if he had known that the world was going to be blown up. Or just that the whole of civilization would be destroyed, that historical continuity would be broken and that the survivors—doubtless Chinese people—would start up again from scratch. Perhaps they would enable socialism to triumph, but their version of it would bear no relation to the one that his parents, his comrades and he himself had dreamed of. Yet if the USSR settled down to peaceful co-existence, socialism would be a long time coming. How many hopes had been disappointed! The Popular Front, the Resistance in France; and the emancipation of the Third World, which had not pushed back capitalism by a single inch. The Chinese Revolution had resulted in the Sino-Soviet conflict. No, the future had never seemed so bleak to André. "My life will have served no purpose," he thought. What he had wanted was for it to be usefully incorporated into a history that led men toward happiness. Doubtless they would find happiness one day; André had believed in that for too long not to still believe in it a little. But it would come about in such a roundabout way that history would have stopped being *his* history.

Nicole's voice broke into his reflections.

"Macha's French is entirely correct; even a little *too* correct, a little stilted."

"I'm so afraid of making mistakes," said Macha.

"One can sense that."

Once more they bent over the typed sheets, smiling at each other and whispering. Nicole, who was usually so hard on women, felt a real friendship for Macha; André was delighted by how well they got along.

"I'd like to look at the translation, too," he said. Even if the future seemed bleak, he must not spoil this moment of tender intimacy. He tore himself away from his ruminations.

* * *

"I'd be glad to sit down," said Nicole. The Uzbek restaurant was charming, with its little open-air enclosures and its exotic clientele—men with flat faces and slanting eyes, wearing square hats; women with heavy black braids, in multi-colored silk dresses. You could eat the best *chachliks* in Moscow there. But the din of the orchestra—and it was the same everywhere—had driven them away as soon as they had swallowed their last mouthful. Macha had suggested a walk. And, since they had walked a great deal during the day, Nicole felt tired. It was annoying: she used to be able to go on for miles, as merrily as André! Now, every evening after their long rambles her legs gave out on her. She did not let it show. But, after all, it was stupid to force oneself. They were going past an empty bench—a rare windfall—and she might as well profit from it. They sat down.

"Well, then, in the end are we able to go to Rostov the Great, or not?"

"I'm afraid not," said Macha.

"And our little trip on the Moskva?"

"I can ask . . ."

"Oh, why don't we simply stay in Moscow!" said André. "There are so many things that we want to see again."

"We shall see them again in any case."

Seeing things again – there had been a time, when she was nearly forty, when that delighted her. But not before that, when she badly needed novelty. Just as she did now. So few years left to live: walking about in Red Square day after day was a waste of time. It was a wonderful square: what an unexpected impact it had made, three years ago. This year, too, on the first day. But already Nicole knew it too well. That was the great difference between their first trip and this one. In 1963, everything was new; this time, almost nothing was. That was probably the source of her slight disappointment.

"And where are we going to spend the evening?" she asked.

"Why not here?" said André.

"On this bench, all evening?"

This year, they did not know where to go in the evenings. Youri seemed very nice—since he did not speak French, relations with him were rather basic—but he worked in his room, and Vassili in his. They had to whisper in order not to disturb the two of them, and, even so, felt that they were intruding. The hotel room was not welcoming. Many cafés had been built in the intervening three years. With their glass walls, they were not ugly from the outside, but inside they were like cheese shops, lacking comfort and intimacy. In any case, by this time of day they were closed. Would it be this bench, then, next to a subway station, in a square smelling of diesel fumes?

"We're fine here," said André. "There's a smell of greenery in the air."

He was fine anywhere. He was not cold in his flannel suit, and Macha found it warm at any temperature over 50°F But Nicole was shivering in her light silk dress. Also, to spend the whole evening on a bench was to feel like the victim of a disaster.

"I'm cold," she said.

"We can go to the bar in the National," said Macha.

"Good idea."

The bar stayed open until two o'clock in the morning; you could pay in foreign currency and have whisky, as well as American cigarettes. She had pointed this out to André and Macha on the day when they lunched there, but they had not responded. Still, Macha had made a mental note of it and she remembered it at the appropriate time. They got up.

"Is it far?"

"Half an hour's walk. Perhaps we'll find a taxi," said Macha.

Nicole wanted a taxi: her legs and feet were hurting. Usually, you could easily find one: there were twice as many as in 1963. This evening quite a number were going by, with their little green eye illuminated in a promising way, but however much you signaled to them they kept moving on relentlessly: they were not allowed to stop on these big avenues. The nearest taxi rank was some distance away; and perhaps there would be a line and no vehicles. Walking and sitting on benches was quite a tough regimen. Moscow was perhaps fine for its inhabitants; Macha would not have wanted to live anywhere else, especially not in Paris (which was surprising, all the same). But how austere it all was for foreigners! Perhaps I've grown old in the last three years, Nicole thought to herself; I am less good at putting up with discomfort. And that will only get worse. "We're in the flower of old age," said André. A strange kind of flower—more like prickly thistles.

"I'm dead tired," she said.

"We're almost there."

"It's no fun, getting old."

Macha had taken her arm. "Come on! You're so young, both of you."

People often said that to her: "You seem so young;" "You're young." An ambiguous compliment, which heralds painful times to come. To stay young is to retain some vitality, some cheerfulness, some presence of mind. What awaits the old, therefore, is routine, gloom, senility. They say: "Old age doesn't exist; it's nothing." Or even: "It's very beautiful, very moving." But when they encounter it, they discreetly cover it up, with words that lie. Macha said: "You're young." But she had taken Nicole's arm. Basically, it was because of Macha that Nicole had been feeling her age so acutely since she arrived. She realized that she had hung onto the image of herself that she had at the age of forty. She recognized herself in the vigorous young woman that was Macha, all the more so as Macha exuded experience and authority, and was as mature as Nicole; they were peers. And then, all of a sudden, a gesture, an inflection of Macha's voice, a considerate action reminded her that there was an age difference of twenty years between them—and that she was sixty.

"What a crowd!" said André.

The bar was smoky and rowdy. There was one free table, wedged between some young Americans, who were laughing noisily, and some middle-aged French people making loud jokes. Some West Germans—only Western currencies were accepted—were singing in chorus. A jazz record was playing, but could scarcely be heard. Still, it was pleasant to rediscover the taste of whisky, the taste of evenings in Paris with André, with Philippe. (It was hot there: they would have sat on a café terrace in Montparnasse.)

"Are you pleased to find yourself back in the West?"

"For a while, yes."

André had burned his bridges. He had written to no one, having scribbled the briefest of notes on Nicole's last letter to Philippe. He smiled in the mornings when she stubbornly bought a copy of *Humanité* which was several days old. He was always the same on trips. He easily forgot Paris; he did not have his roots there.

"Partying conference delegates are worse than a wigmaker's wedding!" he said glumly.

"Do you want us to leave?"

"Of course not."

He was staying to please Nicole; but he would not want to come back. And neither would Macha, who was ill at ease. (There were no Russians there, apart from two heavily made-up women, who were obviously trying their luck.) Yet it was a pleasant spot that opened out into the world beyond or at least gave a glimpse of it. A tall black man, in a red shirt, had started dancing all on his own, and people were marking the rhythm by clapping their hands.

"He dances really well," said Nicole.

"Yes."

André seemed absent. He had contracted a habit some days ago: he pressed a finger against his cheek, at the level of his gums. She said, a little impatiently:

"Are you in pain? Go to see a dentist."

"I'm not in pain."

"Then why are you fingering your cheek all the time?"

"I'm making sure that it's not painful."

He had had a phase when he took his pulse twenty times a day, staring rigidly at the hands of his watch. Little compulsions that are not serious, but which constitute a sign, nevertheless. Of what? That life is grinding to a halt, that senility is around the corner. Senility—she knew the Larousse definitions by heart: their asymmetry had struck her. Youthfulness: the quality of being youthful. Senility: weakening of the body and mind brought on by old age.

* * *

Youri and Nicole had left immediately after lunch. André had stayed with Macha for his Russian lesson. He reached for the small carafe of vodka:

"Enough work for today."

He added disappointedly: "I've lost my memory."

"Not at all; you do very well."

"I don't retain what I learn. I forget as I'm going along."

He drank a mouthful of vodka and Macha shook her head disapprovingly: "I'll never get used to that way of drinking."

She emptied her glass in a single swallow.

"It's true that one month is a derisory amount of time for learning a language," he said.

"Why one month? You have nothing special to do in Paris, do you?"

"Nothing."

"Well then, stay a little longer."

Why not? I'll talk to Nicole about it this evening.

On fine summer days like this, Moscow was very gay. People were pressing around the street vendors selling *kvass* and beer on tap;[5] they were besieging the automatic machines which, for one kopeck, cough up more or less fresh water, and, for three kopecks, soda with a vaguely fruity taste. Their faces expressed good humor.

They were much less disciplined than André had imagined; they crossed the roads when the traffic lights were at red, just as calmly as they did when they were at green. He thought back to the conversation he had had at lunch with Youri.

"Youri didn't convince me," he said.

"Yet I can assure you that he's right," said Macha.

They had been talking about the agreements recently reached with Renault, and André had been astonished that the USSR envisaged making 600,000 individual cars rather than improving its road network and public transportation. But public transportation worked well, said Youri; and building roads before the population felt the need, would be an inept policy: people would clamor for roads themselves when they had cars. Even under a socialist regime, citizens have the right to certain satisfactions of a private kind. The government was making strong efforts to develop consumer goods; they were to be congratulated for it.

"Do you think that you will succeed in building socialism by making more and more concessions to private property?"

"I think that socialism is made for men and not the opposite," she said. "One has to give a little thought to their short-term interests."

"Yes, of course."

What had he imagined exactly? That people's interests here were different? That they were less attached to material goods? That the socialist ideal remained alive in them and replaced everything else for them?

"The Chinese accuse us of losing ground; it's absurd. There's no question of going back to capitalism. But you must realize that this people has had only a life of sacrifices: during the war, and during the period of reconstruction. Even now, we are hardly spoiled. We can't have this austerity imposed upon us indefinitely."

"What you call 'austerity' doesn't seem so striking to me. My own childhood was harder than Vassili's. My mother's life hasn't been easy. She is happy—at least, as far as one can be at 83—but that's because she has so few needs."

"Why do you say 'as far as one can be at 83'? It must be very satisfying to feel that you have a long and very full life behind you."

She was deliberately diverting the conversation. She did not like talking to André about this country, which she considered to be her own: whether he criticized or praised the USSR, she was rather impatient with him.

"You look at things too abstractly," she often said.

He dropped the topic.

"At 83, you don't have any future; and that takes all the charm away from the present."

"If I live that long myself, I think I shall spend my time telling myself the story of my life. It's wonderful to have 83 years behind you! Think of all the things she has seen!"

"Even I have seen a fair number of things. But what's left of them for me?"

"A very great deal, of course. Everything you were telling me yesterday about your period with the Red Falcons,[6] about the electoral bust-ups in Avignon . . ."

"I can tell people, but I don't really remember."

It would be fine, he often thought, if the past were a landscape in which one could wander at will, discovering little by little how routes meander and double back. But this was not so. He could recite names and dates, in the way that a schoolboy recites a well-learned lesson. He had a certain knowledge, and some distorted, faded images, as static as those in an old history book—they sprang up, at random, against a blank background.

"All the same, getting older is enriching," said Macha. "I feel more enriched now than when I was twenty. Don't you?"

"A little richer; but also much less so."

"What is it that you've lost?"

"Youth."

He poured himself a glass of vodka. His third? Or his fourth?

"I hated being young myself," she said.

He stared at her rather remorsefully. He had created her, then abandoned her to a stupid mother and to an ambassador.

"Did you miss having a real father?"

She hesitated: "Not consciously. I was concerned with the future. With escaping from my surroundings. Making my marriage a success. Bringing Vassili up properly. Making myself useful. And then, as I became more mature, I felt the need—how can I put it?—for roots. The past has become important: that is, France. And you."

She looked at him in a trusting way, and he felt guilty; not just because of the past, but because at that moment he would have liked to offer her someone more brilliant as a father.

"Aren't you a little disappointed that I have dried up?"

"Of course not! For one thing, you still have plenty of time in front of you."

"No. It's clear that I shall never produce anything else. Perhaps it might just be possible if I left Paris. But Nicole couldn't put up with living anywhere else. Or with being further away from Philippe."

He had talked about it once, jokingly. And she had replied, jokingly: "You would die of boredom as much as I would." No, he often thought of it longingly. His mother's presence did not weigh heavily: she would not have been a nuisance to them. He would have done some gardening, fished for trout in the green waters of the Gard, walked in the scrubland with Nicole, done some reading, lazed about, and perhaps done some work. Perhaps. But, in any case, that was his only chance. It would never happen in Paris.

"In any case, it doesn't matter much," she said. "I'm of the same opinion as Nicole: you should live in the way you want."

"I'm not sure that that's what she really thinks. And you yourself said that it's a pity!"

"It was just for something to say." She bent over and kissed him.

"I love you the way you are."

"And what way is that?"

She smiled: "Are you looking for compliments? Well, what struck me in 1960—and it remains true—is how you could give yourself to others, and at the same time, be present to yourself. And then the attention that you pay to things: when I'm with you, everything becomes important. And you are bright and cheerful. And I swear that you have stayed young: younger than all the people I know. You've lost nothing."

"Well, if you're pleased with me like that . . ."

He smiled, too, but he knew very well that he had lost something: the fire, the sap that the Italians have such a nice name for: *stamina*. He emptied his glass. That was probably why he sought the joyful warmth of alcohol. Too much so, Nicole said. But what else is left for us, at our age? He touched his gum. It was scarcely sensitive. But a little, nevertheless. If the dentist did not manage to save the tooth that was supporting his bridge, there would be no other solution than dentures. How dreadful! He no longer wanted to be attractive: but at least he wanted people to be able to imagine, on looking at him, that he had *been* attractive. If only he could avoid becoming an entirely sexless being. When he was scarcely beginning to get used to his condition as an adult, he was going to be thrust into that of a very old man. No!

"Does Nicole feel badly about growing old, too?"

"Less than I do, I think."

"Was she disappointed not to go to Rostov?"

"A little."

The irrepressible Nicole, he thought affectionately. As energetic and eager as she was at twenty. Without her, he would have been content to wander around the Moscow streets, chatting about this and that, sitting down on benches. Perhaps in that way he would have absorbed the atmosphere of the city better. But if he had told her that, it would have hurt her, and he did not want that for anything in the world.

"Five o'clock! And she's expecting us at five," said Macha. "We must hurry."

They left the apartment in a rush.

Nicole liked Macha's apartment very much. The courtyard was sad, the staircase dingy, the rusty metal elevator was often stuck, but the three small rooms—one for each of them, plus a kitchen and a bathroom—had been very well arranged, with a few photos, some well-chosen reproductions, fine carpets that Youri had brought back from Asia, and some objects collected by Macha during her childhood travels. As she went down the staircase, Nicole was suddenly nostalgic for her own studio apartment, her furniture, her own objects. It came back to her as it was when she had left it on the last morning, with a large bouquet of roses on her table, as young and fresh as young lettuce. You never saw roses here. And since her arrival—ten days ago—she had heard no music: it was almost a physical privation. She turned the corner of the road onto the big avenue that led to the hotel. In Paris, she knew all the shops on Boulevard Raspail; the faces of many people were familiar to her, and they all spoke to her. These faces meant nothing to her. Why was she so far away from her own life? It was a fine June day. The trees were in heat; the pigeons were flapping about in the pools of soft, fleecy pollen lying on the pavements, and its white flakes were fluttering down around Nicole, getting into her nose and mouth, sticking to her hair, making her head spin. They were fluttering down into the library and sticking to her hair on that afternoon when she had, in a certain way, said goodbye to her body. There had already been signs before that. In the mirror, in photographs, her image had come to look worn, but she still recognized herself in it. When she was chatting with male friends, they were men and she felt herself to be a woman. And then this young man that she did not know—he was so handsome—had arrived with André. He had shaken her hand with a kind of distracted politeness and something had definitively been undermined. For her, he was a young, attractive male: for him, she was as asexual as an eighty-year-old woman. She had never recovered from that look; she had stopped coinciding with her body, which was now an unfamiliar skin, a kind of distressing disguise. Perhaps the metamorphosis had taken rather longer than that, but her memory crystallized it in that image: two doe eyes turning away from her with indifference. From that point on, she had remained unresponsive in bed: you have to like yourself a little to take pleasure in being in someone's arms. André had not understood her, but little by little he had allowed himself to be defeated by her coldness. The memory came back to her every summer, on this very same date, but she had stopped being wounded by it long ago. She usually took in good spirit this vague, springtime nostalgia that the dance of the pollen awakened in her, seeing it as a reminder of a time when the beauty of each day contained promises for the future. But today she felt both tense and listless—ill at ease with herself. "Why?" she asked herself when she arrived back in her room. She sat on the window ledge, watching the cars diving down into the tunnel only to reappear on the other side of Gorky Street: "I think I'm a little bored," she said to herself. She did not find Moscow particularly charming. Being a little bored isn't a serious matter. They were going to leave for Leningrad; they would see Pskoff and Novgorod. She picked up a book. Normally, to be rid of her morose thoughts, she had only to explain them to herself, but the word "bored" had solved nothing—she was still ill at ease. "This is a sad room," she told herself. "Sad room," what does that mean? When Philippe had told her that he was getting married, the bright harmony of the colors of the cushions, the charm of the hyacinths, the fine Nicolas de Staël reproduction had not helped her. All the same, at neutral moments like this, a joyful color, an elegant shape, an agreeable object can be enough to revive your taste for life. Here nothing did so. Neither what was happening in the streets, nor the walls, nor the furniture consoled her. Consoled her over what? "It's André!" she suddenly said to herself. "I see him all the time, yet I never see him." In 1963, Macha was preoccupied with her work: this year she was with them every single minute. For her, that was natural. But didn't André ever want to be alone with Nicole? Had he changed so much? In the past, a very, very long time ago, he was the more passionate one. At that stage she was not ready for passion. To be ready for it you have to be lacking something, to be torn, or to have something to compensate for: in André's case, it was his tough childhood, his mother's austerity, the failure of his love life with Claire. But in her own case it was the opposite: her parents had pampered her, and love was not the most important thing in her life; she wanted to become someone. She was the one who, after sex, left the bed first. He would try to keep holding her against him, murmuring: "Don't go away: it's like being weaned." (She often gave in, a little grudgingly.) And then, throughout their long life together, her need for him and the joy that he brought her had done nothing but grow. Now it was impossible to say which of the two of them was fonder of the other. Linked like Siamese twins: he is my life, and I am his. And yet there it was: it was not hurting him to never see her alone. Had his feelings cooled down? Sometimes indifference comes over people as they grow old: he had not been as upset by the death of his sister as he was earlier by his father's. Should she talk to him about it? Perhaps that would make him sad. She put her book down and stretched out on her bed. Too much for lunch, too much vodka—sleep was overcoming her.

"Where am I? Who am I?"

Every morning, even before she opened her eyes, she recognized her bed and her room. But sometimes, when she slept in the afternoon, she experienced this infantile bewilderment when she woke up: Why am I who I am? As if her consciousness, emerging anonymously from the darkness, was hesitating before taking on an incarnation again. What surprised her—as it does the child when he becomes aware of his own identity—was finding herself back at the heart of her own life and not of a different one: by what stroke of fate? She might not have been born: then the question would not have arisen. "I could have been someone else, but then it would be someone else questioning herself about her self." It gave her vertigo to sense at once her contingency and the necessary coincidence between herself and her history. Nicole, sixty years old, a retired teacher. "Retired"–she had difficulty in believing it. She remembered her first job, her first class, the dead leaves rustling under her feet during an autumn in the provinces. At that stage her retirement day—separated from her by a stretch of time almost twice as long as the time she had already lived—seemed as unreal to her as death itself. But it had arrived. Sometimes she thought nostalgically of the doorway that she would not pass through again, of the waxed corridors, of the sounds of children rushing about and laughing that she would never hear again. She had stepped across other lines, but less well-defined ones. This one was as firm as an iron curtain. "I am on the other side." She got up and recombed her hair. She was certainly putting some weight back on. It was annoying not to have any scales. Half past five. Why was he still not back? He certainly knew that she hated waiting.

She hated waiting, but, as soon as he was there, there was so much warmth in her heart that she forgot she had been waiting for him.

"We couldn't find a taxi. We walked."

"It doesn't matter at all," she said.

"We worked well," André said.

"And you drank a few glasses of vodka."

She invariably spotted the slight distortion of pronunciation, the faint delay in his movements which indicated that André had had a drink or two. They were not yet clearly perceptible signs; she called them "advance signs."

"You have advance signs," she added.

"I drank a little vodka, but I'm showing no advance signs."

She did not press the matter. It was always with a heavy heart that she played the spoil-sport, but she feared for his health, since his blood pressure was a little too high. Sometimes she would wake up with a start: "He risks getting lung cancer; having a heart attack; a stroke."

"Look," said André, "Perfect balance."

He seized Macha by the waist and twirled her around while humming a waltz. It was strange to see him with another woman. Even though she had his eyes, his chin. Nicole sometimes forgot that Macha was his daughter. André talked to her with the words and the charming smiles that he had found for Nicole when they were young. Little by little, she and André had come to adopt with each other the curt tones of friendship; their gestures were almost gruff ones. Whose fault was it? Mine, obviously, she thought rather regretfully. She had been too well brought up, too formal, almost inhibited. He was the one who had immediately decided that they would say "tu" to each other, and sometimes the exuberance of his affection embarrassed her. Little by little, she had slipped back into her former reserved manner: it would have been ridiculous to be an old married couple playing at turtle doves. Nevertheless, she felt vaguely jealous of his complicity with Macha, and reproached herself for not managing to retain that affectionate freshness in her relations with André. Her original rigidity had taken over again: she had never entirely overcome it, because she had never entirely accepted her condition as a woman. (Yet no man could have helped her to adjust to it as much as André had.)

"Do you like dancing?" she asked Macha.

"I adore it—with a good dancer."

"I've never been able to dance myself."

"Really? Why?"

"Because it's the male dancer who leads: I was silly when I was young. After that, it was too late."

"I like being led," said Macha. "It's restful."

"Provided that you are led in the direction you want to go," said Nicole, smiling sympathetically at her.

It was rare for her to sympathize with a woman. With her female students, of course: they were children, adolescents, and one could hope that they would not be like their elders. But adults! The young ones were of Irène's type. They carried out their "career as a woman" with an ostentatious zeal. As if it were a career! The older ones took Nicole back to her rebellious childhood; they reminded her of her mother. "Girls can't do that." She couldn't be an explorer, nor an aviator, nor a captain of an ocean-going ship. Just a girl. Memories of chiffon, organdy, my mother's excessively smooth hands, the soft texture of her arms, her perfume which used to cling to my skin. She dreamed of Nicole marrying someone rich, having pearls and furs. And so the struggle had begun. "Girls *can* do that." She had prolonged her studies, had sworn to confound the destiny set out for her: she would write a sensational thesis, hold a chair at the Sorbonne; she would prove that a woman's brain is as good as a man's. None of that had happened. She had been a student, and an activist in feminist movements. But like the others—those others that she did not like—she had allowed herself to be devoured by her husband, her son, her home. Macha certainly did not allow herself to be devoured by anyone. Yet she accepted her femininity comfortably: probably because she had been living since the age of fifteen in a country where women have no inferiority complex. It was clear that Macha felt inferior to no one.

"Who's taking whom to dinner, where, and at what time?" Nicole asked.

"I've reserved a table, for 7:30, at the Bakou," said Macha. "We have plenty of time for a little stroll beforehand. It's a good time of day."

"Right, let's go for a stroll," said Nicole.

She had left her morose thoughts behind. André had come here to see Macha: it was natural that he should make the most of her presence. She looked forward cheerfully to the evening that all three of them were going to spend together.

* * *

André found the hotel that they stayed at in Leningrad charming. Long corridors and pearl-gray doors opening onto them, with oval panes at the top framed by old-fashioned festoons and hung with silk curtains, which were pink, green or blue according to which floor you were on. In their room there was an alcove, hidden by a curtain, and endearing old furniture: a heavy desk of false marble, a black leather sofa, a table covered by a tablecloth with fringes. Chandeliers with crystal pendants lit up the dining room, where a young, semi-naked woman in marble was adjusting her dress with a naughty smile—or was she taking it off?

"The service is as slow as in Moscow!" said Nicole. "Fortunately, the orchestra isn't too loud."

"It's true that they take their time," said André, watching a waiter going up to a sideboard: he put a glass down on it and stayed gazing at it meditatively. They all moved hesitantly and in a disorganized way, which was bound to exasperate clients who were in a hurry. The bricklayers and the laborers that one saw working in the street, the clerical workers, the shop assistants also looked nonchalant. And yet this country was not full of lazy people, otherwise they would not have been so extraordinarily successful in certain fields. The scientists and technicians probably had special training: they had a different mentality.

"Ah! Here comes the bill," said Macha.

They left. How beautiful the light was at ten o'clock in the evening! At midday, the colors of the palaces were overwhelmed by the bright sunlight. But now, the blues, greens and reds throbbed gently in the fading sun.

"It's a wonderful city," said Nicole.

Wonderful. The grace and splendor of the Italian baroque behind a Nordic glaze. And what gaiety along the banks of the bluish-white Neva river! It was mostly young people walking around in groups singing.

"All the same, you want to go to Pskoff and Novgorod?"

"There's time to do everything," said Macha.

No doubt, but for his own part he would have liked to stay here for ten days. Leningrad, Petrograd, Saint-Petersburg. He would have liked to grasp everything about them, and even—though it was an impossible dream—to grasp everything at the same time. The city besieged one winter's day, with men and women staggering in the snow, and falling over never to get up again; the corpses being dragged across the frozen ground. The corpses strewn over Nevsky Prospekt; the men running; the bullets whistling past; the sailors attacking the Winter Palace. Lenin. Trotsky. Was there not a way to conjure up the great saga that took place during his adolescence and somehow have it superimposed? It seemed so far away then, but so close now, as he trampled over the very places where it had unfolded. The setting had remained, but it did not help to bring the men and the events back to life. Quite the contrary. Historians were partly successful in reviving them, but to follow it all you had to abandon the world of the present, shut yourself up in the silence of your study, alone in front of your book. In these streets the density and weight of reality suppressed the mirages of the past: it was impossible to inscribe them in these stones. But, this evening, there was still Leningrad, on a clear and beautiful night. In 1963, they had come in August; the sun was setting. Today it was not setting. There was a festival. Along the river banks, boys and girls were dancing to the sound of a guitar. Others were sitting and playing the guitar on the benches of the Champ de Mars, to the rustle of lilac: luxuriant clusters of lilac, like those in French gardens, and Japanese lilac, growing more soberly and giving off a peppery scent.

They sat down on a bench. Who were these boys with guitars? Students, office workers, manual workers? He gave up the idea of asking Macha. All too often she could not answer his questions and it bothered her. He was a little disappointed with her as a source of information. Perhaps people mistrusted her because of her foreign origins, or was society here as stratified as elsewhere? She knew nothing about working-class life, or peasant life, or the immense scientific and technical thrust that André would so much have liked some insights into.

"The first time I stayed up all night was when I was fifteen," said Macha. "I was overjoyed. I didn't understand how my parents could stay so calm. It's true that on that day I did think that it's terrible to grow old."

"You don't think so any more?" said Nicole.

"I'm much more at ease with myself than I've ever been," said Macha. "Why, do you miss your youth?"

"No," said Nicole. She smiled at André: "As long as other people are growing old at the same time."

The first time I stayed up all night, André repeated to himself. He became uneasy: this beautiful night of happiness did not belong to him. He could only take part in it: it was not his own. They were laughing and singing: he felt excluded, a tourist. He had never liked being in this position. But then again, in countries where tourism is a national industry, traveling around is a way of being integrated into them. On Italian café terraces, or in London pubs, he was one consumer among others; an espresso coffee tasted the same in his mouth as it did in that of someone from Rome. Here he would have had to get to know people through their work, to work with them. He was excluded from their leisure pursuits because he was excluded from their activities in general. An idler. No one else in the garden was an idler—just Nicole and himself.

And no one else was as old as they were. How young everyone was! He had been young. He could remember the ardent and sweet flavor that life had at that time: this night had it for them, too; they were smiling at the future. What was the present without a future, even amidst the scent of lilac and in the freshness of dawn experienced at midnight? For a moment, he thought: it's a dream, I'm going to wake up, I'll have my body back, I'm twenty. No. He was an adult, an aging man, almost an old man. He looked at them with envious stupefaction: why am I no longer one of them? How could this have happened to *me*?[7]

They walked back from the Hermitage, where they had spent two hours: their third visit this year. They had seen again everything that they wanted to see for a second time. They were leaving the following day for Pskoff; they would visit Pushkin's property. Macha said the countryside was very beautiful and Nicole was delighted at the idea of smelling grass again. Leningrad was a very beautiful city, but you stifled in it. She took the key held out by the floor supervisor, who also gave Macha a note: the Intourist office wanted to see her urgently.

"There'll be some more complications," said Nicole.

"It's probably a matter of settling a few details," said André.

His incurable optimism! He buried himself in his Russian grammar and she opened her copy of *Humanité*.

She was longing for the car journey, countryside, fresh air, some novelty. She knew the Hermitage, Smolny, the palaces, the canals by heart; she did not want to spend another three days here.

Macha came through the door: "Permission refused!" she said, in a furious voice.

"I saw it coming," Nicole said to herself gloomily.

"I did battle with the guy at Intourist, but he can't do anything; he has received orders. It's exasperating. They're exasperating."

"Who are 'they'?" André asked.

"I don't know exactly. He wouldn't tell me anything. Perhaps there are troop movements. But there's probably nothing at all."

The panic that Nicole felt welling up inside her was disproportionate. Her impatience at the slightest obstacle, the fear of being bored—it was becoming neurotic. Come on now. What if they left tomorrow for Novgorod? But there wouldn't be hotel rooms available; everything always had to be arranged in advance. And then the stay in Moscow would be interminable in that case. Quickly, think of something else.

"And what about that trip you had talked about, the monastery on an island?"

"That will be forbidden, too."

"You can always try."

"Oh, no!" said André. "She mustn't start all over again, going through those annoying hoops only to be told 'No' once more. Let's just stay here quietly. To tell you the truth, I don't want to see that monastery."

"Fine. Let's not talk about it any more," said Nicole.

As soon as they had left her, she gave in to her anger. "Three days of boredom here!" Suddenly, everything seemed boring to her: the straight avenues, the monotonous streets, the interminable dinners with music playing, the hotel room, the whole life here and the endless discussions between

Macha and André: he defended the Chinese, whom she hated and feared; he criticized the policy of co-existence at any price which she supported. They kept going over the same ground. Or else André would tell Macha stories that Nicole knew by heart. She was still never seeing him on his own, or, at least, only for moments too brief to get a conversation going: he threw himself into a Russian book and she into a newspaper . . . She leaned her forehead against the window. How ugly that huge ocher and black church was! "Permission refused." If at least she could have discussed it, argued. But everything rested on Macha's shoulders, and perhaps she was too easily discouraged. The dependency was irritating. Nicole had been amused by it at the beginning, but now it weighed on her. In Paris, she stood at the center of her own life, making the decisions herself, with André or alone. Here the initiatives and ideas fell to someone else; she was just one element in Macha's universe. She looked at her books; she had not brought enough, and those that really interested her she had read in Moscow. She went back to the window. The square and the little public garden, the people sitting on benches—everything seemed dull in the flat afternoon light. Time was stagnating. It's terrible—she wanted to say: it's unfair—that time can pass so fast and so slowly at the same time. She was going through the front door of the lycée in Bourg, almost as young as her pupils; she was looking pityingly at the old teachers with grey hair. And, then presto, she had been an old teacher and then the lycée door had closed behind her! For years, her classes of pupils had given her the illusion that her own age was not changing: with each new year she met up with them again, as young as ever, and she believed she was unchanging too. In the ocean of time, she was a rock battered by new waves all the time, but unmoving and not being worn down. And now the tide was carrying her along, would carry her along onto the beach of her death. Tragically, her life was slipping by. And yet it was running out in drips, hour by hour, minute by minute. You always had to wait for the sugar to dissolve, for the memory to subside, for the wound to heal, for the boredom to dissipate. A strange fracture between these two rhythms. My days are galloping past, but each day I languish.

She turned away from the window. What a void there was inside her, all around her, as far as she could see. During the last year she had helped Philippe with his research. At the stage he had reached, she could be of no further use to him. And he lived elsewhere. Reading at random, with no specific purpose, was a way of passing the time that was scarcely more interesting than doing crosswords or playing "Spot the Mistakes." She had told herself: "I shall have time, all my time to myself. What a stroke of fortune!" It is not a stroke of fortune if you find nothing to do with your time. It is even the case, she had realized, that too much leisure impoverishes you. It was on leaving home early in the morning or on coming out of the subway that she would sometimes be struck—in the old days—by the violent, unexpected pleasure afforded by light reflecting on a tiled roof, or the color of a certain sky. While she was walking slowly through the streets, open to experiences, it eluded her. You sense the brightness of the sun much better when it is filtered through closed shutters than when you are faced directly with its torrid harshness.

She had never been able to put up with boredom. And if she was suffering from it to the point of anguish this afternoon, it was because it was overflowing into her future. Years of boredom, until death finally ensued. "If only I had projects, if only I were engaged in some work!" she told herself. Too late. She should have gotten started on something earlier; it was her own fault. Not only her fault. André had not helped her. He had put pressure on her, in an insidious way: "You've worked enough; don't do any more correcting; come to bed . . . Stay in bed a little while longer . . . Come for a walk . . . I'll take you to the cinema." He had crushed all of Nicole's vague desires, without even being aware of it. "All I had to do was not to give in to him," she told herself. She was inventing certain resentments. But that was because she resented what André had done. He had made a decision, without even discussing things with her: "Let's just stay here!" And above all, above all he was not making the least effort to keep Macha at a slight distance; the idea did not even occur to him. Is he less fond of me? In Paris, we are bound together by a network of habits so tight that it leaves no room for any questions. But beneath that shell what remains between us that is living and true? Knowing what he is to me does not tell me what I am for him. "I'll talk to him," she decided. In Moscow. Macha had plenty to do; they were not obliged to keep her with them all the time. And yet what was the good of arranging tête-à-tête sessions with him if he did not spontaneously want them? No. She would not talk to him. She began writing a letter to Philippe.

"Now, this is a functioning church. Do you want to go in?" Macha said.

"Of course," said Nicole. "Oh, what a beautiful golden light!"

On the walls, on the icon screen, the icons gently glowed, and even the shadows were like flowing gold. But the smells made André feel sick: the scent of incense, of candles, and the smell of the poor old women on their knees on the floor, mumbling, groveling and kissing the slabs. It was even more offensive than in Catholic churches. A nasal voice rose from the back, on the left. They went closer. What a strange sight. Men and women—young men and women—were moving in circles around an orthodox priest with a long silky black beard, attired in his finery—all of them holding in their arms babies dressed in white, who were crying. The priest was sprinkling the infants from a holy water sprinkler while chanting prayers. It seemed like a game, with the parents rocking their bawling children and going round in circles.

"Assembly-line baptism! I'd never seen that before," said Macha.

"Do parents often have their children baptized?"

"When they have an old mother who is a believer and don't want to hurt her."

"And what's going on over there?" said Nicole.

There were boxes lined up against the walls: empty coffins. And six had been placed on the floor side by side, each with a dead body in it: the exposed faces, waxen and framed by chinstraps, were all alike.

"Let's leave," Nicole said.

"Does this disturb you?"

"Rather. Doesn't it disturb you?"

"No."

He looked upon his own death with indifference: surviving, surviving one's death seemed to him more arduous than dying. The death of others . . . He had become hardened. At 25, he had sobbed when he had lost his father. And then two years ago, he had buried his sister without shedding any tears, although he had loved her very much. And his mother? Macha thought of her at the same time as he did.

"I'd very much like to see my grandmother before she dies," she said. "Will it hurt you when she dies?"

He hesitated: "I don't know."

"But you adore her!" said Nicole, in a surprised tone. "It will certainly hurt me," she said. "And then it will have a strange effect on me. There will be no one left from the generation before ours. That will push us back one notch further."

They went back to the Nevsky Prospekt by taxi, and sat down in an open-air café. He ordered a cognac: it was not very good, but they did not serve vodka in cafés. Cognac was much more expensive, to discourage drunks. In practice, a lot of people came along with a bottle of vodka in their pocket.

"Are there many religious funerals?"

"No. There, too, it's mostly old women who ask to be buried by the church or bring their dead to the church." Macha hesitated: "All the same, I went into a Moscow church one Sunday morning and I was astonished. There were quite a few men, of early middle age, or even young. Many more than there used to be."

"It's regrettable," said André.

"Yes."

"If people want to believe in heaven, it's because they don't believe in much on earth any more. It means that the policy of material well-being that you are beginning to pursue here is not as successful as you say."

"Oh, well-being! Let's not exaggerate," said Macha. "I've never denied that ideologically we are currently in a period when we are slipping back," she added.

"A period that will last how long?"

"I don't know. There are young men like Vassili and his comrades who are full of enthusiasm. They will fight for a socialism that excludes neither happiness nor freedom."

"It's a fine program," said André skeptically.

"You don't believe in it?"

"I wouldn't say that. But in any case I won't see that kind of socialism myself."

Yes, his discomfort had a name, a name that he did not like but was obliged to use: disappointment. In general, he detested the travelers who came back from China, from Cuba, from the USSR, or even from the USA saying: I was disappointed. They had been wrong to have a priori ideas which the facts subsequently refuted; it was their fault and not the fault of reality. But, in the end, it was something analogous that he himself experienced. Perhaps things would have been different if he had visited the virgin lands of Siberia, or the towns where the scientists were working. But in Moscow and in Leningrad, he did not find what he had been hoping for. What had he been hoping for exactly? It was vague. In any case, he had not found it. Of course, there was a great difference between the USSR and the West. Whereas in France technical progress only deepened the divide between privileged people and those being exploited, here the economic structures were in place to ensure that one day technical progress would benefit everyone. Socialism would end up by becoming a reality. One day it would triumph in the whole world. This was just a matter of a period when things were slipping back. In the whole world—except perhaps in China, but what one knew about that country was uncertain and scarcely reassuring—countries were going through a period when things were slipping back. Admittedly, they would come out of it. That was possible, that was probable. A probability that André himself would never verify. For young people, this moment was no worse than any other, no worse than the period when he was twenty: only, these years which for them were a point of departure represented a terminal point for him, a fall. At his age, he would not witness the revival that was perhaps to follow. The road leading to the good is worse than evil itself, says Marx. When you are young, with an illusory eternity in front of you, you jump to the end of the road in one leap; later, you do not have enough strength to surpass what have been called the incidental casualties of history, and you consider them to be appallingly high. He had counted on history to justify his life: he was not counting on it any longer.

* * *

All things considered, the time had passed quite quickly. Two pleasant days in Novgorod; and in less than a week she would rediscover Paris, her house, her life, and André. He smiled at her:

"You wanted to go into a *dacha*. Well, it's been arranged," he said.

"How kind Macha is!"

"It's a friend's *dacha*, about thirty kilometers away. Youri will drive us there, not this Sunday, but the one after."

"The one after? But we're leaving on Tuesday."

"Of course not, Nicole: you know very well that we decided to stay for ten days longer."

"You decided that, without saying a single word to me!" said Nicole.

Suddenly, there was a red mist in her head, a red fog in front of her eyes, something red shouting out in her throat. He couldn't care less about me! Not a single word!

"But, look, I did; I talked to you about it. I would never have made the decision without talking to you about it. You agreed."

"You're lying!"

"It was on the day I had drunk a little vodka at Macha's apartment, and when you claimed that I had advance signs. We had dinner at the Bakou. When we got back, when we were alone, I talked to you about it."

"You said nothing, ever. You know very well. I can assure you that I would have noted the occasion. You decided without me and now you're lying."

"You've forgotten. Come on, have I ever faced you with a *fait accompli*?"

"There's a first time for everything. And you're lying, into the bargain. It's not the first time that that's happened."

In the past, he never used to lie. But this year, he had lied over little things, twice. He had laughed, and excused himself: "It's my age; you become lazy.

It would have taken too long to explain myself, so I took a shortcut." He had promised not to do it again. He was doing it again. And this time it was more serious than a matter of an empty bottle, of a visit to the doctor that he had skipped. Her anger: only rarely—very rarely—had she been angry with André. But then it was a tornado that carried her thousands of kilometers away from him; and from herself, out of her life, out of her skin, into a horrible solitude that was both glacial and scorching . . .

He looked at her changed, stubborn face, her tight lips; the face that used to frighten him so much, and which still moved him deeply. I told her, and she has forgotten. At that point, she was still enjoying herself here: ten days more, or less, were of no great significance. She had begun to be bored little by little. She missed Philippe. I'm not enough for her; I've never been enough for her. I told her in this room, after our dinner at the Bakou. But like all the people who think they have an infallible memory, she wouldn't admit that she could ever be mistaken. Just the same, she knew very well that he decided nothing without consulting her; and during this trip he had done every single thing that she wanted. An extra ten days in Moscow, it wasn't an enormous thing to swallow.

"Listen, there's nothing dreadful about ten extra days here."

Nicole's eyes were sparkling with rage, one might almost have said with hatred.

"I'm bored! You're not aware of how bored I am!"

"Oh, I'm aware of it! You miss Philippe, and your friends. I know very well that I have never been enough for you."

"Go away, leave me alone. I can't bear seeing you any more. Go away."

"What about Youri and Macha? They're waiting for us downstairs."

"Tell them I have a headache. Tell them whatever you like."

He closed the door, agitated. "That's how bored she is with me!" She had not even protested when he had said to her: "I have never been enough for you." He was not so eager to stay, but Macha was counting on it, and he did not want to hurt her. Nicole should have understood . . . But he lost heart at the idea of quarreling with her. He found any disagreement between them unbearable. Anyway, he would come back straight after dinner; she would surely agree to listen to him. Was there any chance that he really had neglected to talk to her about it? No, he could see himself sitting down on his bed in his pajamas, while she was brushing her hair. What had she replied? "Why not?" or something of that kind. I never decide anything without her, she knows that very well.

As soon as the door closed, tears suffocated her. As if, although he was still alive, she had lost André for ever. In less than a minute the guillotine can cut a head off; in less than a minute an utterance had cut off her links with André. How could she have imagined that they were welded to each other? Because of their past, she took for granted that he was as attached to her as she to him. But people change; he had changed. The fact that he lied was not the worst thing: he was lying out of cowardice, like a child who is afraid of being scolded. The worst thing was that he had made the decision with Macha, without taking her into account; that he had completely *forgotten* her, neglecting to consult her, or even to warn her. She needed the courage to face up to things: in three weeks he has never tried to arrange a tête-à-tête between us. All his smiling, all his affection is for Macha; he doesn't care what I want and don't want. "Let's stay in Moscow then. Let's stay in Leningrad." He enjoyed being here. He took it for granted that she enjoyed it, too. It's not love any more: I am just a habit.

She could not bear to be in the room any longer. She tidied her face up and went down into the street. Walk: she had often walked in order to calm her fears, fits of anger; to get rid of images. Only, she was not twenty any more, or even fifty; she very quickly became tired. She sat down on a bench in a little public garden, opposite a pond where a swan was gliding. People stared at her as they went by; she must look dazed; or perhaps they simply recognized her as a foreigner. He was probably dining with Youri and Macha, in the restaurant at the harbor station, beside the Moskva, as they had planned to do. Perhaps the evening had an unpleasant after-taste for him, but even that was not sure, since he had the art of being caught up in the moment, of blocking out anything that bothered him. He was forgetting her, putting her to one side; he was telling himself that she would have calmed down when he came back. He had always been that way: as soon as he was happy, she must be too. In fact, there had been no real symmetry between their two lives. He had had exactly what he wanted: a home, children, leisure, pleasures, friendships and a little turbulence. Whereas she had given up all her youthful ambitions—because of him. He had never wanted to recognize that. It was because of him that she had become this woman who no longer knew how to spend the time that she had left to live. Someone else would have pressed her to work, would have preached by example. *He* had turned her away from work. Now she found herself empty-handed, having nothing in the world but him, and suddenly she didn't have him. There was an atrocious contradiction in an anger born out of love that kills love. With every second, as she conjured up André's face and voice, she stoked up a grudge which was devastating her. It was like those illnesses where you forge your own suffering; each time you breathe in, it tears at your lungs, and yet you are obliged to breathe. "What's to be done, then?" she asked herself in a stupor as she returned toward the hotel. There was no way out. They would continue to live together, she would bury her grievances; many couples vegetate in this way, in a state of resignation, of compromise. In a state of solitude. I am alone. Next to André, I am alone. I must convince myself of that.

She opened the door of their room. On the bed were André's pajamas; his slippers were on the floor, a pipe and a packet of tobacco on the night table. For a moment he existed poignantly for her, as if an illness or exile had taken him away from her and she were finding him again in these abandoned objects. Tears came to her eyes. She stiffened. She took a tube of sleeping pills from her medicine bag, swallowed two tablets and went to bed.

"I'm alone!" She was stricken with anguish: the anguish of existing, something much more intolerable than the fear of dying. Alone like a rock in the middle of the desert, but condemned to be aware of her useless presence. Her whole body, knotted, clenched, was a silent scream. And then she let herself slip between the sheets and sank into sleep.

When she woke up, in the morning, he was asleep, huddled up with his hand pressed against the wall. She looked away. No impulse pulled her toward him. Her heart was icy and dulled, like a disused chapel where there is no longer even the tiniest night light. The slippers, the pipe moved her no more: they did not evoke the presence of someone dear to her who was absent; they were just an extension of the unfamiliar person who lived in the same room as she did. "Oh, I hate him!" she told herself, in despair. "He has killed all of the love that I had for him!"

She was coming and going about in the room, silent and hostile. Often, when they were young, he had come up against that closed face. "I don't accept . . . One must not . . ." At the time, such severity petrified him. He was older than she, but for a long time he had regarded all adults as elders. Today, she made him impatient: "How long is she going to go on sulking at me?" She was exaggerating. He had done everything to ensure that she was happy during this trip. And during their whole life together. He was staying in Paris because of her . . . Even if she had forgotten their conversation, she should have given him a little credit. It was as if she had leapt at the opportunity. What grudges was she harboring? Did she regret not having a more brilliant husband? In that case, she did not really love him. If she had really loved him, she would not have been bored with him. At the beginning of their marriage, her lukewarmness had hurt him, but he told himself that the day would come . . . He had thought that the day had come. But it seemed not. He had expected only one compensation in old age: Philippe was getting married, and she was retired, so he would have Nicole all to himself. But if she did not love him, if he was not enough for her, if she persisted in her grievances, then this dream of their being alone together was entirely compromised. They would have the sad old age of people who only stay together because, after a certain age, they can't really separate. No, he couldn't believe it. Were they one and the same woman, the one whose smile, even yesterday, radiated affection, and the one with her lips tightened in a furious pout?

"How furious you look!"

She made no reply, and he was gripped by anger, too.

"You know, if you want to leave before me, I'm not stopping you."

"That's exactly what I intend to do."

He was shocked: he had not thought that she would take his offer seriously. Well, let her leave! he said to himself. At least, I know where things stand. I can't delude myself any more; I'm an old habit for her, but she has never truly loved me. I knew that once and then I forgot it. I must remember it. Harden my heart. Let her do what she wants. And I'll do what I want. He thought of the garden at Villeneuve, the smell of cypress trees and roses in the sweltering sun. When I get back from Moscow, I'll leave Paris. I'll set myself up in Provence: I've been too stupid, sacrificing myself for her. It's every man for himself.

Is it true what they claim then, that we can't communicate, that no one understands anyone else? Nicole asked herself. She looked at André, sitting on Macha's couch, with a glass of vodka in his hand, and she thought that she would have to revise their whole past. They had lived juxtaposed, every man for himself, not knowing each other, neither merged nor transparent. Just before leaving their room, in the morning, André had looked at her hesitantly; he would have liked to embark on an explanation. She had opened the door, he had followed her, and in the taxi they had both remained silent. There was nothing to explain. Words would be shattered against this anger, this pain, this stiffening of her heart. So much negligence, so much indifference! In front of Macha, all day long they had played out a polite comedy. How can I announce to her that I'm leaving before André?

He was drinking a fourth glass of vodka; he was free to do so. When he was young, alcohol made him lyrical and charming: he went a little too far, but without becoming incoherent, or falling about. Now—since when?—both his words and his actions became tangled up, and the doctor had said that alcohol and tobacco were doing him no good; he was swallowing his own death in little mouthfuls. Again, fear—more corrosive than anger—made her stubborn. "He drinks too much." She pursed her lips. He was free. He could kill himself in small stages if that pleased him. In any case, they would both finish up by dying, and in certain cases that's just as good as living. There was something senile about the way in which he tried to keep a conversation going in Russian with Macha. She was laughing at his accent; they were as thick as thieves. From time to time he touched his cheek with his finger, in a preoccupied way. Nicole wanted to shout out: "We're not so old, not yet, no!" He had changed; she had noticed it during this trip—perhaps because, although she never saw him, she was seeing him all of the time. He no longer wanted to just let himself live. Previously, living was the only thing he liked. But for him living was a process of perpetual invention, a joyful, unpredictable adventure in which he drew her along. Now he gave her the impression of vegetating: that's what old age is and I don't want it.

Something wavered in her mind. As it does when you have received a blow on the skull and vision is muddled; you see two images of the world, at two different levels, without being able to say what is above and what is below. The two images that she had of her life, of the past and of the present, could not be matched up. There was a mistake somewhere. This moment was a lie: it was not André and it was not Nicole; this scene was taking place somewhere else . . . No, alas! It was the past that was a mirage; that often happens. How many women are wrong about their lives, throughout their lives. Her own had not been the one that she used to tell herself. Because André was impetuous, emotional, she had thought that he cherished her passionately. In truth, he forgot her as soon as he could not see her. Third parties coming between them did not worry her. For her, André's presence was an inexhaustible joy, but hers was not for him. Perhaps I'm even a burden to him; perhaps I've always been a burden to him.

"Macha, we have to settle the question of my departure. You see, I have commitments in Paris."

"Oh, let's not mince words!" said André. He turned toward his daughter: "She's mad at me because she claims that I decided to extend our stay here without consulting her. In fact, as you can imagine, I talked to her about it."

"Of course," Macha said forcefully. "The first thing that he said to me when I suggested that you should stay a little longer was: 'I'll talk to Nicole about it.'"

The complicity between them!

"He didn't do so. He forgot to do it, and he's lying to me."

Again, she was giving herself the appearance of a Gorgon. But for the first time in his life she did not intimidate him. She was wrong, entirely wrong. Macha was trying to patch things up, but she was replying coldly, and watching him pour himself some vodka with blame in her eyes. A pain in the ass, that's what she's in the process of becoming. He defiantly swallowed the vodka in one gulp, Russian style.

"You can get drunk, it makes no difference to me," she said in an icy voice.

"Please, please, don't go back to Paris so quickly; that depresses me," said Macha.

"It may depress you, but it doesn't depress him."

"No, it doesn't depress me."

"You see. At least we're in agreement about that. He'll be able to down ten bottles of vodka without anyone protesting."

"Really, it's not in the least amusing to see you pulling your long face. I think that a short separation will do us both good. When I get back from Moscow, I'll go down to Villeneuve. And I'm not asking you to follow me."

"Rest assured, I won't follow you."

She rose: "We can't bear to see each other any more: let's not see each other any more."

She walked toward the door. Macha took her arm:

"This is stupid. Come back. Talk things out between you."

"Neither of us wants to."

The door slammed.

"You should have stopped her from leaving," said Macha.

"I tried to talk things out this morning; she doesn't want to listen. To hell with her!"

"It's true that you drink rather too much," said Macha.

"Fine. Put this bottle away."

She put the bottle away and came back to sit opposite André, looking perplexed.

"You had both drunk a fair amount at the Bakou. You may have forgotten to talk to her yet believe you did."

"Or else she didn't register the conversation because, being slightly drunk, she fell asleep immediately afterward."

"That's possible, too. But in any case you are both sincere [*de bonne foi*]; so why are you both angry?"

"I'm not questioning her sincerity myself. She is the one who claims that I'm lying. She has no right to do that."

Macha smiled: "I would never have imagined that you could squabble like that . . . like children."

"When we're over sixty? But, just think, what are adults and even old people? Just children swollen out with age."

It was precisely because of their age that this quarrel was so odious to him. Nicole was betraying the whole long period of mutual understanding behind them. If she doubted his sincerity, it must be that she had never entirely had confidence in him; that he had never completely had her respect. And then always keeping a watch on how many glasses he was drinking, so that she could have the pleasure of being a pain. He did not want to think about her any more.

"Pass me *Pravda* and let's get down to work."

"Now?"

"I'm not drunk," he said, a little aggressively.

He began translating an article. After a moment she got up.

"I'm going to telephone to see that Nicole got back safely."

"Why shouldn't she have done?"

"Just that she seemed quite beside herself."

"In any case, *I* won't speak to her."

Nicole had not arrived back. Nor an hour later, at midnight. Or she had probably got back, but was not answering the phone.

"I'll come up with you," said Macha when she stopped the car in front of the hotel. "I want to be sure that she is there."

The floor supervisor gave André his key. So Nicole was not there. The silence and the emptiness of the room brought his heart into his mouth. The taste and effects of the vodka had disappeared, and his anger with them.

"Where can she be?"

He did not like to imagine her wandering through the sleeping city, where all the cafés were closed.

"There's one place open and she may be there: the bar at the National Hotel."

"Let's go there," he said.

Nicole was sitting in front of a glass of whisky, with a slack mouth and a fixed stare.

André would have liked to take her by the shoulders and embrace her. But at the first word he said, her face would change, and harden. He went up to her and smiled shyly. Her face changed, hardened.

"What are you doing here?"

She had been drinking: words were slurred in her mouth.

"We've come to fetch you in the car."

He placed his hand lightly on her shoulder: "Come on, let's have a drink together. Let's make up our differences."

"No wish to. And I'll go back when I'm ready."

"We'll wait for you," he said.

"No. I'll walk back. Alone. I think it's a bit rich that you've pursued me all this way."

"Let me take you back now," said Macha. "Please, do it for me. If you don't, we'll end up waiting until two o'clock, and I have to get up early tomorrow morning."

Nicole hesitated. "Fine. But I'm doing it for you. Just for you," she said.

Light filtered through her eyelids. She kept them closed. Her head was heavy and she was as sad as could be. Why had she got drunk? She was ashamed. As soon as she arrived back she had thrown her clothes all over the place and had collapsed. She had sunk into deep darkness; it was fluid and stifling, oily, and this morning she could scarcely emerge from it. She opened her eyes. He was sitting in an armchair at the foot of her bed; he was smiling and looking at her.

"Darling, we can't go on like this."

Suddenly, it was André again. She recognized him: past and present were one single image. But the iron band remained around her chest. Her lips were trembling. Stiffen herself still more, go straight down to the bottom, drown herself in the deep darkness. Or try to catch hold of this hand held out for her. He was speaking, in an even, calming voice; she loved his voice. No one can be sure what they remember, he was saying. Perhaps he hadn't talked to her, but he was sincere when he maintained that he had. She was no longer sure of anything either. She made an effort.

"Perhaps you did talk to me after all, and I've forgotten. I'd be surprised, but it's not impossible."

"In any case, there's no reason for us to be angry."

She managed to smile: "None," she said.

He came up to her, put his arms around her shoulders, kissed her on the temple. She clutched him to her and, with her cheek against his jacket, she began to cry. The warm voluptuous feeling of tears running down her cheek. What a release! It's so tiring to detest someone you love. He was saying the old words: "My little one, my darling . . ."

"I've been stupid."

"But I've been thoughtless. I should have come back to the subject. I should have understood that you were bored."

"Oh, I'm not as bored as that. I exaggerated."

"I'm bored because I'm not seeing you on your own": the words would not pass her lips. It would have seemed like a reproach. Or a request. She rose and went into the bathroom.

"Listen," he said when she came back into the room. "If you want to leave before me, then do it. But if I went with you, Macha would be very hurt. She suggested yesterday evening that I should leave with you, but that wouldn't be a nice thing to do. I'd very much like you to stay," he added.

"Of course, I'll stay," she said.

She was trapped. Deprived of her anger, disarmed, she would not have the strength to carry out the hostile, and unnecessary, act of leaving. What was waiting for her in Paris?

"I can tell you that I'm starting to find it a long time, too," he said. "Living as a tourist in Moscow isn't much fun all of the time."

"Anyway, as you said, there's nothing dreadful about ten days here," she said.

In the corridor, she took his arm. They were reconciled, but she felt the need to reassure herself of his presence.

* * *

In the darkness of the cinema, André secretly looked at Nicole's profile. Since their quarrel, two days earlier, she seemed a little sad. Or was he projecting his own sadness onto her? Things were not exactly the same between them as before. Perhaps she regretted having agreed to stay another ten days in Moscow? Or else he himself had been more deeply wounded than he had thought by what she had told him and her anger. He could not manage to become interested in the story of this woman pilot. His mind was dwelling on morose thoughts. How could Macha imagine that growing old was an enrichment! Many people think that. It's the years that give wines their bouquet, furniture its patina, men their experience and wisdom. The claim is that each moment is encompassed and justified by the following moment, which itself prepares a more successful future, with even failures finally recuperated. "Each atom of silence provides the chance of a ripened fruit."[8] He had never fallen for that. But neither did he see life in the way Montaigne did, as a succession of deaths: the new-born baby is not the death of the embryo, nor the child the death of the new-born baby. He had never seen Nicole die and come back to life. He even rejected Fitzgerald's idea that "Life is a process of deterioration."[9] He did not have the body he had at twenty, his memory was fading a little, but he did not feel diminished. And Nicole certainly was not. Until very recently, he had been quite convinced that, at eighty, they would still be just like themselves. He did not believe that any more. His incurable optimism, which Nicole smiled at, was less robust than it used to be. There were those teeth that he spat out in his dreams, those dentures that threatened him; and, on the horizon, decrepitude. He had hoped that, at least, there would never be a decline in their love; it even seemed that Nicole would belong to him more when she was old. And now something between them was perhaps in the process of unraveling. How could one distinguish, in their actions and their words, between what was just a routine repetition of the past and what was new and alive? His own feelings for Nicole remained as young as they were at the very beginning. But what about hers? There were no words with which he could ask her the question.

"Pick out some books for yourself," Macha said to Nicole. Their anxiousness to entertain her was a little irritating. It was a good film yesterday, but this afternoon this story of a woman pilot was a real drag. She could read, of course; in fact, what else could she do? Macha was working on a translation, and André was trying to decipher *Pravda* with the aid of a dictionary. She examined the Pléiade volumes lined up on a stand.[10] Novels, novellas, memoirs, short stories—she had read them all, or almost all. But apart from the texts that she had analyzed in classes, what could she remember? She could not recall precisely a single episode of *Manon Lescaut*,[11] which she had dissected sentence by sentence while studying for her degree. And yet she felt lazy at the idea of going back to those pages that she could not conjure up any more. Re-reading bored her. You remember things as you go along, or at least you have the illusion of doing so. You are deprived of what makes reading joyful: that free collaboration with the author that is almost a creation. She was still curious about her own times, and she kept up with the new books coming out. But what did these old books that had made her what she was, and would continue to be, have to say to her?

"Your only problem is what to choose from all these," said André. "It is a problem."

She took a volume by Proust. Proust was different. She waited for the sentences that she knew by heart, and she recognized them with all the happiness that the narrator had in recognizing the musical phrase by Vinteuil.[12] But today she was finding it hard to concentrate. She was thinking: it's not the same any more. She looked at André. What is a presence? There was their long history together, which finally came to die upon the nape of his neck, and she was as familiar with their history, and had forgotten as much of it, as in the case of the texts enclosed in these covers. In Paris, he was present, even when he was some kilometers away. And it was perhaps even in those moments when, leaning out of the window, she watched him going away that he existed in her heart in the most powerful and certain way: his silhouette diminished and disappeared at the corner of the street, marking out with each step the route along which he would come back—the apparently empty space was a force field which, irresistibly, would bring him back to her, as if to his natural place. That certainty was even more moving than a body of flesh and bone. Today André was there in person, at arm's length, but between them, invisible and impalpable, was a kind of insulating layer: a layer of silence. Was André aware of it? Probably not. He would have replied: "Not at all: things are as they were before. What has changed?"

There had been quarrels in their life, but for serious reasons. When one or the other of them had had an affair; or over Philippe's education. They were real conflicts, resolved violently, but quickly and definitively. This time, it had been a swirl of smoke, smoke without fire; and, because of its very thinness, it had not quite dispersed. It had also to be admitted, she thought, that formerly there had been torrid reconciliations in bed: pointless grievances were burned away in the heat of desire, excitement, pleasure; they found themselves facing each other refreshed and joyful. Now, this recourse was lacking. As a result, Nicole kept thinking about things too much. She had been largely responsible for their disagreement: she had thought that he was lying. (Well, why had he lied to her before, even though it was over little things?) It was also *his* fault. He should have come back to the matter, instead of considering it settled in two minutes. She had been too mistrustful, but he had been negligent, and he remained so, since he was not really worried about what was going on in Nicole's head.

Had he become unfeeling? In the midst of her anger, she had thought many unjust things about him. No, he was not senile. Vegetating, no. But perhaps less sensitive than before. Inevitably, since one gets worn down: so many wars, massacres, catastrophes, misfortunes, deaths. When Manon dies, will I cry myself? "There will be no one left to call me: my dear child," she told herself sadly.[13] But that was a selfish thought. Would she regret not seeing Manon any more? She remained vulnerable with regard to André and Philippe. But other people? And at this moment she felt no warmth even toward Philippe or André.

A couple going on together because they have started: was that the future that awaited them? Friendship, affection, but no real reason for living together: is that how it would be? There had been real reasons to begin with. She who bridled as soon as a boy tried to assert the slightest superiority over her had been won over by a kind of ingenuousness on his part, a kind that she had never met in anyone else. She was disarmed by how dismayed he seemed when he sighed: "You are quite wrong!"

Over-protected by her mother, neglected by her father, she had this wound within her: that of being a woman. The idea of one day lying down beneath a man revolted her. By his sensitivity and his tenderness, André had enabled her to become reconciled with her sex. She had accepted sexual pleasure with joy. After a few years, she had even wanted a child; and motherhood had fully satisfied her. Yes, she had really needed André and not someone else. And, for his part, why had he loved her when, because of her aggressiveness, people did not generally like her? Perhaps the harshness and severity of his mother, which he found hard to take, were at the same time necessary to him, and perhaps he had found them again in Nicole. She had helped him to become, more or less, an adult. In any case, she had always had the impression that no woman would have suited him better than she did. Was she mistaken? On her own side, would she have been more fulfilled [*pleinement accomplie*] with someone else? Pointless questions. The only problem was to know what remained between them now. She did not know.[14]

Macha was busy that afternoon; she had left Nicole and André in the hands of a taxi driver, to whom she had given detailed instructions. They got out of the car in a suburb, where they had already been three years earlier and which was a true village at the gates of Moscow. They climbed up a street lined with old *isbas*.[15]

"Don't walk so quickly: I want to take photos," said Nicole.

She had suddenly announced that it was a shame not to take home any photos of their trip, and had borrowed Youri's camera. She had scarcely ever taken any photos. He watched her lining up an *isba* in the viewfinder. "It's because she's bored with me," he thought. In the taxi, they had found nothing to say to each other. Yet there was no longer any problem between them: that was the saddest thing. Perhaps he had become boring. Even during their vacations in Villeneuve, they never saw each other as much as they did here: she was over-saturated with his presence. And because she was bored, she herself was not much fun either. She photographed a second *isba*, and a third. People who were sitting on their doorsteps, chatting in the sun, looked at her with annoyance: one of them said something that André did not understand, but which did not seem pleasant.

"I think that they don't like you taking these photos," he said.

"Why?"

"These *isbas* are pretty, but they find them wretched and they suspect you, an evil foreigner, of wanting to take away images of their misery."

"Fine, I'll stop," she said.

They slipped back into silence. In the final analysis, he had been wrong to extend their stay. What good did it do him, even in relation to Macha? They were going to be apart for so long in any case: two years, three years, more? Would they really like to see each other again soon? Showing her Paris, in 1960, discovering the USSR with her, in 1963, these had been great celebrations. This time he had not experienced the same jubilation, except at the beginning. He loved her very much, and she reciprocated, but they saw the world in such different ways; and neither of them really had a place in the other's life. The charming romantic impressions that he had when he first arrived had fizzled out little by little. It was stupid to have upset Nicole without a good reason, all for the sake of a casual exchange of words: "You have nothing special to do in Paris, do you?—Nothing."

"When it comes down to it, it was silly to extend our stay," he said.

"It's silly if it doesn't even give you pleasure," she said.

"So you regret it then?"

"I regret it if you do."

Fine. They were going to go around in circles again. Something had become jammed in their dialogue; they each took wrongly, to some degree, what the other said. Would they never manage to break out of that? Why should they manage it today rather than yesterday? There was no reason.

They passed under a portico and in front of a church, which Nicole photographed. A little further on, another church with complicated architecture rose from the top of a hill. It dominated the Moskva, beyond which one could see a vast plain, and Moscow, in the distance. They sat down in the grass and looked at the view.[16]

"That's it. On the one occasion when we are alone, we find nothing to say to each other. We don't even want to talk to each other," Nicole thought bitterly. She had thought it would amuse André if they took some photos of Moscow together; the postcards were so bad. And he had lost interest in it; it had even seemed to annoy him. She stretched out on the grass, closed her eyes and suddenly she was ten years old: she was lying down in a meadow, with that smell of soil and greenery against her cheek. Why was a childhood memory so moving? Because time stretched out infinitely, the evening was becoming lost in the distance, and had eternity as its future. "I know what I've missed in this country," she told herself. Except for one night in Vladimir, nothing had touched her profoundly because nothing awoke resonances in her. The moments in her life that had moved her were always those which evoked something other than themselves; they seemed to her like a reminiscence, a premonition, the materialization of a dream, a painting that had come to life, the image of a reality that, in itself, was inaccessible and mysterious. In the USSR, not only did she have no roots, but she had not loved it at a distance as she had Italy or Greece. That was why, here, even beautiful things were never anything more than what they were. She could admire them: she was not enchanted by them. Would André understand that? she wondered. She told herself morosely that it would not interest him. But, all the same, for them to be alone together as she had so much wanted and yet not even profit from it was too depressing.

"I have just understood why nothing in the USSR moves me very much," she said.

"Why?" he said.

He was so much present, so attentive—with everyone, but even more so with her—that she was astonished that she had hesitated to talk to him. It was easy, in the warmth of his look, to explain out loud what she had said to herself privately.

"In short, this trip has disappointed us both a little," he said.

"Not you."

"Yes, in a different way. Too many things have eluded me. I'm no further on than when we arrived. I shall be glad to be back in Paris." He looked at her a little reproachfully: "Although I haven't been bored: I'm never bored when I'm with you."

"And I'm not when I'm with you, either."

"Come on! You shouted it out at me: 'I'm bored!'"

There was real sadness in his voice. She had shouted out her words in anger; she had forgotten them. And he seemed to have been deeply wounded by them. She hesitated, then decided.

"The truth is that I'm very fond of Macha, but seeing you when you're with her isn't at all the same as seeing you on your own. What bored me was never being alone with you. That made no difference to you, but it did to me," she added a little bitterly.

"But there were many moments when we were alone."

"Not many. And you threw yourself into your Russian grammar book."

"You only had to talk to me."

"You didn't want me to."

"Of course I did! I always want you to." He paused for reflection: "It's funny! I had the impression that we were seeing more of each other than in Paris."

"But always with Macha."

"You seemed to be getting along so well with her: I didn't think that she was getting you down."

"I get along with her. But when there is a third person between us, it's not the same thing."

He gave a strange smile: "That's what I often tell myself when you bring Philippe on our weekends away."

She was disconcerted. Yes, she often asked Philippe to go with them; it seemed quite natural.

"That's quite different."

"Because he's my son? He's still a third person between us."

"He won't be any more."

"That obviously upsets you a great deal!"

Were they going to argue again?

"No mother likes her son getting married. But you needn't think that it will make me ill."

They were silent. No. We must not fall back into silence.

"Why did you never tell me that you sometimes found Philippe's presence a nuisance?"

"You've so often reproached me for being exclusive! And then what would I have gained by depriving you of Philippe if I'm not enough for you in any case?"

"What do you mean, you're not enough for me?"

"Oh, you're happy to have me in your life. Provided that you have other things: your son, friends, Paris . . ."

"What you're saying is stupid," she said, astonished. "You need other things than me, too."

"I can do without everything if I have you. I'd be perfectly happy alone with you, living in the country. You told me one day that you would die of boredom there."

Was his dream of retiring to Villeneuve more serious than she thought?

"You prefer the country and I prefer Paris, because we all love the place where we spent our childhood."

"That's not the real reason. I'm not enough for you and when I told you that the other day, you didn't even protest."

She remembered. She was angry. And she had always had difficulty—

when she was knotted up and stiff with anger—in getting out the words that he needed.

"I was angry. I wasn't going to declare my love for you. But if you don't think that I am as attached to you as you are to me, then you're really stupid."

She smiled tenderly. And there was some truth in what she was saying: Macha had scarcely left their side.

"In short," he said, "there has been a misunderstanding."

"Yes. You thought I was bored with you, whereas I was bored of being without you: that's more flattering."

"And I was happy to have you all to myself, but you didn't realize it."

"But why did we misunderstand each other so badly?" she asked.

"Our disappointment put us in a bad mood. All the more so since we didn't want to admit it to ourselves."

"We should always admit everything, to ourselves and to each other," said Nicole.

"Do you always admit everything to me?"

She hesitated: "Almost. And you?"

"Almost."

They laughed together. Why had they been incapable of living together during the past few days? Everything seemed so familiar and so easy once again.

"There is one thing that I haven't told you, and which mattered," she went on. "Since I arrived in Moscow, I've grown old. I've realized that I have so little time left to live: that makes the slightest set-backs intolerable. You don't feel your age, but I do."

"Oh, I feel it," he said. "I even think about it very often."

"Is that true? You never talk about it."

"That's in order not to make you sad. You don't talk about it, either."

For a while, they remained silent. But it was no longer the same silence: just a pause in their finally-renewed dialogue, which would not stop any more.

"Shall we go back?" she asked.

"Let's go back."

He took her arm.

It's a great stroke of luck, to be able to talk to each other, she told herself. It's understandable that, with couples who don't know how to use words, misunderstandings should build up and end up spoiling everything between them.[17]

"I was rather afraid that something had been spoiled between us."

"Me, too."

"But, basically, that was impossible," he said. "It was inevitable that we should end up by explaining things to each other."

"Yes, it was inevitable. Next time, I won't be afraid again."

He gripped her arm: "There won't be a next time."

Perhaps there would be one. But that was not important: they would never again go very far astray from each other. He had not told her absolutely everything that had passed through his mind during the days concerned. And she had perhaps kept little things to herself. That was not important, either. They had found each other again. He would ask questions and she would reply.

"Why did you start feeling old?" he asked.

NOTES

1. In French, the point is that Macha uses the informal mode of address "tu" with her father, but the more formal "vous" with Nicole.

2. In most cases, the changes of narrative viewpoint (from Nicole to André, or vice versa) are marked by a one-line gap in the text. All of the six cases where the gap is larger and contains three stars in a triangular pattern mark significant time-jumps, and four of them also mark changes of location within the Soviet Union. (In only four instances is there no gap at all: scrutiny of Beauvoir's typescript might show whether this is deliberate.)

3. The grammar of the clauses following Macha's words at this point strongly suggests that "comme il craignait de l'avoir peiné" should read "comme si elle craignait de l'avoir peiné"—hence the translation: "as if she were afraid of having upset him."

4. *Aucassin et Nicolette*, a medieval French romance (in the form of a "chante-fable," or combination of prose and verse) by an unknown author, probably dating from the early 13th century.

5. *kvass* is a fermented, mildly alcoholic beverage made from black rye or rye bread, popular in Russia and other Eastern and Central European countries.

6. Red Falcons, the name of various socialist or communist organizations, were popular in Europe and the United States, especially between the first and second world wars, but are still in existence today.

7. The change of narrative viewpoint after this paragraph is the first not to be indicated by a gap in the text. The other three such cases are all in the last few pages of the story.

8. "Patience, patience,—Patience dans l'azur!—Chaque atome de silence—Est la chance d'un fruit mûr!" from *Charmes ou Poèmes* (1922), by Paul Valéry; translated by James L. Brown as *Charmes* (Chico, Calif.: Forsan Books, 1983).

9. "a process of deterioration," from F. Scott Fitzgerald's *Tender Is the Night* (London: Wordsworth, 1995), 240.

10. Pléiade, the "Bibliothèque de la Pléiade" is a French collection of books created in the

1930s. It offers authoritative reference editions of the complete works of classic authors. The "Library of America" series (from 1979) is a rather similar series in the United States.

11. *Manon Lescaut* is a novel by the French author the Abbé Prévost, published in 1731.

12. Vinteuil's sonata is regularly evoked in Marcel Proust's series of novels, *A la recherche du temps perdu* (*Remembrance of Things Past* or *In Search of Lost Time*). It represents an aesthetic ideal that brings back past memories.

13. This is not, of course, a reference to *Manon Lescaut*, but to a real person in Nicole's life. Close comparison with a nearly identical passage in Beauvoir's story "The Age of Discretion" strongly indicates that "Manon" is André's mother, though no name is mentioned in earlier passages in the present text about André's mother.

14. The stretch of narrative from Nicole's viewpoint ends here, again without a break in the text. In this case, however, before narrative that is clearly from André's viewpoint, there follows a paragraph that might be described as "neutral." That is, it comes as close as any sequence in the story to being written from the standpoint of the old-fashioned omniscient narrator, bearing no marks that enable the reader to ascribe it to the mentality of either André or Nicole. Interestingly, it corresponds to—though it does not exactly describe—a taxi journey during which neither finds anything to say to the other, thereby perhaps highlighting by a stylistic device the fact that there is temporarily a kind of stalemate between them that is based upon each one's inability to break through certain mental barriers and take positive steps toward finally overcoming the "misunderstanding" of the title.

15. *Isbas* are Russian log huts.

16. Beyond this point, the narrative is manifestly from Nicole's viewpoint for a while, and both the paragraph that ends here and the previous one can easily be ascribed to André. Nevertheless, it is worth noting that the second has much of the "neutral" quality described in the last note. Furthermore, the first of the two could be an expression of the thoughts of *either* of the main characters at this precise stage in their relationship. It was probably deliberately conceived by Beauvoir in this way.

17. After this point, the final dozen lines or so of the text are probably most naturally seen as the closing section of Nicole's last narrative sequence. But again we may note that they are of such a nature that they might represent the thinking of either of the couple at this stage. That stage, however, is now one of reconciliation, characterized by a communication between them that is the exact counterpart of their alienation and silence in the taxi.

8

My Experience as a Writer

INTRODUCTION

by Elizabeth Fallaize

When Simone de Beauvoir undertook a lecture tour of Japan with Sartre in the autumn of 1966 she had long been a writer with a substantial international reputation. She had published four novels and three volumes of her autobiography, as well as *Le deuxième sexe* (*The Second Sex*) and a number of other philosophical essays. All her major work had been translated into Japanese, and the Japanese translation of *Le deuxième sexe* had been a best seller only the previous year. Beauvoir has described in her memoirs the warmth of the welcome that she received from her Japanese readers.[1] The three lectures that she gave on her tour, of which this is the third, all reflect her confidence in her status as internationally successful writer.

Yet the mid-1960s were also a period in which the philosophical novel no longer held the same sway in France that it had done in the immediate postwar period. A new generation of writers had launched the *nouveau roman* (new novel) in the 1950s; both they and the supporters of the *Tel Quel* group favored formal experimentation and did not believe that the novel should seek to communicate a coherent and consistent meaning.[2] Beauvoir was perceived as an opponent of these new tendencies and had taken part in a public debate in 1964 defending committed literature against its critics.[3]

In her first two lectures in Japan she had taken *Le deuxième sexe* as a starting point and had focused on the situation of women and on the issue of women and creativity. By focusing in her third lecture on her own experience as a writer of fiction and autobiography, Beauvoir was both speaking very personally and returning to the debate about literature in which she had recently been involved in France. It is not surprising that her lecture mounts a vigorous defense of her conception of the task of the writer. Taking up Sartre's definition of the writer's work as a "singular universal" from his earlier lecture, and returning to a central theme of her 1946 article, "Literature and Metaphysics," Beauvoir argues that the writer's task is to use an individual experience to reveal a universal dimension.[4] Whether writing novels or autobiography, the writer has to convey the meaning of lived experience in the world, bringing together the sense of immediate experience and at the same time the universal dimension of that experience in a way that we cannot perceive simultaneously in life. She underlines the necessity of creating a degree of facticity in order to echo the resistance of everyday life to surrendering meaning—a theme that had preoccupied her from her earliest texts on the writing of fiction. The problem poses itself according to Beauvoir in an especially acute form in autobiography—whereas in the novel, the writer's problem is to include sufficient facticity, in autobiography, the accumulation of brute experience could on the contrary overwhelm the construction of meaning. And Beauvoir is very clear here that the writing of autobiography is indeed a construction rather than a recording of meaning. She emphasizes the degree of research that she has to do in order to write her autobiographies and her reconstruction of truths, which she may not have been aware of at an earlier period.

This view of autobiography as a creative construction allows her to firmly reject the view of the *Tel Quel* school that autobiography is not an artistic form as such, belonging, according to the distinction made by Roland Barthes, to the domain of the *écrivant* rather than to the domain of the *écrivain*. Beauvoir describes this view as "absolutely absurd" and goes on to defend her view that autobiography is a form of witnessing ("un témoignage"), which precisely enables the universal to be attained via the individual.[5] However, she does raise difficulties about one aspect of her autobiographical practice and that is her use of a chronological framework. She concedes that its principal disadvantage is the sense that every moment recounted is leading to a culminating point that never occurs. The synthesis of present and future that animates our projects in real life is missing when the past is recounted and yet Beauvoir is committed to a chronological framework because it mirrors her conception of existence as both bound by time and history and as always moving forward into the future. The only means of palliating this disadvantage, she concludes, is to maintain her reader's interest to a point where he or she will themselves take on the creative task and insert their own imagination into the present of the narrative. In order to do this, the writer needs to use all the resources of artistic creation that the critics of autobiography take to be irrelevant to the project. This emphasis on the crucial role of readers is another constant of Beauvoir's writing on literature. In her memoirs she refers frequently to the effect of her readers' letters on her, and her conception of literature as a communication with her readers reinforces their role.

Like autobiography, the novel is presented by Beauvoir as a form of communication that works through a different channel from that of the essay in which a clear line is to be argued; in a work of art the ambiguity of lived experience in the world must be conveyed. She is particularly concerned in this lecture to reject two misapprehensions about her major Goncourt winning novel *Les Mandarins* (*The Mandarins*). The first is that it is a *roman à clef*, and the second that it is a thesis novel (*roman à thèse*). These are both criticisms that Beauvoir had already discussed in her memoirs but she comes back to them here because they go to the heart of the debate about the creation of meaning in the novel, and her conception of what a novel should be. A novel that set out to illustrate a thesis or that simply described reality would not meet her own criteria of recreating the ambiguity of lived experience and would not attain the universal. She therefore rejects these criticisms firmly. One might note, however, that she makes no mention in her lecture of her second novel, *Le sang des autres* (*The Blood of Others*), written during the German occupation, which she concedes in her memoirs to being much more of a thesis novel than she had intended.[6]

Nonetheless, the novel for Beauvoir is essentially a form of communication of meaning, even if that meaning is not conveyed in the same unambiguous way in which it would be in an essay, and she goes on to underline the difference between her own work and that of the leading *nouveau romancier*, Alain Robbe-Grillet, in which there is a deliberate rejection of a signifying fictional universe. Beauvoir's rejection of the techniques of the new novel was nevertheless far from total. At the time of her lecture she had completed her fifth novel, *Les belles images*, which was to be published within a month of her return from Japan. Published twelve years after her previous novel, *Les Mandarins*, *Les belles images* displays quite a radical shift in technique on Beauvoir's part, a shift which she readily agreed had been in part inspired by the theories of the new novel and the criticisms it had made of the traditional novel.[7] However, the technical innovations that Beauvoir introduces do not affect the fundamental purpose of fiction as Beauvoir sees it: through the crisis of a young woman, Laurence, the novel launches a double-pronged attack on the myths that permit both the traditional bourgeoisie and the new technocratic bourgeoisie in France to avoid facing uncomfortable problems such as poverty and starvation. In many ways it stands as one of her most radical fictions.

One can only speculate as to why Beauvoir made no mention of her new novel in this lecture. It is possible that she preferred not to complicate the picture by signaling her new techniques, or that she preferred to wait for the critical reaction to her novel before discussing it herself. A further omission is perhaps more striking: despite having talked at length about the difficulties for women writers in both of her previous lectures, Beauvoir makes no attempt to explain how she herself has managed to break through the barriers that she had described in such detail. Only two or three clues are offered: the first is her emphasis on her own strong sense of vocation as a child—an element she had insisted on in "La femme et la création"—and the second is her recognition that the female first person voice of her autobiography is quite exceptional. Finally, she repeats in this lecture a theme developed at length earlier, and that is the failure of many would-be women authors to rise above the particular and individual to attain the universal. Her own struggle to attain this goal in her writing takes on a particular significance in the light of her conviction that the universal dimension is the barrier at which many women fall.

NOTES

1. See *Tout compte fait* (Paris: Gallimard, 1972), 281–82.

2. The *nouveaux romanciers* included Alain Robbe-Grillet, Nathalie Sarraute, Michel Butor and Claude Simon. The *Tel Quel* group founded in 1960 by Philippe Sollers was focused on the journal of the same name and argued for a purely poetic role for literature.

3. Beauvoir's contribution, translated in this volume as "What Can Literature Do?" appeared in *Que peut la littérature?* ed. Yves Buin (Paris: Union Générale d'Editeurs, 1965), 73–92.

4. Sartre's three lectures given in Tokyo and Kyoto in September of 1966 have been published as "Plaidoyer pour les intellectuels," in *Situations philosophiques* (Paris: Gallimard, 1990; 219–81) and translated as "A Plea for Intellectuals," in *Between Existentialism and Marxism* (London: Verson, 2008; 228–85). Note that Sartre's 1966 lectures are mistakenly dated as 1965 in "Plea," 226.

5. See Ursula Tidd's study of Beauvoir's autobiographical writing as "témoignage," *Simone de Beauvoir Gender and Testimony* (Cambridge: CUP, 1999).

6. See *La force de l'âge*, tome II (Paris: Gallimard, 1960), 623.

7. See for example her interview with Francis Jeanson in his *Simone de Beauvoir ou l'entreprise de vivre* (*Simone de Beauvoir or the Undertaking of Living*) (Paris: Seuil, 1966), 294–95.

MY EXPERIENCE AS A WRITER

by Simone de Beauvoir

TRANSLATION AND NOTES BY J. DEBBIE MANN

Jean-Paul Sartre spoke to you about literature in general. He told you what all writers have in common; for them it is a question of communicating "the lived sense of being-in-the-world" by giving as a product an object which is a singular universal: their oeuvre.[1]

In order to round off his talk, I thought that it would be interesting to choose a specific example, and I chose the one that I know the best, my own. So I am going to speak to you, along the lines laid out by Jean-Paul Sartre, of my own undertaking, of my own experience as a writer.

This experience began with the contradiction about which he spoke: having everything and nothing to say. I got the desire to write very young, at fourteen or fifteen years of age. I was thinking about it for a lot of psychological and familial reasons. The meaning of this project was to make the world my own, to show my life as freely recreated by me. I did not say this to myself, naturally, in those terms, but it is clear that this is what I wanted to do. I endured the world which was given to me sometimes with joy, often with revolt or boredom; I wanted to make it mine in order to justify it in some

"Mon expérience d'écrivain," a lecture given in Japan on September 27, 1966, was published in *Les écrits de Simone de Beauvoir*, ed. Claude Francis and Fernande Gontier (Paris: Gallimard, 1979), 439–57.

way. So I thought I had everything to say: the whole world, life, everything. In my youthful, adolescent diaries, at eighteen, nineteen years old, this leitmotif appears over and over: I will say everything, I have everything to say.[2] That amused me when I reread them because in fact at that time I knew very little of the world, and in reality I had nothing to say. I was promising myself to say everything and I knew quite well that I had nothing to say, absolutely nothing. The proof is that when I had finished my exams, when writing became for me a real and concrete project, I struggled for several years. I still thought that I was going to write, that I had everything to say; and when I found myself with sheets of paper in front of me I sadly realized that I had nothing to say. I think that this tension is shared by all writers at certain points. There are times when one is on vacation and one does not write, when one does not feel like writing, and that is fine; there are times when one writes, times of fecundity, when one has difficulties, but one writes, one is engaged in the work and that is fine too. But there are other times that every writer is familiar with, that are called times of drought, of depression, when one continues to have the desire to write, therefore to say everything, but when, at the same time, one feels empty and dried up. One has nothing more to say and it is a very unpleasant tension. This tension is resolved when from everything or from nothing *something* springs forth. That is to say at the moment when the actual work is conceived. The work is a way of embodying in something this everything which one wants to express starting from a nothingness: the vertiginous void of the blank page. This synthesis was realized for the first time when I wrote the first of my books to be published; it was a novel, *L'invitée* [*She Came to Stay*].[3] I took as a starting point a concrete psychological experience, for I had realized in a startling way the antagonism which brings certain consciousnesses into opposition. Previously I had hardly known anything but friendship or indifference. As for the people whom I did not hold in esteem, who did not interest me, I cared little that they did not hold me in esteem, that they did not like me; thus I had never lived a real antagonism. And then it happened that a friend I was very fond of refused in some ways to enter into true communication; she was somewhat hostile to me. In short, I discovered something that everyone knows: the other's consciousness exists; the other is a subject for himself as I am for myself. In his world I am an object with which he can more or less do as he likes and which he can consider as hateful and unpleasant. I thus had a concrete experience which was at first situated on a psychological level. But as long as one remains on a psychological, that is to say, anecdotal level, the book does not get written. The book began to take shape in my head when

I found a way to move from this singular experience to a universality. I expressed myself as I have just done to you when I understood that it was the problem of the other, the relationship to the other's consciousness, which was tormenting me. From that moment on, all that remained was to create a plot and invent characters and a story, which would allow my singular story to take on a universal dimension, so that everyone, while reading my book, could recognize his own personal preoccupations and communicate with me. This task constitutes the actual artistic work. In this concrete case one can see clearly how from a singular experience I moved on to a universal one. When I succeeded in finding a form which gave this universal dimension to my experience, then the book was conceived. I have often proceeded in an analogous fashion. I have very often started from a universal fact that an experience has singularized for me and which then has become the subject of a work. Very often people have told me, while reading such and such a book, "How strange, you seem to be discovering only today that all men are mortal, that the other's consciousness exists, that one grows old, that it is sad to see people that one loves die: these are banalities."

I respond, "Yes, these are banalities, but the fact is that to be acquainted with them as knowledge [*savoir*], as conceptualized universality, is completely different than to experience them as a personal, lived, and singular experience which keeps its singular dimension even when you universalize it." Therefore the creative task consists either in giving a universal dimension to what you have lived singularly, or in finding a way to singularize a conceptually impoverished knowledge [*connaissance*].

There are cases in which, for me, knowledge [*savoir*] remains at the level of knowledge and in these cases I wish to communicate it in conceptual form. That is when I write essays. They cannot be considered exactly as literary works—although it is a little more complicated because in the essay itself there is a style, a way of writing and a construction. One also communicates through what is shared and misinformative in language. Consequently, it happens that certain essays may be literary works—not all—that depends on the case. As for me, there have been circumstances in which I have chosen to communicate a conviction on the universal plane, on the plane of knowledge. For example, in *Le deuxième sexe* [*The Second Sex*], I was very direct in my exposition. I situated myself on an anthropological, scientific plane without referring to any singular experience or giving way to personal feeling.[4] It has sometimes been pointed out to me that I was much more forceful in my essays than in my novels, which is completely normal since I write an essay precisely when I have clear-cut convictions, when I want to say something precise which implies neither ambiguity nor contradiction for me. In that case I set out my arguments with the clarity and universality that they have in my head. On the contrary, if I want to render the lived aspect of an experience, with its ambiguity and contradictions, with this inexpressible side requiring the creation of a literary work which must close again on silence, then of course, I write in a completely different way. I take care to emphasize these ambiguities, nuances and contradictions which are the very reason for my book, which lead me to compose not an essay, but a literary work which must close again on silence.[5] To try to render this "lived sense of being-in-the-world" of which Sartre spoke, I have resorted, on the whole, to two different forms: first, the novel, then autobiography. I think, moreover, that I will go back to the novel and later again to autobiography. This means that I do not give preference to either of the two forms. They each have their own advantages and characteristics, at the same time as their limitations and difficulties. And I would like to try to examine them one after the other with you.

I started with the novel and for a long time the novel seemed to me to be a privileged genre. It is easy to understand why. It is a question of uncovering a *sense*; but life as we live it day to day is burdened with elements that one could call non-sense: trivial details, contingent details; many things happen which are merely present without signifying anything. In order to derive the meaning of an experience, it is obviously very convenient to distance oneself from this too real world in which we are immersed and to substitute an imaginary world, divested of all of its scoria, dust and uselessness. Writing a novel is in a way pulverizing the real world and only retaining the elements that one will be able to include in a re-creation of an imaginary world: everything can then be much more clear, much more signifying. . . . One will attempt to construct relationships between the characters, a plot, personalities which disclose meanings. A novel is a kind of machine that one creates to illuminate the meaning of our being-in-the-world. There is thus an obvious advantage to the novel; it allows one to eliminate everything that is useless in the world which surrounds us, to do away with the pure facticity of it.

On the other hand, our experience is detotalized in the sense that Sartre gives to this word, that is to say that we never live all aspects of it at the same time. My consciousness is always a surpassing of the present moment. I suffer, but my way of suffering is already a way of putting myself outside of my suffering. For a joy it is the same. I am always at a certain distance from what I am experiencing. I am always in the future and consequently, there is never a total plenitude of the moments I am in the process of living. The novel can, on the contrary, render the meaning which is on the horizon of my experience but which does not manage to be enclosed in it with complete plenitude. Personally, one of the reasons for which I have written is this *inadequacy* of the lived moments and of the reality which haunts my horizon, which invests me without my being able to completely grasp it. I am going to take as an example an experience which greatly struck me: the Algerian war.[6] There were times when I truly lived the horror of that war: when people told me about particularly dreadful episodes, in a chance meeting, when I came across an article in a newspaper. At those times, I was filled with this horror to the point of not imagining that I could think of anything else. But naturally, in the course of the day, I had things to do—I slept, I took walks, the weather was nice—I forgot. And yet the horror was always there. One did not take walks in the same way, the sky was not the same blue it would have been if not for this war. It was on the horizon even when I did not realize it in its horror. I will call this, using Proust's word, the intermittences of the heart.[7] Whether it be in private life or in public life, one encounters these intermittences: realities that are in some ways not present are nevertheless present on the horizon of our experience; however they are not lived in their plenitude at each instant of our lives. There are intermittences and also contradictions. I am and have always been very sensitive to these contradictions because I have a great love for life, and often a great joy in living. But at the same time I have a very keen sense of the tragedy of the human condition, of its horror in certain cases and of the fact that death will come one day for me and for the people I hold dear. But it is almost impossible to have both these thoughts at once. When I am really overtaken by the love for life and feeling very happy, I do not think either of death or of the tragedies which exist for others. If, on the contrary, I am filled with a tragic feeling, either personally or out of sympathy with others, my *joie de vivre*, at that moment, does not exist. I cannot hold both of these attitudes at once; it is absolutely impossible.

On the contrary, if I am writing a novel I can very well sustain these two themes at the same time, as one sustains several themes at the same time in a symphony or sonata, in counterpoint, by mixing them and making them exist together and by having them support each other. For example, this is what I tried to do in *Les Mandarins* [*The Mandarins*].[8] I gave Henri the sense of an action to be done, the taste for life, the taste for engagement: he is a man among men who is happy to be so, who wants to fight along with them. On the contrary, I gave Anne, the female protagonist, a sense of nothingness, death, the futility of all things, the impossibility of attaining the absolute. Anne's point of view disputes Henri's: often Anne thinks that Henri is crazy to get so agitated over earthly things since one will die; but inversely, Henri thinks that it is easy to say to oneself that one will die someday, and in that way escape engagement and action. In the end I do not prove either of them right. That is the advantage of a novel: one can put forth two opposing points of view, keeping them in balance in this silent whole which is the finished novel. It says neither "act" nor "do not act." It says nothing but rather shows a whole set of difficulties, ambiguities and contradictions which constitute the lived meaning of an existence. In a novel, in order to succeed in rendering this lived meaning, one begins by aiming at generalities. In writing *Les Mandarins* I set out to depict the milieu of left-wing intellectuals to which I belonged between 1945 and 1950 (a time which was very important for us as it was for you). Thus I started out with the intent of speaking about all of them. And naturally, I, who was a left-wing intellectual, found myself situated among them. I was part of this group that I was describing, with the result that my singularity is also represented in my narrative. I presented the singular point of view of a left-wing intellectual on left-wing intellectuals; but I took the generality as a starting point.

That is why in my opinion a novel must never be a *roman à clefs*. People believed, which rather bothered me, that *Les Mandarins* was a *roman à clefs*; I was thought to have chosen such-and-such intellectuals and to have described them in an anecdotal way, such as they existed in their singularity. But this is not at all true; that is not what a novel is. On the contrary, it must try, beginning with the singularity which is of necessity at the root of creation, to find the universality of a situation; therefore no character, no episode should be simply anecdotal. One must recast, recreate. That is the task of the novelist. He begins with concrete, singular, separate, scattered experiences in order to recreate an imaginary world in which a meaning is disclosed.

This rules out the novel having "keys" [*clefs*]. If I now compare the novel to autobiography, I find it has a first, quite obvious advantage: when I write my memoirs, I speak of my life, but it is only one object in the world; the world extends far beyond it.[9] By knowledge, sympathy, joint action and imagination, I participate in many lives which are not mine and there are a great number of things which belong to my experience without constituting my own life. I have the advantage, when I write a work of fiction, of being able to talk about everything which surrounds my life but which is not my life: individuals that I have met, who interested me, whom I found sympathetic, whose problems fascinated me. I can try to recreate them; I can try to aim for the universal, beginning with a singularity other than that of my own life.

Once again, it is on the condition that this singularity is not anecdotal, but rather a vehicle of the universal, that it can serve as a mediation between me and the universe. In order to play this role of mediator, I myself must be singularly engaged. I mean that even speaking of things which are not part of my own life, as in *Tous les hommes sont mortels* [*All Men Are Mortal*], a novel of pure imagination in which I tell stories that happened centuries ago, to people who in a sense do not concern me, I must be in on the action.[10] In *Tous les hommes sont mortels*, my singularity is expressed by the interest that I show in the problems of my characters, problems which are close to my own. If it were a question of an experience which had no lived connection with my own, it is quite obvious that I would not be able to give it a lived sense in describing it. I mean that I exclude in this way the novel that has sometimes been called the documentary novel, which is a survey novel. There was a time when writers in socialist countries were deliberately sent to the fields or to the factories. There, they did what was called an apprenticeship. They spent six months in a Chinese village where the inhabitants were picking tea, for example, or in the USSR, six months on a dam, and they were expected to bring back a novel which showed the life of the dam workers or of the peasants who grew tea. Those novels never interested me because they lacked this essential dimension which is precisely the subjectivity of the man who is building a dam or who lives in a village. The author spoke of them in a way that was inadequate on the anthropological level and devoid of any literary quality because all singularity was done away with. If the writer had spoken of his own experience in the village or on the dam, of his difficulties with the workers or the peasants, if he had seen their problems through his own personal experience, he would truly have shown a concrete universal, which is much more interesting than a false documentary. There is an example in your country of a great novel in which the connection between objectivity and subjectivity succeeds admirably; it is the tale of the Genji by Murasaki Shikibu.[11] She describes the Court in a way that appears to be completely objective, recounting intrigues which do not concern her directly. However, her presence can be felt at all times not only because she sometimes says very amiably, "I am stopping; I have a headache; I am putting down my brush; I will not say any more today," but because one can feel that she has lived all of these intrigues herself, that she has the same values as the people about whom she is speaking, the same nuances, the same subtleties of feeling, etc. Finally, as a lady of the Court who is writing a story about the Court, she is present in it at all times. It is not a documentary book, but something much stronger, a true literary work in which a singularity is expressed through universality, in which universality is presented through a singular point of view.

Therefore, a novel must be neither *à clefs* nor documentary; furthermore it must not be a thesis novel [*roman à thèse*] either. It has often been maintained that my novels were thesis novels. I deny it. In my opinion, the thesis novel contradicts the very meaning of the novel. In a novel it is a question of showing existence in its ambiguities and contradictions. Existence is detotalized, always unfinished, always to be continued, existence is never over. If we consider a real experience, we can talk about it indefinitely, look at it from all angles, just as when speaking about a real person, we can indefinitely ask ourselves who she is and what she wants. A novel must pose the same enigmas. One must not wonder, what did the novelist mean? But rather one must examine his characters, saying to oneself, "so they are thus; they do this, they do that; what do I think about it all?" This presupposes that the author has concluded nothing. A thesis novel is a novel which speaks, in the weak sense of the word; it is a novel which preaches a lesson: one must dedicate oneself to the community, one must not be selfish, one must work for others. If that is what one has to say, there is no need to construct a whole complicated story, a whole imaginary world, one has only to say it; one must write an essay. One writes a novel to present together the contradictions, difficulties and ambiguities at the heart of an object which does not speak, a silent object. Thus we exclude the *roman à clefs*, the documentary novel, the thesis novel. One must construct a novel which will truly be a multifaceted object that can never be summed up, which does not put forth any definitive word.

However, even if one follows these precepts, if one tries to communicate through non-knowledge, through the lived, and not starting with the universal, the fact remains that the novel, besides the advantages pointed out earlier, has limitations which come from these very advantages. In the novel—since one chooses an imaginary world—all the scoria and contingencies of the real world are done away with. Yes, but the novel is written to communicate to us the lived sense of things; yet, in life, there is this share of non-sense, of contingency. If I eliminate them too radically, I find myself confronted with an object which will have only a rather distant relation to reality, which will betray it. As soon as an episode or even a detail occurs in a novel, it is immediately situated there in a necessary way. If one begins a novel by saying that it was a beautiful night, it immediately seems important that this night be beautiful. One knows that the beauty of this night is going to be connected with the mood of the hero or with his adventures. The detail is mentioned because the author deliberately wanted it there; it is concerted, necessary. Whereas in life things happen which have no meaning, or at least no necessity. The greatest reproach that can be leveled at the classic novel is that it substitutes for a world in which connections are loose and ambiguous and without necessity, a universe in which there is logic, coherence, necessity. This reproach of the classic novel is made in particular by that school of which Sartre spoke earlier, which is called in our country the "new novel" and whose leader is Robbe-Grillet.[12] He has very often expressed in lectures or in articles his distrust of the narrative. In his film *L'année dernière à Marienbad* [*Last Year at Marienbad*] [1961] there is a character who says with disgust, "Oh, telling a story! . . ." and thinks that as soon as one tells a story one gets so far away from the truth of the lived world that it is completely useless to claim to do it. In his latest novel, *La maison de rendez-vous* [The Rendez-Vous House] [1966], Robbe-Grillet purposely constructed a story which means nothing; it takes place in a house of assignation in Hong Kong and in fact nothing happens. Moreover, insofar as some things do still take place, what follows in the story contradicts them. For example, there is a character who dies in the middle of the book and who is alive at the end, without any attempt to explain this inconsistency. For the author it is a question of constructing an insignificant and totally incoherent object, thus parodying the classic novel which aims for coherence, meaning and necessity. And the school of which Sartre spoke a little while ago, *Tel Quel*, goes even farther.[13] *Tel Quel* thinks that the new novel is still too bound to reality and there is now a dispute between *Tel Quel* and the new novel. *Tel Quel* claims that the practitioners of the new novel themselves fall into academicism, that Butor or Nathalie Sarraute, or Robbe-Grillet himself tell a great deal too much of a story.[14] For them the novel must be a simple construction of words, in which nothing will be contested except the language itself and which will signify absolutely nothing. Such works can indeed have some interest, especially in the critical sphere, but it is quite clear that for authors and readers who continue to wish for communication, they do not provide a satisfactory solution. Perhaps this is why one sees such a large number of autobiographies coming out. They are very numerous. Many people today, women in particular, are writing autobiographies. Perhaps it is because one no longer dares to write a classic novel inasmuch as the younger generation has exposed its difficulties, contradictions and failures. However, one does not want to resign oneself to saying nothing, to communicating nothing.

So one writes autobiographies. In any case, I myself know that I was led to autobiography not at all by the critics of *Tel Quel* or the new novel, but by a personal reflection on the inadequacies of the novel. It annoyed me to only be able to show the world in a distorted way, through plots that were overconstructed, episodes too full of meaning. So I thought that instead of eliminating the contingencies, the facticity as one does in the novel, there was a move in the opposite direction which consisted of finding support in contingence, in facticity. In the novel, the author only brings himself in indirectly. On the contrary, in autobiography it is a question of starting from the singularity of my life in order to find a generality, that of my era, that of the milieu in which I live. This aiming at generality is extremely important because if you merely write a collection of anecdotes, it holds absolutely no interest for anyone. This is the flaw of many of the autobiographies that we are seeing today in France—I am well aware of it because among the manuscripts that I receive there is always a stack of autobiographies; women especially recount their lives without undertaking to ascertain whether the episodes are of any interest to others. They do not surpass the anecdote; they remain in the facticity of daily life. Their narratives are trivial. For an autobiography to be interesting, one must have had experiences that concern a large number of people. And this is why there is a reproach that has sometimes been directed at me, which I find completely unjust, even though a priori it may seem justified: the reproach of narcissism. There are people who have said to me that it takes a great deal of narcissism to talk about oneself for three thick volumes. And in truth, if it were a question of only talking about myself and depicting myself, it would be a very presumptuous undertaking. But I decided to do it because I thought that I was at a time in my life and in my era when I could, in talking about myself, speak of other things. The "I" that I use is actually very often a "we" or a "one" which refers to the whole of my century rather than to myself. Here is an example: I recounted how one night, when I was with some friends in a car on a road in Provence, we suddenly saw a glimmer in the sky, and when we found out it was the first Sputnik, we were very excited.[15] It is obviously of no consequence that I myself saw, on that road, at that moment, a Sputnik. But I think that later, when people wish to understand what it meant for us to see that first Sputnik, they will be able to get a concrete idea of it only by reading the detailed, individualized, singular accounts of people who saw it. Therefore, in writing "I . . ." my intention is to bear witness to my era and to other people who lived along with me the events that I lived. Moreover, this "I" when I say it, is also the "I" of a woman. In this era of transition for women, when they are on the road to emancipation but have not yet obtained it, I think that it is interesting to see a woman's life. The "I" that I use is an "I" which has a general scope; it relates to a very large number of women. Finally, inasmuch as I, like everyone else, have a singular life which has a singular flavor distinct from that of others, inasmuch as I will die, inasmuch as I have known joys, suffering, etc., etc., my "I" encompasses the problems of the human condition in general. Thus I am not talking only about myself; I am trying to talk about something that goes infinitely beyond my singularity. I am trying to speak of everything, and therefore to write a literary work, since for me it is a question of creating a concrete and singularized universal.

There are critics, there are people who maintain that in any case the eyewitness account is not a literary work. In particular, those of the *Tel Quel* school would classify the authors of memoirs, according to the distinction established by Barthes, not among authors [*écrivains*] but among writers [*écrivants*].[16] They maintain that autobiography is a communication through knowledge [*savoir*], in the form of knowledge; one recounts events, cites dates, gives facts, and that consequently this is not a literary work. A literary work must be a communication of the inexpressible, of the incommunicable, a communication through non-knowledge. I find this thesis absolutely absurd because nothing can be more an experience of the lived than the testimony [*témoinage*] given by someone of his life. To say that any type of witnessing [*témoinage*], in other words the account of a lived experience, communicates through knowledge and not through the lived is obviously a contradiction. It is very clear that there is a degree of knowledge in memoirs and autobiographies. I cite dates, give names and refer to real events. But we find this degree of knowledge in the novel as well; it is not less extensive in a work of fiction. In any case, it is a question of communicating through the widest possible knowledge that which cannot be communicated directly: the flavor of my century, the flavor of my life, something that is impossible to render in a direct way. Otherwise it would suffice to make a chronological list of events and dates; there would be no point in writing the books that I offer to the public as my autobiography. In fact, when composing memoirs, it is not at all a question of taking down a dictation from some sort of dictaphone that one might have in one's head. There are people who imagine exactly that, people who have no idea at all of what writing is. They say, "it is not so hard; if only I had time, I would not make such a big fuss; I would sit down at my table and I would write from beginning to end what has happened to me; everyone can do that." Not at all: writing an autobiography is really recreating events that one has behind one in the form of memories. One must bring them back to life, resuscitate them, which requires truly creative work. I have just said that one has the past behind one in the form of memories. But that is expressed badly, because in fact the past is not at our disposal. Chateaubriand had an expression, a very beautiful one; he spoke of the "desert of the past."[17] Indeed, if one goes back to one's past, one sees an immense desert, with here and there, some more or less isolated, scattered objects: vague images whose meaning is often obscure. Actually, it is a question of constructing a story [*histoire*] of the past, by means of a work of logic and of documentation. I make use of everything that I can find in the way of documents: diaries, letters, and also the information provided by books and by the press. Moreover, I note that in order to recreate the past one must recreate one's own life, insofar as one has had a knowledge [*connaissance*] of it, a consciousness; but one must also find the context in which this life took shape insofar as one was unaware of it. The degree of what one was unaware of is just as important in a life as the degree of knowledge. I mean, for example, that between 1929 and 1938 I was depoliticized; I took very little interest in politics. Well, if I were to rewrite the second part of my memoirs, *La force de l'âge* [*The Prime of Life*], I would put much more emphasis on this indifference. It defines me as a French bourgeois intellectual of that era, as the French intellectuals of the time were for the most part depoliticized. Thus, what I was ignorant of situates me as clearly as the conscious experience that I myself had. Therefore, I find myself obliged to gather information about what took place apart from me, at the horizon of my experience insofar as I was unaware of it.

Moreover, a problem arises: in what order am I going to reveal this past? I will not choose that of my spontaneous memories because it is very uncertain. One could choose it, but for me, its vagaries were not acceptable. Many other possibilities were available. One can, when one writes a life, one's own or that of another, divide it into categories: travels, friendships, readings, jobs. Or, more capriciously, one can start from an impression, odor or taste, and wander. There are some very good autobiographies which are constructed in that way. I myself chose another order: the order of time, because I see existence as a constant surpassing of the present toward the future. Consequently, for me, the dimension of time, the historical and practical dimension, is essential. Therefore it was normal for me to follow the order of time. But it is a choice which is not without drawbacks, as I am well aware. A critic has remarked that when one reads an autobiography which follows chronological order one has the impression that the author never reveals anything but preliminaries: this happened in such-and-such a year, and it is useful to know it in order to understand what will happen later. All the events seem to be of secondary importance, non-essentials. One is hopeful that the essential is going to be there at some time, further on; and then suddenly one realizes that one has never reached it. I have sometimes had this same disappointment when reading autobiographies and biographies; one follows the hero, one thinks that he is going toward a plenitude, toward a culminating point in his existence and then suddenly it is over. There is some sort of break, and this moment has never taken place. The reason for this is obvious: in life, the moments are separate, but at the same time they are linked by our projects. In the same moment, I retain my past and at the same time I extend it into the future. Therefore, lived time always has three dimensions: it is past, present and future. On the contrary, if I am talking about an old project, and I say, "At a certain moment I decided to leave for America," this project is old, outdated, surpassed. It is a dead moment of my story [*histoire*]; it does not realize any living synthesis. Synthesis is never achieved in the chronological account. Such an account only reveals flat moments, as it were, laid out next to each other like a sort of rosary, with everything always being in the present. In this way, the account betrays the living movement of a life. Even so, there is a way of giving rise to it—only one. The reader, who is alive, who lives in the flesh and in time, must lend me his own time. While he is reading he remembers everything he has read up to that point; when he sees me at age twenty, he remembers the little girl that I was, and at the same time he wonders what kind of woman I am going to become. Thus he lends me the depth of his own time and the drawback that I told you about will be palliated. But in order for this to happen, I must capture the reader's interest; therefore my book must have a literary quality. By the tone, by the style, by the way in which I speak and tell my story I must charm, win over, retain the reader's freedom; he must freely remain there listening to me and, for his part, carrying out this work of creation which belongs to him. Therefore, it does not at all suffice to lay out the moments of my life one after another, with absolutely no artistry. On the contrary, I must find a way to make them interesting. Another problem is going to arise here, that of choice: among all the events which have happened to me, many hold no interest and in any case, I cannot recount them all; I am therefore obliged to make a choice. This choice is going to be guided by the same principle as in a novel: to draw out a meaning, and thus to retain the elements, the episodes which will help to bring it to light. But since I want to convey what a life is—its taste, its rhythm, its twists and turns—and since, precisely, in a life there are a great many insignificant or trivial or contingent elements, if I make a choice, if I do away with insignificance and contingency, I will give a false idea of my life; everything will seem to be heavy with meaning. This is a very difficult problem. I do not think that it has a solution. Every person who writes his autobiography will lean to one side or the other: sense or nonsense. The reader, for his part, will always find that one says too much or too little. I have been criticized at times, and sometimes rightly for relating details that are of no consequence. In fact, I have sometimes intentionally given details that are of no consequence because one falsifies the face of a life by not underlining its facticity. If I compare the autobiography to the novel on this plane, I see that between them there is a kind of gap, there is a kind of break, as they say in mathematics between series that never meet. In an autobiography, I grasp the facticity of the real, its contingence; but then I risk getting lost in trivial details, missing the meaning of the lived. To describe a lived experience stripped of meaning is to say nothing. On the other hand, when I write a novel, I draw out a meaning, but then I risk making something too necessary and missing the facticity. It is a little like physics; they tell us that to describe light, according to the new theories, one must describe it both in terms of particles and in terms of waves. But if one determines the position of the particle, then the wavelength is uncertain; if, on the contrary, one determines the wavelength, the position of the particle is no longer determined. This is somewhat the same. One must choose. A work will never be able to give both the meaning and the reality at the same time.

There is one last question that I would like to consider and it is this: Why are the autobiography and the novel—that is to say communication through non-knowledge [*non-savoir*]—chosen by the writer? Why prefer this to communication through knowledge? The question arises, for in France today there is a very great vogue for works of documentation, anthropology, and history, works which provide information on the plane of the universal. They are widely read and most of the best sellers fit into this category. So, the question I ask myself is this: Is this vogue due to the current state of literature, which is as I told you, extremely austere and which on the whole seeks to communicate nothing? The people who want communication are obliged to look for it elsewhere. Or is there a decline of literature in general, would our time consider literature to be useless? I think the first hypothesis is the true one: it is because literature partly fails in its task that today people turn away from it and turn toward works of documentation. But in truth there is something that only literature can give. When I read a work of documentation, on a distant country, for example, I find out about one of the parts of my universe without leaving this universe; I remain in my place in the world, in my room, at a certain moment of my life, of my epoch, with Paris around me. I try to incorporate an unfamiliar country into my universe, but I do not leave this universe. On the contrary, if I read a novel or an autobiography or the *Confessions* of Rousseau or Kafka or Murasaki Shikibu, something very different, and very curious happens.[18] Insofar as I am captivated, suddenly it is no longer I who says "I." I am in another world. Of course I remain myself, but I forget myself; I identify with the hero of the novel or with the author of the autobiography; his world with its values and its colors, becomes my own world. I still live in mine, but I leave it; there is a perpetual movement back and forth that results in the world of others becoming mine even while I am still in my world. And not only that, but insofar as there are other readers who also read this book, who like this book, who make Proust's world their own world, for example, I communicate with them through Proust. I am thinking of Proust because it is he who said that the literary work, the literary world is the privileged space of intersubjectivity; that is to say that it is the place where consciousnesses communicate with one another, inasmuch as they are separated from one another. That is a very important thing because the ambiguity of our condition is that we are linked precisely by that which separates us. I mean that I am *I* for myself alone. But each of you is *I* for yourself alone. It is our shared condition that we are radically separated from one another as subjects [*C'est une condition commune que nous soyons sujet d'une manière radicalement séparée les uns des autres*]. So much so that Descartes can base on the intuition of the *I* the most universal philosophy there is. When he discovers by a completely singular intuition "I think, therefore I am" it is an absolutely singular existential truth which is universalized.[19] Likewise, our life has a flavor which is only ours; but this is true for everyone; it is true for each one of us. We are alone to die our own death. No one will die for us. But this is true for everyone. There is therefore a generality in what is the most singular in us. I think that one of the writer's tasks is to break down the separation at the point where we are the most separate, at the point where we are the most singular. This is one of my most comforting, most interesting experiences as a writer; it is in speaking of what is the most singular that I have arrived at what is the most general and that I have touched my readers most deeply. Recently, when I wrote about the death of my mother,[20] I received a great many letters saying, "In speaking of the death of your mother you have spoken of the death of mine, of that of my wife, or my husband, and curiously you have helped me to bear it; even though your book is very somber, you have helped me." Why? It is because when one goes through a painful experience one suffers in two ways; first from the misfortune which strikes you; but also the grief isolates you and you are separate because you are unhappy. If you can write, the very act of writing breaks down this separation; writers often describe painful experiences not because they create literature from just anything at all, in a sacrilegious way, as is sometimes said, but because for them speaking of it is a way of surpassing their grief, their anguish, their sorrow. And it is the same for the people who read, since they no longer feel isolated in their sorrow or anguish, they bear it better. This is why I think that everything that is said on occasion whether from the right or the left against so-called literature "*noir*" is absolutely false. Speaking of the most personal experiences that we can have like loneliness, anguish, the death of the people we love, our own death, is on the contrary a way of bringing us together, of helping each other and of making the world less somber. I believe that this is one of the absolutely irreplaceable and essential tasks of literature: helping us communicate with each other through that which is the most solitary in ourselves and by which we are bound the most intimately to one another.

NOTES

1. Sartre's three lectures given in Tokyo and Kyoto in September and October of 1966 have been published as "Plaidoyer pour les intellectuels," in *Situations philosophiques* (*Philosophical Situations*) (Paris: Gallimard, 1990; 219–81) and translated as "A Plea for Intellectuals," in *Between Existentialism and Marxism* (London: Verson, 2008), 228–85. Note that Sartre's 1966 lectures are mistakenly dated as 1965 in "Plea," p. 226. See "Plea," p. 284, for Sartre's reference to "being-in-the-world as lived experience."

2. The first volume of Simone de Beauvoir's *Diary of a Philosophy Student*, with entries dated 1926–27, was published by the University of Illinois Press in 2006, transcribed by Barbara Klaw and Sylvie Le Bon de Beauvoir; translated by Barbara Klaw; and edited by Barbara Klaw, Sylvie Le Bon de Beauvoir, Margaret A. Simons, and Marybeth Timmermann; the French edition of the entire student diary, *Cahiers de jeunesse: 1926–30*, edited by Sylvie Le Bon de Beauvoir, was published in Paris by Gallimard in 2008.

3. *L'invitée* (Paris: Gallimard, 1943); trans. Y. Moyse and R. Senhouser as *She Came to Stay* (Cleveland: World Publishing, 1954).

4. *Le deuxiéme sexe*, 2 Vols. (Paris: Gallimard, 1949); trans. H. M. Parshley as *The Second Sex* (New York: Knopf, 1952); *The Second Sex: A New Translation by Constance Borde and Sheila Malovany-Chevallier* (New York: Knopf, 2010).

5. See Sartre in "Plea": "how [the writer] can fashion silence with words" (278).

6. The Algerian War (1954–62) was an armed uprising against French rule that led to the independence of Algeria in 1962. Begun by Algerian nationalists on October 31, 1954, the eight-year war was characterized by the brutality of the combat and the use of torture which brought about deep divisions of public opinion in France.

7. Marcel Proust (1871–1922) was a French novelist and author of the seven-volume *A la*

recherche du temps perdu, (1913–27), translated into English by Scott Moncrieff as *Remembrance of Things Past*, (New York: Wordsworth, 2006) and considered one of the greatest achievements in modern fiction. "Les intermittences du coeur" (intermittences of the heart) appears as a subheading at the end of the first chapter of *Sodome et Gomorrhe II*, part of the fifth volume of *A la recherche* entitled *Sodome et Gomorrhe* (Cities of the Plain), published in 1921–22. The narrator observes: "Car aux troubles de la mémoire sont liées les intermittences du coeur." ("For with the troubles of memory are closely linked the heart's intermissions," trans. C. K. Scott Moncrieff).

8. *Les Mandarins* (Paris: Gallimard, 1954), trans. L. M. Friedman as *The Mandarins* (New York: Norton, 1954).

9. Three volumes of Beauvoir's memoirs had been published at the time of her 1966 lecture: *Mémoires d'une jeune fille rangée* (Paris: Gallimard, 1958), trans. J. Kirkup as *Memoirs of a Dutiful Daughter* (New York: World Publishing, 1959), *La force de l'âge* (Paris: Gallimard, 1960), trans. P. Green as *The Prime of Life* (New York: World Publishing, 1962), and *La force des choses* (Paris: Gallimard, 1963), trans. R. Howard as *Force of Circumstance* (New York: G.P. Putnam's Sons, 1964).

10. *Tous les hommes sont mortels* (Paris: Gallimard, 1946), trans. L. Friedman as *All Men Are Mortal* (Cleveland: World Publishing, 1955).

11. The long and complex *Genji monogatori* (*The Tale of Genji*) by Murasaki Shikibu (978–1014), translated by Edward G. Seidensticker (New York: Knopf, 1978), depicts the loves of Prince Genji against the backdrop of an aristocratic and refined court society. One of the greatest works of Japanese literature, it is thought to be the world's oldest full novel.

12. Alain Robbe-Grillet (1922–2008) was a French novelist, film director, screenwriter and leading theoretician of the new novel (*nouveau roman*), that emerged in the 1950s challenging the traditional conventions of the novel with a new conception of time, plot, and character. Among Robbe-Grillet's works of this period are the collection of theoretical essays, *Pour un nouveau roman* (1963), translated by Richard Howard as *For a New Novel: Essays on Fiction* (Evanston, Ill.: Northwestern University Press, 1992); and the following novels translated by Richard Howard (New York: Grove Press, 1994): *Les gommes* (*The Erasers*) (1953), *Le voyeur* (*The Voyeur*) (1955), *La jalousie* (*Jealousy*) (1957) and *Dans le labyrinthe* (*In the Labyrinth*) (1959), *La maison de rendez-vous* (1965); The *nouveau roman* covers a variety of approaches and was applied to the avant-garde novel that emerged in France in the 1950s and produced by writers including Michel Butor, Robert Pinget, Nathalie Sarraute, and Claude Simon in addition to Alain Robbe-Grillet. This group of authors, considered among the most significant writers of the mid-fifties through late sixties period, attached a great importance to the theory as well as the practice of fiction, systematically rejecting the traditional elements of omniscient narrator, plot, chronology, and character as well as Sartre's and Beauvoir's conception of writing as an act of political commitment.

13. *Tel Quel* was a French avant-garde journal published from 1960–1982 by the Editions du Seuil. Founded by writer Philippe Sollers in association with Jean-René Huguenin and Jean-Edern Hallier, *Tel Quel*'s initial objective was to disengage literature from the reigning ideologies of the postwar years. The journal quickly came to be associated with the defense of the *nouveau roman*, viewing it as a viable alternative to Sartre's *engagement* and publishing works by writers such as Alain Robbe-Grillet and Nathalie Sarraute as well as contemporary literary criticism by Michel Foucault, Jacques Derrida, Julia Kristeva, Roland Barthes, and Jacques Lacan. From 1966 to 1970, *Tel Quel* increasingly linked its literary radicalism

with political radicalism, representing a Maoist view of Marxism. From 1974, the journal's critical orientation shifted and it relinquished political involvement.

14. Michel Butor (b. 1926) is a French novelist and essayist, and one of the leading practitioners of the *nouveau roman*. While sharing with the other writers of the *nouveau roman* with whom he was initially associated a view of the novel as a domain of structural experiment, he also insisted that its purpose was to enlarge the reader's understanding of social and historical reality. After his fourth novel, *Degrés* (1960), translated by Richard Howard, as *Degrees* (Urbana, Ill.: Dalkey Archive, 2005), Butor largely abandoned the genre for nonfiction writing and more experimental forms. Among Butor's works of this period, including both novels and nonfiction texts, are *Passage de milan* (A Kite Goes By) (1954), *L'emploi du temps* (1956), translated by Jean Stewart in 1960 as *Passing Time* (New York: Simon and Schuster, 1960), *La modification* (1957), translated by Jean Stewart as *A Change of Heart* (New York: Simon and Schuster, 1959), *Le génie du lieu* (1958, Vol. 1), translated by Lydia Davis as *The Spirit of Mediterranean Places* (Marlboro, Vt.: Marlboro Press, 1986), *Description de San Marco* (1963), translated by Barbara Mason as *Description of San Marco* (Fredericton, N.B.: York Press, 1983), and *6,810,000 litres d'eau par seconde* (1965), translated by Elinor S. Miller as *Niagara, A Novel* (Chicago: H. Regnery Co., 1969); Nathalie Sarraute (1900–1999) was a Russian-born French novelist, dramatist and essayist, as well as an initiator and leading theorist of the *nouveau roman*. She began developing her literary innovations as early as the 1930s. One of the most widely translated and discussed authors of the *nouveau roman* group, her area of investigation focused on a new psychological realism, attempting to translate internal, largely nonverbal sensations into language. In addition to her theoretical essay *L'ère du soupçon* (1956), translated Maria Jolas as *The Age of Suspicion* (New York: G. Braziller, 1963), among Sarraute's works of this period are *Tropismes* 1939; 1957), translated by Maria Jolas as *Tropisms* (New York: G. Braziller, 1967, ©1963), *Portrait d'un inconnu* (1947), translated by Maria Jolas as *Portrait of Man Unknown* (New York, G. Braziller, 1958), *Martereau* (1953), translated by Maria Jolas as *Martereau* (New York: G. Braziller, 1959 [©1953]), *Le planétarium* (1959), translated by Maria Jolas as *The Planetarium, A Novel* (New York: G. Braziller, 1960), and *Les fruits d'or* (1963), translated by Maria Jolas as *The Golden Fruits* (New York: G. Braziller, 1964).

15. The first of a series of artificial Earth satellites, Sputnik I was launched by the Soviet Union on October 4, 1957. It remained in orbit until early 1959, circling the Earth every ninety-six minutes.

16. Roland Barthes (1915–1980) was a French essayist and social and literary critic whose writings on semiotics, the formal study of symbols and signs, helped establish structuralism and the New Criticism which viewed texts as a system of signs. In 1960, Barthes became Director of Studies in "Sociology of signs, symbols and representations" at the Ecole Pratique des Hautes Etudes in Paris and in 1976 he was elected to a chair of literary semiology at the Collège de France. Barthes's first book, *Le degré zéro de l'écriture* (1953), translated by Richard Howard as *Writing Degree Zero* (New York: Hill and Wang, 1968), was an essay on modern literature in which he examined the arbitrariness of the constructs of language. In the essay entitled "Ecrivains et écrivants" ("Authors and Writers") that appeared in his *Essais critiques* (1964), translated by Richard Howard as *Critical Essays*, (Evanston, Ill.: Northwestern University Press, 1972), Barthes distinguishes between *authors* (*écrivains*), who perform a function and work on and with words and *writers* (*écrivants*), who perform an activity and use language instrumentally. For Barthes, "the author is the man who *labors*,

who works up his utterance (even if he is inspired) and functionally absorbs himself in this labor, this work. His activity involves two kinds of norm: technical (of composition, genre, style) and artisanal (of patience, correctness, perfection). . . . The *writer*, on the other hand, is a 'transitive' man, he posits a goal (to give evidence, to explain, to instruct), of which language is merely a means; for him language supports a *praxis*, it does not constitute one. Thus language is restored to the nature of an instrument of communication, a vehicle of 'thought.' . . . The author participates in the priest's role, the writer in the clerk's; the author's language is an intransitive act (hence, in a sense, a gesture), the writer's an activity" (144–47). See "Plea," where Barthes's distinction between *écrivants* and *écrivains* is rendered as "literal writers" and "literary writers" (272).

17. François-René Chateaubriand, viscount of Chateaubriand (1768–1848) was a French author, diplomat, preeminent literary figure in early nineteenth-century France and considered as a founder of Romanticism. A keen observer of and participant in the political scene of his time, Chateaubriand was also an apologist of the Christian faith, historian and essayist. In 1847 he completed his *Mémoires d'outre tombe*, translated by A. Teixeira de Matos as *The Memoirs of François René Vicomte de Chateaubriand* (London: Freemantle, 1902), an autobiography published posthumously (1849–50). The work is divided into four sections (covering Chateaubriand's early years, travels, military career and exile, his literary career during the Consulate and the Empire, his political career under the Restoration and the years of his retirement) and in it the writer provides both an analysis of himself and a vivid account of contemporary French history; The expression "*le désert du passé*" appears in volume one, in the fourth chapter of the fourth book where he describes his first meeting with the officers of his regiment. Chateaubriand mentions, among others, the Marquis de Mortemart, colonel of the regiment, and the Count d'Andrezel, major, stating that he also had contact with them later in his life. "Je les ai retrouvés tous deux dans la suite: l'un est devenu mon collègue à la chambre des pairs, l'autre s'est adressé à moi pour quelques services que j'ai été heureux de lui rendre. Il y a un plaisir triste à rencontrer des personnes que l'on a connues à diverses époques de la vie, et à considérer le changement opéré dans leur existence et dans la nôtre. Comme des jalons laissés en arrière, ils nous tracent le chemin que nous avons suivi dans le désert du passé." ("I met both of them in after years: one of them became my colleague in the House of Peers, the other applied to me for some services which I was happy to show him. There is a melancholy pleasure in meeting people whom we have known at different periods of our life, and in contemplating the changes that have taken place in their mode of existence and our own. Like landmarks left behind us, they trace for us the road which we have followed in the desert of the past" (Vol. 1, 106).

18. Jean-Jacques Rousseau (1712–78) was a Swiss-born French-language philosopher, writer and political theorist whose works inspired the leaders of the French Revolution and the Romantic generation. *Les confessions*, edited by Patrick Coleman and translated by Angela Scholar as *Confessions* (Oxford: Oxford University Press, 2000), Rousseau's account of his life, are considered a founding text of literary autobiography. Written between 1764 and 1770 while Rousseau was in exile from France and published posthumously in 1781 and 1788, Part I deals with Rousseau's childhood, his adventures as a young man, and his relationship with Madame de Warens while Part II covers the period 1742–66 and treats Rousseau's career as a writer, his quarrels with the *philosophes* and his first years of exile. Although inaccurate in terms of detail and self-justificatory as well as self-revelatory, *Les confessions* offer insights into Rousseau's thought and feelings up to 1766 and are recog-

nized as a remarkable attempt to tell the inner truth of Rousseau's life as he saw it; Franz Kafka (1883–1924) was a Czech-born Austrian fiction writer whose works include stories and novellas such as *Das Urteil* (*The Judgment*) (1912) and *Die Verwandlung* (*The Metamorphosis*) (1915), translated by Willa and Edwin Muir in *The Penal Colony, Stories, and Short Pieces* (New York: Schocken Books, 1948), and posthumously published novels such as *Der Prozeß* (*The Trial*) (1925), *Das Schloß* (*The Castle*) (1926), and *Amerika* (1927) (*America*), translated by Willa and Edwin Muir as *The Collected Novels of Franz Kafka* (London: Penguin, 1988). In his *Brief an den Vater* (1919), translated by Ernst Kaiser and Eithne Wilkins as *Letter to His Father* (New York: Schocken Books, 1966), that represents his autobiography, Kafka undertakes an investigation of his own life, concentrating on his father's preponderant role in shaping his existence.

19. René Descartes (1596–1650) was a French mathematician, scientist and philosopher. Descartes' philosophy is founded in what he considered to be evident truths intuited by the natural faculty of reason. His metaphysics centered on the establishment of the individual subject, a being characterized by rational thought. In the fourth part of his *Discours de la méthode* (1637) translated by F. E. Sutcliffe as *Discourse on Method* in *Descartes: Discourse on Method and Other Writings* (Harmondsworth, Eng.: Penguin Books, 1968), Descartes briefly presents the argument best known in its Latin formulation (*Cogito, ergo sum*) although it was originally written in French (*Je pense, donc je suis*) (I think, therefore, I am). In his *Méditations* (1641), (translated as *Meditations* in *Descartes: Discourse on Method and Other Writings*) written in Latin, Descartes applies his system of methodical doubt and finally finds certainty in the intuition that when he is thinking, he must exist, stating *Cogito, sum* (I think, I am). Descartes asserts that thinking must presuppose the existence of the thinking subject. The *cogito* is a logically self-evident truth that also gives intuitively certain knowledge of the existence of the self.

20. Simone de Beauvoir's mother died in 1963 and she recounted this experience in the 1964 work entitled *Une mort très douce* (Paris: Gallimard), trans. P. O'Brian as *A Very Easy Death* (New York: G. P. Putnam's Sons, 1965).

9

Short Prefaces to Literary Works

INTRODUCTION

by Eleanore Holveck

During the thirteen years when these short prefaces were written, 1964 to 1977, Simone de Beauvoir produced an astonishing amount of work. She finished the memoir of her mother, *Une mort très douce* (*A Very Easy Death*) (1964) and the fourth volume of her autobiography, *Tout compte fait* (*All Said and Done*) (1972); two works of fiction, *Les belles images* (1966) and *La femme rompue* (*The Woman Destroyed*) (1968); and her essay on old age, *La vieillesse* (*The Coming of Age*) (1970). She visited the Soviet Union and Japan; 1967 found her traveling to the Middle East during the Six-Day War and taking part in the Bertrand Russell Tribunal investigating United States war crimes in Viet Nam. She witnessed the student riots in the streets of Paris in May 1968, demonstrated with the *Mouvement de la Libération des Femmes* (Movement for the Liberation of Women), distributed the left-wing paper *La cause du peuple* (The Cause of the People) (1970) and signed the abortion Manifesto of 343 in 1971. Yet she found time to compose a charming preface, directed to children, for a translation of fairy tales, in addition to prefaces for a book by a famous photographer, an autobiographical account by a potash miner from Alsace, and a major World War II novel by an important Italian writer.

Perhaps the New York publisher Macmillan asked Beauvoir to write a Preface to an English translation of *Bluebeard and Other Fairy Tales*, based on Charles Perrault's *Contes de ma mère l'oye* (*Tales of Mother Goose*) (1697), because the translator, Richard Howard, was also working on *Force of Circumstance*, which had appeared in French in 1963. At any rate a major feminist writer's imprimatur might reassure women about the place of Mother Goose in the nursery. Beauvoir's Introduction reveals and develops several important philosophical themes from her previous works and sets the stage for prefaces that follow: (1) Childhood is a crucial time for human beings. Human existence is situated and, hence, the past cannot be ignored, but rather it must be acknowledged freely and continuously recreated. (2) In our past, women, especially women from the proletariat, have not been given their due. (3) Authentic human freedom may and must be exercised responsibly as free action even in situations of oppression. (4) Literature is an expression of lived experience from one point of view; it fosters communication with other points of view on the same world.

Beauvoir read Perrault's fairy tales in childhood;[1] she commented that this sometimes led to masochism. "[M]y sister, always forced to be Bluebeard or some other tyrant, would cruelly banish me. . . . [F]rom time to time, trembling, half-naked, I would substitute myself for the royal slave and feel the tyrant's sharp spurs riding down my spine."[2] In *The Second Sex* Beauvoir had argued that fairy tales represent beautiful, passive maidens waiting for active men to love them and rescue them. "Woman is the Sleeping Beauty, Cinderella . . . she who receives and submits. . . . [H]e slays the dragon, he battles giants; she is locked in a tower, a palace . . . she waits."[3] In this 1964 Introduction, however, having recently reflected on the weight of the past, Beauvoir now prefers to recreate the authentic meaning of the fairy tales that influenced her. As a phenomenologist, Beauvoir outlines the constitution of the meaning of these tales; she gives a Marxist-inspired historical account and then points to a moral that emphasizes authentic existential free action.

The tales of Mother Goose were handed down from generation to generation across continents, as peasants wove stories of a just world where powerful, oppressive upper classes were punished for their misdeeds against the poor. For example, the tale of Bluebeard stems from an actual rich landowner, Gilles de Rais, a serial killer of peasant children who was finally hanged. Beauvoir presents Charles Perrault as a shy seventeenth-century gentleman at the royal court who wrote down tales like these from peasant grandmothers because he preferred them to the inferior tales composed by his upperclass lady companions.

The major moral of these stories is the message of Beauvoir's *Pyrrhus and Cineas*, *The Ethics of Ambiguity*, *The Blood of Others*, and *The Useless Mouths*. Act freely in full recognition of past oppression with hope for future liberation. Bluebeard's wife was tricked into marrying him, because his luxurious lifestyle was seductive, but she freely chose to disobey him and found the secret cellar under his castle, which contained the corpses of his previous, murdered wives.

I had never read "Bluebeard" until writing this Introduction, but I must agree that it not only inspires free action, it is a feminist liberation tale. True, the wife must wait to be rescued by her brothers, but it is her united action with her older, wiser sister, who has the courage to climb the tower, be the lookout, and encourage their brothers to hurry, which saves the day. With Bluebeard slain, his rich widow can now buy good husbands for her sister and herself. I have searched a long time for the possible source of the name Anne that Beauvoir gave to the character based on her friend Zaza in the early short story collection, *When Things of the Spirit Come First* and, suddenly, here she is: the wise, loving, courageous, athletic sister who helps free Bluebeard's wife from the horrors of this particular bourgeois marriage, although Zaza's life had no fairy-tale ending. Free independent women have little to fear from Mother Goose. It was perhaps an unwise move on the part of the shy gentleman to allow the tales of Mother Goose to penetrate the King's court.

Beauvoir's Preface to *James Joyce in Paris: His Final Years* is a tribute to her friend and photographer, Gisèle Freund, who was born in Berlin to a wealthy Jewish family, fled to Paris in 1933, and fled again from Paris in 1940. Freund is a living heroine who acted freely to escape oppression and make a unique, creative contribution to major cultural and literary events of her time. Freund's photos bring back fond memories from Beauvoir's student days when she "devoured" countless books by modern writers like D. H. Lawrence, Virginia Woolf, Hemingway, and Kafka, which she borrowed from Adrienne Monnier's book store, *La Maison des Amis des Livres* (The Home of the Friends of Books). In Freund's own preface, entitled "On Photographing Joyce," she recounts that Monnier published *La Photographie en France au dix-neuvième siècle* (French Photography in the Nineteenth Century), based on Freund's dissertation at the Sorbonne, and Monnier introduced Freund to Joyce and many other great writers and artists. Freund's photographs appeared in *Life* magazine and *Time* in the 1930s. Part of this collection was in honor of the publication of Joyce's *Finnegan's Wake* (1939).

Beauvoir comments that many of the writers of the 1930s pictured here—Valéry, Gide, Giraudoux, Aragon, Claudel, Breton—wrote under the illusion of man as solitary individual, psychologically and poetically. Young writers like Beauvoir, in bad faith and ignorance, longed to take their places among their distinguished forerunners, creators of a timeless Literature devoted to ideal Truth and Beauty. But Freund's camera caught authors involved in life. Freund knew that art could present not an idealized world but actual individuals who are firmly placed in their historical, social, economic, political world. For example, a striking photograph of the extraordinary face of Virginia Woolf from 1939 appears here,[4] as well as the equally impressive faces of two unnamed women watching a parade of veterans on *Le quatorze juillet* 1939.[5] The very lines of their faces mirror each other, reflecting the horror of what is soon to come. I am touched by the picture of James Joyce seated across a table from Sylvia Beach and Adrienne Monnier at the former's bookstore, Shakespeare and Company,[6] two Penelopes who organized and launched his *Ulysses*.

Beauvoir describes the 1930s as a flowering and a decline, which contains the seeds of a future harvest. A few writers anticipated *littérature engagée*: Nizan, Saint-Exupéry, and Malraux. Although Beauvoir and her colleagues followed and reformulated this kind of literature, Beauvoir's nostalgia in this Preface for the "dazzling abundance" of the thirties,[7] makes us suspect that committed literature is not the only type she truly admires.

The last two prefaces from 1976 and 1977 illustrate Beauvoir's theory of literature in the 1960s and reveal some of her differences from Sartre. Henri Keller's *Amélie I* appeared in the series *La France sauvage* (Savage France) edited by Jean-Paul Sartre, Michel Le Bris, and Jean-Pierre Le Dantec; their editorial policy statement reflects Sartre's Maoist-inclined period when he promoted writings by workers. In *Search for a Method* (1960), Sartre wrote that all action, whether that of knowing or writing, detotalizes totality. When an individual like Henri Keller knows and articulates his existence as a miner, when he realizes the material conditions of his existence, which circumscribe his fields of possible action, he can then act on one of his possibles; "by transcending the given to—the field of possibles and by realizing one possibility from among all the others . . . the individual objectifies himself and contributes to making history."[8] In the 1970s Sartre modified the theory somewhat. Actions and writings may be "*sauvage*," wild, brutal, uncivilized, lawless in the same sense as a workers' strike. "*Sauvage*" describes a process of effervescence at a point in the social surface when a group affirms their common freedom in action. Freedom is not an individual choice but an eruption, a spontaneous action that forges a group.

Beauvoir's Preface to Keller's book accepts Sartre's notion of detotalized totality, as does her 1966 essay "Mon expérience d'écrivain" ("My Experience as a Writer"), but she interprets from the point of view of the person who intends to write. Henri Keller, no longer a miner but an engineer, is writing his reflection on his past lived experience. His description helps us to "enter into his night," i.e., to relive the experience, which he shares with others, with him. Beauvoir's emphasis is on the action of writing as a living free choice to communicate.

Last, but not at all least, we have Beauvoir's Foreword to the English translation of the great novel of the Italian writer, Elsa Morante (1912–85),[9] *La Storia* (*History*) (1974), one of the finest novels to come out of World War II. Morante was born in Rome to a poor Sicilian father, a clerk, and a Jewish mother who taught school. Beauvoir and Sartre traveled to Rome every year after World War II and usually saw Morante and novelist Alberto Moravia (1907–90), her husband from 1941 to 1963.[10] Morante's first major novel, *Menzoga i Sortilegio* (*House of Liars*) (1948) received the Viareggio Prize; she wrote short stories, poems, and the well-received *L'Isola di Arturo* (*Arturo's Island*) (1958).

Beauvoir's Foreword to *History: A Novel* points out that true history for Morante is "in the hearts and bodies of the anonymous individuals who suffer through them," but I am neither so sure about the anonymity nor that Beauvoir gives sufficient credit to Morante's achievement. Between two chapters summing up the past and the future, seven chapters of Morante's novel are devoted to each year between 1941 and 1947. Each begins with a summary of historical events, but the true story is the birth and death of Useppe Ramundo. From his first movements in his mother's womb, "the little blows he gave seemed more information than protest: I inform you that I am here and, in spite of everything, I'm coping and I'm alive. . . . What are you scared of? You're not alone,"[11] Useppe incarnates the joy of human existence, *la joie d'exister* that Beauvoir describes so movingly in *The Ethics of Ambiguity* as the concrete flesh and blood thickness of the world that underlies all political activity and that should be its final goal.[12] Morante's ability to recreate the world from a child's viewpoint is unmatched and magnificent, and the ultimate core of her novel is summed up by his mother's thoughts at Useppe's death. "[T]he scenes of the human story (History) revolved . . . as the multiple coils of an interminable murder. . . . All History and all the nations of the earth had agreed on this end: the slaughter of the child Useppe Ramundo."[13]

Alberto Moravia commented that Elsa Morante "considered herself the greatest writer—as all writers do,"[14] which obviously irritated him; he complained of her "constant, obsessive affirmation of her own personality and independence."[15] This strong life-affirming spirit enabled Morante to mourn for a generation of children whose lives involved no fairy tales but whose singular, free, *joie d'exister* was dimmed, dampened, and finally snuffed out from 1941 to 1947.

Morante's novel truly represents Beauvoir's position in her 1966 essay "Que peut la littérature?" ("What Can Literature Do?") based roughly on Leibniz, that the world is one totality and that each point of view on that same world expresses itself, communicating with all the others, through literature.

NOTES

1. Simone de Beauvoir, *Memoirs of a Dutiful Daughter*, trans. James Kirkup (New York: World, 1959), 51–52.
2. Ibid., 58.
3. Simone de Beauvoir, *The Second Sex*, ed. and trans. H. M. Parshley (New York: Vintage, 1989), 291.
4. Gisèle Freund and V. B. Carleton, *James Joyce in Paris: His Final Years* (New York: Harcourt, Brace and World, 1965), 101.
5. Ibid., 89; *Le quatorze juillet*, or Bastille Day, is the French National holiday held each year on the fourteenth of July, commemorating the anniversary of the storming of the Bastille Prison in Paris, which occurred in 1789 just before the French Revolution.
6. Ibid., 60.
7. Ibid., ix.
8. Jean-Paul, *Search for a Method*, trans. Hazel E. Barnes (New York: Vintage, 1968), 93.
9. Various dates are given for Morante's birth. I am using the one from Alberto Moravia and Alain Elkann, *Life of Moravia*, trans. William Weaver (South Royalton, Vermont: Steerforth Press, 2000), 134.
10. Typically, in an interview Moravia (*Life of Moravia*, cited above, ibid., 242) mentions only Sartre and Camus, and Beauvoir mentions only Moravia in *Force of Circumstance*, trans. Richard Howard (London: Penguin, 1968), 109.
11. Elsa Morante, *History: A Novel*, trans. William Weaver (New York: Knopf, 1977), 77–78.
12. Simone de Beauvoir, *Ethics of Ambiguity*, trans. Bernard Frechtman (New York: Citadel, 1976), 135.
13. Morante, *History*, 546.
14. Moravia, *Life*, 210.
15. Ibid., 213.

INTRODUCTION TO *BLUEBEARD AND OTHER FAIRY TALES*

by Simone de Beauvoir

NOTES BY JANELLA D. MOY

The stories you are about to read were written down in France, nearly three hundred years ago, by a very learned old gentleman. He wore a white wig, and his name was Charles Perrault.[1] He didn't make up the stories himself, though. They were already old when he found them, so old that no one can tell their age. What is more, they had traveled by word of mouth so far around the globe—from Ireland to India, and all through Europe and Asia—that no one is sure where they first started. A thousand years ago in China, grandmothers were telling their grandchildren the wonderful story of a slit-eyed Cinderella who lost a golden slipper at the ball.[2]

When Perrault dipped his goose-quill pen in ink and set these tales down on paper, every French peasant already knew them. Winter evenings in the country were no fun in those days—no movies or television, and the peasants couldn't read because they didn't know how. When supper was over they would gather around the fireside. The women spun wool on their spinning wheels, while the men repaired their tools and wooden

Introduction by Simone de Beauvoir translated by Peter Green, to *Bluebeard and Other Fairy Tales of Charles Perrault*, translated by Richard Howard, illustrated by Saul Lambert (New York: Macmillan, 1964).

clogs. The only amusement they enjoyed was telling legends and stories of olden times.

One of the things these poor folk liked was imagining a world in which top people met their downfall. From the field in which he worked, the laborer could see, perched high on the hill, the huge and well-fortified castle where his master dwelt. These great lords were sometimes so powerful that they could commit the most horrible crime and go unpunished.

Two hundred years before Perrault's time, there lived a very rich landowner called Gilles de Rais.[3] His home was in Brittany.[4] Over a period of five or six years he had, it was suspected, murdered about three hundred children. But the children's parents were poor people, and nobody listened to their complaints. In any case, they were scared of what might happen if Gilles de Rais got angry with them. But finally he was put in prison, and in the end he confessed his crimes and was hanged. In the country districts of Brittany, people hearing the tale of Bluebeard[5]—his very name would send a shiver through the peasants' thatched cottages—would remember the monstrous Gilles de Rais. They wouldn't think it at all odd that Bluebeard managed to get rid of seven wives without any trouble.

Countless stories like the one about Bluebeard were handed down at night by the fireside, from one generation to the next. Hardly any of them were to be found in books, but the old tales were just as popular in town, even at the King's court. In seventeenth-century France, aristocratic ladies composed fairy stories in notebooks and read them out to their drawing-room guests, who said how nice they were. But the ladies couldn't make up stories as good as the fireside tales, which had grown up slowly over hundreds of years, shaped by country tradition. Like Cinderella, left in the chimney-corner while her sisters went to parties, these popular legends couldn't get beyond the peasants' hovels.

Then, just as happened to Cinderella, a miracle took place. One of the periwigged gentlemen was sensible enough to like Bluebeard and Puss in Boots better than the tiresome efforts of the ladies.[6] He had a magic wand, too: his pen. He decked out nine old tales in magical words, and suddenly they shone like the sun. He was a shy person, and pretended that it was his son who had written the stories down. But his son was a young boy at the time, and it is surely Charles Perrault himself whom we must thank for telling these tales so beautifully, and for making them just as well-loved today as ever they were.

Little by little, Perrault's book (he called it *Tales from Mother Goose*) won everybody over. Millions of copies of it have been printed; it has been translated into almost every language. People read it all over the world and will continue to do so. Today boys and girls have whole libraries of books at their disposal but still love Cinderella and Puss in Boots.

The fairy tales show us that the world is by no means so cut and dried as some grownups think. You must have faith: things which look impossible may not be so at all. If Cinderella had told her fairy godmother that it was all nonsense, that no one could go to a ball in a pumpkin, she might never have got her coach. If Puss in Boots hadn't trusted his own cunning, he would never have turned his master into a noble lord.

Bluebeard's wife behaves very rashly in picking such a husband and then disobeying him; but her rashness also shows courage. What is more, it is all through this young lady that Bluebeard is unmasked and the earth rid of him; and she inherits his vast fortune. Hope, act; heaven will help you if you help yourself. This is the advice that Perrault's tales, in their lighthearted way, have to offer you. They will astonish you, and entertain you, and probably scare you a little too; but I'm certain you'll find them enchanting. And when you are older, I know that among your most precious memories will be your first meeting with the fearsome Bluebeard, gentle Cinderella, and that crafty character, Puss in Boots.[7]

NOTES

1. Charles Perrault (1628–1703), a French poet, writer, and storyteller, is best known for his collection of fairytales entitled *Contes de ma mère l'oye* (*Tales of Mother Goose*) (1697).

2. Cinderella is the ancient tale of a young girl whose loving father dies and leaves her in the care of a hateful, jealous stepmother. Cinderella is treated cruelly by the stepmother and stepsisters and is forced to work as a slave for the family. She eventually meets a prince and is rescued from her life of slavery by trying on a slipper, which fits only her foot.

3. Gilles de Rais (1404–40), a French aristocrat and soldier, fought at the side of Joan of Arc. However, he is remembered for his heinous crimes against young peasant boys. It is said that de Rais lured young boys to his castle where they were raped, tortured, and killed. In 1440, de Rais was found guilty of murdering between 80 and 200 children. He was excommunicated and sentenced to death. The connection between de Rais and Bluebeard is thought to have arisen due to the deaths of two of de Rais's prospective wives and his unparalleled cruelty to the peasant children he captured.

4. Brittany is a region in northwestern France with a distinct Celtic heritage.

5. Bluebeard is the story of a nobleman, who marries a young woman, Fatima. He gives her the keys to every room in his house but forbids her to enter one small room. When Bluebeard is away from home, Fatima opens the door to the forbidden room to discover the dead bodies of Bluebeard's former wives. Bluebeard reappears and prepares to kill Fatima, but she is saved by her two brothers.

6. Periwigged refers to the act of wearing a wig, popular for gentlemen in the seventeenth and eighteenth centuries; "Puss in Boots" is the tale of a granary cat that is left as inheritance to a simple miller's youngest son on the death of his father, the miller. The cat, both intelligent and crafty, helps the miller's son attain wealth, status, and a wealthy bride.

7. This Introduction is followed by a note on the author: "Simone de Beauvoir is one of the outstanding woman novelists and philosophers of our time. She has written several plays and many essays, but is best known for her *Prix de Goncourt* novel, *The Mandarins. Memoirs of a Dutiful Daughter* and *The Prime of Life* are two of her recent books. Mlle. de Beauvoir was born in Paris and lives there today."

PREFACE TO *JAMES JOYCE IN PARIS: HIS FINAL YEARS*

by Simone de Beauvoir

NOTES BY JANELLA D. MOY

So often of late, while walking through this new Paris of freshly whitened façades where a stream of traffic flows along the road between hedges of parked cars, I find myself pausing to ask: What did all this look like in the days when I was young? How I longed to bring back from memory a picture as vivid as one of the illustrations in *Votre Maison*,[1] the old farmhouse transformed into an elegant villa—before and after. This desire of mine was suddenly fulfilled when the photographs Gisèle Freund made during the thirties were placed in my hands.[2]

Deserted highways, peaceful riverbanks; an almost provincial silence emanates from these images in black and white. The sidewalks along the Champs-Elysées belonged to the pedestrians.[3] What makes this crowd look so strange to us today? Is it perhaps because all of them, men and women, are wearing hats?

The rue de l'Odéon had the tranquility of a village; it was here that the bookshop *La Maison des Amis des Livres* was located; if one watched carefully, the owner, Adrienne Monnier, could be seen in the doorway, her hair cut short, her dress long and flowing.[4]

Preface by Simone de Beauvoir, to *James Joyce in Paris: His Final Years*, by Gisèle Freund and V. B. Carleton (New York: Harcourt Brace and World, 1965), vii–ix; © Éditions Gallimard, 1979.

When I was a student, this bookshop symbolized the fascinating world, so near and yet so far, of modern literature; far, because I did not know, as yet, a single one of the authors; near, because I devoured so many of their books, which I borrowed from Adrienne's circulating library. I even discovered their faces in the autographed portraits of famous writers that lined the walls. I eavesdropped when the owner of this sanctuary—who intimidated me with her nun-like apparel and lofty friends—spoke in the most casual and intimate way of famous people whose very names left me somewhat dazed. She would tell some old client, for instance, that she had seen Valéry just the night before, or perhaps that Gide wasn't feeling very well.[5] Léon-Paul Fargue and Jean Prévost were two other writers who could often be seen talking to Adrienne on the most affectionate terms.[6] And sometimes with a beating heart I suddenly saw the most remote and inaccessible of them all materialize before me in flesh and blood: James Joyce, whose *Ulysses* I had read in French with utter amazement.[7]

Not long afterward, however, authors ceased to be as lofty as mythological figures in my life because I finally met one: Paul Nizan, an intimate friend of Jean-Paul Sartre.[8] He, in turn, knew many other writers and spent hours regaling us with tidbits of gossip about their foibles and weaknesses. Gide, Aragon, Jean-Richard Bloch, Chamson, and Malraux were some of the names he let fall so easily.[9] Soon we too were included in this brotherhood, because we had begun to write with patience and the utmost faith.

In spite of the heavy clouds that were gathering over Europe and the world, literature remained the sparkling, brilliant guide star of our lives. After the monumental *Ulysses* appeared in French, a door was opened for us to a new world of foreign writers—D. H. Lawrence, Virginia Woolf, the great American Hemingway, Dos Passos; Faulkner, who totally transformed our concept of what a novel should be;[10] and Kafka who transformed our vision of the world in which we lived.[11] This was an outstanding moment in French literature because so many of the writers who had come to the fore right after the First World War[12] were still, in the thirties, at the very height of their vigorous talent: men like Valéry, Gide, Cocteau, Giraudoux, Aragon, St.-John Perse, Claudel, with his *Le soulier de satin* [*The Satin Slipper*], Breton with his *L'immaculée conception* [*The Immaculate Conception*] and *L'amour fou* [*Mad Love*].[13] Then there were the newcomers clamoring for attention. Giono.[14] Like a bolt of lightening—Céline, with his *Voyage au bout de la nuit* [*Journey to the End of the Night*]. Saint-Exupéry, Malraux.[15] On a less spectacular plane was the poet Henri Michaux (*Un Certain Plume* [*A*

Certain Plume]), Raymond Queneau (*Les Derniers Jours* [*The Last Days*]), and Michel Leiris, whose *L'âge d'homme* [*Manhood*] enchanted us.[16]

All during the thirties, however, most of the books were written under a cloud of illusion. Their authors tried to escape the limits of time by following a tradition that one might call individualistic, psychological, or poetic. Man was pinpointed against his vast solitude or in his singular relationship with those around him. This was the path we all trod.

It took the devastating rise of Nazism in Germany and the Civil War in Spain to open our eyes at last. A large group of intellectuals banded together to fight fascism; we became aware of all the implications of our historical moment. A literature that was committed, *engagée*, appeared even before the name itself had been invented, a literature that embraced the epoch and society, even if this was done merely in an allusive way; but it went far beyond any limited, individual confine. Nizan placed his heroes firmly within the economic and political atmosphere of their times. Saint-Exupéry sketched the outline of a literature of technicians in action as opposed to the literature of pure contemplation created by his forerunners. Malraux utilized firsthand experiences in China and Spain to demonstrate the human destiny that linked men everywhere to one another in a common fate.

Only in retrospect were we able to evaluate fully the important contributions of these predecessors, but even then their originality impressed us and we found the complex richness of their vision utterly fascinating.

On a spring day in 1939, Gisèle Freund invited us to Adrienne's bookshop to see her portraits—many of which are reproduced here—projected in color upon a screen. The place was crowded with famous writers. I don't remember who was there; what has stayed eternally in my mind, however, is the sight of the chairs lined up in rows, the screen glowing in the darkness, and the familiar faces bathed in beautiful color: Giono, for one, resting on a hill overlooking the Provençal countryside; Sartre smoking a pipe with a slightly melancholy, somewhat ironic smile touching the corners of his mouth. All the consecrated authors as well as the new talents with a still-uncertain future drifted across the screen before our eyes. The camera had captured them with a precision that was often cruel; faces in need of a shave, each little hair standing on end, a sight that prompted Sartre to murmur, as he went out, "We all look as if we'd just come back from the war."

War—we thought about it sometimes but we never dreamed that an entire epoch was about to disappear, that the very core of our lives would soon be shattered. On the contrary, we looked forward to a new life, when our own generation of writers, like our elders before us, had won recognition. In truth, a whirlpool of darkness and blood was about to engulf the world, destroying us with it, the beings we had been, for when we found ourselves alive again, reborn and radically different, the entire universe about us had changed.

Ours was no Golden Age, as I am the first to admit, not being a believer in lost paradises. It was a time in which only sheer ignorance or perhaps bad faith protected us from the full impact of that unbearable anguish that might have been our destiny. But I keep an ardent memory of those days, and not just because they happened to coincide with my youth. With their contradictions and their turbulence, the thirties had an extraordinary character, for they were, at one and the same time, a flowering and a decline. The past still lingered on in them, and even took on vivid and fecund forms: seeds of future harvests were already sprouting.

That is why—quite apart from their intrinsic beauty—the photographs in this book have moved me so deeply; they evoke in all their radiant diversity those last moments when I still lived heedless and unaware of the drama that was about to engulf us all. Looking back, I am amazed at the variety, the force, the dazzling abundance the thirties offered us as writers. If you allow yourself to dream over the images Gisèle Freund has torn from oblivion, you, too, will capture the poignant flavor of those far-off years.[17]

NOTES

1. *Votre Maison* (Your Home) is a French magazine.

2. Gisèle Freund (1912–2000) studied sociology and art in Frankfurt and nineteenth-century French photography at the Sorbonne. As a photojournalist, Freund photographed numerous South and Latin American artists as well as many of her personal friends who were prominent European and American artists and writers.

3. The Champs-Elysées (Elysian fields) is a famous boulevard in Paris stretching from the Arc de Triomphe to the Tuileries Gardens and is the site of many grand processions.

4. The rue de l'Odéon is a street in Paris located on the left bank. In the 1920s and '30s, when Adrienne Monnier owned her bookshop, this street was famous for its numerous bookshops and the famous writers who visited this area; Adrienne Monnier (1892–1955) was a French poet and publisher, as well as the owner of the bookstore called, in English, *The Home of the Friends of Books*. Her circle of friends included famous American and French authors and philosophers who frequented her bookshop where their portraits were displayed.

5. Paul Valéry (1871–1945) was a French poet, writer, and literary critic. Valéry's prose piece—*La soirée avec Monsieur Teste* (*An Evening with Monsieur Teste*) (1896)—and his books of poetry—*La jeune parque* (The Youngest of the Fates) (1917) and *Charmes* (*Charms*), which includes "Le cimetière marin" ("The Graveyard by the Sea") (1922)—are considered

his most famous works; André Gide (1869–1951) was a French writer who ranged from psychological novelist, to literary critic, to homosexual and social activist. His most famous work, *Les nourritures terrestres* (*Fruits of the Earth*) (1897), proved influential on younger French writers

6. Léon-Paul Fargue (1876–1947) was a French poet writing in Paris and a member of the Symbolist poetry movement; Jean Prévost (1901–44), a French author, was killed in the *maquis* or French Resistance movement at Vercors in 1944; his works include *Le sel sur la plaie* (Salt on the Wound) (1934) and *La chasse du matin* (The Hunting of the Morning) (1937).

7. James Joyce (1882–1941), born in Dublin, Ireland, was a poet and novelist. His inventive use of language and the interior monologue made his writing both innovative and fresh. Works like *Dubliners* (1914), *A Portrait of the Artist as a Young Man* (1916), *Ulysses* (1922), and *Finnegan's Wake* (1939) are considered Joyce's greatest works. In particular, the novel *Ulysses*, which tells the story and adventures of Leopold Bloom, has received great acclaim since its publication in 1922 by Joyce's friend Sylvia Beach.

8. Paul Nizan (1905–40), a French philosopher and writer, resigned from the Communist Party in 1939 and died fighting against Germany in the Battle of Dunkirk during World War II. Two of his best-known works are *Antoine Bloye* (1933) and *La conspiration* (*The Conspiracy*) (1938); Sartre's foreword to a 1960 edition of Nizan's 1931 essay, "Aden, Arabie," introduced him to a new audience; Jean-Paul Sartre (1905–1980), a philosopher, writer, playwright, and literary critic, was the long time companion of Simone de Beauvoir. He may be best known for his philosophical treatise, *L'être et le néant* (*Being and Nothingness*) (1943) and *Qu'est-ce que la littérature?* (*What Is Literature?*) (1947).

9. Louis Aragon (1897–1982), a French poet and novelist, studied medicine during World War I, joined the Communist Party, and became a leader of the French Resistance during World War II. *Feu de joie* (Fire of Joy or Bonfire) (1920) was Aragon's first collection of poetry, and *Le crève-coeur* (The Heartbreak) (1941) was one of five books of poetry recording the Nazi occupation of France; Jean-Richard Bloch (1884–1947) was a French novelist and essayist. His novels included a romance, *Kurdish Night* (1925) and *Sybilla* (1932). Bloch's essays—"*Offering with the Policy*" (1933) and "*Birth of a Culture*" (1936)—made him a respected and well-known intellectual; André Chamson (1900–1983), a French novelist and historian, a veteran of the Spanish Civil War and the French Resistance, may be best known for *Le puits des miracles* (The Well of Miracles) (*Nouvelle Revue française*, 1945); Georges-André Malraux (1901–1976), a French novelist, wrote *La condition humaine* (*Man's Fate*) in 1933, a work that gave him international fame. Malraux was also very interested in art and art history, which was the topic of many of his writings. During World War II, he served in the French Resistance, and as Minister of Information, and later Minister of State for Cultural Affairs, under French President Charles de Gaulle.

10. D. H. Lawrence (1885–1930), a famous British novelist, poet, and literary critic, was the son of a poor coal miner and school teacher. He is best known for his sexually explicit novels like *Lady Chatterley's Lover* and *Sons and Lovers*; Virginia Woolf (1882–1941) was born in London and became a famous British novelist. Her father, also a writer, educated Woolf at home and encouraged her writing. As a result of her mother's death, and later her brother's and father's deaths, Woolf suffered several emotional breakdowns during her life. Her novel, *Mrs. Dalloway* (1925) was a cutting-edge work resulting from Woolf's innovative use of stream of consciousness writing. Her essay, "A Room of One's Own,"(1929) focused

on newly developed feminist views. Experiencing depression, Woolf took her own life by drowning in the Ouse River; Ernest Hemingway (1899–1961) was an American author born in Chicago, Illinois; he became a newspaper writer at age seventeen. In the 1920s, he lived in France and associated with other famous American (expatriate) authors such as F. Scott Fitzgerald and Gertrude Stein. Hemingway's novels were published in America and abroad in the 1930s and '40s. Some of Hemingway's most famous novels were *The Sun Also Rises* (1924), *A Farewell to Arms* (1929), and *For Whom the Bell Tolls* (1939); John Dos Passos (1896–1970) was born in Chicago, Illinois. He received a Harvard education and became a prominent writer, commenting on what he saw as the corrupting influence of capitalism in government and on American society. Dos Passos is best known for his three novels, *The 42nd Parallel, 1919*, and *The Big Money*, which were published together in 1938 as the trilogy *U.S.A*; William Faulkner (1897–1962), an American short story writer born in Mississippi, often wrote about the South. Although he never completed high school, Faulkner's novels are considered some of the greatest and most remarkable works of the twentieth century. A few of his works are *The Sound and the Fury*, *Absalom, Absalom!* and *Go Down Moses*.

11. Franz Kafka (1883–1924), born in Prague (a part of Austria at that time), was the son of a Jewish shopkeeper. Prior to World War I, Kafka published several short stories. However, his novel *Der Prozess* (*The Trial*) written in 1914, was one of the three unfinished novels, including *Das Schloss* (*The Castle*), and *Der Verschollene* (retitled *Amerika*), that were considered Kafka's finest works and were published posthumously by his friend and biographer Max Brod.

12. World War I (1914–1918), known as The Great War, was fought among Germany, France, Great Britain, Russia, and Austria-Hungary, with America entering the war against Germany and the Axis forces in April of 1917.

13. Jean Cocteau (1889–1963) was a French artist and writer influenced by cubism, surrealism, and Catholicism. *Les enfants terribles* (*The Holy Terrors*) (1929) is considered his most influential piece of writing. In the 1930s, Cocteau began producing films in France, and in 1949 he took a theatrical tour in the Middle East. He was painting frescos and murals in cathedrals at the age of seventy; Jean Giraudoux (1882–1944) was a French playwright, novelist, and politician known internationally for his plays—*Amphitryon 38* (1929) and *Ondine* (1939). He also wrote powerful essays and literary studies such as *Racine* (1930); St.-John Perse (1887–1975) was a French diplomat and poet. His poetic career grew after he moved to the United States in a self-imposed exile. His poem *Exile* was written in 1944; Paul Claudel (1868–1955) was a French poet, playwright, and diplomat. *Le soulier de satin* (1929) is one of his best-known works; André Breton (1896–1966), French poet, essayist, and one of the founders of the Surrealist movement, initially studied medicine and Freudian psychiatry. He soon realized his calling was to write poetry and he discarded his medical ambitions after working on a neurological ward during World War I. In 1924, Breton published "Manifeste du Surréalisme" ("Surrealist Manifesto"), which analyzed his views of psychology and how truth functions through Surrealism. He also published books of poetry, including *L'amour fou* (1937) and prose, such as *Nadja* (1928).

14. Jean Giono (1895–1970), a French novelist who was predominantly self-taught, wrote over fifty novels in addition to plays and essays throughout his lifetime. Several of his novels were translated into English, including *Blue Boy* and *Joy of Man's Desiring*.

15. Louis-Ferdinand Céline (1894–1961) was a novelist and a physician who became famous with the publication of his novel *Voyage Au Bout de la Nuit* (1932); Antoine de Saint-

Exupéry (1900–1944) was a French poet and aviator. His last and most famous book, *Le Petit Prince* (*The Little Prince*), was written in 1943. Saint-Exupéry was lost in action while on a military flight during World War II.

16. Henri Michaux (1899–1984) was a French painter and poet, whose most famous artistic work was *Un Certain Plume*, a book of sketches about Monsieur Plume; Raymond Queneau (1903–1976) was a French poet, novelist, and publisher. *Zazie dans le métro* (*Zazie in the Metro*) (1959), Queneau's internationally known novel, was made into a movie in 1960 by film director, Louis Malle; Michel Leiris (1901–1990), a French ethnologist and writer, had an intense interest in African and Central American cultures. His autobiography, *L'âge d'homme*, was published in 1939.

17. The text is followed by: "Simone de Beauvoir, Paris, 1965."

PREFACE TO *AMÉLIE 1*

by Simone de Beauvoir

TRANSLATION BY MARYBETH TIMMERMANN

NOTES BY JANELLA D. MOY

This book is the true story of a youth that is consumed in a potash mine in Alsace twenty years ago.[1] With fascinating precision, it introduces us to the techniques of an exhausting and dangerous job that—at least to my knowledge—has never been described. But its value surpasses, and by far, that of a simple document. In a darkly passionate tone, the author reconstitutes an entire human experience for us—the experience of a "wood-louse of a man who scrapes at the salt nine hundred meters down." He tells us of his fatigue, his fear, his resignation, his rebellion, his suffering: "A suffering measurable in centigrade degrees, in dry temperature, in liters of sweat lost, in the number of scabs on the skin where the potash penetrates like an acid, like a tongue of fire." He has us enter into his night: an exhausting obscurity that "consumes both the living strength of man and his thoughts." Yet something human remains in these annihilated individuals, each of whom feels like "the twin brother of the other." This humanness is found in the relationships that they maintain with each other. Henri Keller tells us about them

Préface by Simone de Beauvoir, to *Amélie 1: Chronique d'un mineur de potasse*, by Henri Keller (Paris: L'Harmattan, [1976], 1997).

at length. He evokes them in their similarities and their differences; each one tied to the others in camaraderie or hostility; each one enclosed in the solitude of an existence which a tragically ordinary accident often cuts short or mutilates forever.

In order to describe this condition to us, Henri Keller had to, at least in part, escape from it. Having perfected an important technical innovation, and having convinced the engineers to accept it, he himself obtained the title of engineer. Although he still works in a mine—a manganese mine in the south of Morocco[2]—it is no longer as an underground miner. But his past still consumes him. And even after twenty years, it is the voice of "number 886" that he makes us hear.

NOTES

1. Henri Keller's chronicle of life in the Amélie I potash mine in the beginning of the 1950s was written in memory of two miners killed in a mining accident. Potash, an important industrial chemical, is an impure form of potassium carbonate obtained through mining processes and used in the production of glass, soap, and fertilizer. Historically potash has been mined in Alsace, a region and province of eastern France, bordered by Germany on the east and Switzerland to the south.

2. See Henri Keller's, *Azougar: Fragments de vie dans l'atlas* (Azougar: Fragments of Life in the Atlas Region) (Paris: L'Harmattan, 1998), an account of life in a manganese mine in Morocco. Manganese is a gray-white metal that is essential in the production of iron and steel. Morocco, located in northwestern Africa on the Atlantic coast, won its independence from France in 1956.

FOREWORD TO *HISTORY: A NOVEL*

by Simone de Beauvoir

NOTES BY JANELLA D. MOY

History is Elsa Morante's latest novel.[1] However, don't expect to find in these pages glorified accounts of ancient or modern crises that have rocked the world. True, each chapter begins with a summary of world events, but the author does not see History as the upheavals reported in newspapers and described in books. For Morante, History is the hidden repercussion of these events in the hearts and bodies of the anonymous individuals who suffer through them, usually without understanding what is taking place.

The central character of this story—most of which takes place between 1941 and 1947—is Ida, whom Morante describes as a poor woman with a limited, underdeveloped mind. She is trying to raise her bastard son, Useppi. The innocent child and his uncomprehending mother are surrounded by a world of meanness and misery that afflicts old and young alike. Through Ida, Useppi, and many other characters, we get an intricate picture of Rome during those times. The experience of the vague and anguished daily lives of these people is, for Elsa Morante, the only truth. And while the life de-

Foreword by Simone de Beauvoir, to Elsa Morante, *History: A Novel*, translated from the Italian by William Weaver (Franklin Center, Pennsylvania: The Franklin Library, 1977).

scribed may be unfamiliar to us, little by little it becomes very real. Not only do we believe in Ida; the specifics of her world hypnotize us.

Some will say that Ida's is a materialistic world, for she is concerned only with finding shelter, clothing, and food for her son and herself. Elsa Morante's answer is to make us deeply aware of the extent to which the human spirit is revealed through the existential necessities of physical survival. Hunger, for example, is more than a tightening of the stomach; it can also create a world of subtle sensation and poetic fantasy. Even the humblest life is a unique human adventure.

At the end of the book, Ida envisions "the scenes of the human story (History) . . . as the multiple coils of an interminable murder." Yet Morante concludes, "History continues . . ." We cannot transcend the individual, according to Morante. With remarkable mastery—without facile effects, without useless pathos—she makes us feel the uniqueness of each human being.[2]

NOTES

1. Elsa Morante (1918–85), a famous Italian novelist, wrote about the impact of World War II on European society, particularly the common people, which can be noted in her novel, *La Storia: Romanzo* (*History: A Novel*) published in 1974. Her first novel, *Menzogna E. Sortilegio* (*House of Liars*) (1948) won the Viareggio Prize and her last novel, *Aracoeli* (1982) won the *Prix Médicis étranger*.
2. The foreword concludes with the following: "Simone de Beauvoir, Paris, 1977."

10

Notes for a Novel

INTRODUCTION

"Necessity but [unintelligible]"

by Meryl Altman

> *I started [writing] a vast novel; the heroine was to live through all my own experiences; she was to be awakened to the meaning of "the true life," enter into conflict with her environment, then be disillusioned by everything: action, love, knowledge. I never knew what the ending was because I ran out of time and gave up halfway through.*[1]

"In my young days, I wrote a great deal: but nothing that seemed worthwhile to me," wrote Simone de Beauvoir in 1979, introducing her earliest completed novel manuscript when it appeared as *Quand prime le spirituel*—almost forty years after Gallimard and Grasset had rejected it.[2] And when biographer Deirdre Bair asked her about a "collection of loose papers dating from 1928," which appears to include at least part of the manuscript you are about to read, she responded (according to Bair) "I am astonished . . . I wrote little more then than crude, confused blunderings, all of which I destroyed."[3]

That *Quand prime*, an unsentimental, demystifying exploration of female sexuality with a firm anti-Catholic stance, found no publisher until its author was already celebrated may say more about the French cultural climate in the 1930s than about its intrinsic literary quality, more evident to readers today. By contrast, the much earlier fragment you are about to read is in no way a polished product, and one is not led to lament the novel manuscript to which it refers as a lost masterpiece. What we have here is not even a draft of the planned narrative, though such a draft appears to have been completed: the fragment ends with a formal yet passionate dedication to Beauvoir's friend Zaza (although she is not named)[4] and a firm resolve to recopy the text and send it to a well-known critic, with an eye toward publication.[5] Rather than a draft as such, what has come down to us is a loosely associated set of "notes to self," including outlines, to-do lists, statements of purpose, lists of "themes," notes for further reading, sketches for other philosophical and literary projects, and even what may be notes taken for the philosophy courses Beauvoir was then pursuing at the Sorbonne and/or for the dissertation on Leibniz she was writing under the direction of Léon Brunschvicg.

Nonetheless the fragment is well worth studying for what it reveals about Beauvoir's early preoccupations and influences, at an important juncture in her intellectual development, a key moment of transition where she was freeing herself both from the Christian schema and from the Gidean cult of sincerity and *inquiétude* that had helped pry her loose from her Catholic upbringing in the first place. It also provides invaluable insight into the methods of thinking and writing Beauvoir evolved during a long, intense apprenticeship, with numerous false starts. If additional evidence were needed of her intellectual independence and autonomy, to give the lie to the old legend (to which she herself contributed) that she was malleable clay or a *tabula rasa* before Sartre "took her in hand," such evidence is here as well: even her own memoirs describe her as isolated from fellow students until asked to join Sartre's study group, but here in the fragment we see her vigorously projecting the organization of a group of her own, on ambitious terms, and probably somewhat earlier. And like the diaries, this manuscript shows that she was working out her own ethics and her own epistemology, and pulling together her own synthesis, including the authors they were studying for the *agrégation*, the influences of teachers like Brunschvicg and Jean Baruzi, and more diffuse features of the intellectual culture of her day. The list on page IV, "necessity, freedom—disquiet and salvation—choice and obligation"[6] names the jumping-off point, not only for those who would later be called "existentialists," but for every intellectual of that generation; and she plunges into the questions, taking no received point of view for granted.

But strikingly, Beauvoir works through these issues (or plans to) not by means of a treatise or system, but by means of a "heroine's text," a love story that is also a *Bildungsroman* or novel of development, where the central character, "Denise," would gain in emotional and intellectual maturity by learning to create her own values and "choose herself."[7] The turning point, apparently, would be the heroine's decision to send a man some sort of written declaration—presumably a declaration of love?—which would commit her, engage her, irrevocably. The written-down self would then be more fixed, more fully engaged, than the lived and living self, which might well continue to fluctuate; the writer realizes this because when she rereads her own earlier pages, she both does and doesn't recognize herself in them. Serious metaphysical issues (the nature of the self, of reality, the role of time) then come into play, along the lines explored by Bergson and others: "am I a substance, posited once and for all?" asks the writer, or possibly the heroine.[8] The metaphysical question about substance then leads to an ethical awareness—"does one have the right to commit tomorrow?"[9] Can I ethically make a promise *now* that would formally bind the different selves I may later become? Answering the question in the negative, Beauvoir would go on to invent a revolutionary design for personal life, whose social and political conclusion—"the principle of marriage is obscene"—would culminate in *The Second Sex*.[10] The young writer's almost ruthless quest for honesty and "authenticity of this act"[11] (VI verso) would echo through the decades to come; so would her never-questioned belief in *writing* as a central and defining aspect of human life.

A clear advance from the raw adolescent emotion of the 1926 and 1927 diaries, the fragment still lacks the self-lacerating, corrosive irony of *Quand prime*, where Beauvoir would turn earlier selves into self-deceived, unreliable narrators; and all these texts are years away from the retrospective shaping and even-handed, bemused adult perspective of *Mémoires d'une jeune fille rangée* (*MJFR*). What does emerge in the fragment is a discipline, a plan, a step toward maturity, an attempt to make systematic and intelligent sense of that raw mess of emotion which would nevertheless remain her ur-material, as philosopher, novelist, and feminist, to the end of her life. Where the diaries show us a young girl polishing the mirror of her developing self, the loose leaves of the fragment are the working notes of a writer who knows where she is going—which paradoxically makes them harder to decipher, and more challenging to translate. To a large extent these are puzzle pieces, which the reader's conjectures must reassemble: a good reminder perhaps of the extent to which despite her voluminous texts "Beauvoir" remains a character we (readers and feminists) create, in a process of interpretive collaboration that can never be completely finished.

That observation emerges from the fragmentary state of the papers, an accident of history. But it is also the question that Beauvoir intended to stage in the projected novel, posed and dramatized by a self in the process of creation and discovery, seen now from within and now from without, seeking a balance between other people's expectations and her moral obligation to be true to herself, while simultaneously wondering, which of these contradictory and oscillating versions is really *me*? The fragment is "life writing" in two senses, both because the novel Beauvoir is drafting is partly autobiographical, and because she (like her heroine) is creating and mapping a life and a self through the very act of narration and writing. As she tells herself in her diary, as she repeats in her published memoir, "My life will be a beautiful story which will become true as I go along telling it to myself."[12] But a full life, like a well-made novel, has other characters, which often escape authorial control—as she would realize when she discovered that her cousin Jacques, whom she had idealized and imagined she might marry, had other involvements: "This beautiful story which was my life, it was becoming false as I went along telling it to myself."[13] Here we find an early draft of what Beauvoir would later call "le mirage de l'Autre," the mirage of the Other, which she'd continue to explore in the "Mme de Préliane" novel she wrote while teaching at Marseille,[14] in *Quand prime*, and perhaps most successfully in *L'invitée*; and there is an evident connection with Sartre's description of the Look of the Other, "which steals my world from me."[15]

Other lifelong themes are visible in the fragment. Should one seek self-definition, and salvation, through another person, or only through oneself? How can one avoid solipsism, not to mention loneliness, and still escape the equally narcissistic trap of the *femme amoureuse* who devotes herself exclusively to love (what has been described as Beauvoir's "death's head" as a novelist)?[16] There is also the difficulty of being a passionate woman in love with a less than passionate man, in a culture where female desire is defined as either passive, or deviant.[17]

In some ways what we see is Beauvoir "becoming modern," loosening the grip of her Catholic upbringing even as she partly preserves its vocabulary ("spiritual progress" [*progrès spirituel*], "salvation" [*salut*]).[18] It may be worth underlining how pervasive this language was, even within respectable academic philosophy, and how serious a contender Catholicism remained for the soul (so to speak) of a young woman who had retained what she called "the taste for the Absolute."[19] Another aspect of her modernity is the attempt (diagrammed on XIII recto) to use *film* as a way of representing different levels (or "planes") within the self, and staging the "mirage of the Other" by literally showing an audience, on different screens, the different images and stories unfolding for each member of a couple, unbeknownst to the other. It is very difficult to see how this could have *worked*, either entirely onscreen or as part of a stage performance; but it is a useful reminder of her very early interest in all sorts of films, from the most radical experiments to the most banal and formulaic—Eisenstein to Buster Keaton, *Un chien andalou* to *Broadway Melody*—which paralleled her interest in avant-garde experiments with narrative and point of view in literature (Dos Passos, Richardson, Woolf).[20]

One delight for the scholar and intellectual biographer is the reading list, which recalls what James Baldwin calls somewhere "the book hunger of the lonely adolescent" and prefigures the intellectual omnivore who would read voluminously in order to write *The Second Sex*, disdaining no sort of source and twining together literature, philosophy, novels, social science, and personal experience. Was this early reading list a self-improvement project, a list of things recommended to her that she intended to buy or read, or a reading list she put together for someone else, in one of her didactic moods? Perhaps it does pertain to the novel project, as a list of books for a character or characters to be reading? Or perhaps it is a retrospective list, the sort of "balance sheet" Beauvoir was in the habit of drawing up periodically (New Year's day, her birthday, the end of the month), to monitor her self-development, a habit of self-reflection and self-correction first inculcated by the nuns at the *Cours désir*.[21] Books listed range from the austere and severe metaphysical *Réflexions sur l'intelligence* of Thomist philosopher Jacques Maritain to *Battling Malone*, a best-selling thriller about a British boxer.[22] Some very recent popular works are included, such as André Beucler's sexy bestseller *Gueule d'amour* (later a film with Jean Gabin) and *Tels qu'ils furent* (conservative, nostalgic, rosy, written by a member of the Académie Française whose style Zaza described as boring enough to encourage suicide).[23] Was Beauvoir perhaps informing herself about what worked, what succeeded, in vernacular narrative? Alongside lighthearted "*romans gai*" we find several of Plato's most abstruse dialogues, classical Greek drama, and Dante's *Divine Comedy*. There is also a fair amount of poetry, which Beauvoir loved throughout her life, though apparently she never tried to write any—the only genre, I believe, for which this can be said—and again her interest ranges broadly from the mystical Rabindranath Tagore, through the Parnassien/late symbolist Verhaeren (melancholy to the point of masochism), to surrealist André Breton and modernist Apollinaire. Some books reflect the official curriculum of the Sorbonne (Vendryès on language appears to have been part of studying for the degree of "Latin-Langues," as according to Zaza's letters he was one of the examiners),[24] and some are clearly sources for the dissertation on Leibniz; others, like the Tagore poems and the Suarès book of literary criticism, are things she and Zaza seem to have been reading and discussing together.[25] Some are books we know from other sources she loved; some she ought by rights to have hated. The persistence of her interest in mysticism, which may reflect the influence of her teacher, Jean Baruzi, an expert on Saint John of the Cross, is especially intriguing (and needs further study). The list as a whole testifies to her enormous drive to understand and synthesize, her passionate desire to create "a Work where I will say absolutely *everything*."[26]

Another pleasure of this fragmentary text is the sheer sense of life it gives—for instance, the phrase in a different handwriting which makes it easy to imagine someone (but who?) sitting next to her in a lecture or in the library saying "quick, can I borrow a piece of paper"—a sense of plenitude, to use her word, of an intellectual and creative and emotional life all mixed together, and of a determination to understand everything, and face everything, with maximum intellectual courage but also with hope: "rêver les yeux grands ouverts et non les yeux fermés." To dream with her eyes wide open.

* * *

In considering the literary origins and ambitions of this fragment, it's helpful to remember that as she grew up Beauvoir read through the classic English as well as French texts in the *Bildungsroman* tradition—*Little Women*, Jane Austen, George Eliot (especially *The Mill on the Floss*),[27] Virginia Woolf's novels and essays, even Dorothy Richardson's *Pilgrimage* (which she describes, not unfairly, as "*interminable*"[28]) and Rosamond Lehmann's *Dusty Answer* (in French, *Poussière*).[29] The "women and literature" courses created in the wake of *The Second Sex* would be quite similar to the course Beauvoir set herself as a girl. *Dusty Answer* in particular was an enormously important book both to her and to Zaza, one they turned to, along with Alain-Fournier's *Le grand Meaulnes*,[30] not just as budding novelists and literary critics, but for help in making sense of their own lives, particularly of the way men behaved and how one ought to behave oneself in response. But according to *MJFR*, the reading led Beauvoir to a *writer's* vocation, a decision to become, not Maggie Tulliver, but George Eliot (*MJFR* 195).

Beauvoir had written since childhood, and had always wrestled with combining the romantic and the realistic traditions. Her very early story about an Alsatian girl who saved her family foundered when she learned that the real Rhine river did not flow where the story needed it to be (*MJFR* 73). And she sought, as girls always have, in novels, plays, and poems, for clues about what might happen to her, and cues about what and how (and whom) to choose. At one point in the diary, facing difficulties in her on-again-off-again-not-quite-a-love-story with her cousin Jacques, she calls for help and strength, as if calling on patron saints, to Alissa and Violaine, the self-abnegating heroines of André Gide's *La porte étroite* and Paul Claudel's *L'annonce faite à Marie*, respectively.[31] *The Second Sex*, too, would turn to novels about women, novels by women and also by men, for intimate and expert testimony about women's lived experience that wasn't offered by the social science of Beauvoir's place and day. At the same time, *The Second Sex* would provide a reason-based critique of the fantasy life women base on novel reading: a critique that novels by and about women have often provided as well.[32] At the time of the fragment, Beauvoir also intended to move a step beyond what was possible for George Eliot and become a novelist of ideas in an overt and less gender-bound way. She brought all the skeptical tools of her philosophical education to bear on the questions, who can a woman be, what can a woman do, how can a woman find love and happiness and also think, and live, on her own terms.

Like *The Second Sex*, the fragment draws on, and attempts to harmonize, both literary and philosophical traditions. It integrates a number of Beauvoir's previous attempts at writing, and a number of her future attempts would build on it. Checking against the diaries, as they become available, and the accounts she gives in her memoirs of her early life, one finds a great deal of consistency, repeated revisitings of primary intellectual and emotional material—not surprising in itself, especially because Beauvoir consulted her diaries and later her letters as working documents. This text however is not a diary, and it is not letters. Rather, it reflects on both letter-writing and diary-writing—and reading, and rereading—as techniques for understanding both self and others.

The central incident of letter-writing seems fairly close to the story, told in *MJFR*, of Simone's momentous decision to write to her cousin Jacques and declare, if not precisely her love, at least her profound affection, despite the fact that as the man in the case it remains his role to take the lead, and that "I know I may appear ridiculous."[33] In her 1926 diary she refers to the writing of this letter as *one of the few acts she can think of that she has truly willed.*[34] Lest this seem excessive, we must remember the strength of the prohibition against female sexual agency in the haute bourgeoise Catholic milieu. Simply for having fallen in love with her South American cousin, a love that turned out to contravene her mother's wishes, Zaza (in real life) excoriated herself in a letter addressed to God, saying that everyone she knows considers her to have become a "fille" (whore) and that she more or less agrees with them. Letters between lovers or potential lovers circulate as significant and sometimes compromising commodities, much as they do in *Liaisons dangereuses* or *The Princess of Cleves* or Poe's "Purloined Letter."[35] One should not underestimate the seriousness of the risk Beauvoir's heroine was taking, the vulnerability to ridicule and humiliation comparable to what happens to Judy in *Dusty Answer*, when the man she assumes is in love with her (after a steamy D. H. Lawrence–like scene involving a boat) responds rather coldly to a love letter she has sent him: "Well . . . if a man wants a girl to—marry him he usually asks her himself, don't you see?"[36]

So it seems that Beauvoir intended to incorporate earlier stages of her own intellectual and emotional development, and perhaps "cure" herself of them in curing the heroine or showing how the heroine would move through and beyond them—through sensibility to sense, as Austen might have put it—though ideally without becoming insensible to love. "Story about the scarab," for instance, refers to an autobiographical story she'd begun to write much earlier, around the age of 17 (see *MJFR* 265): "Eliane," a girl who is not like the others, finds a precious scarab in the grass and clenches it in her hand, refusing to show it to her companions: "She felt sufficiently strong in herself to defend her one possession against blows and blandishments, and to keep her fist tightly closed all the time."[37] What started as a *cri de coeur* of the awkward age may now be a way to document and dramatize that preliminary stage of the maturing self. But an upside-down annotation in the middle of one thematic outline reads, "was that me?—I was crazy—that madwoman is dead: but not so dead that the void does not remain—a few days pass—desire."[38] Perhaps this is emotion recollected in tranquility, but the tranquility is not entirely calm. Similarly, when she writes "mensonge de Gide," Gide's "lie," and "mensonge d'un certain culte du moi"—the lie of a certain "cult of the self"—she is bravely renouncing belief in two cherished heroes, Gide and Maurice Barrès, on whose autobiographical and pedagogical works she had patterned herself; but their influence, as I'll discuss below, would be enduring.

It is important to be cautious about overly autobiographical readings. Some of the experiences Beauvoir seems to give Denise are not her own, but *Zaza's* ("Sud-americain" refers to Zaza's failed romance with the South-American cousin, frowned on by her parents); then also in XVIII a scene of recognition and self-recognition that in *MJFR* is attributed to Simone refinding Zaza at the start of the school year, is instead given to Denise refinding "M.," probably Maurice. A moment later we learn about Denise that "*elle* ne pleure jamais"—*she* never cries—which means that Denise is *not* Beauvoir, at least not the Beauvoir of the diaries, who regularly dissolves into tears. It is quite tempting to identify "Maurice" with cousin Jacques, especially in IX, which includes one of Jacques's habitual phrases, "à quoi bon" (what's the use) and his suggestion that a reasonable way of life involved conforming outwardly to social norms. The course of the romance, insofar as one can trace it, appears to follow roughly the same roller coaster as in *MJFR*; in XVI, the discussion of the incompatibility between the two also echoes both the diary and *MJFR*; examples might be multiplied. However, the central emotion of the fragment, the anguish of a desiring heroine who can do nothing, or very little, to advance her own story and affect her own destiny, seems to draw as well on Zaza's experiences with Merleau-Ponty. Beauvoir seems also to have intended a second heroine, or "foil,"[39] named Jeannine, to whom some of Zaza's experiences are given. But some interchanges with Jeannine appear to parallel Simone's discussions in *MJFR* with the Sorbonne friend she there calls Blanchette Weiss—a "friendship of youth and not childhood friendship," with superficial and arriviste tendencies and a taste for gossip. ("Weiss" also appears in the fragment under her real name, Georgette Lévy, in a way that makes clear [in contrast to *MJFR*] that Beauvoir took her seriously as a philosophical interlocutor, at least for a time.)

Other characters seem to be included so that the heroine can have conversations with them, ideas can emerge and things can happen. Some also represent "themes," as in a morality tale. "Sombreuse," who seems to be based on "Suzanne Boigue," Beauvoir's colleague at the Équipes Sociales, stands for the possibility of social good works, another stage Beauvoir and her heroine have passed through and are moving beyond. Madeleine represents the traditional feminine vocation (pouring the tea, etc.), which the heroine rejects and yet regrets. "J. Rivière," who is mentioned as a source, is not cousin Jacques but Jacques Rivière, a real critic and novelist of that name. Simone and Zaza were fascinated by the relationship between Rivière and his best friend (and brother-in-law) Alain-Fournier, the author of *Le grand Meaulnes*; they passed back and forth the published volume of letters between the two and borrowed from the "formulas" by which the two young men sought to define themselves. Rivière's name here seems to be shorthand for a somewhat cold, overmethodical temperament with which he reproached himself, in contrast to Fournier, who was more imaginative, more of a poet; Fournier is described as a "peasant" where Rivière is a "metaphysician," and so forth. Of particular interest to Beauvoir was Rivière's self-portrait in his novel *Aimée* as a person who lacked the vocation of happiness.[40]

Different readers may find different ways to put these puzzle pieces together, however, and later novelistic reworkings of her own experience

(*L'invitée, Les Mandarins*) should serve as a reminder that Beauvoir was consciously planning and structuring a work of fiction here, and as a caution against viewing this fragment as (even) more naive than it is. Another cue is given by the *dramatis personae* pages (XXI and XXII), where she sometimes seems to be redividing the qualities she'd earlier assigned to various characters. We might also reflect that the "Jacques" and the "Zaza" we feel we know from the memoirs are also fictional, or at least textual, creations—would it be too much to say that "Maurice" in the fragment is a rough draft for "Jacques" in *MJFR*? Indeed, the young cousin Beauvoir felt she knew and loved was himself a highly conjectural creature, reconstructed from a single letter she received from him, a few key conversations, and analogies and predictions based on the experiences of others, including many drawn from . . . novels. This in a way is the central theme of the fragment, the way Other People ("autrui") can be largely imaginary, until we recognize, like Alice in Wonderland arguing with the Red King, that it may be they who have imagined us.

And yet some of the incidents that may appear most wildly overromantic or even melodramatic—such as "their parents want to separate them"[41]—are things that actually happened to Zaza, ultimately (at least as Beauvoir would see it) with fatal consequences. Zaza's own texts augment the sense one gets from *MJFR* of an existence nearly as circumscribed as that of the Princess of Cleves, one that was common in the haute bourgeois milieu Beauvoir herself narrowly escaped. Beauvoir would later reflect that one side of her remained somewhat invested in romance plots of the "Delly" sort—(the Delly books are like Harlequin romances, or Mills and Boon).[42] But some of what seems least realistic in the heroine's text is real: and the restriction of real women to these unrealistic scripts is not only tragic but (as Adrienne Rich would later put it) "shared, unnecessary, and political."[43]

* * *

But to speak of the literary separate from the philosophical, as I have been doing, is to falsify what is most original about the project: the complete interwovenness of philosophical thinking and literary expression. VI recto is headed "essai d'une éthique," "Essay toward an Ethics," or "attempt at an ethics"; on the other side of the paper, she returns to the scene of the heroine rereading her notebook, debating whether to write to "M." At first one might imagine that VI recto is here by accident, a separate fragment of class notes, that it doesn't belong in the novel, but it does: the same issues arise on both sides of the sheet. In XVII she has added in blue, "write an essay of 10 large pages about the personality."[44] One feels this might not have improved the flow of the narrative! And yet the relevance to the heroine's dilemma of the questions asked there—what about the personality is given, what is made, are we what we wish to be or merely a collection of our history and our habits, do we have a choice about who we are or become—is clear.[45]

To a large extent, questions about the stability of the self, the relation between the social self and the deep self, and the persistence and coherence of the self through time, are Henri Bergson's questions. The cryptic comment that begins "le temps mêlé d'identique et de même," which we have translated as "Time mingled with the identical and the same," perhaps signals agreement with his analysis, in *Essai sur les données immediates de la conscience*, of how human notions of time differ from, are radically incommensurable with, our understanding of space as homogeneous, quantitative, and divisible—so that attempts to understand time in terms of space, while inevitable in ordinary language, are merely metaphorical. Why this matters (to Bergson, as to Beauvoir) is because the inner or deep self of consciousness is then shown to be radically different from the social self of common sense and everyday habit; this in turn means that human action must be free and undetermined. Bergson himself, in a famous passage that Beauvoir copied into her diary, compares the way consciousness can operate to free a hidden self with the creation of a novel or a work of art:

> Now, if some bold novelist, tearing aside the cleverly woven curtain of our conventional ego, shows us under this appearance of logic a fundamental absurdity, under this juxtaposition of simple states an infinite permeation of a thousand different impressions which have already ceased to exist the instant they are named, we commend him for having known us better than we knew ourselves. [46]

Readers of Proust will find these ideas familiar and perhaps remember that Bergson was Proust's brother-in-law and one of his teachers; the problematic fluctuations of the self when confronted by its own past, present, and future is well-captured, I think, by Proust's term "les intermittences du coeur," the intermittences of the heart. But Beauvoir says she intended her presentation of this "dédoublement," or doubled reality, to be different from Proust's:[47] how, I am not sure. Perhaps his irony did not suit her, or she disliked his taste for gossip; or perhaps his resignation to the impossibility of coinciding with oneself seemed too passive, insufficiently heroic.

It also seems important that Bergson legitimated the role of reflection and intuition in philosophy. When she writes about enthusiastically recognizing her own experience in his theories about the social self and the deep self,[48] she is simply applying his own method, which leads to a sort of philosophy of the everyday, long before Sartre would discover that you could make phenomenology out of a glass of beer or an apricot cocktail, and even longer before the encyclopedic compilation of "l'expérience vécue," lived experience, in *The Second Sex* would lead to the insight that the personal is political. Compare her diary:

> It amuses me to think about what J[acques] would say if he knew that on the subject of my love for him, I ask questions about the one and the many, about finite and absolute modes, about ideas and being. He probably would not understand because few people can understand what it is *to feel ideas* and that just because a love is not sentimental does not necessarily mean that it is intellectual. (In fact, it is often one or the other.) But there is a deeper question, and I am once again curiously finding myself thinking the same things as last year about this incommunicable self. [emphasis added] [49]

Perhaps this is simply the born philosopher, the sort of girl Zaza's family would make fun of for wondering aloud at the dinner table why tomato or herring tasted different in different mouths (*MJFR* 355). Or perhaps this is the birth of an influential and new intellectual style.

Page VII consists of notes about Leibniz, the subject of a thesis, or "diplôme," she was writing for Brunschvicg,[50] and at first glance they might simply seem not to belong with the novel draft. But the basic question Beauvoir (and Denise) pose about the self—am I a substance posed once and for all—can be broken down further: (1) *is the self a permanent substance* leads to the question, (2) *are there permanent substances at all*, and then (3) we come up against the basic question of metaphysics: *what* is *substance, anyhow*.[51] Leibniz's themes—whether ideas are innate or acquired, and what are the smallest building blocks of everything—are also taken up by Bergson, though in different language, and, at least in Beauvoir's view, they appear to bear on the questions about whether consciousness is free, when applied (as she intends to do) to "the relationship of the possible to the existent—of the individual to the species."[52] One possibility is that she is taking questions that come out of metaphysics, that come out of trying to understand Leibniz—what is substance, what are the basic units of reality, how are material and immaterial substances (bodies and souls, in one way of putting it) related, is matter all one thing or lots of different little things—and applying the Bergsonian questions to that: what happens when you add the dimension of time and the possibility, the inevitability, of change?

To a secular mind formed in the late twentieth century, Leibniz's metaphysics seems so shaped by his submission to a Christian omnipotent and omniscient Deity as to admit little or no meaningful choice; its usefulness is thus hard to see; but Bertrand Russell, for instance, whose influential book Beauvoir includes on her reading list, argued it was possible to take Leibniz's metaphysics without his theology. Today Leibniz's view seems incompatible with real human freedom and contingency, though he himself claimed otherwise.[53] That the issue is a complex one can be seen from her quotation, from a letter Leibniz wrote in 1696, "Descartes who doubted too much, also abandoned doubt too easily."[54] In context, she may be using it to refer to the rigor of Cartesian method rather than to belief in God, but the verb in question in the original is *peccavit*, "he sinned."

Characteristically—though for my present purposes, somewhat unhelpfully—Beauvoir is not particularly interested in doing history of philosophy here (not making notes on what one philosopher thought in contrast to another, never asking how an idea developed or was transmitted). Rather she is asking, in the most rigorous way possible, *what is actually the case*: the ideas of others are tools or paths toward figuring that out. The reading list shows that she had not at this point ruled out a mystical solution (Plotinus) or even an orthodox one (Maritain); even the essentialist view of substance presented in the most difficult Platonic dialogues still seemed worth studying.

The links between the fragment and her own later philosophical work, however, seem to fall less under metaphysics and more in the fascinating terrain where ethics overlaps epistemology. In love, do I engage my whole (real) *moi* (as in xvii), or am I creating my (new, but real) *moi* in expressing my love, or am I . . . simply being seduced into becoming a false *moi*, something I must reject in order to choose myself? And can I choose myself by choosing someone else? By the time of *Pyrrhus et Cinéas*,[55] it will be clear that the answer to the second question is, *no*—it's a bad mistake to make someone else your project, and devoting oneself "altruistically" (what is called in the fragment "salut par lui," "salvation through him") is a classic example of bad faith. The particular application of that point to *women* will have to wait until *The Second Sex*. And how to achieve what she calls in the fragment "equilibrium in an other,"[56]—whether this is even possible—will remain an open question for even longer.[57]

* * *

In speaking of the "moi," it would be remiss not to discuss the profound influence of Maurice Barrès—especially since his name is almost wholly unknown now, except to those who specialize in the decadent origins of French fascist thought, or those interested in the minutiae of the Dreyfus affair, where he distinguished himself as an extreme right-wing, ultra-Nationalist anti-Semite.[58] When Beauvoir writes in the fragment, "the lie of a certain cult of the self," she is referring to his trilogy, *Le culte du moi*, three philosophical novels which Barrès originally published separately as *Sous l'oeil des barbares* (1888), *Un homme libre* (1889) and *Le jardin de Bérénice* (1891). The word "cult" could be applied to the status Barrès enjoyed among followers who called him "prince de la jeunesse," the Prince of Youth. But in "cult of the self" it evokes a combination of religious worship, and "cultivation," a sort of agricultural or gardening metaphor. The novels propose an early form of "self-help" which involved adapting the spiritual exercises of Ignatius Loyola to a more secular but equally strenuous form of meditation—one that did not however preclude enjoyment of good cigars, prostitutes, and so forth. Rather than pray to God, one might make a novena to the proto-Romantic writer Benjamin Constant, for example, or give vent to ecstatic effusions, e.g., "I rushed eagerly toward this night, oh my beloved, oh Myself, in order to become a god."[59]

Jacques' suggestions to his cousin that one should try to live like everyone else, while secretly preserving the integrity of one's deeper self—thus continuing to enjoy inward feelings of superiority to one's milieu without paying the social costs of nonconformity—could come straight out of Barrès. It was perhaps a measure of the desperate predicament of bourgeois youth that several generations of otherwise intelligent young men were taken in by the narcissistic sentimental pseudo-Hellenizing semicareerist bad faith of these texts; but many (including for a time Alain-Fournier and Rivière) revered and cherished Barrès as a mentor: "He taught us the grandeur of *inquiétude* and of desire," wrote Rivière in a letter, while explaining that Barrès's second trilogy, which preached the return to the land in the interests of national and spiritual "renewal," left him cold.[60] Barrès claimed to have saved hundreds of boys and young men from suicide. Perhaps this is one further example of what Michèle le Doueff has called Beauvoir's "genius for the inappropriate."[61] And yet, it is hard to see how she could have done without him, in a way; because he provided an indispensable support to her spirit of resistance. Many passages from her early diaries echo the governing sentiment of *Sous l'oeil des barbares*: "What! to be just like the others! To define myself, that's to say, to limit myself! To end up reflected in those minds that will deform me in ways that correspond to their own minds!"[62] And in 1926, she conscientiously practiced his method in her diary: "I must cultivate these nuances of my self, both out of respect for the treasure deposited in myself, and for others."[63] By the time of the fragment, she sees through Barrès; but the tears she has shed at the stupidity of others—at the banality of their conversation and of their preoccupation with money, status, and what is and isn't "done"—and her need to resist at least inwardly in order to survive, and study, and write leave their traces here. One sign is the reference to the "scarabée" image, which she glosses in *MJFR* as follows: "This little fable expressed my most obsessive worry: how to defend myself against other people; for though my parents did not spare me their reproaches, they demanded my confidences."[64] Another is in the brief interchange: "What are you thinking, Denise?" "Nothing, Mother," which evokes the whole drama of the Beauvoir family during the daughter's adolescence:

> My mother would come in and out, coming and going and leaning over my shoulder all the time: . . ."What are you thinking about? What's the matter with you? What are you looking like that for? Of course, I'm only your mother, you won't tell me anything."[65]
>
> I would gaze in the looking-glass at the person *they* could see: it wasn't *me*; I wasn't there, I wasn't anywhere; how could I find myself again? . . . Sometimes I used to think that strength would fail me and that I would have to give in and become like all the others.[66]

Perhaps "autrui," whose terrifying look has the power to annihilate one's own painstakingly constructed sense of self-worth, is really always one's parents. And perhaps if there was a stark choice between self-worship and self-sacrifice, between self-love and self-hatred, self-worship must be the right answer, sick-making as some of its expressions may be. Barrès ends *Sous l'oeil des barbares* with an address to his ten-year-old self, with whom he has attempted to keep faith: "Little boy, you weren't wrong to despise those pompous asses."[67] To my ear, some of the same sense of having escaped with one's skin persists in Beauvoir's work as late as *MJFR*. Barrès is at his best in evoking the terrifying power of social conformity: "We are the barbarians, they chanted, arm in arm, we are the believers. We gave a name to everything; we know when it's appropriate to laugh and when one must look serious."[68] This is still the refrain of the Theban chorus at the opening of Sartre's *Les mouches*. But as Beauvoir would humorously recognize in *MJFR* and *La force de l'âge*, while she and Sartre had a great deal in common with the poets of *inquiétude*, their highly bourgeois and individualistic form of resistance to bourgeois individualism had its limitations.

By the time of *Quand prime le spirituel* it will be precisely Marcelle's concentration on her inner life ("vie intérieure"),[69] her split consciousness ("dédoublement") bordering on narcissism, along with Chantal's diary or "carnet intime," that inspires Beauvoir's bitterness and disgust: her own experiences (and some of the very same ones) are described there, but as if distorted by the eyes of hostile readers. Already by the time of the fragment, Barrès figures mostly as a skin Beauvoir is in the process of shedding. But one must take more seriously the continuing influence of André Gide, even though the quotation from his *Nourritures terrestres*—"may what really matters be in the look"[70]—is described as a lie, a "mensonge," and even though one character delights in exposing the "Gidisms" of another.[71]

Like many of her generation, Beauvoir had taken Gide to her heart as an ally against the Catholic piety that threatened her on two fronts: its anti-intellectualism, and the strict bourgeois morality that would confine women to family and deny them sexual self-expression. When Jacques introduced her to *Nourritures terrestres* it became a sort of secular breviary and bed-table book for her, as for a whole segment of bourgeois youth—dubbed "les inquiets" by moralist Marcel Arland—who rejected their parents' system of values without necessarily finding anything to put in its place (the alternative of concrete, activist politics, engagement with the social world, was barely on the screen for Beauvoir or most of her friends). Young men especially seem to have seen in *Nourritures terrestres* what a later generation would see in Kerouac's *On the Road.* Gide preaches the doctrine of sincerity, changeability, openness to experience (including to sexual experience), a sort of Whitmanesque, "natural" rootlessness; there is an exaltation of caprice and whim, an ecstatic (though not particularly specific) celebration of desire, and an injunction to live in the moment. In *MJFR*, Beauvoir recalls taking to heart the touchstone phrase of his alter ego, Menalque—"Family, I hate you! locked doors, stifling rooms"[72]—though she displays some retrospective irony at Gide's expense and her own: "Menalque's curse assured me that in finding my home dull I was serving a sacred cause."[73] As she later understood, that individualist revolt against bourgeois norms, whether in its positive form (the romance of the open road) or its negative one ("à quoi bon?"), was itself bourgeois to the core. Even by the time of our fragment Beauvoir has become disillusioned with disillusionment, perhaps after watching Jacques fail his exams because he couldn't see the point of studying for them.

Moreover, we see in the fragment the beginning of her awareness that *inquiétude* and sincerity can themselves be a sort of insincere, or at least inauthentic, *pose*: underneath "lie of Gide" we find "one gives oneself strong emotions in order to create the illusion that it's worth while to have them,"[74] and later (XVII verso): "There are people who act in contradictory ways to persuade themselves that's what they are like."[75] The quest for self-knowledge through writing (and/or through love) incorporates an uneasy awareness that one is creating the self by performing it for somebody else (in conversation, in letters, in a novel), in ways one cannot fully control or predict. If one puts Gide's rhapsodies about the need, almost the duty, to cultivate the intensity of individual sensation or (as a later generation of *inquiets* would have it) live for today, alongside Bergson's analysis of the mutability of the self in time, one arrives at the question, *how can I know when I am really sincere*, which is not a question Gide (or Jacques) would have found intelligible. Perhaps she is moving from an ethic of sincerity toward an existentialist ethic of authenticity; certainly the use of "comédie" begins to gesture toward later definitions of false consciousness and "bad faith." And perhaps phrases like "she chooses that life be tragic," "nostalgia for old sufferings"[76] even gesture toward the critique of specifically feminine forms of masochism and bad faith that she'll make in *The Second Sex*. As with Barrès, Beauvoir's treatment of Gide in the fragment might be a form of what she'd later call "liquidating her past"[77]—an interesting metaphor, as liquidation preserves the asset in usable form for future projects.

* * *

But meanwhile, how was the novel supposed to end? Readers were meant to track Denise's "spiritual progress" ("progrès spirituel"), but where was she going? Bair remembers Beauvoir explaining that it was "'too perplexing' to create a story based on friends when she had no idea what was happening to them" (Bair 147). But the conventions of the heroine's text also posed a problem, specific to the genre she had chosen. Stories of the heroine's sentimental education are pedagogical and ethical: the good will be rewarded, the others punished, and the task of the heroine, to negotiate her limited agency in the narrow space of respectable femininity, can end only in death or in marriage. It is true that the reading list included in the fragment, and what we know from other sources about Beauvoir's reading at the period, includes a number of controversial, unconventional, "New Woman" heroines, strong women who resist possession while enjoying the power of their own sexuality. But we should not be too quick to rejoice in these "modern" alternatives. *MJFR* records an argument with "Herbaud" about the heroine of Michael Arlen's bestselling *The Green Hat*:—"one doesn't *have* an Iris Storm," she remembers saying[78]—but Arlen's vibrant, self-sufficient, defiantly sexual flapper dies in the end a martyr to her own desire for sexual "purity," a fate not terribly different from what happens to the hyper-Christian Alissa at the end of Gide's *La porte étroite*. *Battling Malone* and *Gueule d'amour* both end with the sexually proud and strong woman being shot to death by the lover who can stand no more, and both texts seem to demand the reader's sympathy for the killer. Even the lesbian heroine of Victor Margueritte's scandalous bestseller, *La garçonne*, which Beauvoir's father held up to her as a warning,[79] ends up happily married like the heroines of the bourgeois stories Beauvoir's parents favored, in which women with professional ambitions are tamed. "Surely it was time somebody invented a new plot," as Virginia Woolf's playwright Miss La Trobe muses in *Between the Acts*.[80] But in the 1920s, few new plots were available.

Beauvoir would try many more times before she got the shape of the story right, not as novel but as *Mémoires d'une jeune fille rangée*, where her own "which-man-will-she-choose" story ends on a happy note with Sartre, and Zaza . . . Ah. "For many years, I felt that I had paid for my freedom with her death."[81] But when she sketched the 1928 version, Beauvoir had not yet concluded her famous pact with Sartre; and Zaza was still very much alive.

In the pages you are about to read, Zaza is everywhere, as dedicatee, source of additional experiential "data," alternative heroine, and (perhaps most importantly) as reader. On September 3, 1927, Zaza wrote to Simone:

> There's one book I'm waiting for impatiently, one which will have a value for me that no other book could have, and that's your book. I seem already to see very clearly what it will be; if it won't be annoying or disagreeable to you, bring me when you come at least some of the pages you've written: it seems to me I almost deserve it, and I know I need it. There's nothing sweeter in the whole world than to feel there's someone who can understand you, someone on whose friendship you can absolutely count.[82]

What Zaza provided at Gagnepan was the sense that Beauvoir was not, after all, a monster: that other women felt as she did; that she could be both a brilliant scholar and a woman like other women. She was not, after all, "unique," and she was not alone. What she was writing, what she would write, would be something of which others, other women especially, stood in passionate and desperate need.

Whether the love expressed in the fragment dedication is sexual, whether one should call the relationship queer, or lesbian, or anything else, no longer seems important to me in the way it once did. What does seem important is the affirmation of bonds between women as real and significant, even in this text replete with the agonies of the heterosexual plot. What can I call that? Feminist.

Meanwhile the fractious but ultimately satisfying love-hate relationship between literature and philosophy would come to fruition as that collective *Bildungsroman*: the second volume of *The Second Sex*.

NOTES

1. Simone de Beauvoir, *Memoirs of a Dutiful Daughter*, trans. James Kirkup (Harmondsworth, England: Penguin, 1963), 252 (hereafter referred to as *MDD*). Translation altered. "Je commençais un vaste roman; l'héroïne traversait toutes mes expériences; elle s'éveillait a 'la vraie vie,' entrait en conflit avec son entourage, puis elle faisait amèrement le tour de tout: action, amour, savoir. Je ne connus jamais la fin de cette histoire car le temps me manqua et je l'abandonnai à mi-chemin." *Mémoires d'une jeune fille rangée* (Paris: Gallimard, 1958), 349 (hereafter referred to as *MJFR*).

2. "J'ai beaucoup écrit dans ma jeunesse: mais rien qui me parût valable." Introductory note, *Quand prime le spirituel* (Paris: Gallimard, 1979), vii; the text was translated by Patrick O'Brian as *When Things of the Spirit Come First* (London: Fontana, 1982). (The English version did not include this introductory note.)

3. Deirdre Bair, *Simone de Beauvoir: A Biography* (New York: Vintage, 1990), 626. Bair's rendering of the document differs significantly from the text given here, no doubt for reasons of a technical nature; in particular, she often reads "je" where we read "elle." This is especially unfortunate because it makes the document seem like diary jottings rather than a draft toward something less purely subjective and more ambitious.

4. The dedication "in remembrance of the weeks we spent together in Gagnepan," which permits us to assign the manuscript a rough date, refers to a visit Beauvoir made in September 1928 to her close friend Elisabeth La Coin, who is given the pseudonym "Zaza Mabille" in *MJFR*. The country estate called Gagnepan, which belonged to Zaza's grandmother, is in Gascony, near Aire-sur-Adour; the La Coins had the habit of spending part of every summer there, much as the Beauvoir family vacationed with relatives at Meyrignac and in the Limousin. See *Zaza: Correspondence et carnets d'Elisabeth La Coin 1914–1928* (Zaza: Letters and Diaries of Elisabeth La Coin 1914–1928) (Paris: Editions du Seuil, 1991). See also Maurice de Gandillac, *Le siècle traversée: Souvenirs de neuf décennies* (Spanning the Century: Memories from Nine Decades) (Paris: Albin Michel, 1998).

5. "Have R. Fernandez read it if possible." Literary critic Ramon Fernandez, known for his defense of Proust, wrote for the prestigious *Nouvelle revue française*. He would later become quite conservative. Beauvoir attended a lecture he gave in February 1928 on the topic "Intellectuel et Société" and was inspired by his view of the intellectual's mission to unite internal and social worlds. She wrote in her diary, "A hard destiny but a lofty one, and that's exactly what I have lived and want to make my novel from . . . Fernandez is one of those people that five years from now I'll want to have met." ("Dure destinée: mais haute, et c'est tout cela justement que j'ai vécu et dont je veux faire mon roman. . . . Fernandez est un de ceux dont d'ici cinq ans il faut avoir fait la connaissance.") Simone de Beauvoir, *Cahiers de jeunesse 1926–1930*, ed. Sylvie le Bon de Beauvoir. (Paris: Gallimard, 2008), 438–39. See also

458–59: "Je suis une intellectuelle, il faut le rester (oh! exaltation, promesses après la belle conférence de Fernandez)." ("I am an intellectual; I must remain one [Oh! exaltation, promises after Fernandez's wonderful lecture].") By the time of *MJFR* her enthusiasm for the "new humanism" of Fernandez and his group of young writers had cooled, even retrospectively—"je ne les suivis pas" (271), "I didn't follow them."

The fragment has come down to us on scrap paper—as Sarah Gendron notes below, twenty-two of the twenty-four pages seem to be checks from the BPF (Banque Populaire Française) that have been cut in half, and another is note paper on which there is an advertisement for a pen company ('Onoto')—an indication of Beauvoir's well-known frugality. So the decision she announces at the end of the fragment, to buy several new notebooks for recopying her manuscript, is in itself a sign of serious intention and ambition.

6. "nécessité, liberté—inquiétude et salut—choix et exigence."

7. For the classic discussions of the "heroine's text" in French and English literature, see Nancy K. Miller, "Emphasis Added: Plots and Plausibilities in Women's Fiction," *Subject to Change* (New York: Columbia, 1988); Rachel Brownstein, *Becoming a Heroine* (New York: Viking, 1982); see also Rachel Blau DuPlessis, *Writing beyond the Ending* (Bloomington: Indiana, 1986) and *The Pink Guitar: Writing as Feminist Practice* (London: Routledge, 1990).

8. "suis-je une substance une fois posée?" "Posée" is sometimes translated as "posited," but can also mean simply "set down" or "set forth," or be equivalent to the English "to pose" as in, "poser une question," "to ask a question."

9. " a-t-on le droit d'engager demain?"

10. See *Le deuxième sexe* 2 (Gallimard 1949/1976), 254, my translation: "le principe du mariage est obscène parce qu'il transforme en droits et en devoirs un échange qui doit être fondé sur un élan spontané . . ." "the principle of marriage is obscene because it transforms into rights and duties an exchange which ought to be based upon a spontaneous impulse." Margaret Simons has discussed the emergence of this issue in Beauvoir's student diary with reference to a fellow-student, Barbier. See Margaret A. Simons, *Beauvoir and The Second Sex: Feminism, Race, and the Origins of Existentialism* (Lanham, Md.: Rowman and Littlefield, 1999), 195. The diary passage (for May 6, 1927) reads in part: "I had just seen Barbier again . . . one instant I held in my hands an entirely new life . . . the horror of the definitive choice, is that it engages not only the self of today, but that of tomorrow, which is why basically marriage is immoral." See also Meryl Altman, "Simone de Beauvoir and the Sexual Revolution," Proceedings of the 10th Annual Symposium of the International Association of Women Philosophers-IAPH, Barcelona, October 2002.

11. "authenticité de cette acte."

12. "Ma vie sera une belle histoire qui deviendrait vraie au fur et à mesure que je me la raconterais" (*MJFR* 234). The Penguin translation reads, "My life would be a beautiful story come true, a story I would make up as I went along" (*MDD* 169).

13. "C'est que je venais de faire une cuisante découverte: cette belle histoire qu'était ma vie, elle devenait fausse au fur et à mesure que je me la racontais" (*MJFR* 442). "I had just made a very painful discovery: the fine story of my life was gradually going wrong as I went on making it up" (*MDD* 316).

14. *La force de l'âge* (Paris: Gallimard, 1960), 118–23; translated by Peter Green as *The Prime of Life* (Harmondsworth: Penguin, 1965). The unfinished Marseille novel, which dealt with the relation between an older woman artist and a younger woman who admires her, seems a crucial step in Beauvoir's evolution toward *L'invitée* (Paris: Gallimard, 1943), trans-

lated by Yvonne Moyse and Roger Senhouse as *She Came to Stay* (New York: World Publishing, 1954). As far as I know, no draft of the Marseille novel has survived.

15. Jean-Paul Sartre, *L'être et le néant: Essai d'ontologie phénomenologique* (1943; Paris: Gallimard, Collection Tel, 1976), 295: "Ainsi tout à coup un objet est apparu qui m'a volé le monde." Translated by Hazel E. Barnes as *Being and Nothingness: An Essay on Phenomenological Ontology* (1957; New York: Routledge, 2005), 275: "Thus suddenly an object has appeared which has stolen the world from me." But see Simons, *Beauvoir and The Second Sex*, 232, and Sonia Kruks, *Retrieving Experience: Subjectivity and Recognition in Feminist Politics* (Ithaca: Cornell University Press, 2001), for an account of how Beauvoir and Sartre differ on this point. Beauvoir's own first brush with this shock of nonrecognition appears to have had to do with Zaza, to judge from the direct accounts given in *MJFR* and in *La force de l'âge*, and from the chapters about Françoise's childhood that are deleted from *L'invitée*. See Beauvoir, *Philosophical Writings*, ed. Margaret A. Simons, Marybeth Timmermann, and Mary Beth Mader (Urbana: University of Illinois Press, 2004), 31–76.

16. "Françoise d'Eaubonne, dans sa critique des *Mandarins*, remarquait que tous les écrivains ont leur 'tête de mort' et que la mienne—figurée par Elizabeth, Denise, et surtout Paule—c'est la femme qui sacrifie à l'amour son autonomie" (*La force de l'âge*, 95). "Françoise d'Eaubonne, in her review of *The Mandarins*, observed that every writer has his King Charles' head, and that mine—as exemplified by Elisabeth, Denise, and above all by Paula—is the woman who sacrifices her independence for love" (*The Prime of Life*, 80).

17. Beauvoir would dramatize this difficulty repeatedly, before finally analyzing it in *The Second Sex*: literary antecedents include Rosamund Lehmann's *Dusty Answer* and Gide's *La porte étroite*, while real-world sources include Zaza's difficulties with Merleau-Ponty and other incidents involving "Suzanne Boigue," "Lise," and "Clairaut" (Gandillac). In the fragment she explores one result of frustration—fantasies of rape, or near-rape—an effect of oppression *The Second Sex* will both critique and explain.

18. See Margaret Simons, "Introduction," Simone de Beauvoir, *Diary of a Philosophy Student: 1926–27*, trans. Barbara Klaw, ed. Barbara Klaw, Sylvie Le Bon de Beauvoir, Margaret A. Simons, and Marybeth Timmermann (Urbana: University of Illinois Press, 2007). In the 1926 diary, Beauvoir contrasts herself to Merleau-Ponty, who is still a communicant; Simons comments, "in rejecting Merleau-Ponty's appeal to faith, Beauvoir claims a modernist position, affirming the process of becoming and the critique of reason" (44).

19. "Un antique goût de l'absolu," *La force de l'âge*, 53; *Prime of life*, 43. The vocabulary of *salut* (which can be translated as health, rather than salvation, but retains its normative cast) continues to echo through her philosophical writings right up through *The Second Sex*.

20. See Emmanuel Leclerq, "Le cinéma selon Simone de Beauvoir: les visages et les myths" ("The Cinema According to Simone de Beauvoir: Faces and Myths"), *Les temps modernes*, June–July 2002, No. 619, 185–248. "Ce qui est cependant frappant, lorsqu'on établit la liste des films qu'elle a cité dans son oeuvre, c'est à quel point elle recouvre l'essentiel de l'histoire du cinéma" (185). "What is striking is, once one puts together the list of films she cites in her works, how fully it covers the essential canon of film history." The 1926 diary mentions seeing *Rien que des heures* (*Nothing but Time*), a 1926 surrealist silent film by Alberto Calvalcanti, which the current Facets catalogue calls a "landmark in the tradition of documentary." From diaries it would seem that she frequented the Studio des Ursulines, where experimental films were shown, before Sartre could have influenced her to do so. For a discussion of Bergson's views on film and human consciousness, which also seem

relevant here, see Donato Totaro, "Time, Bergson, and the Cinematographical Mechanism," *Offscreen* 2001, January 11, 2001, http://www.offscreen.com/.

21. The nuns gave her her first notebook as part of a religious retreat: "Je notais sur un carnet les effusions de mon âme et des résolutions de sainteté" (*MJFR* 102). "I wrote down in a special notebook the outpourings of my immortal soul and my saintly resolutions" (*MDD* 74).

22. Jacques Maritain, *Réflexions sur l'intelligence et sur sa vie propre* (Reflections on Intelligence and Life Itself) (Paris: Nouvelle librairie nationale, 1924); Louis Hémon, *Battling Malone, pugiliste* (Paris: Bernard Grasset, 1925).

23. André Beucler, *Gueule d'amour* (Lady Killer) (1926; reprint, Paris: Gallimard, 2003); Edouard Estaunié, *Tels qu'ils furent* (The Way They Were) (Paris: Perrin, 1927); *Zaza*, 54.

24. *Zaza*, 119.

25. See *Zaza*, especially 138, where Zaza responds in the warmest terms possible to Simone's gift to her of the poems of Tagore: "c'est bien un livre de nous deux et pour nous deux." "It's very much a book about the two of us and for the two of us."

26. "une oeuvre où je dirais tout, *tout*" (*MJFR* 335). Translated in *MDD* as "It is to be a work . . . which will *tell all*." (242).

27. Louisa May Alcott, *Little Women* (1869; reprint, Harmondsworth: Penguin, 1995); George Eliot, *The Mill on the Floss* (1860; New York: Dover, 2003).

28. Dorothy Richardson, *Pilgrimage*, (1915–38; New York: Virago, 1994); *MJFR* 63.

29. Rosamond Lehmann, *Dusty Answer* (1927; reprint, New York: Harcourt Brace Jovanovich, 1975).

30. Alain-Fournier (Henri-Alban Fournier), *Le grand Meaulnes* (1913; reprint, Paris: Livres de poche, 1971).

31. *MJFR* 294; André Gide, *La porte étroite* (*Strait is the Gate*) (1909; reprint, Paris: Gallimard, 2001); Paul Claudel, *L'annonce faite à Marie* (*The Tidings Brought to Mary*) (1910; reprint, Paris, Gallimard, 1993).

32. A number of novels that were important to Beauvoir at this stage of her life also take up the theme of the young *man* whose overidealized understanding based on novel-reading leads to an inability to function in real life. *Étienne* and *Monique* by Marcel Arland, *Aimée* by Jacques Rivière (1922; reprint, Paris: Gallimard, 1993) are a few. One could trace the theme back to Flaubert's *Sentimental Education* (which might name the genre) and *Madame Bovary*, and behind them to *Don Quixote*. *Le grand Meaulnes*, too, can be discussed as a *Bildungsroman*, though it also belongs to a slightly different genre that Beauvoir calls "le merveilleux" and says she sometimes attempted to imitate without success.

33. Jacques Champigneulle, called in *MJFR* Jacques Laguillon. "*Ridicule*" was a word Beauvoir's mother used for anything that violated her sense of bourgeois social decorum.

34. *Diary of a Philosophy Student*, 162.

35. *Zaza*, 69. The correspondence of Fournier and Rivière also discusses an undercover correspondence between Fournier and a young woman met on the train, disapproved of by both sets of parents and leading to possible blackmail. And we should not forget that the melodramatic conclusion of *L'invitée* turns on Xavière's reading of letters received by Françoise—a literary convention with a real-life antecedent. Choderlos de Laclos, *Les liaisons dangereuses* (*Dangerous Liaisons*) (1782; reprint, Paris: Gallimard 2003); Mme. de la Fayette, *La princesse de Clèves* (1678; reprint, Paris: Livres de poches, 1973).

36. *Dusty Answer*, 276.

37. *MDD* 192; "Elle se sentait assez fort pour défendre son unique bien contre les coups et contre les caresses, et pour tenir toujours sa main fermée" (*MJFR* 265). Translator James Kirkup has rendered the word for what the heroine finds in the grass, "scarabée," as "beetle" (*MDD* 191).

38. "étais-ce moi? j'étais folle-cette folle est morte: mais point tant que le vide ne demeure-quelques jours passent—le désir."

39. Again, this is a characteristic trope of the "heroine's text": both Alissa and Violaine have more ordinary feminine sisters for whom they sacrifice themselves, in Maggie Tulliver's case it is her blonde cousin Lucy, Jo's childhood sweetheart Laurie marries her sister Amy, and so on.

40. The correspondence was cut short by Alain-Fournier's tragic death in 1914. Rivière went on to become André Gide's right-hand man as editor of the NRF, and a friend of Claudel (who later reconverted him to Catholic practice). *Aimée* was a book Beauvoir liked very much when her cousin Jacques gave it to her. Jacques Rivière and Alain-Fournier, *Correspondance 1904–1914*, new edition revised and edited by Alain Rivière and Pierre de Gaulmyn, (Paris: Gallimard, 1991) (Zaza and Simone read a shorter and somewhat expurgated version).

41. "les parents veulent les séparer"

42. *La force de l'âge*, 73: "Il m'en reste un petit côté Delly, très sensible dans les premier brouillons de mes romans."

43. Adrienne Rich, "Translations," *Diving into the Wreck* (New York: Norton, 1972).

44. "faire une dissertation de 10 grandes pages sur la personnalité."

45. "The personality" is named in *MJFR* as the subject of a paper or *dissertation* Beauvoir wrote for a class with Jean Baruzi, who seems to have thought highly of it. See Simons, *Beauvoir and The Second Sex*, 188.

46. "Si maintenant quelque romancier hardi, déchirant la toile habilement tissée de nôtre moi conventionnel, nous montre sous cette logique apparente une absurdité fondamentale, sous cette juxtaposition des états simples une pénétration infinie de milles impressions diverses qui ont cessés d'être au moment où on les nomme, nous le louons de nous avoir mieux connus que nous ne nous connaissons nous-mêmes." Quoted in Beauvoir's *Diary of a Philosophy Student*, 59. Henri Bergson, *Essai sur les données immediates de la conscience* (1927; reprint, Paris: Presses Universitaires de la France, 1944), 99; translated by F. L. Pogson as *Time and Free Will: An Essay on the Immediate Data of Consciousness*, (London: George Allen and Unwin, 1910), 133.

47. VI (recto) under the section "Essai d'une éthique" (Essay toward an Ethics).

48. *MDD* 207; "dans ses théories sur le moi social et le moi profond je reconnus avec enthousiasme ma propre expérience" (*MJFR* 287). Kirkup has "the social ego and the personal ego."

49. *Diary of a Philosophy Student*, 251–52; "Cela m'amuse de penser à ce que dirait J[acques] s'il savait qu'à propos de mon amour pour lui je pose les questions de l'un et du multiple, des modes finis et de l'absolu, de l'idée et de l'être. Il ne comprendrait pas sans doute, parce que peu de gens peuvent comprendre ce que c'est de *sentir les idées*, et qu'un amour pour n'être pas sentimental n'est pas pourtant intellectuel; en fait il est souvent l'un ou l'autre; mais il y a une question plus profonde, et je me retrouve curieusement devant mes pensées de l'année dernière sur ce moi incommunicable . . . [emphasis added]" (*Cahiers de jeunesse*, 336–37).

50. Apparently this thesis has been lost. According to *MJFR*, it was as an expert on Leibniz

that Beauvoir was first invited to join Sartre's study group (reviewing for the *agrégation*), but Leibniz himself failed to hold their interest very long.

51. Starting from the other direction, one might first ask, are there permanent substances (at all) and then, if there are, is the self like that, or different. One might also note the way these issues interweave with the existentialist claim that "existence precedes essence," and later with feminist critiques of "essentialism."

52. "mettre sur le rapport du possible à l'existant—de l'individu à l'espèce-"

53. G. W. Leibniz, *Philosophical Texts*, translated and edited by R. S. Woolhouse and Richard Francks (Oxford: Oxford University Press, 1998); see especially Leibniz's letter to Arnold, 43, 63–64, and 94.

54. As Leibniz puts it in a letter to Joh. Bernoulli dated August 23,1696, Descartes "failed doubly, by doubting too much and by too easily taking leave from doubt" ("sed ille dupliciter peccavit, nimis dubitando et nimis facile a dubitatione discedendo" cited in Heidegger SvG:29). http://mail.architexturez.net/+/Heidegger-L/archive/msg06799.shtml.

55. Beauvoir, *Pyrrhus et Cinéas* (Paris: Gallimard, 1944), translated as "Pyrrhus and Cineas" (1944), in *Philosophical Writings*, 89–149.

56. "équilibre en une autre."

57. From *The Prime of Life* (153): "and I still had not achieved any final resolution of my most serious problem: how was I to reconcile my longing for independence with the feelings that drove me so impetuously toward another person." "Et je n'avais pas définitivement résolu le plus sérieux de mes problèmes: concilier le souci que j'avais de mon autonomie avec les sentiments qui me jetaient impétueusement vers un autre" (*La force de l'âge*, 178).

58. See Liz Constable, "'Ce bazar intellectuel': Maurice Barrès, Decadent Masters, and Nationalist Pupils," in *Perennial Decay: On the Aesthetics and Politics of Decadence*, ed. Liz Constable, Dennis Denisoff, and Matthew Potolsky (Philadelphia: University of Pennsylvania Press, 1999); and also David Carroll, *French Literary Fascism: Nationalism Anti-Semitism, and the Ideology of Culture* (Princeton: Princeton University Press, 1995). I am indebted to Liz Constable for helpful conversation as well.

59. "J'avais hâte de cette nuit, ô mon bien-aimé, ô moi, pour devenir un dieu." Maurice Barrès, *Le culte du moi: Sous l'oeil des barbares* (The Cult of the Self: Under the Watchful Eyes of the Barbarians) (1888), *Un homme libre* (A Free Man) (1889), *Le jardin de Bérénice* (Bérénice's Garden) (1891) (Reprint, Paris: Livre de poche, 1966), 105, my translation; and later: "The religious orders created a hygiene for the soul which seeks to love God; a similar hygiene will advance us in the adoration of the Self." "Les ordres religieux ont crée une hygiène de l'âme qui propose d'aimer Dieu; une hygiène analogue nous avancera dans l'adoration du *Moi*" (163); Foucault's phrase, *le souci de soi*, usually translated as "Care of the Self," also comes to mind to describe this breathtakingly self-satisfied form of ascesis, which is not unrelated to some of the sorriest examples of sadomasochism's indebtedness to Catholicism (e.g., Paul Claudel and Marcel Jouhandeau). Constable calls this a "Christomorphic . . . exercise of the senses," and points out its indebtedness to Baudelaire; she quotes another critic, Michel Beaujour, to the effect that it "modelizes the fantasies of an ego-trip" (296).

60. "Il nous a appris la grandeur de l'inquiétude et du désir." I: 177 (October 12, 1905).

61. Michèle le Doeuff, *Hipparchia's Choice: An Essay Concerning Women, Philosophy, etc.* (Oxford: Blackwell, 1991), 35.

62. Constable quotes *Sous l'oeil des barbares*, 241.

63. *Diary of a Philosophy Student*, 54; "je dois cultiver les nuances de mon moi et par respect pour le trésor déposé en moi-même, et pour autrui." Beauvoir refers directly to the second volume of the trilogy in her diary: "Oh! this profound necessity in me not to be what others desire me to be but what I am—it would be cowardly for me to steal away—cowardly to lie. But I am so weak that I desperately wish for one who understands. I am 'the free man' who suffices to himself alone, but all the same, to read in a friendly glance that one is right. . . ." (*Diary of a Philosophy Student*, 92). "Oh! cette profonde nécessité en moi de n'être pas ce que les autres désirent que je sois mais telle que je suis—ce serait lâche de m'y dérober—lâche de mentir. Mais j'y suis si faible qu'éperdument je souhaite un qui comprenne. Je suis 'l'homme libre' qui se suffit à soi seule; mais tout de même, lire dans un regard ami qu'on a raison. . . ." (*Cahiers de jeunesse*, 92–93).

64. *MDD* 192; "Cet apologue traduisait le plus obsédant de mes soucis: me défendre contre autrui; car si mes parents ne m'épargnaient pas leurs reproches, ils réclamaient ma confiance" (*MJFR* 265).

65. *MDD* 226–27; "Ma mère entrait, sortait, allait, venait, et se penchait sur mon épaule . . . Elle réclamait ma complicité et si je manquais d'allant, elle s'inquiétait. A quoi penses-tu? qu'est ce que tu as? Pourquoi fais-tu cette tête-la? Naturellement à ta mère tu ne veux rien dire." (*MJFR* 313).

66. *MDD* 193; "Je regardais dans la glace celle que leurs yeux voyaient: ce n'était pas moi; moi, j'étais absente, absente de partout; où me retrouver? . . . 'Vivre c'est mentir,' me disais-je. . . . Quelquefois, je pensais que les forces allaient me manquer et que je me résignerais à redevenir comme les autres" (*MJFR* 268).

67. "Petit garçon, tu n'avais pas tort de mépriser les cuistres" (150).

68. "Nous sommes les barbares, chantent-ils en se tenant par le bras, nous sommes les convaincus. Nous avons donné à chaque chose son nom; nous savons quand il convient de rire et d'être sérieux." (104).

69. See *MJFR* 470 for a description of the mockery Sartre and his male friends displayed toward "états d'âme" and "vie intérieure," which they seem to have regarded as a narcissistic and perverse swamp cultivated by "delicate souls."

70. "que l'important soit dans le regard" [*sic*].

71. André Gide, *Nourritures terrestres* (*The Fruits of the Earth*) (1897; reprint, Paris: Gallimard Folio, 1977).

72. *MDD* 194, translation altered; "Famille je vous hais! foyers clos, portes refermées" (*MJFR* 268).

73. "L'imprécation de Menalque m'assurait qu'en m'ennuyant dans la maison je servais une cause sacrée" (*MJFR* 268).

74. "on se donne de fortes émotions pour avoir l'illusion que cela vaut la peine de les avoir."

75. "Il y a des gens qui font les actes au contraire pour se persuader qu'ils sont ainsi."

76. "elle choisit que la vie soit tragique . . . nostalgie des anciennes souffrances."

77. *Force de l'âge*, 21.

78. "On *n'a pas* un Iris Storm," *MJFR* 454; "I admired Iris: her loneliness, her free-and-easy life, and her proud integrity. I lent the book to Herbaud. 'I have no liking for women of easy virtue,' he told me as he handed it back. . . . 'I find it impossible to respect any women I've had.' I was indignant. 'But one doesn't "have" an Iris Storm.' 'No woman surrenders herself with impunity to a man's most intimate embraces.'" (*MDD* 324).

79. Victor Margueritte, *La garçonne* (*The Bachelor Girl*) (1922; reprint, Paris: Flammarion, 1978); *MJFR* 247, *MDD* 178.

80. Virginia Woolf, *Between the Acts* (New York: Harcourt, 1941), 215.

81. "Ensemble nous avons lutté contre le destin fangeux qui nous guettait et j'ai pensé longtemps que j'avais payé ma liberté de sa mort" (*MJFR* 503).

82. "Il y a un livre que j'attends avec impatience, qui aura pour moi une valeur qu'aucun autre ne peut avoir, c'est le vôtre. Il me semble que je vois bien déjà ce qu'il sera; si cela ne doit pas nous ennuyer et vous être désagréable, apportez-moi ici au moins quelques-uns des pages que vous avez écrites: il me semble que j'ai presque un peu droit et je sais que j'en ai besoin . . . il n'y a pas au monde une chose plus douce que de sentir qu'il y a quelqu'un qui peut vous comprendre et sur l'amitié de qui vous pouvez compter absolument" (9).

NOTES FOR A NOVEL

by Simone de Beauvoir

TRANSCRIPTION BY SARAH GENDRON,
JUSTINE SARROT, AND SYLVIE LE BON DE BEAUVOIR
TRANSLATION BY SARAH GENDRON
NOTES BY SARAH GENDRON, MERYL ALTMAN,
AND SYLVIE LE BON DE BEAUVOIR

I
3rd part: decides to write—8 days pass: realizes as she sets herself before her table that she has not made up her mind—had thought she would write who she was and that the act of writing would express a being against which she could do nothing—realizes that she is free to choose herself [*libre de se choisir*]—[1]
When one says "I love" one takes oneself for a complete whole—
Love creates itself at each instant—

Am I a *substance*, posited [*posée*] once and for all?[2]

Plan:
I. Astonishment: effort to bring together images—philo[sophy]—impression and regret,
rereads the story while searching for it—astonishment in seeing there.
plan—

tells herself stories—
astonishment in seeing oneself so similar to oneself—promises to help her—drowsiness—

Upon awaking: she chooses that life be tragic—
Awakening: pathos that envelops her—Madeleine's phrase and her portrait: how do they not know—need to scream her tenderness out loud—

II.
Ideas to put at the end of her spiritual progress
Time mingled with the identical and the same (yes, undoubtedly)—and that one must not seek in today either one's diversity alone nor one's sameness—but oneself—*duration versus the instant*—[3]
the self—
and the marvelous world reconstructed in oneself alone—and
the recreation of the real on another plane
In love: impression that one's very being depends upon
something other than oneself—who am I? without this resistance
nothing in me would manifest itself—

III
the death of others (with respect to Pierre de Rêmes)—
the voraciousness of others—of Maurice—
in the period of deliverance, all the temptation to love once
again—nostalgia
for old sufferings . . . remorse almost . . .
that often we affirm first about ourselves what is least us—a false us, in uncertain wanderings, because we know that the rest will surely be discovered—
(G[eorgette] Lévy and me)[4]—

IV
Theme 7—necessity, freedom—disquiet [*inquiétude*][5] *and salvation—choice and obligation—*
The lie of the social.[6]
the lie of admiration—the lie of a certain cult of the self[7]—
the lie of Gide "may what really matters be in the look"[8] as one gives oneself strong emotions in order to create the illusion that it's worthwhile to have them—not the lie but the uselessness of love—

V
I describe a thought and do not judge it—I point out the connections that

might be made in the course of the thought, without admitting that they are really of value;
it is my impression about intelligence that I paint, not the fruit of this intellectual work, which will perhaps come later—

VI [Recto]
Essay toward an Ethics
the stumbling block is death—death is in time, thus free oneself from time—but (and here is the problem) not by turning away from things that are in time, and envisioning them in the category of the timeless—
the first condition is to believe in it—
the 2nd " " "
the 3rd " " "
To spiritualize the emotions—
utility of the work of art—
manage to split one's consciousness in two [*dédoubler*]: to be a spectator of what we do in time—but not like
Proust does, not at all—

finish describing this temptation of the worst and move on to the question: but what am I waiting for—4th dimension—
then *fear*—the uselessness of this?
distinguish between the two questions: self—and the rest?
and decide that even in the horror of the second one must stick with the first, which perhaps will resolve itself in that way—
(describe the moments when exaggerated sensitivity limits everything—a little farther)—*

VI [Verso]
At the moment of writing him in order to go to see him—
(imagine the thing: M would come with them to the country, etc.)—
hesitates—rereads her notes of the fortnight
sees that she believed she was only amusing herself but that here she is choosing—and that she is choosing to try again—authenticity of this act—(difficulty of the *choice*—does one have the right to commit [*engager*] tomorrow? (preserve her freedom)—farther

struggle between the first part and the second—

*The lines beginning with "finish describing . . ." until "a little farther" are written upside down on this page. The first two lines ("finish describing this temptation of the worst and move on to the question: but what am I waiting for—4th dimension—") were crossed out.

Link to the first part—show the whole path
traveled, the useless detours—etc.—
Liberated, she had found nothing in herself but emptiness [*vide*]—
had turned to the outside—returning to the self—
proclaiming her own values—remaking the world—
the first part of her task is achieved:
and the discovery of the world, of materials that she will use—
the conquest of oneself—the first part only—
the world is going to open up: the quest—creation—life—
(I. self—II. the non self—III. how will we join them together?)

VII
Book I of [*Leibniz:*] *New Essays* [*on Human Understanding*]*: innate ideas—*

"I would like no limit to be set to our analysis, definitions to be given of all terms which allow for them, and demonstrations—or the means for them—to be
provided for all axioms which are not primary. . . ."[9] (ed. [Emile] Boutroux, p.173)—
See also Erd. 87–339–343 Gerh. V 432–433.[10] Descartes who doubted too much, also abandoned doubt too easily—and also p. 278 ed. Boutroux.

"The truths that we start by being aware of are indeed particular ones, just as
we start with the coarsest and most composite ideas. But that does not alter
the fact that in the order of nature the simplest comes first, and that the reasons for particular truths rest wholly on the more general ones of which they
are mere instances."[11] ([ed. Boutroux], p. 189–190)*

Apply this to the relationship of the possible to the existent—of the individual to the species—

VIII

Outline

1st part
a) Family—the routine life
b) Deliverance: dream—relapses—love of self—
detachment,

*The quotation beginning "The truths . . ." has been crossed out.

boredom

c) Salvation through him—admiration pathos of existence[12]—collapse

2nd part

Erosion that continues—social responsibilities [*oeuvres*]—work—books—pity—love—

IX [Recto]

Outline for the 2nd part—

I. Farewell to Paris—promise of faithfulness—
vacation—conversations with her sister
—her brother and Jeanne whom she discovers—
attempt to construct an ethics—
why not live like them?
(it is the erosion that is beginning)

II. Return to Paris: resumption of activities, of her friendships—awareness
of her horrible solitude, of the necessity of choosing and that
no one can help us to be—
at least I will always have myself

III. 1st interaction with Maurice—what's the use?[13]
She tries to understand and understands only too
well: there is nothing there—her ethics collapses—
new vision of the world—
meets Monique—

IV. Continuation of her love—conversation with

IX [Verso]

Will renew

X

[IV. Continuation of her love—conversation with] Sombreuse—work,
social responsibilities [*oeuvres*], no longer bring her anything—
conversation with Monique—with Jeanne—
meets Pierre de Rêmes—
life is lived and *is not thought.*

V. Following up her love that is beginning to
unravel—suffering—effort to live
in the instant—why one
cannot—Jeanne abandons her—

VI. Disintegration of love and awareness of the nothingness where she tosses and turns—
suicide attempt—does not dare—begins to
try to numb herself—at this moment, review of all the books, of all the ethics, review of her entire life—

VII. story of the South American—burns
all bridges—non-marriage*—

VIII. Or maybe not: thought, research, spiritual and emotional drought—and then come back to Maurice in a magnificent union of her ability to feel and her heart, hopeful and full of life

---

she is going to try to write a book in order to not lose herself—
and then uselessness of herself—and then this love where she tries to put herself to use
—and then nothing—

---

from her moral doctrine first disappears the 2nd part: to be of service, then the 1st: to be—
to be somebody is more worthwhile than to do something—

XI [Recto]
Dream with eyes wide open and
not with eyes closed. The purity of
things is absolute but not relative;
things are perfectly beautiful;
it is perfect beauty that is not sufficient.
(write this to Ponti)[14]—about the dream—
(and not about philo[sophy]—)—
Plenitude of these instants and
not their humility—

XI [Verso]
To G[eorgette] Lévy: this landscape is enough for me:
To write: the mere gesture of placing this before me and looking at it: it's true, but so what? Unless the landscape then appeared
necessary—my existence has a

*The French reads "non-mariage." It is not clear whether the line between "non" and "mariage" is a hyphen or a dash. If it is a hyphen, the English would read "burns all bridges—non-marriage," which would seem to fit best with what follows. If it is a dash, we would understand it as "burns all bridges—no—marriage," as if not *all* bridges were burned after all.

necessity: if you admit that one can suppress death and prolong such moments to infinity, you will admit that
joy becomes something necessary, that
stops me in my tracks and obviates my desire to debate—I agree with you; that is what I am looking for.
But my joy is debatable,
at least when I no longer feel it,
so, [it] isn't *that*—

XII
Perfection—The Good—Utility
Conclude by showing why I believe this impression to be necessary.

XIII [Recto]
They embrace: A and B in each
other's arms. B' fills all of screen a and A' all of screen b so much so they are in one another's arms, both equally large—then A' becomes very pale and scenes follow one another in b; in a, B' is always [illegible]__________ several images,—the entire scene between A' and B.'* All interior life is unfolding in the background on the screen.

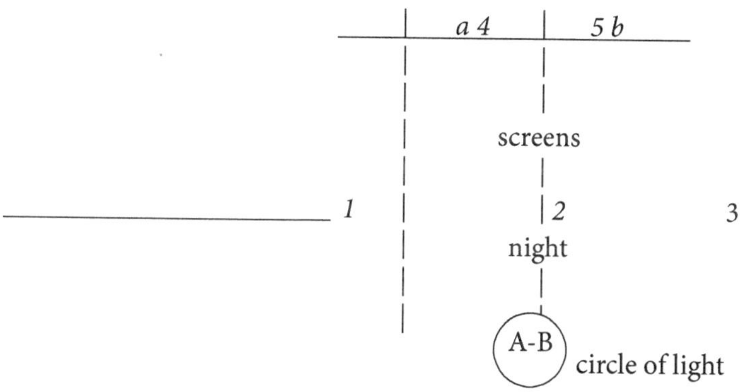

B wants to watch a;
Or again the screen becomes opaque.
4: screen where A sees his/her life
5: screen where B sees his/her life
2: opaque wall

Asks A' to tell everything
A describes a; on b we
see very different images born.

*Single quotation marks follow all capital A and B's in the original except for the first two ("A and B in each other's arms.").

better

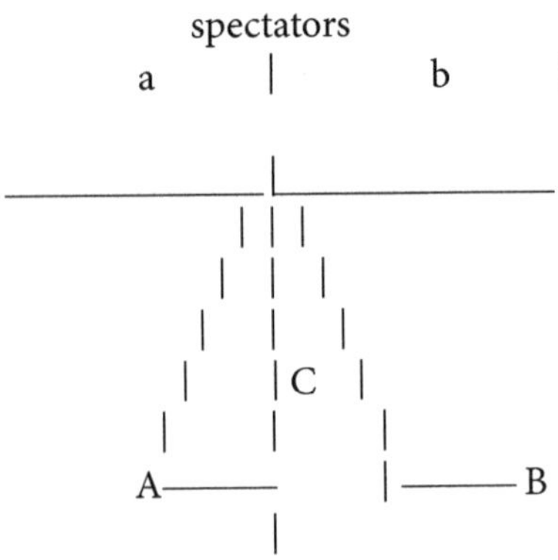

[sketch later crossed out]

[Upside down on the same sheet]
During vacation, write a play about the following Gidisme: the same event seen by 3 or 4 different beings—find a *mise en scène* that expresses this.

3 compartments:	A-B and a phonograph c—	c°		C+		C+
	A C and a phonograph b—		+B		°b	B+
	B C and a phonograph a—	A+				
				+A		°a

XIII [Verso]
Prologue: Jacques and Jeannine—They love each other.
Their parents want to separate them—
Promises to not forget each other—
Each of their lives: in 2 separate compartments—

Their encounter—

XIV [Recto]
It should be said that he continues to refuse—
that she also knows that he can do nothing—
and his remorse*—

*The passage, "It should . . . remorse" is written on the right side of the page, from top to bottom so that if the page were held right-side-up, these lines would appear to the right and sideways.

Insist on these *poetic* rules that command her life—which makes the most idealist novel seem vulgar when compared with this mystery to which she enslaves herself—tell of her love and of that together*—

Torture for Denise, who accuses herself of not knowing how to keep Maurice with her—
when she wants to try it, her torture of dreaming that she could dare to hope
to diminish this suffering that overwhelms [*dépasser*] her and that she lives in a heartrending sympathy†—

XIV [Verso]
I.
The Misunderstanding
Essay

XV [Recto]
Le cycle du printemps—Tagore[15]—
St. Augustin—L. Bertrand[16]—
Poèmes barbares—L. de Lisle[17]—
Vie de Haydn—Mozart—Métastase Stendhal[18]—
Pascal, Ibsen, Dostoïevsky—Suarès[19]—
Un nouveau Moyen Age[20]
Maurice de Guérin[21]—

Mireille—Opéra[22]*—Gueule d'amour*[23]*—Réflexions sur l'intelligence*[24]

Memory actualized in images differs profoundly from this pure memory (in this sense the past is conserved in the present)‡—

XV [Verso]
Le bachelier sans vergogne—Marchon[25]—
Proust—Léon Pierre-Quint[26]—
Apollinaire vivant—Billy[27]—
L'Evangéliste—Daudet§[28]—
La philosophie de Leibniz—Russell[29]—

*The passage, "Insist . . . together," is on the left side of the page, written from bottom to top.

†The passage, "Torture . . . sympathy," is on the right side of the page, written from top to bottom.

‡The passage, "Memory . . . present," is on the right side, written from top to bottom.

§The list beginning "Le bachelier" and ending "Daudet," is very faint, barely legible.

Discours de métaphysique—Leibniz—
Le livre de chants—Heine[30]—
Le problème moral—Jean Baruzi[31]—
Les pas perdus—André Bréton[32]—
81 chapitres sur l'esprit et les passions—Alain[33]—

Le sophiste }
} Plato
Philèbe }

St. François d'Assise—Chesterton[34]—*La divine comédie*—Dante—
Entretiens sur la métaph[*ysique*]—Malebranche[35]—
La recherche de la vérité—Malebranche[36]—
Tels qu'ils furent—Estaunié[37]—
Le language—Vendryès[38]—
Solitudes—Estaunié[39]—
Battling Malone—Louis Hémon[40]
Les soirs—Les débâcles—Flambeaux noirs—Les Apparus dans mes chemins—Les extases illusoires, les vignes de ma muraille—
Verhaeren[41]—
Théâtre d'Eschyle—
Ennéades—Plotinus—
Le désir de Dieu chez Plotin—René Arnou[42]—

XVI [Recto]
****
basis of human life.
(Feeling of
continuity.)*
****

this blame comes back to Monique—
then from her to Maurice—goes to see him after a sad evening—
chatting about freedom—that was too perfect—pain†—

so what was she waiting for?
Perhaps for him to take her and throw her across his horse that would

*The passage: "basis of human life. (Feeling of *continuity*)" is not in the handwriting of Simone de Beauvoir.
†The lines, "basis ... continuity" and "this blame . . ." "too perfect—pain" are written upside-down.

carry her away in spite of herself, panting, submissive, toward a tower
where happiness would guard her
jealously—for him to order this defeat
to which for him she would have the cowardice to consent, helpless to consummate it for herself alone—
he didn't ask for anything;
he didn't approach; he left her alone
with her pain of living—and he didn't
ask her at all to take part in his own [pain]*—

XVI [Verso]

Plan

Profoundly shaken by the beauty of what they are realizing—
tears,†—desire to leave—
there is nothing left—the instants die—
torment all the greater for being shared—
finds herself weak again—Sombreuse—no—
tears at night like a little girl: enough—goes to see him—leaves him with a heart heavy with waiting, never fulfilled—still, the joy of being able to do something for
his joy—his severity—he is right—but how she suffers!—
seeks him in books—everywhere—cannot bear her
suffering—wants to come closer (why torture us so?)
impossible—
Everyone abandons her—constructs on their greatness a bitter joy‡—
yet remain united—
boredom slips in between them—joy of leaving—
conversations about literature—about art (music and painting)—almost brutal

---

*The passage, "so what was she . . . his own [pain]," is written on the right-hand side of the paper.

†"tears" is written above "realizing."

‡The French reads "se construit sur leur grandeur un âpre joie." It is difficult to know how to interpret this. It could be that "she" is the subject of "se construit"—in which case these words imply that she receives a bitter joy in the greatness she perceives in those who abandon her (perhaps precisely *because* they abandon her). However, the subject of "se construit" might also be the bitter joy, in which case we might understand it to mean that those who abandon her take some pleasure in abandoning her, but it is but a bitter joy that is created from this act. This second option seems to fit better with the line that follows: "yet remain [plural form of the verb] united." In other words, even though the joy created and which they receive from abandoning her is bitter, they remain, nonetheless, united (in their abandonment).

opposition (she often leaves in
anguish, feeling everything has been ruined) however with him alone, she is in harmony—
it is exactly the inverse of the habitual hostility that is the shame of love—
their love recognized brings them together in an accepted complicity—
it is in friendship that they contradict each other—not to take pleasure in offending—but because inevitably they differ from one another—

XVII [Recto]
Theme 1—About oneself—a) In ch. 1 model of equilibrium in an other—portrait of her in her friends—her self is engaged in the mechanical—then in ch. 2: can't dreaming be the truth—an act through which the repressed self expresses itself. Oscillation between her two selves—in ch. 3: reign of the true self discovered—it is this alone that lives—show in ch. 4, in the impression that this gives someone else, how there is oscillation or slippage again from one plane to the other: during pure contemplation, the first self makes itself disappear [*s'abolir*]; as soon as she performs old gestures, the old self comes back and she wonders whether the first [self] wasn't just a figment of the imagination [*chimère*]; her body is not yet emancipated. When she remains in her interior world she is sure of her *reality*[;]
when she wants to express it outside, routine takes her back: since she is conscious of *opposing herself* [*s'opposer à elle*], this suggests that she is not yet saved (insist upon this).[43]
b) further in the 2nd part when she writes to Maurice astonishment about this again, that this could express itself, but conscious however this time that it is really her in her entirety; no more strangeness but sense of the irreparable
*Write an essay of 10 large pages about the personality**
in the 3rd part, she rediscovers this impression that she is putting on an act, that this intellectual personality
because she believes that there is inside her an unchanging given†
she pretends to have this intellectual personality but in fact does not;
in the act (that is, the temptation to drop everything and to come see him), she realizes that it's really all of her that's completely engaged there—remembers the 1st part. This happens because the self is not yet accustomed [illegible] to its

*The following phrase is written between the lines in a different color, blue ink, suggesting a later addition: "Write an essay of 10 large pages about the personality."

†The following phrase is written between the lines in a different color, blue ink, suggesting a later addition: "because she believes that there is inside her an unchanging given."

*freedom**
new position; the memory of the old one is more present to it than even the new,
or considers it to be finished†
one experienced it in an act, one still remains in a vague dream world. The act, once complete, teaches us about the force of this; we become accustomed to it; thus we are astonished, when we accomplish the act, to see that it really was *we*, who did it, that we were living what we had thought we only imagined.
we are what we wish to be [*voulons être*]‡
The horror of *indecision* is precisely here, in not knowing our *real* selves (as in the 3rd part when she writes to Maurice for the 1st time).

(in letters one can study a decision in the pure state, but a *presence* can intimidate us, affective and physical elements and so forth come into play: words which stick in one's throat, and so on. *Study this*)§

> *The act* is *the affirmation* of ourselves—did this "ourselves" then *not exist* [*n'était pas*] before the act? Or were we just unsure that it existed? Does the act acquaint us with ourselves, or does it create us? (among the most important points) But *are* we everything we don't know we *are*? Make the distinction between act and *choice*, in Part One she doesn't *choose*. In part three she chooses. The role of *words* in this affirmation of self (a phrase of Madeleine's, a conversation with Monique) Meditate on this, and develop it—
> *3rd part complement*‖
> become what you are? do you know yourself? do you see yourself?#
>
> (a letter is sent at 2 times: one writes it without thinking that one will send it—one sends it without thinking that one wrote it.)**

*The following word is written between the lines in a different color, blue ink, suggesting a later addition: "freedom."

†The following phrase is written between the lines in a different color, blue ink, suggesting a later addition: "or considers it to be finished."

‡The following phrase is written between the lines in a different color, blue ink, suggesting a later addition: "we are what we wish to be."

§The following passages are crossed out: "in letters one can study a decision in the pure state, but a *presence* can intimidate us, affective and physical elements and so forth come into play: words which stick in one's throat, and so on. *Study this*."

‖The following phrase is written between the lines in a different color, blue ink, suggesting a later addition: "*3rd part complement*."

#The following passage is enclosed in a box: "The act is the affirmation. . . . do you see yourself?"

**The following passage is written in blue ink, suggesting a later addition, and crossed out: " (—a letter is sent at 2 times: one writes it without thinking that one will send it—one sends it without thinking that one wrote it)."

XVII [Verso]
There are people who act in contradictory ways to persuade themselves that's what they are like—(J. Rivière perhaps a little). P. de Rêmes will be like this—
Denise will become conscious of this: she has the impression she's putting on an act but she isn't. While he believes he's sincere, which he is not.

Jeannine: no inner life despite her intelligence—
Monique: inner life, knowledge but she doesn't feel strongly about it—
Sombreuse: action
P. de Rêmes: dilettante of the inner life—
Maurice: lost in his inner life, impossible to get it under control—

How does an evolution come about?
sometimes one asserts that one is sure of a position, one puts it aside and goes deeper into the other out of curiosity; without realizing it, one gets used to the latter and if one suddenly comes face to face with the former, one is conscious of having departed from it—

Sometimes on the contrary it is the 2nd idea that one puts aside and which silently makes its way in us—
and one becomes aware that in each . . .*
collapse of the other, sadder than the 1st way.

XVIII [Recto]
Powerlessness of love—their solitude—
compassion [*attendrissement*]—
 and where are the words that have never been said?—
Portrait of Maurice and of the future disappointments that will bring this one back anew and sometimes it's he who would like and she who doesn't want—
Yielding and springing back up—
his regrets and how oppressive their power is now—

that the subject would not be chosen by each but, so to speak, would emerge in the course of the discussion itself and that someone would then take responsibility for going into it more deeply, without anything being arranged ahead of time—etc.
That the secretary each time would summarize the essential points of the discussion and the conclusions reached. That we should have a written

*The following passage is crossed out: "and one becomes aware that in each."

list of the members of the group and send them the minutes when they are unable to attend. Only to take in members who have committed themselves to attending. Everything depends on how much interest the few interesting students we can reach will bring to this project, and on the degree of mutual understanding that can be reached—Only do something if we have the means to do it seriously, but if so, it might be fruitful*

As the school year begins—excitement about her life—
Her joy that is waiting and the entire resumption of contact—2 long pages to write tomorrow—with Jeannine: rejoices that they are getting along well, and yet feels that she would not even want anyone to judge them as inferior but totally
foreign—that they are not worth these nuances.†

XVIII [Verso]
The soul and the body
D. climbs the staircase, estranged from P. and all the rest, why?
when she sees M. who she hadn't realized was on her mind she understands (or rather does not understand) that the anticipation of his presence had cast a shadow over everything else.
D's irritation before the sadness that she believes to be weakness and imagination; *she*
never cries.
A few dismal days: void after the great revelation and in
this void, doubt about what used to be—astonishment—awakenings—the absent taste of life—then lunch and the horrible impression of routine: *portrait of her family*—story about the scarab—etc.

was that me?
I was crazy—that madwoman is dead: but not so dead that the void does not remain—a few days pass—desire . . .‡

XIX
Shows the books to Jeannine—J. explains, understands: jealousy—M. enthusiasm that she shows—vague uneasiness: that's it, evidently, better than D. had seen. But it is reduced to a thing that can be debated

*The passage, "that the subject . . . it might be fruitful," is upside-down, on the bottom of the page.

†The passage, "As the school year . . . not worth these nuances," is upside-down and is mixed in with the text above.

‡The passage, "was that me . . . desire," is upside-down.

and summarized, it is no longer a "head" [?]; try through this to [illegible drawing of a large M or A?]
speak of her deeper life: the nonsense of J. who makes fun of the world, but ironically by staying on the same level. She puts herself 1st and scorns the others for being lower: that still classifies her among them. Denise is simply elsewhere: misunderstanding of which J. is not aware, sure of always
understanding everything: she understands everything in intellectual terms, she *feels nothing*—She isn't endowed with this deep sympathy, which alone can uncover a soul
Denise keeps her friendship: these things cannot be said. It is a friendship of youth and not childhood friendship: moreover, does not clash with J[eannine]who permits her to maintain her illusion: they are of the same opinion,
which is why D's reason condemns the malaise in her heart.

Jeannine *social climber*: objections of Denise; how they are refuted—to top it off, J. believes in these reasons that she gives—*

tomorrow: 3 pages—finish J. and up until Maurice's party—
contempt for the world: Jeannine continues to cultivate it—
the excuse: contempt for scholastic success: J. seeks it—
the excuse—
Later notices that she admires but does not let herself be influenced: "when it seemed to her that her friend was getting ahead of her . . . jealousy."
when she lagged behind, sighs and regret—

XX [Recto]
She did not doubt that life was beautiful—nor that beings were beautiful—only that this beauty was sufficient
(with Monique)—

he is not there—practice of the other—leaves a note inviting him over for tea; he does not come—comes the following day—
Madeleine stays with them—(doubt, anguish, nausea . . .)—
Sees him again: everything forgotten—joy—Champs Elysées—elation of the instant—wants to tell him about it—their mutual suffering—

*A triangular drawing separates this last line and the lines that follow.

and they are no longer self and the other but two children alone together—
fear of this love that is coming—
around 40 pages

goes to see him, joy! joy on the Champs Elysées*—
irreparable—love returns—surprised that she disperses herself in such useless analyses—what does it matter? live in the instant—
tea, he doesn't come—then he does come—his coldness (?)
and again a tragic failure: for love is too big to play around with

renew
prohibition
they reject†

XX [Verso]
Ch. I—Begin with the scene with M—follow her during the walk—
Arrival at the department store: impression of the new school year—
anticipation of life that is opening up. 1st resumption of contact—a tea party, then a dinner-party, then a soirée—returns home and recovers her serenity—

The coffee is served—Denise stretched out in a corner dreams of her childhood in this study—
the way he looks today baffles her; describe it, however and explain this—"naturally it is Madeleine who serves the coffee" says her mother—
acknowledgment by D.—why can't I ever be like Madeleine—

The impression of routine will be produced the following day—today she is not living it—

thus she deftly conjured away the disharmony between the ongoing rhythm of our inner thoughts and the series of objects that tend to turn up, and she brought some beauty into the present and filled this present with the memory of the past.

XXI
Write the struggle of a young man who does not live for the world—of a young woman who lives for the world—have them meet in the Limousin

*The lines "goes to see him, joy! Joy on the Champs Elysées" were inserted between the lines that precede and follow them.

†The words "renew . . . reject," appear on the bottom, far right-hand side of the page.

country and wander at night by the marshes, hearing the distant voices of men—she feels the exigencies of his God [*de son Dieu*] and reveals this to him [the young man], thus helping to push him away from her.—
he suffers from her too ardent love of the world and of the wet leaves—

the transcendent—immanent link { conflicting conceptions of the world—

art—literature—
spiritual life—and inner life—
charity and love of self—
she: her impression that he "is leaving her behind"—dialogue with his God from which she is excluded—
has the impression of being a soul to be saved—that he lies in wait for her—
she fears his pity and his indulgence, which *knows*—
he: suffers from this resistance in her—doesn't really understand and feels that she doesn't understand his love transposed toward God—
their ideas on marriage: sacrament or human choice. Impossible to live together. "my God here I am" in the garden heavy with roses
and she, blinded by her own tears as she hears the whistle of the train, rushing her onward toward some new and unknown passion—

They'll have to be very young and very excessive—
The young woman will come to give lessons to the young man's sister—
3–4 months (July to October)—

XXII

Portrait of Maurice

Until the age of 20 pursued his studies—presented at conferences—occupied himself with good works—then disgust with this, *disquiet* [*inquiétude*] that eats away at him—turns away from literature, from everything—amuses himself by founding a journal, which turns out well—but always in pain, tormented, and the reticence about his torment—
At times very serious—infinitely so, at other times, the opposite, not ironic, but *bitter* and almost sneering (depict him faithfully)—return of tenderness and then irritation, not this "to hell with everything" attitude that I sometimes attributed to him, sometimes tender, ready to give up everything "ah! I will make her happy"—then the impossibility of that—discontented with his apparent inconstancy, which he nonetheless knows is right;—gives up in the end: "I'm an idiot!" And this is the indecisive year

when he moves toward denying everything and separates from Denise—then the betrayal in effect—

Pierre de Rêmes

This affectation: this irony that I attributed to Maurice. It amuses him to be complicated; he turns it into poems. Treats joy as a game, pretends to take nothing too seriously—artist—a kind of double life between his life and his works [*dédoublement*]: doesn't engage himself in depth in any of the things he does—indulgence and not hate—

long conversations with Denise where she will expound to him upon his "Gideisms," where they will look for stances to take about life; description of this charming intimacy—

insist on the portraits of people—do a few of them carefully—

Sombreuse—

XXIII [Recto]

In remembrance of the weeks we spent together in Gagnepan[44] and especially of that night when we said so many things—and of those very things we said. In remembrance of all that part of life which belongs to the two of us and which we will never forget—

S. de Beauvoir, 24 September, 1928

For the

What are you thinking about Denise—"nothing, Mother!" And was this even a lie?

Necessity but [unintelligible]—pose the question of salvation—about the possibility

of optimism—

Renunciation*—

XXIII [Verso]

Buy 4 large format notebooks with graph paper,

long, each one 90 pages—(from 50–60 lines per page and

around 50 characters per line)—recopy the 1st part of my novel in its entirety

during vacation (after having redone the outline of each chapter in July and

*The passage beginning with "For the . . ." and ending with "Renunciation" is upside-down on the page. In addition, the words "For the" were crossed out.

looking at each passage again for style little by
little as I will recopy it)—
have at least two copies typed by the beginning of the school year—
all the while recopying the 2nd part until the end of January—
have R.[Ramon] Fernandez read it if possible—

NOTES

"Notes for a Novel," tentatively dated 1928, is comprised of twenty-three leaves of holograph notes on small sheets of paper, almost all of which are bank deposit slips from the BPF (Banque Populaire Française). The exceptions are p. 16 (recto and verso)—which is a sheet of business stationary from the Onoto fountain pen company—and p. 23 (recto and verso)—which is a plain sheet of unlined notepaper. The manuscript is housed in and published by courtesy of the Department of Special Collections, Memorial Library, University of Wisconsin-Madison. © Sylvie Le Bon de Beauvoir.

1. "Libre de se choisir" can mean "to choose herself," as well as "to choose *for* herself," as in the conclusion of *L'invitée*, where Beauvoir writes of Francoise's decision to kill Xavière: "Elle avait enfin choisi. Elle s'était choisie" (Paris: Gallimard, 1943), 503; trans. Yvonne Moyse and Roger Senhouse as *She Came to Stay* (New York: Norton, 1954), 404.

2. Questions about whether the self is a fixed, self-identical substance, once and for all, and her discussion on the following page of how human experience of time and space as both unified and multiple makes that problematic, draw upon Henri Bergson's *Essai sur les données immediates de la conscience*, 1927, repr. Quadrige 2003, trans. F. L Pogson as *Time and Free Will: An Essay on the Immediate Data of Consciousness* (London: George Allen and Unwin, 1910). XVII below returns to this philosophical question of the self, which was apparently intended to be the major philosophical theme of the projected novel.

3. Again, see Bergson, and Altman's introduction preceding this translation. The entire passage in French reads, "Le temps mêlé d'identique et de même (oui, sans doute)—et qu'il faut chercher dans aujourd'hui ni sa diversité ni sa similitude—mais lui-même—la durée contre l'instant—le moi. et le monde merveilleux en soi seul reconstruit-et la recréation du réel sur un autre plan—Dans l'amour: impression que son être même dépend de quelque chose autre qu'elle- qui suis-je? sans cette résistance rien de moi ne se manifesterait—"

4. Georgette Lévy, Beauvoir's fellow philosophy student and friend from the Sorbonne (see, e.g., Beauvoir, *Diary of a Philosophy Student: 1926–27* [Urbana: University of Illinois Press, 2006], 230, 265).

5. *Inquiétude* has no exact English equivalent. An important keyword of the period, it was used by and about Gide and others, and applied to a kind of adolescent "*nouveau mal de siècle*" experienced by people like Beauvoir's cousin Jacques. See *Memoires d'un jeune fille rangée*, 269–272, 278.

6. Beauvoir may be referring here to the way the whole of social life can be a lie, especially the way "oeuvres sociales"—good works of the sort engaged in by Garric et al.—turn out to be a lie; the whole philosophical mistake of seeing things in social terms.

7. "*Culte du moi*" refers to the theories/plan for life espoused by Maurice Barrès in his

trilogy of novels (*Sous l'œil des barbares/ Un homme libre/ Le jardin de Bérénice*). As we see in the student diaries, Beauvoir had been very taken by this (following the lead of Alain-Fournier and Jacques Rivière) but now she has outgrown it.

8. See André Gide, *Les nourritures terrestres* (*The Fruits of the Earth*) (1897; Paris: Gallimard [Livre de Poche], 1964), 21: "Que *l'importance* soit dans ton regard, non dans la chose regardée."

9. The English translation is from book one, chapter one of *Leibniz: New Essays on Human Understanding*, by G. W. Leibniz; trans. Peter Remnant and Jonathan Bennett (Cambridge: Cambridge University Press, 1981), 75.

10. *Erd.* refers to Joannes Eduardus Erdmann, ed., G. W. Leibniz, *Opera Philosophica Omnia—quae exstant latina gallica germanica omnia.* (The Complete Surviving Philosophical Works in French, Latin, and German) (G. Eichleri, 1840) ; *Gerh.* presumably refers to C. I. Gerhardt, ed., Gottfried Wilhelm Leibniz, *Die philosophischen Schriften* (*Philosophical Writings*) (Berlin: Weidmann, 1875–90).

11. The English translation is from book one, chapter one, of *Leibniz: New Essays on Human Understanding*, 84.

12. "pathos of existence," "*pathétique de l'existence.*" In the original, there is a very faint line underneath the "n" of "*admiration*" and the "p" of "*pathétique.*" If we read the line as a dash separating "*admiration*" and "*pathétique de l'existence,*" we might understand these words as "Salvation through him—admiration—the pathos of existence—collapse." However, if we read the line as an accidental pen mark, we might read these words as "Salvation through him—pathetic/heartrending admiration of existence—collapse." The adjective, "*pathétique,*" may thus apply to "admiration" rather than "existence."

13. *À quoi bon?*—what's the use?—is a recurring refrain in Beauvoir's early philosophical essay, *Pyrrhus et Cinéas* (Paris: Gallimard, 1944), translated as "Pyrrhus and Cineas" in Beauvoir's *Philosophical Writings* (Urbana: University of Illinois Press, 2004), which argues for engagement with the world through concrete, self-chosen projects. In the opening dialogue (drawn from Plutarch) Cinéas can't see the point of the conquests Pyrrhus, king of Epirus, is planning—if each victory just leads to another campaign, why not just stay home and rest? Cinéas may remind us of cousin Jacques: "Je le pressais d'écrire; j'étais certain qu'il ferait de beaux livres, s'il voulait: 'À quoi bon?,' me répondait-il. Et le dessin, la peinture: 'À quoi bon?' A toutes mes suggestions, il opposait ses trois petits mots. 'Jacques s'obstine à vouloir bâtir dans l'absolu; il devrait pratiquer Kant,' notai-je un jour avec naïveté." *Memoires d'une jeune fille rangée*, 301. The English version reads:"I would urge him to write; I was sure he had some fine books in him. 'What's the use?' he would reply. What about drawing and painting? He had the gifts. He still replied: 'What's the use?' He countered all my suggestions with those three little words. 'Jacques still persists in wanting to build on absolute foundations; he should study Kant; he won't get anywhere like this,' I naively noted in my diary one day." *Memoirs of a Dutiful Daughter*, trans. James Kirkup (New York: Harper Colophon Books, 1974), 217–18.

14. Ponti: Maurice Merleau-Ponty, Beauvoir's friend and fellow philosophy student, whom she first met in June, 1927; see Beauvoir's *Diary of a Philosophy Student*, 1926–27, 274, 281–82, etc.

15. Rabindranath Tagore, *Le Cycle du printemps* (*The Cycle of Spring*), trans. H. Mirabaud-Thorens (Paris: Stock, 1926).

16. Louis Bertrand, *St. Augustin*, 1913.

17. Charles Marie René Leconte de Lisle (1818–94), Parnassien poet and French translator of Greek tragedy; *Poésies barbares* (*Poems on the Barbarian Races*) (Paris: Librairie Poulet-Malassis, 1862).

18. Stendhal [Marie-Henri Beyle], 1793–1842, *Vies de Haydn, Mozart et Métastase* (*The Lives of Haydn, Mozart and Métastase*) (1817).

19. Andre Suarès, *Trois hommes: Pascal, Ibsen, Dostoïevski* (Three Men: Pascal, Isben, Dostoïevski) (Paris: Gallimard, 1913).

20. Nicolas Berdiaeff, *Un nouveau Moyen-Age: Réflexions sur les destinées de la Russie et de l'Europe* (*The New Middle Ages: Reflections on the Destinies of Russia and Europe*) translated from the Russian (Paris: Plon, 1927).

21. Maurice de Guérin, French poet, 1810–39. His sister Eugénie was known for her journals and letters.

22. *Mireille* is a five-act opera with music by Charles Gounod and libretto by Michel Carré, based on the poem by Frédéric Mistral. It was first performed in 1864 at the Théâtre Lyrique.

23. André Beucler, *Gueule d'amour (Lady Killer)* (1926).

24. Jacques Maritain, *Reflexions sur l'intelligence et sur sa vie propre* (Reflections on Intelligence and on Life Itself) (Paris: Nouvelle Libraierie Nationale, 1924).

25. Albert Marchon, *Le bachélier sans vergogne* (The Shameless Bachelor) (Paris: Grasset, 1925).

26. Léon Pierre-Quint [Léon Steindecker], "*Marcel Proust, sa vie, son oeuvre,*" *suivi de* "*Le comique et le mystère chez Proust*" (*Marcel Proust: His Life and Work, followed by Comedy and Mystery in Proust*) (Paris: Sagittaire, 1927).

27. André Billy, *Apollinaire Vivant* (Living Apollinaire) (Paris: Editions de la sirène, 1923); Memoir of the modernist poet (1880–1918).

28. Alphonse Daudet (1840–97), *L'évangéliste* (*The Evangelist*) (Paris: Dentu, 1883); a novel.

29. Bertrand Russell, *La philosophie de Leibniz. Exposé critique* (Paris: F. Alcan, Bibliothèque de Philosophie Contemporaine, 1908), trans. Jean Ray and Renée J. Ray of *A Critical Exposition of the Philosophy of Leibniz* (Cambridge: University Press, 1900).

30. Heinrich [Henri] Heine (1797–1856), German-Jewish poet who lived in Paris after 1831, *Livre des chants*, translation of *Buch der Lieder* (*Book of Songs*) (1827).

31. Jean Baruzi, editor, *Philosophes et savants Français du XXe Siècle III. Le problème moral* (French Philosophers and Scholars on the 20th Century III: The Moral Problem) (Paris: Librairie Félix Alcan, 1926).

32. André Breton, *Les pas perdus* (*The Lost Steps*) (Paris, 1924).

33. Alain [Émile-Auguste Chartier], *81 chapitres sur l'esprit et les passions* (81 Chapters about the Spirit and Passions) (Paris: l'émancipatrice, 1917).

34. G[ilbert] K[eith] Chesterton (1874–1936), English writer and journalist; *St. François d'Assise* (Paris, Plon [coll. "Le roseau d'or"], 1925), French translation by Isabelle Rivière of *St. Francis of Assisi* (1923).

35. Nicolas de Malebranche (1638–1715), "*Entretiens sur la métaphysique, et la religion,*" *suivis d'extraits des* "*entretiens sur la mort*" (Dialogues on Metaphysics and on Religion, followed by Extracts from Dialogues on Death) (1688; Paris: Armand Colin, 1922).

36. Malebranche, *De la recherche de la vérité où l'on traite de la nature de l'esprit de l'homme, & de l'usage qu'il en doit faire pour éviter l'erreur dans les sciences. Quatrième*

édition revue et augmentée de plusieurs éclaircissements (*The Search after Truth. In Which Is Treated the Nature of the Human Mind and the Use That Must Be Made of It to Avoid Error in the Sciences.* 4th Edition Reviewed and Enlarged with Several Elucidations) (Amsterdam: Henry Desbordes, 1688).

37. Édouard Estaunié (1862–1942), Novelist and engineer; *Tels qu'ils furent* (The Way They Were) (1927).

38. Joseph Vendryès (1875–1960), *Le langage, introduction linguistique à l'histoire*, (*Language: A Linguistic Introduction to History*) (1921) (reprint Albin Michel, 1968).

39. Estaunié, *Solitudes* (1922).

40. Louis Hémon, *Battling Malone, pugiliste* (Paris: Le Livre Moderne Illustré, 1926).

41. Emile Verhaeren (1855–1916), Belgian symbolist free verse poet; *Les soirs* (Evenings) (1887), *Les débâcles* (*Debacles*) (1888), *Les flambeaux noirs* (Black Torches) (1891), Les apparus dans mes chemins (The Apparitions on my Paths) (1891), *Les villages illusoires* (Illusory Villages) (1895), *Les vignes de ma muraille* (The Vines on my Wall) (1899). Beauvoir must have mistakenly referred to his *Les villages illusoires* as *Les extases illusoires*.

42. René Arnou, *Le désir de Dieu dans la philosophie de Plotin* (The Desire for God in the Philosophy of Plotinus) (Paris: F. Alcan, 1921).

43. Beauvoir's discussion of the deep self of inner reality vs. the social self, which is involved with routine gestures, what others see us as, again reflects her reading of Bergson's *Essai sur les données immédiates de la conscience* (*Time and Free Will: An Essay on the Immediate Data of Consciousness*).

44. Gagnepan: the country home of Beauvoir's close childhood friend, Elisabeth LaCoin, known as Zaza.

Contributors

MERYL ALTMAN is professor of English and Women's Studies at DePauw University in Indiana. Her essays about Simone de Beauvoir have appeared in *Feminist Studies, Hypatia, le Cinquantenaire du Deuxième Sexe*, and *Critical Quarterly*. She has also published on Faulkner, Sappho, Djuna Barnes, and various topics in feminist theory and the history of sexuality and writes regularly for the *Women's Review of Books*.

SYLVIE LE BON DE BEAUVOIR, the adopted daughter of Simone de Beauvoir, is editor of several volumes by Simone de Beauvoir including *Lettres à Sartre* (1990); *Journal de guerre* (1990); *Lettres à Nelson Algren: Un amour transatlantique* (1997); *Correspondance croisée*, with Jacques-Laurent Bost (2004), and *Cahiers de jeunesse* (2008).

ELIZABETH FALLAIZE (1950–2009) was pro-vice chancellor of the University of Oxford. In 1989 she was the first woman ever appointed an Official Fellow of St. John's College, Oxford, and, in 2002, she was awarded a professorship in French literature. She was coeditor of *French Studies* (1996–2004) and a series editor for the Oxford University Press. Her books include: *The Novels of Simone de Beauvoir* (1988); *French Women's Writing: Recent Fiction* (1993); *Simone de Beauvoir: A Critical Reader* (1998); *French Fiction in the Mitterrand Years,* cowritten with Colin Davis (2000); and *The Oxford Book of French Short Stories* (2002). She was appointed by the French Government an Officier dans l'ordre des palmes académiques in 2002 and promoted to Commandeur in 2009.

ALISON S. FELL is professor of French Cultural History at the University of Leeds, UK. She has published several books and articles on twentieth-century French women's history, thought, and writing, including *Liberty, Equality, Maternity in Beauvoir, Leduc and Ernaux* (Legenda, 2003). Her current research project focuses on women and the First World War, and her monograph on this topic, entitled *Back to the Front: Women and the Legacy of the First World War in France and Britain, 1914–1933*, will be published in 2012.

SARAH GENDRON is professor of French Language and Literature at Marquette University. She received her PhD in French from the University of Wisconsin-Madison. The author of *Repetition, Difference, and Knowledge in the Work of Samuel Beckett, Jacques Derrida, and Gilles Deleuze,* Gendron has published in the areas of literary and aesthetic theory, propaganda studies, and foreign language pedagogy. Gendron's current research focuses on the relationship between art, language, and genocide.

DENNIS A. GILBERT is currently a doctoral candidate in French at Boston College and a lecturer in French at the University of Massachusetts, Boston. His principal areas of scholarly interest include Jean-Paul Sartre, Simone de Beauvoir, Albert Camus, dramatic theory, and literary criticism. His dissertation is entitled "Sartre's Esthetic of Theater: From Childhood Gesture to Postwar Action."

LAURA HENGEHOLD is the author of *The Body Problematic: Political Imagination in Kant and Foucault* and other articles on Michel Foucault, Simone de Beauvoir, and feminist philosophy with French antecedents. She teaches feminist philosophy and political philosophy at Case Western Reserve University in Cleveland.

ELEANORE HOLVECK (1942–2009) was associate professor in the philosophy department at Duquesne University, where she initiated the Women's and Gender Studies Center and served, during the 1990s, as chair of the philosophy department. Her specializations were the philosophical novel and the ethics of Immanuel Kant. She authored *Simone de Beauvoir: Philosophy of Lived Experience* (2002).

After graduating first in French and then in Philosophy, **TERRY KEEFE** spent much of his career teaching and researching at Leicester University, UK. During the 1980s he was head of the French department and dean of the Faculty of Arts there, before becoming professor of French Studies at Lancaster University in 1988. His publications include monographs on Simone de Beauvoir, a book on the changing moral perspectives of Sartre, Camus, and Beauvoir, and coedited books on both Zola and autobiography. He took early retirement at Lancaster University, where he is now emeritus professor.

J. DEBBIE MANN holds the rank of professor in the department of foreign languages and literature at Southern Illinois University Edwardsville where she teaches French language and French and francophone literature and culture. Recent publications include articles on works by Andrée Chedid, Jacques Poulin, and Louis Hémon.

FREDERICK M. MORRISON (1943–2007) was associate professor of Spanish in the department of foreign languages and literature at Southern Illinois University Edwardsville. Translator and annotator Veronique Zaytzeff began collaborating with him in 1991. Their work includes *Musorgsky Remembered*, sections of *Shostakovich Reconsidered*, and Beauvoir's "Literature and Metaphysics" and "Merleau-Ponty and the Pseudo-Sartrianism."

CATHERINE NAJI has taught Women's Studies in University College Cork and Galway, Ireland. Her primary degree is in French and Philosophy, her master's is in Women's Studies and her PhD is from The University of Newcastle Upon Tyne. Her doctoral thesis has Simone de Beauvoir's work threaded through it and *The Useless Mouths*, in particular, plays a large part. She has written about the "illegal" journeys of some Moroccan women who risk their lives in a dangerous sea crossing and for this reason has compared them to Beauvoir's "useless mouths."

JUSTINE SARROT, a French student of International Marketing and Management at Southern Illinois University Edwardsville from 2001–2002, is currently working in customer relationship management and client satisfaction development with Primagaz.

MARGARET A. SIMONS, distinguished research professor emerita, Southern Illinois University Edwardsville, is author of *Beauvoir and The Second Sex* (1999); editor of *Feminist Interpretations of Simone de Beauvoir* (1995) and *The Philosophy of Simone de Beauvoir: Critical Essays* (2006); and coeditor of Beauvoir's *Philosophical Writings* (2004), *Diary of a Philosophy Student: 1926–27* (2006), and *Wartime Diary* (2009).

LIZ STANLEY is professor of sociology and director of the Centre for Narrative & Auto/Biographical Studies at the University of Edinburgh, UK. A sociologist and social theorist, one trajectory of her work concerns feminist epistemology and ontology; another engages with feminist theorists of the past. Alongside her interest in the early Beauvoir, she is head of a major project researching the letters and manuscripts of Olive Schreiner (*www.oliveschreinerletters.ed.ac.uk*).

URSULA TIDD is senior lecturer and head of French Studies at the University of Manchester, UK. She is the author of *Simone de Beauvoir, Gender and Testimony* (Cambridge University Press, 1999); *Simone de Beauvoir* (Routledge "Critical Thinkers" series, 2004) and *Simone de Beauvoir* (Reaktion Books, 2009) and articles and chapters on Beauvoir's autobiographies, fiction, and philosophy. She has given papers at conferences on Simone de Beauvoir in France, Sweden, Germany, China, the US, Canada, and the UK. Her current major projects are writing a monograph on the Francophone Spanish Holocaust writer Jorge Semprún (forthcoming with Legenda/MHRA 2012), and coediting a collection of essays (with Jean-Pierre Boulé) on contemporary international cinema read through the lens of Beauvoirian theory (forthcoming with Berghahn Books 2012).

MARYBETH TIMMERMANN is a certified French to English translator of the American Translators Association and recently taught an online translation course for the University of Illinois at Urbana-Champaign. She was a contributing translator and assistant editor of Beauvoir's *Philosophical Writings* (2004) and an assistant editor of *Diary of a Philosophy Student: 1926–1927* (2006).

VERONIQUE ZAYTZEFF (1937–2010) was associate professor emerita in the department of foreign languages and literature at Southern Illinois University Edwardsville. She translated from French and Russian. Her translations include *Musorgsky Remembered*, several articles in *Shostakovich Reconsidered*, and Beauvoir's "Literature and Metaphysics" and "Merleau-Ponty and the Pseudo-Sartrianism." She collaborated on translations with Frederick M. Morrison until his untimely death in 2007.

Index

abortion, Manifesto of, 343 (1971), 305

absurd: Bergson on, 339; Camus' definition of, 132–33, 143–45; contradictions in Soviet Union as, 230, 234–35, 241; language as clue to, 85n45. See also *The Useless Mouths* (Beauvoir)

action: call for free action with hope for liberation, 306–7; literary creation as form of, 138, 192, 197; negative portrayal of human condition as means of prompting, 133; novel's depiction of, 94, 95, 109; for self and for others, 140–41; types of, 84n34; of writing as free choice, 308–9, 322–23. *See also* communication

Aeschylus, 150n3. *See also* Orestes

aesthetics. *See* communication

"L'âge de discrétion." *See* "The Age of Discretion" (Beauvoir)

agency: autobiographical, 155; Catholic prohibition against female sexual, 335; loss of faith in, 95

"The Age of Discretion" (Beauvoir): characters of "Misunderstanding" compared with, 214, 215, 217; textual sequences of "Misunderstanding" compared with, 213, 217–18, 274n13

aging. *See* "Misunderstanding in Moscow" (MaM, Beauvoir)

Aimée (Rivière), 337, 350n32, 351n40

Alain (Émile-Auguste Chartier), 364

Alain-Fournier (Henri-Alban Fournier), 334, 337, 342, 350n35, 351n40

À la recherche du temps perdu (Proust), 115, 121n2, 208n18, 274n12, 297–98n7

Alcott, Louisa May, *Little Women*, 334

Algerian War of Independence (1954–62): awareness of horror and forgetting of, 286; *Clarté* debates in context of, 192; Leduc on, 185; mentioned in "Misunderstanding in Moscow," 228; opposition to, 162; pessimism about community in context of, 194–95; summary of, 187n13, 297n6

INDEX

Algren, Nelson, 27, 169

All Men Are Mortal (Beauvoir), 288

All Said and Done (Beauvoir): break from chronological in, 155; on *Clarté* debates, 206n1; context of writing, 305; on writing preface for *La Bâtarde*, 167, 169–70

Altman, Meryl, on "Notes for a Novel": Bergsonian themes, 5; *Bildungsroman* model, 2; fragmentary puzzle pieces, 6–7; introduction and notes to text, 329–54, 374–77

ambiguity and contingency: awareness of, 17; of characters in novels, 93; concept of, 207n10; inherent in fictional writing, 128; of intention vs. reception of theater, 131; literary creation in face of, 192; of lived experience, 4, 279, 285, 289, 292; Sartre's lack of comprehension of, 18–19; singularity and commonality of "I" in, 199–200. See also *The Ethics of Ambiguity* (Beauvoir)

Amélie 1 (Keller), Beauvoir's preface to: editorial comments, 308–9; notes to text, 323; text, 322–23

America Day by Day (Beauvoir), 94, 129, 156, 161

American literature: French enthusiasm for, 2–3, 94–95, 107–8; French fatigue with, 108–9; as model for French writers, 109–10. *See also* "An American Renaissance in France" (Beauvoir); and *specific writers*

"An American Renaissance in France" (Beauvoir)

—EDITORIAL COMMENTS: context and concerns, 94–95; notes to text, 110–12

—TEXT, 107–10; note printed with, 112n15

—TOPICS DISCUSSED: American literary models for French, 109–10; French enthusiasm for American literature, 2–3, 94–95, 107–8; French fatigue with American literature, 108–9

L'Amérique au jour le jour (Beauvoir), 94, 129, 156, 161

anguish: of absence and presence, 177; in Beauvoir's early diaries, x; communication of, 204–5; of empty freedom, 145–46; of knowledge of and forgetting of war, 286; moral acts accompanied by, 141, 150n7. *See also* "Misunderstanding in Moscow" (MaM, Beauvoir); *The Useless Mouths* (Beauvoir)

L'année dernière à Marienbad (film), 290

Anouilh, Jean, 13, 21, 22, 130

Antigone (Sophocles), 104, 106n1

Apollinaire, Guillaume, 333, 363

Aragon, Louis, 316, 319n9

Arland, Marcel, 341, 350n32

Arlen, Michael, *The Green Hat*, 345–46, 353n78

Arnou, René, 364

Ars, Curé d' (aka Jean-Marie Vianney), 185, 187n12

L'asphyxie (Leduc), 167–68, 170, 174

Aucassin et Nicolette (anon.), 232, 273n4

audiences: creative task of, 279, 289, 294; French, of American literature, 94–95, 107–10; impact of spoken word on, 128, 134; invited into phenomenological syntheses of writers, 194; letters to Beauvoir from readers, 279, 296–97; literature vs. reality distinction for, 201; of novel vs. drama, 93, 103, 104, 105–6; prisoners as, 138

Audry, Colette, 168

Augagneux (critic), 98

Austen, Jane, 334, 336

authenticity: of act of marriage, 331, 348n10; of existential free action, 306–7; of novel, 199–200, 207–8n11. *See also* inauthenticity; self

autobiography: "Camille" in, 101n5; as construction and reconstruction, 278–79, 292–93; decision to write novel vs., 295–97; elisions and problems of meaning in, 294–95; harbinger of, 157; historical events underlying, 161–62; increased number of, 290–91; as literary work and "living synthesis," 3, 292, 294–95; motives for writing, 154–55, 158–60, 291–92; novel compared with, 287–88, 295; philosophical work misrepresented in, 5; preface for *La Bâtarde* as perspective on, 172; resources used, 293; self-narration vs. self-knowledge in,

153–54; from singularity to generality in, 291–92; time and narrative in, 155–56; as witnessing ("un témoignage"), 278, 292. See also *All Said and Done*; *The Force of Circumstance*; *Memoirs of a Dutiful Daughter*; "My Experience as a Writer"; "Notes for a Novel"; *The Prime of Life*; "A Story I Used to Tell Myself" (all Beauvoir's)
avant-garde, 298n12, 333. See also *Tel Quel* (journal)

Le bachelier sans vergogne (Marchon), 363
bad faith: of Barrès's texts, 342; characters representing, 12, 52, 84n39; collaborationist stance of, 20–21; as protection, 318; salvation through other as example of, 341
Bair, Deirdre, 329, 345, 347n3
Baldwin, James, 333
Balzac, Honoré de: biographical information, 121n1; hero in novels of, 95, 114, 119; literary world of, 201; on reality, 200; Shakespeare's Lear compared with Goriot, 208n15; WORKS: *La comédie humaine* (*The Human Comedy*), 114, 119, 121n1; *La Père Goriot*, 201, 208n15
Barrès, Maurice: Beauvoir influenced by, 122n6, 341–43, 344; Beauvoir's renouncing of, 336; biographical information, 122n6; "cult of the self" idea of, 122n6, 342, 356, 374–75n7; French influenced by, 116; on social conformity, 343
Barthes, Roland: biographical information, 299n16; *écrivant* and *écrivain* distinction of, 278, 292, 299–300n16; as exemplar of structuralism, 192; as *Tel Quel* contributor, 298–99n13
Baruzi, Jean, 330, 334, 351n45, 364
Bastille Day celebrations (14 July), 308, 310n5
Bataille, George, 193
La Bâtarde (Leduc), Beauvoir's preface to
—EDITORIAL COMMENTS: Beauvoir as mentor and muse to Leduc, 168–69; Beauvoir's autobiography viewed through, 172; Leduc's influence on Beauvoir, 169–70; notes to text, 186–87; others' influenced by preface, 168, 171–72; summary of *La Bâtarde*, 167
—TEXT, 174–85
—TOPICS DISCUSSED: autobiographical narrative, 180–81, 182–83; Beauvoir's reflections on, 167, 169–70; characteristics of Leduc's writing, 174–75; choices, 170–71, 177–79; claiming identity as writer, 179–80; communication, 6; eroticism, 183–84; language within things, 181–82; Leduc as case study, 170, 175–77; moral candor, 184–85
Battling Malone (Hémon), 333, 346, 364
Baty, Gaston, 21, 22
Baudelaire, Charles, 101n8, 352n59
Beach, Sylvia, 308
Beaujour, Michel, 352n59
Beauvoir, Simone de
—INFLUENCES ON: American novels, 94–95; Barrès, 122n6, 341–43, 344; Bergson, 5, 331, 339–41; Dos Passos, 93, 316; George Eliot, 154; Faulkner, 93, 316; Gide, 344–45; Hemingway, 93, 193, 316; Husserl, 5; Kafka, 193, 316; Kierkegaard, 15–16; D. H. Lawrence, 307, 316; Leduc, 169–70; Sartre, 5, 6, 11, 13–14, 21; Woolf, 193, 316
—LIFE: Algren correspondence, 27, 169; Beauvoir as character we create, 7, 331; death, 97n8; family vacations, 347n4; first notebook, 350n21; Jacques idealized, 332 (*see also* Champigneulle, Jacques); job in radio, 12–13, 18, 19, 30n5, 128; job in teaching, 19, 31n19; mother's death, 301n20 (see also *A Very Easy Death*); nostalgia for 1930s, 308, 315–18; questions about actions during war, 128, 131; reading, 306, 307, 316, 333–35, 350n32, 363–64; resistance to being like others or what they expect her to be, 342–43, 353n63; sense of self-worth and awareness of inner life, 343–45; sense of writing vocation as child, 280, 282–83, 334–35; Sorbonne education, 333; Vitold as lover of, 22–23. *See also* Beauvoir-Sartre relationship; literary career and writings; philosophical development and ideas; travels and tours; *and specific works*
Beauvoir-Sartre relationship: Beauvoir's

changing views of literature in context of, 191–92; mutual influences in, 13–14; philosophical disagreements in, 133–34; resistance to bourgeois individualism and, 343; travel in Flanders, 24; travel in Germany, Austria, and Alsace, 23; travel in Japan (lecture tour), 277–78, 280n4, 297n1; travels in Soviet Union (1960s), 193, 214; travels to Rome, 309

becoming, reality as, 200, 208n14

being and doing: rejection of separation in, 29, 75, 87n76; Sartrean movement from doing to being, 69, 86n68; type of action matters in, 84n34. *See also* communication; lived experience; self-and-other

Being and Nothingness (Sartre), 14, 133–34

Les Belles Images (Beauvoir), 195, 214, 279–80, 305

Benjamin, Walter, 28–29

Berdiaeff, Nicolas, *Un nouveau Moyen-Age*, 363

Berger, Jean, 33, 206n1

Bergson, Henri: Beauvoir influenced by, 5, 331, 339–41; on becoming, 208n14; referenced, 4; on social and deep self, 339–40, 377n43; works: *Time and Free Will* (*Essai sur les données immediates de la conscience*), 5, 339, 377n43

Bertrand, Louis, *St. Augustin*, 363

Bertrand Russell Tribunal, 305

Beucler, André, *Gueule d'amour*, 333, 346, 363

Beyle, Marie-Henri. *See* Stendhal (pseud. of Marie-Henri Beyle)

Bildungsroman, 2, 330–31, 334, 350n32

Billy, André, 363

Bizos, Paul, 99

Black Boy (Wright), 110, 112n14

Blancpain, Marc: Beauvoir interviewed by, 157–62; biographical information, 162n1

Bloch, Jean-Richard, 316, 319n9

Blondeau, Lucien, 22, 33

The Blood of Others (Beauvoir): Beauvoir's comments on, 26, 27; body and embodiment in, 96; context of writing, 13; critics' label of "thesis novel," 3, 289; free action with hope for liberation in, 307; narrative strategy in, 215; timing of publication, 91

Bluebeard and Other Fairy Tales (Perrault)

—BEAUVOIR'S INTRODUCTION TO: editorial comments, 306–7; history of fairy tales, 311–12; note printed with, 314n7; notes to text, 313–14; text, 311–13

—STORIES IN: Beauvoir on reading, 306; Bluebeard, 306, 312, 313, 313n5; Cinderella, 311, 312, 313, 313n2; Puss in Boots, 312, 313, 314n6

Boigue, Suzanne (Sombreuse in "Notes"), 337

Bontemps, Roger, 33

Bost, Jacques-Laurent, 115, 121n3

Les bouches inutiles. See *The Useless Mouths* (Beauvoir)

bourgeoisie: individualist revolt of, 343, 344–45; meanings of, 35, 82n7; psychological focus of, 114

Boutroux, Emile, 358

Breton, André, 316, 320n13, 333, 364

Brioude, Mireille, 171

Bris, Michel Le, 308–9

The Brothers Karamazov (Dostoevsky), 120, 122n11

Brunschvig, Léon, 330, 340

Buin, Yves, 206n1

Butor, Michel, 280n2, 290, 298n12, 299n14

Les cahiers de jeunesse (The Student Diaries, Beauvoir): Beauvoir's reflections on, 283; centrality of, x; "Notes for a Novel" juxtaposed to, 330. See also *Diary of a Philosophy Student: 1926–27*

Caldwell, Erskine, 107, 111nn5–6

Caligula (Camus): as exemplar of existentialist theater, 132–33, 143–46; violence in, 148–49

Caligula (Gaius Caesar Augustus Germanicus), 150n12

Calvalcanti, Alberto, 349–50n20

Camus, Albert: on the absurd, 132–33, 143–45; biographical information, 111n7, 123n12, 149–50n1, 186n2; character's moment of liberty in works of, 120; circle of, 168; as

exemplar of modern tendencies in theater, 137; fatigue with American literature, 108; WORKS: *Caligula*, 132–33, 143–46, 148–49; *The Misunderstanding* (*Le malentendu*), 143; *The Myth of Sisyphus* (*Le mythe de Sisyphe*), 132–33; *The Stranger*, 132, 143. See also *Combat* (newspaper); Gallimard (publishing house)
Carleton, V. B. See *James Joyce in Paris* (Freund and Carleton)
Carré, Michel, 363, 376n22
Cartes des quatres (Group of Four), 21. *See also* Baty, Gaston; Dullin, Charles
Catholicism: anti-intellectualism and bourgeois morality of, 344; Beauvoir's transition from, 330; Ignatius Loyola and meditation exercises in, 342; mysticism and, 334; in philosophical discourse, 332; prohibition against female sexual agency in, 335; sadomasochism's indebtedness to, 352n59
La cause du peuple (paper), 305
Caussimon, Jean-Roger, 33
Céline, Louis-Ferdinand, 316, 320n15
Cervantes, Miguel de, *Don Quixote*, 350n32
"C'est Shakespeare qu'ils n'aiment pas." *See* "It's Shakespeare They Don't Like" (Beauvoir)
Champigneulle, Jacques: Beauvoir's concept of love and, 340; Beauvoir's declaration of affection for, 335–36; Beauvoir's idealization of, 332; Gide's *Nourritures terrestres* and, 344; misreading fictional characters as, 336–37, 338; name in *Memoirs*, 350n33; on self and others, 342; urged to write, 375n13
Chamson, André, 316, 319n9
characters: Beauvoir as one we create, 7; as choices of a way out, 131, 145–49; conscious of their roles in drama, 130; displaced by social groups in naturalism, 114; as embodiment of philosophical ideas, 12, 14, 26, 39, 83n15; ethical choices in extreme situations, 95–96, 104 (see also *The Useless Mouths*); exterior conditions vs. interior awareness of, 115–17; hero of traditional novel, 114, 134; identification with, 201; militant feminism of, 216–17; moment of liberty in novel, 120–21; necessity of development of, 193; in novels vs. theater, 93, 102–4, 105–6; opposing points of view of, 286–87; psychological analysis of, 95–96, 114–15, 145; sexual development of, 216–17; solipsist stance rejected by, 16; tableaux vivants combined with particular, 23. *See also* heroine's text; interior monologue
Charmes (Valéry), 273n8
The Charterhouse of Parma (Stendhal), 115–16, 120, 122n4, 201, 208n16
Chartier, Émile-Auguste (Alain), 364
Chateaubriand, François-René de, 162n3, 293, 300n17
Les chemins de la liberté. See *The Roads to Freedom* trilogy (Sartre)
Chesterton, G. K., 364
children: anthropological study of, 198, 201, 207n4; fairy tales for, 306–7, 311–14; viewpoint of, 309–10, 324–25
The Children of Sánchez (Lewis), 198, 201, 207n4
circumstances. *See* lived experience; situation
Clarté (journal): literary debates in, 192–93, 206n1, 277. *See also* "What Can Literature Do?" (Beauvoir)
Claudel, Paul, 316, 320n13, 335, 351n40
Cocteau, Jean, 21, 130, 316, 320n13
Cold War: Sputnik's launch in, 291, 299n15. *See also* "Misunderstanding in Moscow" (MaM, Beauvoir); Soviet Union; United States
Combat (newspaper), 108, 111n7, 121n3
The Coming of Age (Beauvoir), 305
committed literature (*littérature engagée*): anticipation of, 308; Beauvoir's expanded definition of, 194, 203; concept of, 209n26; emergence of, 317–18; literary debates about, 192–93, 206n1. *See also* literature as way of communicating meaning
communication: across individuals' specific

situations, 199; aging couple's perspectives on, 6, 215, 219, 256–65, 269–72; Nazi censorship of and propaganda in, 18; as reintegration into community, 205; separation as heart of, 199–200; in structuralism vs. committed literature debates, 193; theater's success dependent on, 147, 149; "with others by means of being," 191. *See also* action; literature as way of communicating meaning; "Misunderstanding in Moscow" (MaM, Beauvoir)
Communist Party of the Soviet Union, Twentieth Congress, 162, 163n8
community: literature as creating transparency in, 205–6; literature as search for, 194–95
concentration camp experiences: ethical content of choice in, 117–18; exterior conditions vs. interior awareness of, 115–16; silence in writing about, 116–17
concrete and real: American literary models of, 94–95; Beauvoir's need for, in literature, 133–34; joy of, 309–10, 324–25; language for expressing, 109–10; of lived experience, 4, 15, 17; of novel vs. drama, 93, 104–6. *See also* lived experience
Confessions (Rousseau), 296, 300–301n18
conscience (consciousness): existence of multiple, 6; in freeing hidden self, 339; as free or not, 340; uses of terms, 120, 122n10, 141, 150n6. *See also* French terms (meanings and translations)
Constable, Liz, 352n59
Constant, Benjamin, 342
Contat, Michel, 214
Courtivron, Isabelle, 169, 171
Crane, Stephen, 94
critics. *See* literary and theater critics
cross-genre works, 12–13, 26. *See also* existentialist novel; literature as way of communicating meaning

Dangerous Liaisons (Laclos), 336
Daniel, Robert, 99
Dante, *Divine Comedy*, 333, 364
Dantec, Jean-Pierre Le, 308–9
Daudet, Alphonse, 363
Dayan, Josée, 135n3
Deguy, Jacques, 213, 214, 218n2
Delly books, 338
Descartes, René: biographical information, 301n19; doubt of, 341, 352n54, 358; "I think, therefore I am" formulation of, 86n68, 296, 301n19
detective story. *See* Hammett, Dashiell
Le deuxième sexe. See *The Second Sex* (Beauvoir)
dialogue of novel vs. drama, 103–4, 105–6
Diary of a Philosophy Student: 1926–27 (Beauvoir): Beauvoir's reflections on, 283; on essential separation of human existence, 340; on film, 349–50n20; on love for Jacques, 335; on marriage, 348n10; on Merleau-Ponty, 349n18; "Notes for a Novel" compared with, 331; on novel as ideal philosophical form, 191; sense of vocation in, 282; spirit of resistance in, 342–43, 353n63. See also *Les cahiers de jeunesse* (The Student Diaries, Beauvoir)
dictatorship and tyranny: characters representing, 12, 47, 68, 84n34, 86n65; possibility of avoiding complicity in, 16–17; small complicities vs. collaboration in, 18–21. *See also* Nazi Occupation; silence
disclosure: concept of, 206n2
disengagement: characters as representing, 38–40, 44, 48–50, 83n16, 84n28, 84n37. *See also* solipsism
Divine Comedy (Dante), 333, 364
Don Quixote (Cervantes), 350n32
Dos Passos, John: Beauvoir influenced by, 93, 316; biographical information, 110n2, 320n10; French standing of, 94, 107; narrative techniques of, 93; WORKS: *Manhattan Transfer*, 107, 111n3
Dostoevsky, Fyodor Mikhaylovich, 105, 106n2, 120, 122n11
drama. *See* film; theater and drama; *The Useless Mouths* (Beauvoir)
Dreyfus affair, 342
Drôle de jeu (Vailland), 115, 121n3
Ducis, Jean-François, 100, 101n6

Duhamel, Georges, 179, 186n6
Dullin, Charles: biographical information, 101n4; circle of theater friends, 13; drama school of, 150n3; *The Flies* directed by, 21, 131; *King Lear* directed by, 92, 98–100, 101n2
Dusty Answer (Lehmann), 334, 336, 349n17

Eaubonne, Françoise d,' 349n16
Ecole d'Art Dramatique (Paris), 150n3
editorial changes: punctuation, 218n2. *See also* translations; *and "editorial comments" under specific works*
The Egoist (Meredith), 120, 122n11
Eisenstein, Sergei, 333
Either/Or (Kierkegaard), 16
Eliot, George, 154, 334, 335
engaged literature. *See* committed literature (*littérature engagée*)
Équipes Sociales, 337
Erdmann, Joannes Eduardus (Erd.), 358, 375n10
essays: Beauvoir on form and style of, 284–85. See also *The Ethics of Ambiguity* (Beauvoir); literary career and writings (Beauvoir); *The Second Sex* (Beauvoir)
essentialism: critiques and rejection of, 17, 352n51
Estaunié, Edouard, *Tels qu'ils furent*, 333, 364
ethics: in choices of concentration camp internees, 117–18; of commitment to marriage, 331, 348n10; epistemology overlapping with, 341; fragmentary notes on, 338, 357; situational nature of, 15–16, 145–49. *See also* existentialist ethics
The Ethics of Ambiguity (Beauvoir): adventurer as moral type in, 84n35; on attachment to being, 206n2; on communicating with others by means of being, 191; on free action with hope for liberation, 307; on human experience as "detotalized totality" (Sartre), 193; "Introduction" to, 13, 15, 206n2, 207n10; joy of human existence in, 309; "tragic ambiguity" in, 207n10; on writers Ponge and Bataille, 193; writings leading to, 15
L'être et le néant (Sartre), 14, 133–34
everyday: philosophy of, 340. *See also* lived experience
evil: as coming to men through men, 142–43
existentialism: detotalized totality in, 193, 195, 198–99, 204, 207n5, 285–86, 289, 308–9; existence as preceding essence in, 352n51; postwar popularity of, 13, 91, 129; role of necessity in, 38, 83n14; Sartre's defense of, 91; sense of postwar expectation regarding, 12–13
"L'existentialisme est-il un humanisme?" (Sartre), 13, 91
existentialist ethics: concrete experience underlying, 4, 15, 17; as grounded, collective, and shared, 26; *Pyrrhus and Cineas* as basis for, 14
existentialist novel: action properly handled in, 95; Barrès's trilogy on cult of the self, 342, 353n63; Beauvoir's defense of, 2–4, 91, 279; body in, 96, 119–20; concept of, 3–4, 118–19; decline of popularity in 1960s, 277–78; focus on metaphysical and moral choice in, 95–96; intentions to write, 335; labeled "thesis" novels by critics, 3, 5–6, 289. See also *The Blood of Others*; literature as way of communicating meaning; *The Mandarins*; "Notes for a Novel"; *She Came to Stay* (all Beauvoir's)
existentialist psychoanalysis, 96
existentialist theater: concerns about "thesis" in, 146–47, 148; definition of, 133–34, 145–49; as theater of freedom, 130–31. See also *Existentialist Theater* (Beauvoir)
Existentialist Theater (Beauvoir)
—EDITORIAL COMMENTS: circumstances of recordings, 129; discovery of 78 rpm records of, 2, 129; existentialist theater concept, 133–34; notes to text, 149–50; other theatrical writings and, 127–28; plays discussed, 130–33; Sartre's "Forgers of Myths" compared, 129–30
—TEXT (transcription), 137–49
—TOPICS DISCUSSED: Camus' *Caligula*, 132–33, 143–46; discoveries possible in philosophical literature, 3; existentialist

theater defined, 133–34, 145–49; Sartre's *Flies*, 6, 130–31, 137–41; Sartre's *No Exit*, 131–32, 142–43; Sartre's theatrical experience in prison, 135–36n10

facticity: autobiographical elisions of, 294–95; autobiography supported in, 291; in autobiography vs. novel, 278; novel's elimination of unnecessary, 285–86
"A Fair in the Middle Ages" (Beauvoir), 30n5
fairy tales. See *Bluebeard and Other Fairy Tales* (Perrault)
Fallaize, Elizabeth: on autobiographical writing, 6; introduction to short articles about literature, 91–97
Farewell to Arms (Hemingway), 107, 111n3, 320n10
Fargue, Léon-Paul, 316, 319n6
Farigoule, Louis (Jules Romains), 179, 186n4
fascism, 317, 342. *See also* Nazi Occupation
fatality: tragedy as mirror of, 136n11
Faulkner, William: Beauvoir influenced by, 93, 316; biographical information, 111n2, 320n10; French standing of, 94, 107; Hammett compared with, 108; narrative techniques of, 93; WORKS: *Light in August*, 120, 122n11; *Sanctuary*, 107, 111n3
Faye, Jean-Pierre, 206n1
Fayette, Mme. de la, 336. See also *The Princess of Cleves* (anon.)
Feigl, Joe, 106
Fell, Alison S.: on Beauvoir and Leduc's relationship, 2; introduction to Beauvoir's preface to *La Bâtarde* (Leduc), 167–73
feminism: of character and other's response to, 216–17, 226, 231–32, 247–48, 267–68. See also *The Second Sex* (Beauvoir); sexuality; women's issues and liberation movement
"La femme et la création" (Beauvoir), 280
La femme rompue (Beauvoir), 213, 217–18, 305. *See also* "The Age of Discretion"
"La femme rompue" (Beauvoir), 218
Fernandez, Ramon, 347–48n5, 374
Fichera, Virginia M., 11
fiction: autobiography compared with, 287–88, 295; autobiography's relation to, 153, 155–56, 157–58; Beauvoir's short story cycle, 13; production of true stories, 154. *See also* literature; novel; theater and drama
film: Beauvoir's interest in, 332–33, 349–50n20; by *nouveau romancier*, 290
Fitzgerald, F. Scott, 265, 320n10
Flaubert, Gustave, 350n32
The Flies (Sartre): Beauvoir influenced by, 6, 11, 21; concerns about "thesis" of, 147; as exemplar of existentialist theater, 130–31, 137–41; multiple meanings in, 22; mythological background of, 130–31, 145–46, 150n3; New York premiere of, 129; performance of, 13, 21; Sartre's dramas preceding, 135–36n10; social conformity ideas and, 343; violence in, 148–49
La force de l'âge. See *The Prime of Life* (Beauvoir)
The Force of Circumstance (Beauvoir): on autobiography, 153; historical events underlying, 154–55, 161–62; on literary critics and existentialism, 91; literary critics on, 205; *The Mandarins* compared with, 159; missing parts of, 156; on Moravia, 310n10; title of, 158; translator of, 306
"Forgers of Myths" (Sartre), 2, 129–30, 136n10
Foucault, Michel, 298–99n13, 352n59
Fournier, Henri-Alban (Alain-Fournier), 334
France: American literature's reception in (*see* "An American Renaissance in France"); German Occupation (*see* Nazi Occupation); wars of, 162; wartime profiteers in, 184. *See also* Algerian War of Independence (1954–62); French literature; French Resistance; Paris
La France sauvage (Savage France), 308–9
Francis, Claude, 27–28, 133–34
freedom: absolute (Sartre), 14, 82–83n8; acting freely with hope for, 307; aspects of socializing, 14, 36, 82–83n8; circumscribed beyond individual choice, 23; concept of separation of, 207n9; differences between Beauvoir and Sartre, 13, 14; ethical choice juxtaposed to, 118; novel vs. theater and

different constraints of, 106; Orestes' story as concrete meditation on, 139–41; reconception of, 145; resistance and unintended consequences for, 20–21; self-and-other in relation to, 65, 67, 86n61; situational context of, 134; as spontaneous action, 309; writing's role in, debated, 192–93

free will: character's expression of, 78; character's first exercise of, 59–60, 65, 85n52; character's lack of, 58–59; self-and-other in relation to, 65, 86n61

French Cultural Services, 129

French language: reflexives in, 82n5; structural features of, in translation, 28. *See also* French terms (meanings and translations); translations

French literature: "academicism and preciosity" of, 3, 109; American realism as model for, 94–95, 107–10; historical context of writing, 2, 95; naturalism in, 105, 114; philosophy's place in, 118–19; psychological novels of, 95–96, 114–15; role of body in, 96, 119–20; traditional vs. modern novel, 113–14. *See also* existentialist novel; theater and drama; and *specific writers*

French Resistance: dichotomy of collaboration vs., 128; expressing experience of, 109; postwar divisions of, 162; prison especially for partisans, 150n10; questions about, 131; term for, 111n11

French terms (meanings and translations): chef de chantier, 40, 83n18; Grand Guignol, 100, 101n7; histoire, 153; maître, 35, 82n6; salut, 87n83, 332, 349n19; Vaucelles/"vaut-elle," 12, 25, 82n2. See also *conscience* (consciousness)

French writers: American literary models for, 2–3, 94–95, 107–10; fatigue with American literature, 108. *See also* "New Heroes for Old" (Beauvoir)

Fresnes Prison (Paris), 142, 150n10

Freund, Gisèle: biographical information, 318n1; photographs by, 307–8, 315–18. See also *James Joyce in Paris* (Freund and Carleton)

The Fruits of the Earth (Gide), 344

Gallimard (publishing house), 168, 174, 329

Gallimard, Gaston, 168

Galster, Ingrid, 19, 128, 131, 136n16

Gautier, J. J., 99–100

gender divisions: autobiographical context of, 155; complicity with ruling group in, 20–21; in Nazi occupation, 18; women as category in, 29–30, 80, 87n81. *See also* sexual division of labor; women's issues and liberation movement

Gendron, Sarah: notes to "Notes for a Novel," 374–77; on paper for "Notes for a Novel," 348n5

Genet, Jean, 93, 97n8, 170, 174, 186n3

Genji monogatori (Murasaki), 288–89, 296, 298n11

Gerhardt, C. I. (Gerh.), 358, 375n10

German Occupation. *See* Nazi Occupation

Gide, André: abstract domain of, 109; Beauvoir influenced by, 341–45; Beauvoir's reading of, 335; Beauvoir's renouncing of, 336; biographical information, 111n9, 122n6, 150n4, 186n6, 319n5; circle of, 316, 351n40; on fear of influence, 110; French influenced by, 116; on lack of restraint (*disponibilité*), 139; Leduc's reading of, 179; new literary models for, 94–95; reputation in 1930s, 316; on sexual frustration, 349n17; WORKS: *The Fruits of the Earth*, 344; *Strait Is the Gate*, 335, 346

Gilbert, Dennis A.: on Beauvoir's voice, 2; introduction to *Existentialist Theater*, 127–36; notes to *Existentialist Theater*, 149–50

Giono, Jean, 316, 317, 320n14

Girandoux, Jean: abstract domain of, 109; biographical information, 111n9, 320n13; characters of, 130, new literary models for, 94–95; reputation in 1930s, 316; studio theater movement and, 21

God's Little Acre (Caldwell), 107, 111n5

Gogh, Vincent Van, 182, 185, 186–87n10

Gontier, Fernande, 27–28, 133–34

good: as coming to men through men, 142–43

Gounod, Charles, 363, 376n22
Grasset (publishing house), 329
Greek drama, 333. *See also* Orestes
The Green Hat (Arlen), 345–46, 353n78
Guérin, Maurice de, 363, 376n21
Gueule d'amour (Beucler), 333, 346, 363
Guicharnaud, Jacques, 134

Hallier, Jean-Edern, 298–99n13
Hammett, Dashiell, 94, 108, 109, 111n8
Hegel, Georg Wilhelm Friedrich, 15, 16, 21, 84n35, 87n80
Heidegger, Martin, 16
Heine, Heinrich (Henri), 364, 376n30
hell: as Christian belief vs. theatrical fabrication, 132; as coming to men through men, 142–43
"Hell is—other people!" (*No Exit*, Sartre), 132, 142
Hemingway, Ernest: Beauvoir influenced by, 93, 193, 316; Beauvoir's reading of, 307, 316; biographical information, 110–11n2, 320n10; French standing of, 94, 107; narrative techniques of, 93; WORKS: *Farewell to Arms*, 107, 111n3, 320n10
Hémon, Louis, *Battling Malone*, 333, 346, 364
Hengehold, Laura: introduction to "What Can Literature Do?" 191–96
heroine's text: example of feminist hero, 216–17; traditions of, and modern alternatives, 345–46, 353n78. *See also* "Notes for a Novel" (Beauvoir)
"Une histoire que je me racontais." *See* "A Story I Used to Tell Myself" (Beauvoir)
histories: based in hearts and bodies of anonymous individuals, 309–10, 324–25; construction of, 293; dialectic between personal and collective, 153–54; mining (*see* Keller, Henri). *See also* autobiography
History (Morante), Beauvoir's foreword to: editorial comments, 309–10; note printed with, 325n2; notes to text, 325; text, 324–25
Holveck, Eleanore: introduction to Beauvoir's prefaces to others' works, 305–10
Howard, Richard, 306
Hughes, Alex, 173n17
Huguenin, Jean-René, 298–99n13
Huis clos. See *No Exit* (Sartre)
human condition: as carnal, 96, 120; "I" and intersubjectivity of, 201–2, 296–97; indissoluble interconnection in, 16; "intermittences of the heart" in, 286–87, 339; literature as concrete meditation on, 139; literature as safeguarding the human in, 205–6; negative portrayal as means of prompting action, 133; specific situation of each individual as part of, 198–99. *See also* self-and-other; separation
human existence: essence preceded by, 352n51; joy in, 309–10, 324–25; literature as only means of encompassing totality, 204–6. *See also* existentialism; lived experience
humanism, 13, 91, 119–20
hunger. *See* Nazi Occupation; *The Useless Mouths* (Beauvoir)
Husserl, Edmund, 5, 154

"I": as final vs. developing substance, 331, 348n10; possibility of intersubjectivity of, 201–2, 296–97; as representative of large group (women), 291–92; singularity and commonality of, 199–200. *See also* individual; subjectivity
inauthenticity: characters representing, 12; *inquiétude* as potential, 344–45
individual: conditioning and autonomy of thought of, 120; knowledge at level of, 284; as self-directing, 15–16; specific situation of, and human condition, 198–99; traditional novel as celebrating, 114; universality conveyed via experience of, 278–80, 282, 283–84. *See also* lived experience
individualism: bourgeois notion of, 343, 344–45; self removed from Other in, 15
Indochina, 162
In Dubious Battle (Steinbeck), 110, 112n14
information: autobiography as strictly, 292; form and content in, 202; lack of reader's identification with, 201; literature's

relationship to, 197–98, 207n3, 295–97; subjectivity absent in, 288
inquiétude: concept of, 374n5; as potentially inauthentic, 344–45; transition from, 344–45; transition to, 330
interior monologue technique, 116
intersubjectivity, 201–2, 296–97
"Introduction to an Ethics of Ambiguity" (Beauvoir), 13, 15, 206n2, 207n10
L'invitée. See *She Came to Stay* (Beauvoir)
"Is Existentialism a Humanism?" (Sartre), 13, 91
isolation: communication in context of, 6. *See also* separation
"It's Shakespeare They Don't Like" (Beauvoir): Beauvoir's comments on, 92; notes to text, 100–101; "The Novel and the Theater" juxtaposed to, 127–28; text of, 98–100

Jaccomard, Hélène, 170
James, Henry, 94
James Joyce in Paris (Freund and Carleton), Beauvoir's preface to: editorial comments, 307–8; note printed with, 321n17; notes to text, 318–21; text, 315–18
Japan lecture. *See* "My Experience as a Writer" (Beauvoir)
Jayet, René, 101n3
Jeanne avec nous (Vermorel), 22
Jeanson, Francis, 156
Jesus Christ, 41, 44, 79, 84n23, 84n29
Jewish people, 18, 20. *See also* concentration camp experiences
Jollivet, Simone, 13, 99, 100, 101n2, 101n5
Joseph, Gilbert, 136n16
Jouhandeau, Marcel, 174, 186n3
Les jours de notre mort (Rousset), 115, 121n3
Jouvet, Louis, 21
Joyce, James: biographical information, 122n5, 209n25, 319n7; circle of, 316; interior monologue technique of, 116; literary world of, 203; photographs of, 307–8; WORKS: *Finnegan's Wake*, 308; *Ulysses*, 122n5, 308, 316. See also *James Joyce in Paris* (Freund and Carleton)

Kafka, Franz: Beauvoir influenced by, 193, 316; Beauvoir's reading of, 307, 316; biographical information, 106n2, 208n17, 301n18, 320n11; desire to write, 209n23; literary world of, 201, 203; naturalism of, 105; search of, 203; WORKS: *Letter to His Father*, 296, 301n18; *The Metamorphosis*, 203, 209n22; *The Trial*, 203, 209n22
Kant, Immanuel, 15
Keaton, Buster, 333
Keefe, Terry: introduction to "Misunderstanding in Moscow," 213–18; notes to "Misunderstanding in Moscow," 273–74
Keller, Henri: background and writing of, 308–9, 323n1; WORKS: *Amélie 1* (potash mining account), 322–23; *Azougar* (manganese mining account), 323n2
Kemp, Robert, 99, 100
Khrushchev, Nikita S., 163n8
Kierkegaard, Søren: on anguish and moral acts, 141; Beauvoir's reading of, 15; biographical information, 150n7; on situational nature of social life in ethics, 15–16; WORKS: *Either/Or*, 16
King Lear (Shakespeare), 92, 98–100, 100–101n2, 208n15
Kirkup, James, 351n37, 351n48. See also *Memoirs of a Dutiful Daughter* (Beauvoir)
knowledge: anguish of forgetting despite, 286; in autobiography, 153–54, 292; at universal vs. individual levels, 284
Kosakievicz, Olga Dominique, 13, 21, 33, 83n16
Kristeva, Julia, 298–99n13
Kruks, Sonia, 26

Lacan, Jacques, 298–99n13
La Coin, Elisabeth ("Zaza"), 330, 347n4, 349n15, 349n17; childhood home of (Gagnepan), 377n44; on Estaunié's *Tels qu'ils furent*, 333; Merleau-Ponty's relationship with, 337, 349n17; presence in "Notes for a Novel," 346–47; shared reading with Beauvoir, 333–34; on Tagore's poems, 350n25
language: long-term purifying vs. daily influences on, 109; particular voice

underlying, 200. *See also* French language; French terms (meanings and translations); translations
Last Year at Marienbad (film), 290
Laubreaux, Alain, 98, 100n1
Lawrence, D. H., 307, 316, 319n10
Le Bon de Beauvoir, Sylvie: on Beauvoir and the spoken text, 134; on Beauvoir Series, ix-x; Beauvoir's relationship with, 194; notes to "Notes for a Novel," 374–77
Le Conte de Lisle, Charles Marie René, *Poems on the Barbarian Races*, 363, 376n17
lectures: Japan tour, 277–78; US tour, 94, 129, 156. *See also* "Is Existentialism a Humanism?" (Sartre); "My Experience as a Writer" (Beauvoir); recordings
Le Doeuff, Michèle, 342
Leduc, Violette: absence and presence in writings of, 176–78; Beauvoir as mentor and muse of, 168–69; Beauvoir's correspondence with, 173n5; Beauvoir's relationship with, 2; biographical information, 186n1; characteristics of writing, 174–75; choice to become writer, 170, 171–72; existentialist potential of writings of, 173n17; obsessive passion for Beauvoir, 168–69, 173n7; WORKS: *L'affamée* (The Starveling), 169, 174, 178; *L'asphyxie* (*In the Prison of Her Skin*), 167–68, 170, 174; *Les boutons dorés* (The Golden Buttons), 180; *Ravages* (Ravages), 170, 174, 176, 183; *Thérèse and Isabelle*, 183n; *Trésors à prendre* (Treasures for the Taking), 169, 177–78, 185; *La vieille fille et le mort* (The Old Maid and the Dead Man), 178. See also *La Bâtarde* (Leduc)
Left Bank of Paris: bookstores of, 307, 308, 315–16, 317; fame of, 318n4
Leger, Alexis (pseud. Saint-John Perse), 316, 320n13
Lehmann, Rosamund, *Dusty Answer*, 334, 336, 349n17
Leibniz, Gottfried Wilhelm: on Beauvoir's reading list, 363–64; Beauvoir's writing about, 330, 333, 340–41, 351–52n50, 358; biographical information, 207n7; on Descartes' doubt, 341, 352n54, 358; on expressing the world, 199; on monads, 207n8, 310; quoted, 358; reference to, 193–94
Leiris, Michel, 317, 321n16
Letraz, Jean de, *Moumou*, 99, 101n3
Letters to Sartre (Beauvoir), 2, 129
Letter to His Father (Kafka), 296, 301n18
Lévy, Georgette (Blanchette Weiss in "Notes"), 337, 356, 360, 374n4
Lewis, Oscar, *The Children of Sánchez*, 198, 201, 207n4
Les liaisons dangereuses (Laclos), 336
Light in August (Faulkner), 120, 122n11
literary and theater critics: Beauvoir's confrontation with, 2–4; duties of, 100; on literature about anguish and death, 205; on novel as dead (and response to), 113, 120–21; on play vs. production, 25–27; Shakespeare not popular with, 92, 98–100; on thesis novels, 3, 5–6, 289; on writer's intention, 202
literary career and writings (Beauvoir): *Clarté* debates, 206n1, 277; on impossibility of writing in midst of despair, 204–5; language used precisely in, 28; "liquidating her past" in, 345; moral and political engagement in, 11, 13; readers' letters and, 279, 296–97; short articles introduced, 91–97; transition from Catholicism to *inquiétude*, 330; transition from *inquiétude*, 344–45; transpositions of characters and people in, 214; voice in recordings, 2, 134; works translated into Japanese, 277–78. *See also* autobiography; existentialist novel; heroine's text; literature; literature as way of communicating meaning; novel; prefaces and introductions to others' works; theater and drama; *and specific works*
literature: advantages of autobiography vs. novel, 287–88; Beauvoir's need for concrete world of, 133–34; *Bildungsroman* tradition in, 2, 330–31, 334, 350n32; engagement with modern world in, 148–49; facticity and construction of meaning in, 278; faith in, 313, 316–17, 331; function of, 5, 194–

95, 199–206; information's relationship to, 197–98, 295–97; letter- and diary-writing conventions in, 335–36, 350n35; material, manner (style), and search as constituting, 203; mediocrity in, 174; place in world of 1960s, 198; search for answers in, 194–95, 202–3, 334–35; structuralism vs. committed literature debates about, 192–93, 206n1; as sublimation, 192. *See also* American literature; autobiography; essays; fiction; French literature; heroine's text; literary career and writings (Beauvoir); nonfiction books; novel; writers

"Literature and Metaphysics" (Beauvoir): on author and novel, 208n19; disclosure in, 206n2; on discoveries possible in philosophical literature, 3; on novel and communication, 207–8n11; referenced in Japan lecture, 278; on temporal, qualitative reality grasped by human consciousness, 194

literature as way of communicating meaning: action of, 138, 192, 197; another's life in, 3; autobiography as communicating lived experience, 291–95; Beauvoir's preoccupation with, 3, 6, 91–92, 191–94; characters' role in, 12, 14, 26, 39, 83n15; complexity of being in, 191; concrete meditation on human condition in, 139; encompassing totality in, 204–6; evidence of, 296–97; fairy tales in context of, 306–7, 311–14; intersubjectivity in, 201–2, 296–97; novel as communicating lived experience, 285–87, 288–91; novel vs. autobiography, 287–88; novel vs. essay, 279–80; other modes of communication compared with, 4–5, 199–200, 207–8n11; Ricardou's rejection of, 206n1. *See also* communication

littérature engagée. *See* committed literature (*littérature engagée*)

Little Women (Alcott), 334

Littré, Emile, 181, 186n8

lived experience: action and writing based in, 308–9, 322–23; ambiguity of, 4, 279, 285, 289, 292; Beauvoir's focus on describing, 154; chronological framework for, 278–79, 293–94; concreteness of, in existentialist ethics, 4, 15, 17; desire to say everything about, 282–83, 334; detotalized experience of, 193, 195, 198–99, 204, 207n5, 285–86, 289, 308–9; history based in, 309–10, 324–25; literature's potential for conveying, 155–56, 191, 204–5, 207–8n11, 285–97; past, present, and future dimensions of, 295; "personal is political" based in, 340; photographs as capturing, 308; unawareness of particular situation and, 293; writers' task to convey, 278–80, 282, 283–97. *See also* concentration camp experiences; "My Experience as a Writer" (Beauvoir)

Locey, Elizabeth, 168

The Long March (Beauvoir), 163n7

Lorde, André de, 101n8

love: affirmation of Beauvoir's and Zaza's, 346–47; Beauvoir's concept of, 335, 340; independence of self vs. salvation through other and, 341, 349n16, 359, 375n12

Lúkacs, Georg, 202, 208n20

Macmillan (publisher), 306

La maison de rendez-vous (Robbe-Grillet), 290

La Maison des Amis des Livres (bookstore), 307, 315–16, 318n4

Malebranche, Nicolas de, 364

"Malentendu à Moscou." *See* "Misunderstanding in Moscow" (MaM, Beauvoir)

Malraux, Georges-André: biographical information, 123n12, 319n9; character's moment of liberty in works of, 120; circle of, 308, 316; committed literature of, 317; reputation in 1930s, 316

MaM. *See* "Misunderstanding in Moscow" (MaM, Beauvoir)

The Mandarins (Beauvoir): "ambiguities and contradictions" of existence in, 4; Beauvoir's comments about misconceptions of, 159, 279–80; characters balancing commitment and literary experimentation in, 193; communication difficulties in, 215; as harbinger of autobiography, 157; "intermittences of the heart" overcome in, 286–87; review of, 349n16; US tour details in, 156

Mann, J. Debbie: notes to "My Experience as a Writer," 297–301
Manon Lescaut (Prévost), 266
Marchon, Albert, *Le bachelier sans vergogne*, 363
Margueritte, Victor, 346
Marise-Manuel (actor), 33
Maritain, Jacques, 333, 341, 363
marriage: questions about, 331, 348n10
master/slave relationship, 77, 87n80
meaning: autobiographical elisions and problems of, 294–95; novel's illumination of being-in-the-world, 282, 285–86. *See also* literature as way of communicating meaning
media: potentially valid use of, 197; radio dramas during Occupation, 12–13, 18, 19, 30n5, 128. *See also* information
Melville, Herman, 94, 109, 112n13, 120, 122n11
Memoirs of a Dutiful Daughter (Beauvoir): on Arlen's heroine, 345–46, 353n78; author's voice in, 331; books referenced in, 154; Gide's Menalque in, 344; Jacques and Zaza in, 335–37, 338, 350n33, 375n13; philosophical work misrepresented in, 4; "scarabée" image in, 343; solipsistic universe of, 153, 154; on *When Things of the Spirit Came First*, 329
memory and memories: aging and, 232, 240, 242, 245, 246, 252; as isolated and vague, 293. *See also* autobiography
Meredith, George, 120, 122n11
Merleau-Ponty, Maurice: Beauvoir's correspondence with, 360; Beauvoir's rejection of faith of, 349n18; biographical information, 375n14; literary debates and, 192; Zaza's difficulties with, 337, 349n17
The Metamorphosis (Kafka), 203, 209n22
metaphysical novel. *See* existentialist novel
Michaux, Henri, 316–17, 321n16
Middle Ages: guilds, craftsmen, and town structure in, 24–25; radio programs about or set in, 12, 19, 30n5. See also *The Useless Mouths* (Beauvoir); Vaucelles (fictional fourteenth-century Flanders town)
The Mill on the Floss (Eliot), 154, 334
mining history. *See* Keller, Henri
Mireille (opera), 363, 376n22
mise en scène, 21–22
Mistral, Frédéric, 363, 376n22
"Misunderstanding in Moscow" (MaM, Beauvoir)
—EDITORIAL COMMENTS: belated publication and popularity of, 1; Bergsonian themes, 5; characters, setting, and political dimension, 214; context of writing, 213; feminist hero, 216–17; literary quality of story, 213–14; narrative strategy of two viewpoints, 215–16; notes to text, 273–74
—TEXT, 219–73; André's viewpoint (sections), 221–23, 226–30, 233–37, 240–44, 248–50, 253–56, 257, 259–60, 262–64, 265–66, 268–69; neutral viewpoint (paragraphs), 268, 269; Nicole's viewpoint (sections), 219–21, 223–26, 230–33, 237–40, 244–48, 250–53, 256–57, 258–59, 260–62, 264–65, 266–68, 269–73
—TOPICS ADDRESSED: absurd contradictions, 230, 234–35, 241; aging, 215–20, 221, 224, 229–30, 237–42, 250, 252–53, 265–68, 272; books and literature, 219, 223, 224, 226, 232, 235, 245, 252, 266; boredom, 235, 243, 245, 251–52, 253, 257, 259–60, 265, 266, 268, 270–72; communication, 6, 215, 219, 256–65, 269–72; death, 246, 252, 253, 254, 261, 265–66; dreams, 230, 249, 260; familial attachments, 222, 225, 226, 227, 236, 242, 245, 247, 253, 261, 269, 271; feminism (and "super women"), 216–17, 226, 231–32, 247–48, 267–68; happiness, 226, 250; identity, 246; memory and memories, 232, 240, 242, 245, 246, 252; optimism, 251, 266; politics, 221, 222–23, 227–28, 233, 235–36, 239, 241–42, 252, 255; regrets, 228–29, 232, 236, 243; religious beliefs, 233, 253–55; sexuality, 216–17, 227, 243, 244–45, 267–68; specific settings, 220, 223–24, 231, 237–38, 244, 248–50, 253
MJFR. See *Memoirs of a Dutiful Daughter* (Beauvoir)
"Mme de Préliane" (unfinished Marseille novel, Beauvoir), 332, 348–49n14

Moby Dick (Melville), 109, 112n13, 120, 122n11
modern and modernity: Beauvoir's becoming, 332–33; Camus as exemplar of, in theater, 137; literature's engagement with, 113–14, 148–49; situation as basis for theater in, 145–49
Molière, 134
monads, 199, 207n8, 310
"Mon expérience d'écrivain." *See* "My Experience as a Writer" (Beauvoir)
Monnier, Adrienne: biographical information, 318n4; bookstore of, 307, 315–16, 317, 318n4; photograph of, 308
Montaigne, Michel Eyquem de, 265
morality: adventurer as moral type and, 84n35; concerns about theater and, 146–47; fairy tales and authentic existential free action, 306–7; situational context of, 145–46. *See also* ethics; existentialist ethics
Morane, Jacqueline, 22, 33
Morante, Elsa: Beauvoir and Sartre's visits with, 309; biographical information, 325n1; WORKS: *History*, 309–10, 324–25
Moravia, Alberto, 309, 310
Morrison, Frederick: notes to "A Story I Used to Tell Myself," 162–63
Mort de quelqu'un (Romains), 179
Une mort très douce (Beauvoir), 205, 296–97, 301n20, 305
mother-daughter relationships: Beauvoir-Leduc relationship in context of, 168–69; in Leduc's *La Bâtarde*, 167, 175, 182–83, 184; Leduc's works as examples of, 170. See also *A Very Easy Death* (Beauvoir)
Mother Goose tales. See *Bluebeard and Other Fairy Tales* (Perrault)
Les mouches. See *The Flies* (Sartre)
Moumou (Letraz), 99, 101n3
Mouvement de la Libération des Femmes, 305. *See also* women's issues and liberation movement
Moy, Janella D.: notes to "An American Renaissance in France," 110–12; notes to Beauvoir's prefaces to others' works, 186–87, 311–13, 318–21, 323, 325; notes to "It's Shakespeare They Don't Like," 100–101; notes to "The Novel and the Theater," 106; notes to "What Can Literature Do?" 206–9
Murasaki Shikibu, *The Tale of Genji*, 288–89, 296, 298n11
"My Experience as a Writer" (Beauvoir)
—EDITORIAL COMMENTS: autobiography as construction and reconstruction, 278–79; Beauvoir's sense of writing vocation as child, 280; *Clarté* debates as background to, 194, 277; existentialist novel's decline of popularity, 277–78; notes to text, 297–301
—TEXT, 282–97
—TOPICS DISCUSSED: autobiography and novel compared, 287–88, 295; communicating lived experience via autobiography, 291–95; communicating lived experience via novel, 285–87, 288–91; critics' views of her other novels, 4, 289; decision to write autobiography vs. novel, 295–97; detotalizing totality, 285–86, 289, 309; literature as invitation into phenomenological syntheses, 194; sense of vocation as child, 282–83; writing first novel (*She Came to Stay*), 283–84
mythology: Camus' definition of absurd and, 132–33; evil and good illustrated in use of, 142–43; hell as Christian belief vs. theatrical fabrication, 132, 142; as means of avoiding censure in Sartre's *Flies*, 130–31, 139–41. *See also* Orestes

Naji, Catherine: introduction to *The Useless Mouths*, 11–32; notes to *The Useless Mouths*, 82–87; translation techniques of, 28–30
narrative identity concept, 154
Nausea (Sartre), 154
Nazi Occupation (June 1940 to November 1945): allegations of collaboration in, 128, 131; American literature banned in, 94, 107; Beauvoir's radio dramas for national station during, 12–13, 18, 19, 30n5, 128; Beauvoir's teaching post lost in, 19, 31n19; *Caligula* as reflective of, 133, 143–45; censorship in, 18, 20; *in extremis* situation of, 16–17, 26–27; food shortages and conditions in, 1, 17–19; isolation in, 6;

mythic gods as representing, 141; profits in, 184; Sartre's playwriting in prison, 137–38; small complicities vs. collaboration in, 18–21; *The Useless Mouths* written and performed in, 12–13, 16–17, 22–23; writing about experience of war and, 95, 96, 97n12. *See also* silence

Nazism (Germany), 317

"New Heroes for Old" (Beauvoir)

—EDITORIAL COMMENTS: discovery of text, 2; notes to text, 121–23; philosophical novel and context, 95–96

—TEXT, 113–21; notes printed with, 113n, 123n13

—TOPICS DISCUSSED: body in literature, 96, 119–20; ethical content of choice, 117–18; exterior conditions vs. interior awareness of characters, 115–17; philosophical novel concept, 3–4, 95–96, 118–19; psychological novel, 114–15; traditional vs. modern novel, 113–14

new novel movement: Beauvoir's adaptation of techniques of, 280; Beauvoir's rejection of, 279; concept of, 3, 298n12; examples of, 206n1; existentialist novel compared with, 277–78; founder of, 208n13; literary debates about, 192–93, 206n1; narrative rejected in, 290–91; writers of, 280n2. *See also* novel; *Tel Quel* (journal); "What Can Literature Do?" (Beauvoir)

New Woman as literary heroine, 345–46

Nietzsche, Friedrich, 140–41, 150n5

nihilism, 12

Nizan, Paul, 308, 316, 317, 319n8

No Exit (Sartre), 21, 131–32, 142–43

nonfiction books: anthropological biography of Mexican family, 198, 201, 207n4; lack of reader's identification with, 201; popularity of, 197–98, 295–96. *See also* information

"Notes for a Novel" (Beauvoir)

—EDITORIAL COMMENTS: autobiographical perspective, 336–38; Beauvoir's becoming modern, 332–33; Beauvoir's comments, 329, 347n3; characteristics of text, 329–30; dedication (and dating), 330, 347n4; discovery of, 1–2; *dramatis personae*, 338; ending of novel, 345–46; fragments as puzzle pieces, 6–7, 331; heroine's text, 2, 330–31, 336–38, 351n39; influences on, 5, 331, 339–45; letter- and diary-writing conventions, 335–36, 350n35; "life writing," 332; literary and philosophical ideas interwoven, 334–36, 338–41; notes to text, 374–77; paper used for text, 348n5; sense of self-worth and awareness of inner life, 334, 343–45; translations, 347n3, 351n37; Zaza's presence in, 346–47

—TEXT, 355–74; I: decision to write, love, self, astonishment, 355–56; II: spiritual progress, 356; III: death of others, 356; IV: necessity, freedom, *inquiétude* and salvation, choice and obligation, 356; V: description of thought, 356–57; VI: ethics/heroine's reading, 357–58; VII: Leibniz, 358; VIII: outline, 358–59; IX: outline, 359; X: outline; love and awareness, 359–60; XI: dream with open eyes/landscape and joy, 360–61; XII: perfection, the good, utility, 361; XIII: A's and B's screens/love, 361–62; XIV: his refusal, poetic rules, torture/misunderstanding, 362–63; XV: reading list, 363–64; XVI: human life and continuity/beauty and suffering, 364–66; XVII: self and personality/contradictory actions, 366–68; XVIII: love and solitude/soul and body, 368–69; XIX: understanding and social relations, 369–70; XX: doubt, joy, love/impressions and routine, 370–71; XXI: struggles, spiritual life, resistance, 371–72; XXII: Maurice and Pierre described, 372–73; XXIII: dedication, 373; XXIV: notes about writing and review, 373–74

—TOPICS DISCUSSED: communication with Other, 6; modernity, 332–33; "necessity, freedom . . . choice and obligation," 330; questions about self, 338–41, 355–56, 366–67, 374n2; reading list, 333–34, 341; self-and-other and ethics, 331–32

nothingness, 283

Un nouveau Moyen-Age (Berdiaeff), 363

nouveau roman. *See* new novel movement

novel: action writing in, 94–95, 108, 109; communication of lived experience in, 285–87, 288–91; communication of meaning via, 199–200, 207–8n11, 279–80; as dead or not, 113, 120–21; decision to write autobiography vs., 295–97; facticity in autobiography vs., 278; as ideal philosophical form, 191–92; "intermittences of the heart" overcome in, 286–87, 339; limitations of, 289–91; social changes and French cultural place of, 195; theater techniques compared with, 92–93, 102–6. *See also* characters; existentialist novel; literature as way of communicating meaning; new novel movement

novel, types of: documentary, 288, 289; modern vs. traditional, 113–14; naturalistic, 105, 114; observational (exterior conditions vs. interior awareness of characters), 115–17; psychological, 95–96, 114–15; *roman à clefs*, 279, 287–88, 289; *roman à thèse* (thesis), 3, 5–6, 118, 279, 289; romances (Harlequin and Delly), 338. *See also* existentialist novel; new novel movement

"The Novel and Metaphysics" (Beauvoir), 91

"The Novel and the Theater" (Beauvoir)

—EDITORIAL COMMENTS: introduction, 92–93; "It's Shakespeare They Don't Like" juxtaposed to, 127–28; notes to text, 106; writing *The Useless Mouths* reflected in, 92–93

—TEXT, 102–6; note printed with, 102n

objective motivation, 140–41

Of Mice and Men (Steinbeck), 107, 111n5

optimism, socialistic and technocratic, 205

L'ordre (Order, periodical), 25

Orestes: as concrete meditation on freedom, 139–41; situation of, 145–46; summary of myth, 150n3

Other/others: action for self and for, 140–41; Beauvoir and Sartre's differences concerning, 13–14; discovery of consciousness of, in existentialist novel, 3, 4, 283–84; early considerations of, 2–3, 6; film for depicting, 332–33; identification with, 201; independence of self vs. salvation through, 341, 349n16, 359, 375n12; in Leduc's writings, 167, 175, 176–79; "mirage" or existence of, 6, 332; resistance to expectations of, 342–43, 353n63; self removed from, 15; shock of non-recognition, 332, 349n15. See also *The Blood of Others* (Beauvoir); communication; self-and-other; separation

Paris: drama school in, 150n3; film in, 349–50n20; liberation of, 158, 162, 163n4, 204; prison in, 150n10; streets in 1930s, 315; student riots in (1968), 305. *See also* Left Bank; Nazi Occupation

Partisan Review (journal), 94

Pascal, Blaise, 120, 122n9

Perrault, Charles: Beauvoir's characterization of, 306–7, 311, 312; biographical information, 313n1; WORK: *Tales of Mother Goose* (*Contes de ma mère l'oye*), 306, 312–13. See also *Bluebeard and Other Fairy Tales* (Perrault)

"personal is political," 340

personality: Beauvoir's paper on, 351n45; questions about, 338–39, 366–67. *See also* individual; self

philosophical development and ideas (Beauvoir): Beauvoir's writing about, 4–7; context of rapid changes in, 16–17, 26; evidenced in "Notes for a Novel," 330, 334–36, 338–41; existentialism reluctantly adopted in, 13; literature as means of, 191–92; literature juxtaposed to, 4–5; philosophy of the everyday, 340; puppet theater interests in, 12; theology removed from, 341. *See also* literature as way of communicating meaning; *specific concepts (e.g., Other/others); and specific works*

philosophical novel. *See* existentialist novel

photography collections, 307–8, 316–18

Pierre-Quint, Léon (Léon Steindecker), 363

Pinget, Robert, 298n12

Piscator, Edwin, 129

Pitoëff, Georges, 21

Plaisir des hommes (periodical), 25

Plato, 333, 341, 364

Pléiade volumes, 266, 273–74n10
Plotinus, 341, 364
plots: extreme situations as, 95–96, 104 (see also *The Useless Mouths*); in novels vs. theater, 102–6. *See also* characters; existentialist novel; literature; literature as way of communicating meaning; new novel movement; novel
Poe, Edgar Allan, 100, 101n8, 105, 106n2, 336
Poems on the Barbarian Races (Le Conte de Lisle), 363, 376n17
point of view: characters' opposing, 286–87; children's, 309–10, 324–25; individuality of, 194; narrative strategy of two or more, 215–16. *See also* lived experience; "Misunderstanding in Moscow" (MaM, Beauvoir); situation
politics: Beauvoir's reflections on, 293; literature distinguished from, 193; Maoist period, 308–9; "personal is political" view of, 340. *See also* "Misunderstanding in Moscow" (MaM, Beauvoir)
Ponge, Francis, 193
Pour une morale de l'ambiguïté. See *The Ethics of Ambiguity* (Beauvoir)
prefaces and introductions to others' works (Beauvoir): context of writing, 305; on history and writing of fairy tales, 311–13; "history based in hearts and bodies of anonymous individuals" idea in, 309–10, 324–25; as insights into Beauvoir's own work, 2; introductions to, 167–73, 305–10; lived experience concept in, 308–9, 322–23; nostalgia for 1930s in, 308, 315–18. See also *Amélie 1* (Keller); *La Bâtarde* (Leduc); *Bluebeard and Other Fairy Tales* (Perrault); *History* (Morante); *James Joyce in Paris* (Freund and Carleton)
Prévost, Abbé (Antoine François), 266
Prévost, Jean, 316
The Prime of Life (Beauvoir): on autobiography, 153; concerns about "work" in, 191; consciousness in, 154; endpoint of, 158; on independence of self vs. salvation through other, 341, 349n16, 352n57; philosophical development in, 17; philosophical work misrepresented in, 4; politics discussed in, 293; use of phrase, 161
The Princess of Cleves (anon.): absence of lived experience from, 109, 338; character's moment of liberty in, 120; as first French novel, 122n10; letters in, 336; summary and attribution of, 111n12
Proust, Marcel: biographical information, 121n2, 208n18, 297–98n7; French influenced by, 116; on "intermittences of the heart," 286–87, 339, 357; on intersubjectivity, 201, 296; literary world of, 203; Pierre-Quint on, 363; Vinteuil's sonata referenced, 266, 274n12; WORK: *À la recherche du temps perdu* (*Remembrance of Things Past*), 115, 121n2, 208n18, 274n12, 297–98n7
"The Purloined Letter" (Poe), 336
Pyrrhus and Cineas (Beauvoir): as basis for existentialist ethics, 14; context of writing, 13; disclosure concept in, 206n2; on empty ethics, 26; on free action with hope for liberation, 307; Kierkegaardian influence on, 15–16; salvation through other rejected in, 341; summary of, 375n13

Quand prime le spirituel. See *When Things of the Spirit Came First* (Beauvoir)
Queneau, Raymond, 193, 317, 321n16
"Que peut la littérature?" *See* "What Can Literature Do?" (Beauvoir)
"Qu'est-ce que la littérature?" (Sartre), 131, 149, 150n14

Rabelais, François, 120, 122n8
Radio-Paris, 19
Radio-Vichy (Radiodiffusion Nationale): Beauvoir's programs for, 12–13, 18, 19, 30n5, 128
Rais, Gilles de, 306, 312, 313n3
Ravages (Leduc), 170, 174, 176, 183
readers. *See* audiences
realism and reality: Beauvoir on showing doubled reality, 339; in French literature, 110; literature as providing meaning vs.,

295; Lúkacs's defense of, 208n20; writers' relation to, 200–203. *See also* concrete and real; lived experience; situation
recordings: Beauvoir's voice in, 2, 134; reference leading to discovery of, 129. See also *Existentialist Theater*; "A Story I Used to Tell Myself"
The Red and the Black (Stendhal), 114, 119, 121n1
Remembrance of Things Past (Proust), 115, 121n2, 208n18, 274n12, 297–98n7
Renard, Jules, 182, 187n11
Ribowska, Malka, 135n3
Ricardou, Jean, 197, 203, 206n1, 209n23
Richardson, Dorothy, 334
Ricoeur, Paul, 154
Rivière, Jacques: Barrès revered by, 342; circle of, 350n35, 351n40; in "Notes," 337, 368; WORK: *Aimée*, 337, 350n32, 351n40
The Roads to Freedom trilogy (Sartre) (*The Age of Reason, The Reprieve,* and *Troubled Sleep*): characters of, 119; as exemplar of philosophical novel, 95–96, 118; publication of, 13, 91
Robbe-Grillet, Alain: biographical information, 208n13, 298n12; on distrust of narrative, 290; literary world of, 201; as *nouveau romancier*, 279, 280n2; on reality, 200; on writing as search, 202; WORKS: *La maison de rendez-vous* (The Rendez-Vous House), 290
Romains, Jules (aka Louis Farigoule), 179, 186n4
Roman 20—50 (journal), 213–14
roman à clefs, 279, 287–88, 289
roman à thèse (thesis novel), 3, 5–6, 118, 279, 289
"Roman et métaphysique" (Beauvoir), 91
"Roman et théâtre." *See* "The Novel and the Theater" (Beauvoir)
Rousseau, Jean-Jacques, 170, 296, 300–301n18
Rousset, David, 115, 121n3
Roy, Jules, 115, 121n3
Russell, Bertrand, 305, 341, 363
Rybalka, Michel, 1–2, 129, 214
Sachs, Maurice, 176, 177, 178, 179, 181, 183, 184
Saint-Exupéry, Antoine de, 308, 316, 317, 320–21n15
Saint-John Perse (pseud. for Alexis Leger), 316, 320n13
salvation: political engagement and subjective, 140–41; "salvation through him," 341, 349n16, 359, 375n12; self-definition and, 332
Sanctuary (Faulkner), 107, 111n3
Le sang des autres. See *The Blood of Others* (Beauvoir)
Sarraute, Nathalie: biographical information, 299n14; circle of, 168; as *nouveau romancier*, 193, 280n2, 290, 298n12
Sartre, Jean-Paul
—LIFE: biographical information, 122n7, 149n1, 186n3, 209n24, 319n8; circle of, 316, 351–52n50; imprisonment of, 19, 135–36n10, 138, 142, 150n2, 150n10; photograph of, 317; politics, 193, 308–9; questions about actions during war, 131; US tour, 129–30. *See also* Beauvoir-Sartre relationship
—LITERARY IDEAS: American novels as influence, 95; character's moment of liberty, 120; *Clarté* debates, 206n1; *La France sauvage* series edited, 308–9; function of literature (action), 138; Leduc's writing, 174; literature as communication, 206n1; literature as not exercise of language, 203; "lived sense of being-in-the-world," 282, 285; playwriting in prison, 137–38; tragedy and fatality, 136n11; *The Useless Mouths*, 2; writer's task, 278, 282
—PHILOSOPHICAL IDEAS: absolute freedom, 14, 82–83n8; Beauvoir as influence on and influenced by, 5, 6, 11, 13–14, 21; Beauvoir on disagreements with, 133–34; Beauvoir's distinction of her work from, 4–5; detotalized totality, 193, 195, 198–99, 204, 207n5, 285–86, 289, 308–9; doing and being, 86n68; engaged freedom, 140; ethical ambiguities uncomprehended, 18–19; existentialism reluctantly adopted,

13; Kierkegaard and, 16; Look of the Other, 332, 349n15
—WORKS: *Bariona*, 136n10; *Being and Nothingness*, 14, 133–34; "Forgers of Myths," 2, 129–30, 136n10; "Is Existentialism a Humanism?" 13, 91; *Nausea*, 154; *No Exit*, 21, 131–32, 142–43; "A Plea for Intellectuals," 280n4, 297n1; *Saint Genet*, 170; *Search for a Method*, 308; "What Is Literature?" 131, 149, 150n14; *Words*, 181. See also *The Flies*; *The Roads to Freedom* trilogy
sciences: novel's place next to, 120
The Second Sex (Beauvoir): Beauvoir's reading before, 333; Beauvoir's reflections on form and style of, 284–85; Beauvoir's writing about sex and gender before, 11, 331, 345; curriculum changes following, 334; on fairy tales, 306; impartiality of, 159; Japanese translation of, 277–78; Leduc's works as examples in, 170; literature's place in, 335; lived experience in, 340; on sexual frustration, 349n17; shift from being one of them to one of us, 86n67; translation of title, 30
self: film for depicting levels of, 332–33; narrative identity of, 154; questions about, 338–41, 355–56, 366–67, 374n2; resistance and unintended consequences for, 20–21; social and deep, 339–40, 342, 366–67, 377n43
self-and-other: concept of, 14; freedom and free will in relation to, 65, 86n61; fundamental nature of, 16, 38, 83n14; "independence of self vs. salvation through other" idea and, 341, 349n16, 359, 375n12; questions and writing about, 331–32; separation impossible in, 29; struggling together in, 66, 80–81, 86nn63–64, 87n82, 87n84. *See also* communication; Other/others; self; separation
Semprun, Jorge: biographical information, 206–7n3; as *Clarté* debate participant, 206n1; on content, 208n21; on engaged literature, 203, 209n26; on nonfiction, 197–98, 207n3; on search for form, 202
separation: as essential human condition, 340; of freedoms, 207n9; as heart of communication, 199–200; impossible in self-and-other, 29; potential of literature to surpass, 204–6, 296–97; rejection of, in being and doing, 29, 75, 87n76. *See also* communication; self-and-other
service du travail obligatoire (Compulsory Work Service, STO), 17
sexual division of labor: persistence of, 80, 87n81; useful/useless defined by, 12, 15. *See also* gender divisions; *The Second Sex* (Beauvoir); *The Useless Mouths* (Beauvoir); women's issues and liberation movement
sexuality: Catholic prohibition against female agency, 335; frustration of, 332, 349n17; as Leduc's key to the world, 183–84. *See also* gender divisions; *The Second Sex* (Beauvoir); sexual division of labor; women's issues and liberation movement
Shakespeare, William, *King Lear*, 92, 98–100, 100–101n2, 208n15
Shakespeare and Company (bookstore), 308
She Came to Stay (Beauvoir): Beauvoir's reflections on, 283–84; context of writing, 13, 348–49n14; decision to kill in, 374n1; existence of Other in, 6, 332; letter writing and conclusion of, 350n35; literary critics' responses to, 3–6; novel's origin in concrete experience, 4; Shakespeare and, 92; Xavière's death echoed in *The Useless Mouths*, 72, 87n73
silence: level of acceptance implied in, 19–20, 63, 81, 86n58; refusing complicity of, 63, 86n59; in writing about concentration camps, 116–17
Simon, Claude, 280n2, 298n12
Simons, Margaret A.: Beauvoir interviewed by, 4–5; notes to "New Heroes for Old," 121–23; notes to "What Can Literature Do?" 206–9; on questions about marriage in Beauvoir's diary, 348n10
singularity. *See* subjectivity
situation: autobiography based in, 154–55, 161–62; as basis for modern theater, 145–49; concept of, 133–34, 158–59; concreteness provided by, 15, 17; generality

and singularity in, 287; man defined by, 145–46; point of view compared with, 194; specific to each individual in the world, 198–99; writers and reality in, 200–201

social relationships: antagonism in, 283–84; bleak potential offset by friendships in, 132, 142–43; breakdown in extreme situation, 12, 14, 16–17, 26–27, 60–61, 85n54; class divisions in, 20–21; commitment in, 17, 20–21; ethics and situational nature of, 15–16; freedom in context of, 14, 36, 82–83n8; naturalism's focus on groups and, 114; as potential lie, 374n6. *See also* communication; Other/others; self; self-and-other; separation; situation

Socrates, 120, 122n8

solipsism: "alone" in *The Useless Mouths*, 38, 39, 50, 58, 60, 65, 66, 70, 75, 87n71; avoidance of, 332; Beauvoir's shift from, 11, 17; characters as representing, 12, 39, 50, 83n15, 84n37; characters' rejection of, 16; as element in adventurer position, 84n35; self in, 15; unintended consequences of, 20–21. *See also* disengagement

Sollers, Philippe, 280n2, 298–99n13

Sophocles, *Antigone*, 104, 106n1

Soviet Union (USSR): anti-Stalinism in, 163n8; Beauvoir and Sartre's travels in, 193, 214; choice to support, 162; colloquium on novel in, 200, 208n12; Sputnik's launch, 291, 299n15; Stalinization in, 192. *See also* "Misunderstanding in Moscow" (MaM, Beauvoir)

Spanish Civil War, 317

spoken word or text: Beauvoir's voice, 2, 134; impact on audiences, 128, 134. *See also* theater and drama

Sputnik I (satellite), 291, 299n15

Stanley, Liz: introduction to *The Useless Mouths*, 11–32; notes to *The Useless Mouths*, 82–87; translation techniques of, 28–30

St. Augustin (Bertrand), 363

Stein, Gertrude, 320n10

Steinbeck, John, 94, 107, 110, 111nn5–6, 112n14

Steindecker, Léon (Léon Pierre-Quint), 363

Stendhal (pseud. of Marie-Henri Beyle): in Beauvoir's reading list, 363; biographical information, 106n2, 121n1, 208n16; hero in novels of, 95, 114; literary world of, 201; naturalism of, 105; WORKS: *La chartreuse de Parme* (*The Charterhouse of Parma*), 115–16, 120, 122n4, 201, 208n16; *Le rouge et noir* (*The Red and the Black*), 114, 119, 121n1

"A Story I Used to Tell Myself" (Beauvoir)

—EDITORIAL COMMENTS: implications of recording, 2; introduction, 6, 153–56; notes to text, 162–63

—TEXT (transcription), 157–62

—TOPICS DISCUSSED: Blancpain's introductory remarks, 157–58; fiction vs. autobiography, 160–61; historical events in autobiography, 161–62; motives for writing autobiography, 158–60; summary of, 154

Strait Is the Gate (Gide), 335, 346

structuralism: literary debates about, 192–93, 206n1

Studio des Ursulines (Paris), 349–50n20

studio theater movement, 13, 21–23

Suarès, Andre, 333, 363

subjectivity: commonality and, 199–200; to generality, in autobiography, 291–92; to generality, in situation, 287; objectivity combined with, 288–89. *See also* "I"; individual

"The System of Doctor Tarr and Professor Fether" (Poe), 100, 101n8

Tagore, Rabindranath, 333, 350n25, 363

The Tale of Genji (Murasaki), 288–89, 296, 298n11

Tel Quel (journal): on autobiography's place, 292; Beauvoir's rejection of stance, 195, 278–79; committed literature challenged by, 192–93; founding of, 280n2; on new novel, 277–78, 290–91; objective and political stance of, 298–99n13. *See also* new novel movement

Tels qu'ils furent (Estaunié), 333, 364

Les temps modernes (TM, journal): committed literature ethos of, 192–93; editorial team of, 121n3; founding of, 13, 91, 150n14

theater and drama: Beauvoir's desire to write, 11, 21; Beauvoir's research and writing radio programs, 12–13, 18, 19, 30n5, 128; as both written and performed, 127; characters known through being-for-others in, 93; as concrete action and situation, 128, 133–34; costumes vs. content in, 98–99; crisis alleged in, 147–48; engagement with modern world in, 148–49; of fatality vs. freedom, 130–31; intention vs. reception of, 131; metatextuality in, 130–31; modern tendencies in, 137; novel techniques compared with, 92–93, 102–6; philosophy's place in, 118–19; present-day vs. 1940s audiences of, 26; social and psychological analysis in, 145; studio theater movement in, 13, 21–23; tableau vivant form in (passion plays), 23; violence and the macabre in, 101n7, 148–49. *See also* characters; existentialist theater; film; spoken word or text

theater schools, 148, 150n3

Le théâtre (periodical), 25

Théâtre de la Ville (Théâtre Sarah Bernhardt), 92, 98–100

Théâtre des Carrefours (earlier, Les Buffes du Nord), 11, 22, 33

Théâtre du Grand Guignol, 100, 101n7, 101n8

Le théâtre existentialiste. See *Existentialist Theater* (Beauvoir)

Théâtre Sarah Bernhardt (Théâtre de la Ville), 92, 98–100

theatrical metatextuality, 130–31

"thinking reed" concept, 120

Thoreau, Henry David, 94

Tidd, Ursula: on autobiographical writing as construction, 6; on Beauvoir's recording, 2; introduction to "A Story I Used to Tell Myself," 153–56

Time and Free Will (Bergson), 5, 339, 377n43

time and narrative: in autobiography, 155–56; human notions of, 339; narrative identity in, 154

Timmerman, Marybeth: notes to "It's Shakespeare They Don't Like," 100–101

TM. See *Les temps modernes* (TM, journal)

Tous les hommes sont mortels (Beauvoir), 288

Tout compte fait. See *All Said and Done* (Beauvoir)

tragedy as mirror of fatality, 136n11

translations: Beauvoir's works into Japanese, 277–78; goals in, 28–30; masculinization of language in earlier version, 27–28; of *Memoirs of a Dutiful Daughter*, 351n37, 351n48; of "Notes for a Novel," 347n3, 351n37; of *Ulysses* into French, 316

travels and tours (Beauvoir): Brazil, 161; China, 161, 163n7; Flanders, 24; Germany, Austria, and Alsace, 23; Japan lecture tour (1966), 277–78; Rome, 309; Soviet Union (1960s), 193, 214; summarized for 1964–77, 305; US lecture tour (1947), 94, 129, 156, 161

Treich (critic), 100

Trésors à prendre (Leduc), 169, 177–78, 185

The Trial (Kafka), 203, 209n22

truth: individual's conditioning and autonomy of thought in, 120; objective, about World War II, 117–18; in stories, 154; writer's search and discovery as manifesting, 203

Union of Communist Students in France (UECF), 206n1. See also *Clarté* (journal)

United States: Beauvoir's lecture tour in (1947), 94, 129, 156; investigation of war crimes of, 305. *See also* American literature

universality: in essay format, 284–85; writers' task to convey, via individual experience, 278–80, 282, 283–97. *See also* existentialism

L'univers concentrationnaire (Rousset), 115, 121n3

useful/useless: belfry as symbol of, 24–25, 42, 62, 84n26, 85–86n57; category of, 29–30; gender and power divisions underlying definition, 12, 15, 45, 58, 84nn31–32, 85n47; nameless ordinary people and, 82n4; ontological and ethical approach to, 14, 27–28

The Useless Mouths (Beauvoir)

—EDITORIAL COMMENTS: characters' faulty logic highlighted, 57, 61, 64, 68, 75, 76, 85n44, 85n56, 86n60, 86n66, 87n77, 87n79; character's shift from being one of them to one of us, 69, 86n67; context of writing, 1,

13, 16–17; cross-genre form of, 12–13, 26; on free action with hope for liberation, 307; gender marginalization and resistance, 128; historical context of writing, 17–19; "I know" highlighted in, 57, 72, 76, 85n46, 87n72, 87n78; literary critics' responses to, 25–27, 93; multiple meanings of, 20, 21, 22–23; notes to text, 82–87; "one" highlighted, 44, 56, 66, 70, 78, 84n28; opening night of, 91, 93; ordinary people nameless in play, 82n4; performance of, 11, 22, 33; philosophical and ethical concerns, 13–17, 27–28; plot summary, 12; significance in Beauvoir's writing, 11; small complicities vs. collaboration in, 18–21; structure of, 23, 24; translations of, 27–30; writerly aspects, 23–24, 87n74. *See also* Vaucelles; useful/useless

—TEXT, 33–81; Beauvoir's comments on, 26, 27, 29; characters, setting, and performance, 11, 22, 33; dedication, 19, 28, 33; First Tableau, 34–37; Second Tableau, 37–45; Third Tableau, 45–56; Fourth Tableau, 56–61; Fifth Tableau, 61–68; Sixth Tableau, 68–73; Seventh Tableau, 73–79; Eighth Tableau, 80–81

Vailland, Roger, 115, 121n3

Valéry, Paul: abstract domain of, 109; biographical information, 111n9, 318–19n5; circle of, 316; new literary models for, 94–95; reputation in 1930s, 316; WORKS: *Charmes* (referenced), 273n8

La vallée heureuse (Roy), 115, 121n3

Vaucelles (fictional fourteenth-century Flanders town): alternative moral action of, 74–81, 87n75; belfry and its significance, 24–25, 28, 37, 40, 42, 62, 83n11, 84n26, 85–86n57; bourgeoisie in, 35, 82n7; as collective ethical unity at end, 14, 27; as composed of men, 36, 83n8; irony of town's name, 12, 25, 82n2; model for, 24–25; Occupation linked to, 20–21; setting of, 33; town governance in, 24–25, 40, 82n6, 83n20

Vendryes, Joseph, 333, 364

Verhaeren, Emile, 333, 364

Vermorel, Claude, *Jeanne avec nous*, 22

A Very Easy Death (Beauvoir), 205, 296–97, 301n20, 305

Vianney, Jean-Marie (Curé d'Ars), 185, 187n12

La vieillesse (Beauvoir), 305

Viet Nam war, 305

violence, 101n7, 148–49

Vitold, Michel, 22–23, 25, 33

Vitsoris, Georges, 33

Votre Maison (magazine), 315

West-East Colloquium on the Contemporary Novel (Leningrad, 1963), 200, 208n12

"What Can Literature Do?" (Beauvoir)

—EDITORIAL COMMENTS: Beauvoir's changing views of literature, 191–92; Bergsonian themes, 5; literature as communication, 3, 6, 193–94; literature as search for community, 194–95; Morante's novel as exemplar, 310; notes to text, 206–9; publication context, 192–93

—TEXT, 197–206

—TOPICS DISCUSSED: engaged literature, 203; information vs. literature, 197–98; literature as communication, 199–200; literature's function for writers, 204–6; writers and reality, 200–203

"What Is Literature?" (Sartre), 131, 149, 150n14

When Things of the Spirit Came First (Beauvoir): Beauvoir's reflections on, 329; context of writing, 13; existence of Other in, 332; inner life and split consciousness in, 343–44; "Notes for a Novel" compared with, 331; precursors for character in, 307; publisher's initial rejection of, 329

Whitman, Walt, 94

witnessing ("un témoignage"), 278, 292

The Woman Destroyed (Beauvoir), 213, 217–18, 305. *See also* "The Age of Discretion"

"The Woman Destroyed" (Beauvoir), 218

women: Catholicism as threat to, 344; complicity with ruling men, 20–21, 73; "I" of autobiography as, 291–92; novels by and about used in *The Second Sex*, 335;

sacrifices and sexual frustration of, 332, 349nn16–17; struggles of women writers, 280; uninteresting autobiographies of, 291; viewed as "useless mouths" by men, 12, 15, 25, 28, 29–30, 40, 42, 45, 83n17, 84nn31–32. *See also* gender divisions; sexual division of labor

women's issues and liberation movement: Beauvoir's involvement with, 305; community in context of, 194–95; fairy tales in context of, 306–7. See also *The Second Sex* (Beauvoir)

Woolf, Virginia: Beauvoir influenced by, 193, 316; Beauvoir's reading of, 307, 316, 334; biographical information, 319–20n10; on novel plots, 346; photograph of, 308

work: definitions of, 15, 45, 84n31; as escape from brute fact in existence, 143

World War I, 316–18, 320n12

World War II: expressing experiences of, 109; human drama played out in bodies, 120; nostalgia for the period preceding, 317–18; objective truth about, 117–18. *See also* concentration camp experiences; Nazi Occupation

Wright, Richard, 94, 110, 112n14

writers: balancing commitment and literary experimentation, 193; choosing to write autobiography vs. novel, 295–97; claiming identity as, 170, 171–72, 179–80; experiencing a drought and then springing forth, 283; literature's function for, 204–6; misconceptions about practice of, 292–93; photographs of, 307–8, 316–18; public vs. private lives of, 159; reality's relation to, 200–203; search and discovery of, 202–3; singularity of vision of, 147; task of (universal conveyed via individual), 278–80, 282, 283–97. *See also* literature; "My Experience as a Writer" (Beauvoir)

Zaytzeff, Veronique: notes to "A Story I Used to Tell Myself," 162–63

Zaza. *See* La Coin, Elisabeth ("Zaza")

BOOKS IN THE BEAUVOIR SERIES

Series edited by Margaret A. Simons and Sylvie Le Bon de Beauvoir

Philosophical Writings
Edited by Margaret A. Simons with Marybeth Timmermann and Mary Beth Mader
Foreword by Sylvie Le Bon de Beauvoir

Diary of a Philosophy Student: Volume 1, 1926–27
Edited by Barbara Klaw, Sylvie Le Bon de Beauvoir, and Margaret A. Simons, with Marybeth Timmermann
Translation and Notes by Barbara Klaw
Foreword by Sylvie Le Bon de Beauvoir

Wartime Diary
Edited by Margaret A. Simons and Sylvie Le Bon de Beauvoir
Translation and Notes by Anne Deing Cordero
Foreword by Sylvie Le Bon de Beauvoir

"The Useless Mouths" and Other Literary Writings
Edited by Margaret A. Simons and Marybeth Timmermann
and Foreword by Sylvie Le Bon de Beauvoir

Political Writings
Edited by Margaret A. Simons and Marybeth Timmermann
and Foreword by Sylvie Le Bon de Beauvoir

Feminist Writings
Edited by Margaret A. Simons and Marybeth Timmermann
Foreword by Sylvie Le Bon de Beauvoir

Diary of a Philosophy Student: Volume 2, 1928–29
Edited by Barbara Klaw, Sylvie Le Bon de Beauvoir, Margaret A. Simons, and Marybeth Timmermann
Translation and Notes by Barbara Klaw
Foreword by Sylvie Le Bon de Beauvoir

The University of Illinois Press
is a founding member of the
Association of University Presses.

UNIVERSITY OF ILLINOIS PRESS
1325 South Oak Street Champaign, IL 61820-6903
www.press.uillinois.edu